DRUID'S DAUGHTER

THE OLD WORLD TRILOGY: BOOK ONE
A FAE WAR CHRONICLES SERIES

DRUID'S DAUGHTER

JOCELYN A. FOX

Druid's Daughter
Copyright © 2018 by Jocelyn A. Fox

All rights reserved. No part of this publication maybe reproduced, stored in a retrieval system, transmitted in any form or by any means without prior written permission of the publisher. The rights of the authors of this work has been asserted by him/her in accordance with the Copyright, Designs and Patents Act 1988.

This is a work of fiction. The names, characters, places, or events used in this book are the product of the author's imagination or used fictitiously. Any resemblance to actual people, alive or deceased, events or locales is completely coincidental.

Book design by Maureen Cutajar
www.gopublished.com

ISBN 13: 978-1731364418

Chapter 1

"Connall said he heard a banshee in the glen yestereve." Gwyneth glanced up at her cousin in the flickering light of the tallow candle, trying to see if Siobhan showed any sign of surprise at the mention of a coming death.

"You still believe in such things?" Siobhan replied calmly, not even looking up from her mending.

Gwyneth swallowed a curse as she pricked her finger with her needle. She looked at her cousin again, trying to see if Siobhan was serious or jesting. It was hard to tell sometimes – Siobhan was two years older, almost fifteen, and would probably be married soon. Everyone in their clan and the village knew it, and Gwyneth thought that Siobhan was putting on airs.

"I'm just saying what Connall heard," she hedged. For some reason, she still wanted her cousin's approval. They'd grown up together, after all. They'd both had brothers, but they had died as babes. Gwyneth thought she remembered a sister, too, older than her, but the memories were more like dreams. She knew better than to ask her Ma or Da about dead children, so her cousin was the closest thing to a sibling that Gwyneth knew, particularly since their families lived across the dirt road from one another. Siobhan, with her fiery red hair and pale skin, always outshone Gwyneth when they walked together to market, but Gwyneth didn't much care – she'd rather play football with the older boys than flutter her lashes at them. All Gwyneth felt when she thought about her eventual marriage was a clenching like a hand closing into a fist inside her gut. She didn't want to tie her life to a man. She'd much rather run in the forest and follow the deer and find the best wild berries, a skill much touted by Da and his brother, Siobhan's father.

"Well, Connall is a stupid boy, then," Siobhan said loftily.

"Maybe you're a stupid girl," Gwyneth muttered around her finger as she licked the blood from the needle prick. She only had enough courage to say it then, when her words would be mangled and Siobhan wouldn't understand her. Siobhan kept mending her father's shirt with small, neat stitches, holding the cloth close so she wouldn't squint. Gwyneth scraped together enough mettle to ask clearly, "So will you not go to the Beltane fire, if you don't believe in the old ways?"

"There's quite a difference between going to the Beltane fire and believing in banshees," replied Siobhan with a little smile.

That little smile set Gwyneth's blood to boiling. She wasn't quite sure why, but the feeling rose up in her like water rushing down the river after a flood. "Oh, is there, then? Suppose you'll tell me how exactly you think that is. Next you'll be saying you want to go live in the Pale." She snorted in derision.

"And what would be so bad about that?" Siobhan demanded, now finally looking up from her mending. "If an O'Donnell son wanted to wed me and take me to Dublin, I'd go." She raised her chin, her hair curling like flames around her pale, beautiful face.

"Then you'd be a traitor to your blood," Gwyneth replied, her mending forgotten now. She felt as if she didn't know her cousin at all. How could Siobhan say such a thing? Why would she want to go live among the English, hew to their laws and customs, leave their wild land behind for the smoke and slop of the city?

Siobhan shook her head. "You understand little, Gwyneth. You live in a world of your own making in that silly head of yours. Let me guess, you still leave out dishes of milk for the *aos si* and leave berries in little baskets at the roots of hawthorn trees."

Gwyneth felt herself coloring, and she knew Siobhan would be able to see it, even in the flickering light of the dim candle. She swallowed hard. She *did* dream about the *aos sí* and the Tuatha De, but she had no power over dreams. "Your father still observes the old ways."

"My father is an old man," Siobhan replied with another little shake of her head.

It was true – Siobhan's father was older than Gwyneth's own father by almost a dozen years, and though he still stood tall and strong as an oak, his beard was nearly silver.

"Then I suppose I belong among the old folk," Gwyneth replied in as cutting a voice as she could muster. "I, for one, don't wish to scurry away to live in Dublin among the English dogs!"

"You would rather run wild and unwashed in the hills, listening to boys speak about banshees and believing in the Sidhe," Siobhan said in the tone that mothers used when talking about the ridiculous thoughts that occurred to young ones.

Gwyneth felt her heart pounding in her chest. She took a few deep breaths, dizzy with anger. And then she said, finally, spitting the words at Siobhan: "I hope the banshee was foretelling *your* death. Perhaps then you'd not mock the old ways!"

And with that, she seized her mending, heedless again of the needle, and stalked out of the little room, pushing aside the wooden door and stomping across the road made soft by the late summer rain. The night brushed at her face with gentle fingers. She stopped before opening the door of her own home, tilting her head back and looking up at the stars. Believing in the Tuatha De was no more improbable than the tales of the saints peddled by the missionaries that occasionally made their way up into the wild country beyond the English Pale.

The English believed their land to be tamed. They had been giving more and more land grants to the Protestants, because they somehow believed that seeding their own people in the land of Ireland would make it theirs. They had never been up in the wild hills, in the moors where few Christian missionaries, Catholic or Protestant, dared to venture. The Tireoghain, north of the Pale, declared itself for no English lord. Those lords, after all, had never leapt over the fire at Beltane, extinguished their own house coals to relight the hearth from the sacred flames, left out dishes of milk by the door for the *aos sí*, used the ash of the Beltane fire to bless their own skin. And Samhain…Gwyneth shivered. She had always loved the old celebrations, and that held true for Samhain too, but there was almost fear in her love of the darker festival, the ritual that foretold the coming of winter. For the day and night of Samhain, the people of the village were other people. They painted their faces and changed their voices. Some wore masks to trick the *aos sí*, to avoid being taken into the Otherworld. The veil was thin on Samhain, but it was thin on Beltane too.

"Stop lurking outside the door, child," called Gwyneth's mother.

Gwyneth folded her mending over her arm and walked into their home. Her father had built it with his own hands before marrying her mother. The main walls were built of stone, carefully hewn and fit together to withstand even the fiercest winter gale. She remembered a little of when her father and uncle had built the two rooms added on to the largest main room of the home – but that was when there had been three children in the family and a fourth on the way. Now, there was almost too much room, even though the house was not large. Only the richest could afford to have one room for each of their children to sleep within, and a separate bedroom for their father and mother. It was not gold, though, that gave Gwyneth her own room within the house; it was sorrow and loss.

Her mother sat by the fire, a tall, slender woman who looked much younger than her thirty years. Travelers often mistook

Gwyneth and her for sisters; but unlike other women that might have simpered at such a statement, Gwyneth's mother did not take it as a compliment. The strangers were often left stuttering or silent at her severe look as they realized their error.

"Come sit by the fire and finish your mending," Gwyneth's mother said calmly without looking up from her own work.

Gwyneth obediently sat on the stool across from her mother, her neck prickling as it always did when her mother gathered knowledge silently. Sometimes the villagers called it the third eye, other times they called it the Sight, but whatever it was, Gwyneth had never spoken of it directly with her mother. She just waited until the feeling of a thousand small hands plucking at her clothes and pressing against her skin faded.

"Why must you say such things to your cousin?" Her mother still did not pause in her embroidery, her needle flashing in and out of the cloth like a little darting fish. Her golden hair gleamed in the light of the fire, drawn into a neat braid at the nape of her neck. Gwyneth had started to notice white hairs in her father's beard, but she still did not see any sign of age in her mother.

"She speaks ill of the old ways," Gwyneth said finally. She didn't need to tell her mother *what* she had said to Siobhan, because her mother already knew.

"The old ways do not speak to everyone," said her mother after a long moment, "and you cannot force them to understand."

"She speaks to me as though I'm a child," muttered Gwyneth as she licked the end of her thread and squinted at the needle.

"If you allow yourself to become angry at little things such as words, then perhaps you still are a child," her mother said.

"I am not a child, Mother!" Gwyneth protested. "I helped you birth three babes this past fortnight, and you sent me to help Widow Donnelly with her fever on my own!"

Her mother seemed not to have heard her. "Perhaps it is for the best, with Beltane fast approaching..."

"I am not going to jump over the fire with a boy from the village, if that is what you are afraid of," said Gwyneth. Did her mother think that she paid no attention to the lessons of midwifery that she had been taught? Some village girls were stupid enough to think that they couldn't be gotten with child their first time lying with a man, but she knew better. "I do not love the old ways so much as to want a Beltane babe," she said into the quiet, her voice crackling like the flames in the hearth.

Her mother chuckled. "Ah, Gwyneth, I remember when I did not want children."

Gwyneth bridled. First Siobhan, now her mother. Why did everyone think that she was an ignorant child who didn't know what she wanted? "I have no desire for children because I think it stupid to die in childbirth or tie myself to a man in such a way."

"You will think differently soon," her mother said. "Finish your mending. And after, you may go to apologize to your cousin."

"I will not," she said stiffly.

"You will," said her mother in that same unshakeable calm.

It was just the two of them, as it was on the nights when her father traveled to other villages and towns with the wool from their sheep and the cloth that her mother wove. The wool was fine, but it was the brilliant colors her mother dyed the cloth and the delicate patterns she coaxed into the weave that fetched good coin. She had such skill with the needle that Gwyneth's father often returned with dresses and shirts for weddings and feasts, repeating his customers' requests in his low voice. He never forgot an order.

Sometimes Gwyneth could not understand why they were not richer than they were; it seemed to her that with her mother's skill as a midwife and with the needle, and with the size of their flock of sheep, they could have moved into a larger stone house, perhaps even to one of the larger towns near Lough Neagh. She had heard one of the women in the village saying proudly that Brigit O'Dogherty's needlework and cloth was famed as far as Dublin, and some of the English ladies in the Pale had taken a liking to it – though Gwyneth's father had never traveled as far as Dublin. Even so, they had never gone hungry, and they owned two mares, one only for riding and the other for both riding and heavy work like pulling stumps from fields. The villagers sometimes remarked on the good health of all the O'Dogherty animals, and the prosperity of the garden that Gwyneth and her mother tended behind their stone house.

They sat in silence for a long while, the snapping of the logs in the fire the only sound in the room. Gwyneth wished fiercely that she had inherited some skill with the needle, but she stitched with none of her mother's ease and speed.

"It is nothing to do with inheritance," her mother said. "It is everything to do with patience and time."

Gwyneth sighed. She could not remember a time when her mother didn't answer her thoughts. She hadn't realized that all mothers did not do this until just a few years ago, when Siobhan had laughed at her for stating very surely that her mother would know if she even thought of skipping chores. She'd begun to suspect that it was not relegated just to her and her father as she accompanied her mother on her midwife and healer duties.

"Tomorrow we will gather the blooms for our threshold," her mother said. "And I must ride to the pasture to see to the lambs. I may stay the night."

Gwyneth nodded. She was not afraid to spend the night alone. Like most girls of their clan, she was taught how to wield a dagger and shoot a bow just the same as the boys. Unlike most girls, she'd continued to practice until she was a better shot than all her age except for Rhys O'Connor. He vexed her – she had been faster than him until about a year ago, and he hadn't even bragged about it when he'd beaten her in a footrace to the brook by the crossroads.

"Rhys O'Connor is from a good family," her mother said. Gwyneth wasn't sure if she imagined the hint of approval in her mother's voice.

She preferred to think that she did. Her mother just smiled and set aside her embroidery.

"Rhys O'Connor is in Dublin to finish his schooling," Gwyneth muttered. She hadn't seen much of him in the past year, and she told herself she did not care at all as she watched her mother hang the copper kettle over the fire. Her mother was more apt to answer questions when she was making tea, for whatever reason. "Mother, tell me about your mother's grandmother again?"

"I have told you of her many times," Brigit said as she selected the dried herbs to add into the teapot.

"I never tire of hearing it," Gwyneth said truthfully.

"My mother's grandmother was said to be a *bandrui*," said Brigit, sitting down and taking up her embroidery again.

"And it is said that *her* mother's grandmother was a daughter of Tlachtga, daughter of the druid Mug Ruil," said Gwyneth. Speaking of the women in her family, the female druids who had once stood alongside the men in places of power in the land, always kindled a spark of warmth in Gwyneth's chest. Lately, a sense of longing accompanied that spark, soured it into something sharper that pricked her like a needle lodged behind her breastbone. She didn't understand the feeling, but then again, there were many feelings that she did not fully understand yet, stepping over the threshold from childhood into womanhood.

"You know this story," her mother said. "Why do you ask *me* to tell it?"

"Because I think that maybe someday you will tell me something more," Gwyneth said.

"What more do you think there is to tell?" Her mother arched an eyebrow.

Gwyneth shrugged. Her earlier anger had made her brave. "Because I know that you are not like other mothers, and we are not like other families."

Something flashed in her mother's eyes.

"I know that something is different about us," Gwyneth continued, even though she knew this was one of the few ways to ignite her mother's anger. "I know something is different about you and I know something is different about me."

"You must stop saying such things," her mother said, green eyes sharpening and gleaming like emerald flames. People said that Gwyneth had her mother's eyes. She wondered if hers sparked like that when she was angry. She hoped so.

"Why?" she pressed. "Why must I stop saying what I feel – what I *know*?"

She expected her mother to tell her she was a foolish child, to chastise her for wishful thinking or fantasies, but instead her mother, her calm, unshakeable mother went very pale and still.

"Because they will come and take you away from me," her mother said so quietly that Gwyneth was sure she hadn't heard her mother correctly.

Gwyneth felt her hands go slack, the mending sliding into her lap. "What?"

"Mark my words, Gwyneth," Brigit said in a louder voice. "If a stranger comes into the village, you must not go anywhere with him. You must not speak to him, you must not aid him, and you must come to me. Only me, do you understand?"

Gwyneth frowned. "I don't understand."

"You do not *need* to understand, child," her mother said. She leaned forward and grabbed Gwyneth's wrist in a hard grip. "I thought I had escaped it with you, but I see now that you still carry the mark of my blood."

Gwyneth held very still, eyes wide. In the corner of her mind, she noted that her mother's hand around her wrist hurt, that there might be bruises the next morning; but she didn't say anything, holding her breath, waiting for her mother to say something more. The fire leapt higher in the hearth, and at the corner of Gwyneth's eye the flames looked to be white and emerald, though she knew that couldn't be so.

Her mother shook Gwyneth's wrist a little. "Promise me you will heed my words. Promise me you come straight to me if you encounter any strangers in the village."

"Mother, it is Beltane," Gwyneth said. "There are always strangers in the village during the feasts."

"You will know," her mother said, peering into Gwyneth's eyes and pulling on her wrist. "You will know. You must come to me when you see him."

"I – I will," she said. She felt trapped, like a rabbit in a snare, with her mother staring so fiercely into her face. After a long moment, her mother released her. She resisted the urge to rub her wrist, even though it stung. The fire sank back into the hearth, flickering with its gold and orange hues, and Gwyneth told herself that she had imagined the dancing of the shadows on the walls and the tightening of the air in the room. She glanced up at her mother, who had gone back to her embroidery in silence, as though she hadn't just issued some dire warning and the flames hadn't leapt into strange colors at her voice.

Gwyneth cleared her throat. "I'll find our Beltane branch tomorrow, and start gathering the flowers. I saw some primroses about to bloom in a meadow near the lightning-struck oak..."

Her mother nodded, needle dipping into and out of the cloth stretched in its circular frame.

"And I will take my bow with me," Gwyneth said.

"Only the small game," cautioned her mother.

"I will shoot whatever steps in front of my bow," Gwyneth replied, bending over her mending again with the conversation back in familiar territory.

"And then who will carry it back?"

"I will," she replied. "I'm as strong as any boy..."

It was only later, as she lay on her pallet beneath her blanket, that Gwyneth let herself think about her mother's words again. She took a deep breath, wondering if she would dream again tonight. It would be a fitting end to such a day. As her eyes slid closed, she thought she saw a glow hovering in the corner of the room like a firefly...no, *two* glows, floating together in the thickest part of the shadows. She heard the silken echoes of their whispers, the translucent beauty of their fluttering wings cutting through the veil of sleep enveloping her.

Strange indeed, but it was not the first time that her dreams had curled mistily into the last moments before slumber. She greeted the dream like an old friend, familiar and well-worn, like her favorite boots, as her eyes closed, and she drifted into the velvet embrace of the night.

Chapter 2

The day dawned clear and cold. Gwyneth heard her mother in the main room and let herself have the luxury of a few more moments beneath the blankets, stretching and wriggling her toes. It was only in recent years that her father had paid herdsmen and shepherds year-round to care for their flock. She'd honed her skills with a sling and later with a bow as she helped her father watch over their sheep, and in those days, there had been no lazing about in the warmth of the blankets. Sometimes she missed waking up with the dew dampening her blanket, the smell of the morning fresh about them and the dawn just beginning to show pearly gray over the hills.

Her mother greeted her with a bowl of porridge and a cup of tea already set on the table. Gwyneth nodded in thanks.

"You should apologize for your harsh words to your cousin today," her mother said, already dressed for riding in trousers and a long cloak to ward off the early morning chill that still lingered in the air even this close to Beltane.

Gwyneth wrapped her hands around the warmth of the chipped teacup. Perhaps if she didn't say anything, her mother would let the matter drop.

"Gwyneth," her mother pressed.

She stalled further by taking a sip of her tea. Her mother always poured it with just enough time to cool to the right temperature – no one burned their tongue on a cup of Brigit's tea, ever. It was another one of those small things that Gwyneth filed away along with all the others that she'd noticed. She felt like a magpie collecting bits of glass and shards of broken mirror; her observations fascinated her, drew her toward them with a pull so strong she couldn't resist, but she knew their edges were sharp. She felt her mother's eyes fastened upon her with an unrelenting gaze.

"I will go speak to Siobhan before I go to collect our Beltane branch," Gwyneth said grudgingly. She didn't like giving in, even though she knew that her words had been harsh. She didn't *really* want Siobhan to die. The thought sent a little chill down her spine. She took another sip of tea and looked up to meet her mother's gaze.

"You are not a child anymore, Gwyneth," Brigit said.

"I should think not; I've been taller than you for nigh on a year now," Gwyneth replied, trying for a smile. Her mother didn't seem to find it funny.

"You need to understand," her mother said, "that leaving childhood behind…it means leaving behind some of the protections of a child. Do you understand?"

"No," Gwyneth replied. She took another swallow of tea. It was entirely too early in the morning to be having such a serious conversation. "I don't understand, Mother. You hint at these things and then you won't explain them."

"I do not explain them because I fear you will find out yourself too soon, and to speak of them myself is to speak names aloud, to give them power." Brigit looked troubled, her golden hair pinned neatly in a bun at the nape of her neck, her unlined face grave.

Gwyneth frowned. She'd only ever seen her mother look so grave when she knew that one of her patients would die. The babes especially left her mother troubled. "Mother, if I am not a child anymore, perhaps it would be best to just tell me."

She stood carefully straight as her mother looked at her silently, wishing that she'd taken the time to neaten her hair and change out of her nightshift. But then she told herself that her mother either believed what she'd said – that she was not a child – or she was simply saying words to say them, which wasn't her mother's way.

Finally, Brigit nodded. "We will speak of everything when I return."

"Why not now?" The words escaped Gwyneth before she could restrain herself. She winced, knowing that her protest sounded childish. Her mother leveled a stern look at her.

"We will speak of everything when I return," she repeated.

This time, Gwyneth bowed her head in acceptance, like she supposed a mature young woman should. Her mother seemed satisfied, although Gwyneth thought she saw the hint of a smile on her mother's mouth as she turned away and picked up her cloth bundle of supplies.

"I should be back by tomorrow dusk," her mother said. "Moira O'Connor should not have her babe before then, but if she does, you will attend to her. It is her third child and should not be a difficult birth."

Gwyneth flushed with pride. "Yes, Mother."

Brigit nodded. "There is porridge in the large pot, and stew in the small. Do not forget to eat," she said sternly. She gestured to a cloth packet on the table. "Take that with you when you go to find the Beltane branch."

"Aye, Mother," Gwyneth said obediently. She bowed her head and her mother kissed her forehead. For a moment, she wished that her mother would embrace her as she'd done until about a year ago. But to crave such affection was for children, she decided. It felt strange, this balancing act between what she had known and what she was becoming, but if her mother thought her a woman, then she would act as one. And finally – *finally* – when her mother returned from the winter pastures, she would be told all those secret and hidden things that flickered like shadows just out of her reach.

Brigit left, and Gwyneth latched the door behind her mother; she heard the hooves of the riding mare canter down the dirt road. She ate her porridge quickly and washed her face, drinking another cup of tea and banking the fire. Setting out by herself in the forest always gave her a little thrill of excitement – becoming a woman hadn't changed *that*, she thought. As she changed into shirt and trousers, she surveyed her wiry body. "Becoming a woman hasn't changed much else, either," she muttered. She had a bit of a bosom, but not much – not like Siobhan, whose ample curves were well admired by the village lads and many of the older men, to tell truth. But on the whole, Gwyneth thought that perhaps womanly curves would get in the way of running and hunting and climbing trees. A large bosom looked to be terribly uncomfortable when riding.

She shrugged and finished dressing. Maybe if she didn't have a large bosom, men would leave her alone and the lads would only see her as a competitor when it came to shooting an arrow true and setting the best snare for a rabbit. She contemplated her route for the day as she pulled on her boots and walked outside into the cool morning to feed the half-dozen chickens in their coop by the side of the house. She smiled at the nanny goat, which always amused her with its wall-eyed yet serious gaze. The chickens clucked and fussed like old women as she tossed in their feed; the rooster, in his separate pen, stared at Gwyneth accusingly when she sprinkled the handful of feed into his enclosure, as though she personally were responsible for separating him from the hens.

After giving the goat a little scratch on the top of its head, Gwyneth slipped back inside to collect her provisions for the day. Over her shirt, she wore a quilted green vest, her dagger at her belt and her lunch in its cloth packet inside her belt pouch. She checked the dozen arrows in her quiver, though she'd checked them all over last time she'd come back from hunting, running her fingers down the shafts and over the fletching to make sure they'd fly true. After a moment of indecision, she also tucked her well-worn sling into her belt, its leather smooth from years of use. She added four smooth river stones into her belt pouch to nestle alongside her food. A sling was a child's weapon, but she was the best in the village with it.

She grimaced a little. Now she had to go speak to Siobhan. She drew back her shoulders as she pulled the door closed behind her. The early morning light warmed everything with a delicate touch, dew still shimmering on blades of grass and beaded on spider webs. Gwyneth took a deep breath of the spring air. It was the season of rebirth, and the whole earth smelled of renewal.

She knocked on the door of her aunt and uncle's house, which was smaller than her own but just as well made. She watched a sparrow alight on the thatch roof while she waited. The little bird ruffled its feathers and jabbed its beak into the thatch, no doubt making a breakfast of the insects that hid among the straw. Gwyneth smiled a little as she watched. What would it be like to be a bird, to have wings and fly? She was reminded suddenly of the Small Folk in her dreams, the ones with wings like dragonflies. The memory of the dream came to her with the crystalline clarity of an actual experience, so forcefully that it knocked her off balance and she took a step back to steady herself.

The door opened. "Good morning, Gwyneth."

"Good morning, Aunt," she replied, dipping her head in respectful greeting. Her aunt had once been the great beauty of her village, a day's ride to the east. She had an easy smile and was still beautiful despite the threads of white in her hair and the plumpness to her matronly figure. "May I speak to Siobhan, please?"

"She isn't feeling well this morning, I'm afraid," her aunt replied.

"Oh, may I help? If it's womanly complaints, I could make a tea…" Gwyneth took a step forward, but so did her aunt, filling the doorway and putting out her arm against the frame.

"Perhaps later," she said, her voice still kind. "She does not feel well enough to have any visitors."

"Visitors?" Gwyneth repeated, a bit confused. She wasn't a *visitor* – she was family.

"I'll come and fetch you when she feels better this evening," said her aunt with a smile. She didn't remove her arm from the door.

"Could you tell her..." Gwyneth paused. Would she be fulfilling her duty if she passed the message through her aunt? "I meant to tell her this myself, Aunt."

"I can pass any message you'd like," her aunt said.

"I said something unkind yesterday eve," said Gwyneth, straightening her back. She felt her neck going hot with shame, but this was part of what it was to be grown, wasn't it? "Please tell her that I am sorry for the words I spoke in anger."

"You two are like sisters," said her aunt with a fond smile, though it didn't quite reach her eyes. "I am sure she thought nothing of it."

"Will you please tell her?" Gwyneth pressed. She didn't quite know why she felt a sense of urgency in making sure that Siobhan received her apology.

"I will," her aunt replied.

"Thank you, Aunt. I hope she feels better soon. I am going to find our Beltane branch today, and some blossoms. Would you like me to bring one for your home as well?"

"Only if you allow me to bake a loaf of bread in return," her aunt said.

Gwyneth grinned. Her aunt was one of the best bakers in the village – her uncle joked sometimes after a few cups of ale that it was his wife's bread and not her beauty that enticed him to marry her. She bowed her head respectfully again. "Thank you, Aunt."

"Good hunting, Gwyneth," her aunt replied with a smile, and then she closed the door.

Gwyneth turned her feet toward the forest, her step lighter now that she had discharged her duty. She hoped Siobhan wasn't afflicted too badly with womanly pains – she'd never been troubled by her own monthly courses much, and for that much she was grateful, although the whole business was an annoyance that she'd rather do without, given the choice. Sometimes she wondered why the gods had created such trials for women. Her mother did not say that suffering was a woman's lot, like some women of the village, but Gwyneth thought that it would be easy to say something like that, to try to put a reason to the pain.

She knew the moors and the forest to the east of the village well enough that she let her thoughts wander while her feet found the path. Now and again a raven flew up from the long grasses, cawing at her. She nodded respectfully to each one. Ravens were intelligent birds. She saw the shine of a soul in their eyes when they alighted in the same tree as her, and she left the innards of deer for them to eat when she hunted.

She checked the snares she'd set the day before in the forest, finding a large rabbit in one. Murmuring soothingly to the panicked creature as she gathered it into her hands, she quickly snapped its neck, putting an end to its fright. With a few quick cuts of her dagger, she gutted the rabbit, its innards steaming in the cool air. She used a few handfuls of grass to wipe most of the blood off her hands, cleaned her knife, and stuffed some dry grass in the rabbit before she tied a hempen cord around its hind legs and then to her belt. She judged that the day would be cool enough that the field-dressed meat wouldn't spoil, especially if she cooled it in the stream for a while as she ate her lunch. After collecting the snare, she reset it in another likely area a few minutes' walk away. Her other snares hadn't netted anything, and she was careful not to disturb them.

She'd learned the ways of the forest by following her father and uncle when she was barely old enough to walk. Somehow, her father had known that she would be quiet, even as a young child, observing their every move and marking it in her own young memory. The boys of the village had discovered that she was the best at hiding during their games because she could hold herself so still that even the birds thought she was a part of the tree. She learned how to mimic birdsong and the sounds of other animals, became a good tracker and a better hunter, though at first it was hard for her to kill the bright-eyed deer that had sometimes walked up to her so trustingly. Hunting was one of the few things in which she had been gifted patience – like her mother's patience with the needle, she realized now as she threaded her way through the trees, following the slight indentation of a game trail toward the clear, cold brook that ran through this portion of the forest.

By the time the sun reached its noon zenith, painting the shadows dense and short, Gwyneth had shot two more rabbits, though one she'd ruined the meat because her arrow pierced its intestines. She left that one for the ravens and other scavengers after saying a quick apology to the spirit of the little animal. Its body would still return to the earth, but she didn't like it when her arrow missed its mark. All the same, the brace of rabbits at her belt would make a fine stew and she was sure her mother would be happy to have fresh meat after her day of riding.

Gwyneth settled cross-legged on her favorite mossy rock by the brook. At noon, a patch of sun filtered through the branches and cast just enough warmth onto this spot. Sometimes she pretended it was a throne, and she was queen of all the forest, although that game had come to seem a little silly to her lately. In her most elaborate imaginings, the tree nymphs all emerged from the shadows and walked before her throne in a beautiful processional. Sometimes Gwyneth still sensed the presence of something *other* in the trees. It was one of her favorite parts of the forest, because she always felt a sort of kinship with the presence in the trees. She opened her packet of food and ate her bread and cheese thoughtfully. Perhaps her childhood games weren't so silly after all.

As she finished her lunch, shaking the crumbs out from her kerchief and folding it neatly, Gwyneth paused. The chatter of birds and rustle of small animals in the trees had gone silent. Sunlight streamed through the branches, and the sky overhead that Gwyneth glimpsed through the latticework of the trees still shone brilliant, cloudless blue, but a pall fell over the forest. She picked up her bow and slid an arrow from the quiver on her back, walking with gliding and silent steps into the shadow of a nearby oak. She stood and listened intently, her eyes sweeping through the dappled forest, watching for any movement. She held carefully still, moving only to breathe, settling into that quiet, watchful place where her mind emptied of all thoughts and she simply became a vessel for her senses: the sights and sounds and smells of the forest, all with their story to tell.

The breeze brought her a scent that she would have missed had she not been in that quiet place. The breeze smelled of blood. She looked upwind, examined the forest carefully and slipped from the safety of her oak to the next large tree, a wych elm whose oval, saw-toothed leaves provided a large pool of shadow around its trunk. She trod carefully, the green seeds of the wych elm like pebbles beneath her boots.

The forest still sat silent and watchful around her, the quiet laying unnatural and thick. Gwyneth flexed her fingers around her bow, carefully nocked her arrow and put just a bit of tension on the string. She felt the presence in the wood of the tree beside her, as though she were standing beside another person. She tried to open her mind, tried to understand if the tree wished to tell her anything. The breeze brought again the scent of blood, the strange, sweet smell of a badly wounded creature. Gwyneth hoped it was not a deer staggering around after taking a mortal blow from a hunter. She hated cleaning up others' mess, and she disliked seeing the animals suffer when less skilled hunters didn't make a clean kill and either lacked the skill or the patience to track their wounded quarry.

The underbrush rustled. Something large was moving toward them, staggering, by the sound of its uneven steps. Gwyneth brought up her bow, steadying herself to put the creature out of its misery when it emerged into view. But there came a crash and a grunt, something that sounded remarkably...*human.* Her breath caught in her throat as her feet carried her forward, away from the shelter of the shadows. She still held up her bow, the string half-taut. Her mind raced but she shoved her thoughts away.

She made out a shadowy figure in the undergrowth, her view partially obscured by a bush. Out of instinct, she slid behind a tree as the stranger coughed, dragged in a ragged breath, and staggered upright again. He wore a sword at his hip. She drew her bowstring back, stood tall, and stepped out from behind the tree. "Stand fast and declare yourself," she said, her voice ringing through the trees.

The man turned, nearly lost his footing, and put a hand against the nearest tree – a hawthorn, Gwyneth noted peripherally. She couldn't see his face well in the shadows, but there was something familiar about him. His pale skin shone with sweat and his arm gave out as he slumped against the tree. Yet he grinned, his white teeth flashing, and said breathlessly, "Standing…might be a problem." With his back pressed against the hawthorn, Gwyneth glimpsed the gleam of dark blood shining wetly from his side. She stepped closer, lowering her bow to point at the ground but still holding it ready, and tried to see his face.

He turned to her obligingly. She felt her mouth open soundlessly as shock coursed through her.

"You've grown, Gwyneth," Rhys O'Connor said, his gray eyes flashing even in the shadows.

"You're – in Dublin," she said, hearing her voice as though from far away.

Rhys gave half a grin, took a breath to answer her, and then his eyes rolled up and he slid down the tree, leaving a trail of blood on the bark. Gwyneth shoved her arrow back into her quiver and shouldered her bow, leaping forward to steady him before he toppled completely to the ground. She managed to keep him somewhat upright, sitting against the trunk of the tree.

Her mind whirled with questions: what was Rhys O'Connor doing here, in the woods of the Tireoghain, when his family said he was finishing his studies in Dublin? And why was he bleeding like a hapless deer shot by a clumsy hunter? She shook his shoulder lightly, glancing about the forest. He groaned and opened his eyes, one of his hands going instantly to his side, pressing against the bloody ruin of his shirt.

"Is there still danger?" she said urgently. "Did whoever wounded you – are they still pursuing you?"

"*Baobhan sith,*" he panted. His face contracted with pain. "Killed her…last night." He raised his eyebrows. "So…no."

Gwyneth pressed the back of her hand to his forehead to check for fever. She didn't remember Rhys as the type to willingly tell falsehoods, but he certainly couldn't have killed a *baobhan sith* – a woman with cloven hooves rather than feet who seduced men before killing them and draining them of blood. She believed in those tales as much as any other lass that had grown up in the shadow of the old forests and the grace of the old gods, but one didn't speak of such creatures as though they were real. "All right, lay still," she said in the calm, soothing voice that she'd learned from her mother. "Let me look."

"She was…fast," Rhys said. "Got her…claws into me…"

Gwyneth gently pulled his hand away from his side. She noticed that his hands were rough with callouses – certainly not the hands she expected of a scholar pursuing his studies in Dublin. She carefully peeled away the tatters of his shirt, trying not to let any shock show on her face. It was a bad wound, laying his flesh open clean down to the white gleam of ribs, and it looked as though he'd been savaged by some wild animal – but she couldn't think of an animal whose claws would be that far apart.

"I'll be right back," she said to him reassuringly. He caught her wrist with surprising strength, his fever-bright gaze pinning her in place. "I'm going to gather some moss by the brook to staunch the bleeding," she told him. Her wrist ached – it was the same place where her mother's fingers had bruised her the prior night.

Rhys blinked and took a struggling breath. He nodded and released her. She shifted her bow on her shoulder and walked with quick strides toward the brook. If he'd truly been wounded the night before, he had lost a lot of blood, and his grip had been strong for a man who'd been wandering in the forest for hours. She rubbed her wrist. Her mind saw fit to dredge up her mother's words as she touched the bruise:

If a stranger comes into the village, you must not go anywhere with him. You must not speak to him, you must not aid him, and you must come to me.

Her mother had been so insistent, so intent on securing her promise. What had made her unshakeable mother so focused on the threat of a stranger?

"Well, Rhys is *not* a stranger," she muttered as she knelt and pulled up thick pads of moss from the rocks. She sniffed it and touched an edge to her tongue: it was not the best type for clotting blood, but it was still good to use and much better than nothing at all. She started thinking of the other herbs she would need as she walked back toward the hawthorn tree.

There was only the smear of blood on the trunk of the tree, but it took Gwyneth less than a minute to track the shambling Rhys through the undergrowth. She found him leaning against a birch, his blood lurid against the pale bark.

"I told you not to move," she said, brandishing the moss at him. Didn't he understand he was badly wounded?

He flashed that infuriating half-grin at her. "Always were good…at giving orders."

"Well, apparently not good at giving orders that stubborn men will *obey*," she retorted. "What are you thinking, trying to travel in this condition? You'll kill yourself!"

"Better than Orla and Aedan killing me," he muttered.

"What?"

He shook his head and clenched his jaw. "I have to…return."

"Return to *where*? There's only the village – *our* village – for leagues!"

"I shouldn't...I can't..." He lost his breath and swayed, clutching his side. Gwyneth grabbed his other arm and pulled it over her shoulder.

"Your wound needs tending," she said. He smelled sharply of blood and smoke, a strange kind of smoke that she'd never smelled before and that set the hairs on the back of her neck to standing on edge.

"Terrible...worst Paladin," he mumbled to himself. He seemed to be losing his grip on consciousness, because he leaned heavily on her. Gwyneth staggered at his weight – he'd *grown* in the past year since she'd seen him. He didn't look only three years older than her. She took a step forward and he stumbled along with her, but they'd barely been walking for a minute when he went suddenly limp. Gwyneth yelped in surprise at the sudden change in weight as he dragged her down. She managed not to fall, going to one knee hard enough for bright pain to bite into her kneecap, but after a moment of struggle she realized he was too heavy for her. She laid him down as gently as she could, packed his wounds with the moss and bound his side tightly with strips torn from his already-ruined shirt. It was difficult to get the strips of cloth under him, but she managed with some liberal cursing and pushing at Rhys's limp form.

After binding his wound, she checked his heartbeat at his jaw, pressing two fingers to the soft part of his throat. It felt alarmingly weak, but she wasn't sure if that was because she felt the edges of her own panic. He didn't make a sound as she gripped him under the arms, trying not to jostle his wound, and dragged him into the knuckle of an ancient oak's roots, hiding him from view as much as possible.

"I'll be back," she told him, though he didn't show any sign of hearing her. She left her water skin near his hand and wished she hadn't eaten all her lunch before finding him, but he probably wasn't hungry anyway, the state he was in. She stood and scrubbed her hands on her trousers. Led by the same instinct that always guided her in the forest, she asked the oak tree, "Watch over him, please?"

She felt a sort of shiver in the air, took that as a reply, and spun on her heel, dashing away through the trees toward the village, her mind emptying again as she focused her attention on wringing every bit of speed from her legs. There would be time enough to ask Rhys questions later, after she made sure he didn't die from that strange wound, the wound he said was from a *baobhan sith.* Gwyneth grimaced and pushed herself to run faster, the dappled gold of the sun flashing over her and the forest watching as she raced toward home.

Chapter 3

By the time Gwyneth reached home, she'd compiled a list of all the herbs she'd need. Panting, she untied the brace of rabbits from her belt and opened the door to the root cellar, slipping down the rough-hewn stairs and depositing the meat in the cool, dark storage space. There was ample room, since this year's crops had just been planted and they'd eaten most of the food stored in the root cellar over the winter. She took a few deep breaths of the earthy air, feeling the chill that only came from being underground. Then, legs still burning from the run through the forest, she climbed out of the root cellar, shut the wooden doors, and quickly walked into the house.

"Meadowsweet and yarrow," she said as she pulled out the satchel that her mother had given her on her twelfth birthday. A healer's satchel, she'd told the younger Gwyneth. Her mother wore an identical one to any call, though the leather of her mother's satchel felt supple as skin to the touch, worn and oiled with age. Gwyneth's satchel still looked new in comparison, the leather just beginning to soften. "Coltsfoot and comfrey." She found the herbs in their places hanging by the bundle on the crossbeam overhead, and she grabbed a roll of clean linen from the wicker basket on the table that also held the precious glass vials of rare and expensive remedies. Gwyneth did not know all the names of these yet, but she did not think that Rhys would need them. She finished packing her healer's satchel and pulled its strap over her head. She pulled on her cloak, clasping it at her throat. After a moment of indecision, she shouldered her bow and quiver again. With his talk of the *baobhan sith,* she wasn't entirely sure that Rhys was in his right mind. Perhaps those who had wounded him were still tracking him, she thought as she stepped outside and walked to the little paddock beyond the hencoop. She didn't understand why anyone would want to hunt and kill a poor student from Dublin...but then again, it was pretty clear that there was much Rhys hadn't told her. Maybe he wasn't a student in Dublin at all.

"Come on then, Pip," she said, clucking her tongue at the bay mare, which knew how to both pull a plow and listen to a rider on her back. The mare placidly chewed her last mouthful of grass as she raised her head, ears pivoting at the sound of Gwyneth's voice. Gwyneth slid the halter over Pip's head and led her over to the stump that she'd used to mount for as long as she could remember. She nudged Pip with her knees and clucked her tongue; the mare listened to her better than anyone, maybe because they'd grown up together, Pip from a bandy-legged foal to a hardy work horse, and Gwyneth from a wild, shrieking banshee of a child into an apprentice healer.

Pip stepped out onto the dirt road and snorted when Gwyneth pointed her in the direction of the moors and the forest. Gwyneth wrapped one hand in Pip's mane, made sure her seat was secure, and gave Pip another squeeze with her knees. The bay mare started forward at an easy trot, but Gwyneth immediately asked her to go faster. With a toss of her head, Pip eased into a canter. She was not a dainty lady's horse, and her gait was not as smooth as their riding horse, but Gwyneth kept her seat with grim intent.

When they reached the forest, they had to slow out of necessity as Pip wove through the trees and Gwyneth kept an eye out for low branches – a danger to her – and windfall – a danger to Pip. This time, she found Rhys exactly where she'd left him, nestled between the roots of the oak. As Pip obediently halted by the tree, Gwyneth thought she saw something out of the corner of her eye – something shaped like a woman but the colors of the tree, bark for skin and leaves for hair – but when she turned her full attention to the flash of movement, there was nothing. The echo of a laugh shivered through the air, not quite loud enough for Gwyneth to actually hear.

She slid down from Pip's back and took a deep breath. It was time to focus. This was the worst wound she'd ever treated by herself – she'd always had her mother to watch, to provide quiet instruction or to correct her if she was about to do something wrong. She felt like she was walking along the edge of a cliff, and it made her dizzy as she knelt next to Rhys. Dark, sticky blood stained the roots of the tree beneath him. He looked worse than when she'd left.

"I told you I'd be back," she said as she pulled her mortar and pestle from her satchel and set it on the leaves. She didn't know if he could hear her, but her mother said that it was always better to speak and not be heard than leave someone hurting without any comfort. "And here I am. I'm going to make a poultice for your wound, just some yarrow to stop the bleeding, meadowsweet and coltsfoot to help the flesh knit back together cleanly, and comfrey to help it all along." She continued to narrate as she ground the herbs and added water to make a thick paste. "Normally, I'd heat a poultice, but there's no fire since we're in the woods, and so it'll be cold."

Rhys gave no sign that he heard, laying still except for the rise and fall of his chest. She studied him as she cut a length from the linen and dampened the cloth with water, pulling aside the shreds of his shirt to clean the wound as best she could. Just as she'd noticed that his hands were not the soft, pampered hands of a scholar, neither was his body. His chest was well muscled and several scars, some fresh, marked his skin. Most of them looked to be cuts, as though he'd been training seriously with daggers or perhaps a blunt training sword. She glanced at the scabbard at his waist. What use did a village boy from the northern moors have for such a blade?

He still didn't stir as she daubed the blood from his side. The wounds still hadn't clotted well. Gwyneth grimaced and decided to apply the poultice – she could clean the deep cuts with a better eye after they were out of the forest. They would need stitches, but that could wait until she'd gotten him settled by the hearth in their main room. With the little bowl of her mortar held in one hand, she slid close and began applying the paste directly to his wounds with a firm touch. He jerked at that, and she pressed her hand to his chest to steady him, becoming aware that she was almost straddling him in the close confines of the oak's roots.

"Lay still," she said. "I'll do my best to be quick. This will help stop the bleeding."

Rhys turned his face away as she worked. She wondered if it was because he didn't want her to see his pain. His chestnut hair curled against his forehead with his cold sweat.

"Can you sit up? I'll bandage you and then there's just the ride back," she said.

He pushed himself to his elbows at her request, but then he looked at her sharply.

"No," he said hoarsely.

She wrapped the linen bandage tightly around his torso. He closed his eyes and bit back a sound of pain.

"No to what?" she asked, sitting back and surveying her work. It wasn't the neatest bandaging she'd ever done, but it would do.

"I can't…go back with you," he said.

"You can't stay here in the forest," she replied, scrubbing her hands clean on the front of her trousers. "It's going to be cold tonight, and you'll catch your death with that wound. You can't even stand up."

She watched as he tried to push himself to his feet. He managed, leaning heavily on one of the roots, but they both knew that his legs were unsteady as a new fawn's. She gathered her things back into her satchel and stood as well. Somehow, she felt different than when she'd left the house this morning in search of their Beltane branch.

"I'll be fine," he said. "I need to…get to…" He stopped, looked at her and closed his mouth.

"Get to where? The village is the only shelter for leagues," she said, repeating her earlier statement. "Are you sure you didn't hit your head when that animal attacked you?"

She noticed that his eyes appeared more blue than gray in this light. Pip nosed her shoulder, and she stroked the horse's velvety muzzle.

"You should have let me die," Rhys said miserably, in a voice so low she almost didn't hear him.

"What?" Gwyneth straightened. "Why would I let you die? You think I'm so hardhearted as that?" She crossed her arms over her chest. "Or so incapable?"

"No," he said, "no, it's not…that."

"Then what is it?" She raised her eyebrows. "I'm not going to stand here arguing with you all day, Rhys O'Connor. I'll just come back tonight when you're half dead from the cold and put you over Pip's back like a butchered deer."

"Of course you would," he said, almost to himself.

"You are not in your right mind," she said, even though she wanted to let loose a harsher tirade. Her body thrummed with a peculiar mixture of anxiety and excitement: anxiety that perhaps she wasn't capable of dealing with these wounds on her own, and excitement at the chance to prove herself. She imagined the look of pride that would cross her mother's face when she returned from her journey to the pastures.

Rhys slid down to one knee, breathing heavily. She knelt alongside him, the coolness of the ground seeping through the cloth of her trousers. Rhys finally met her eyes. "If you stay out here, you will die. You've lost too much blood, and something will kill you: the cold, a wild beast, or whomever is hunting you." She shrugged. "If you somehow survive all that, then it might be starvation or thirst. None of them are easy ways to die."

"I don't fear death," he said, his eyes blazing.

"I never said you did," she replied, amazed at her own patience. When she listened to herself, she heard a woman speak. She raised an eyebrow and tried to adopt the stern expression her mother wore when dealing with a difficult patient. "Now, what will it be – come along nicely, or like a trussed deer?"

"I cannot put you in danger," he said, shaking his head. He turned his head to the side and went very still.

"What danger?" Gwyneth pressed. He didn't answer and wouldn't meet her gaze. She studied him, and then said quietly, "You aren't living in Dublin for your schooling."

He turned his head and gazed at her warily, but he pressed his lips together and said nothing.

Gwyneth sat back on her heels. "You don't want to tell me, fine. But I'm not a dullard, Rhys." She reached for his wrist as though going to check his pulse and then turned his hand palm up, looking pointedly at his callouses. "You don't have the soft hands of a scholar."

"You haven't met the same scholars I have," he muttered, pulling his hand free of her grip and looking away.

"Stop that," she said in irritation. "Stop saying little things and then not explaining them." She shook her head. "I'm saving your life, you know. The least you could do is tell me what's going on."

Something almost pleading entered his eyes. "Truly, Gwyneth, I do not want to put you in danger. I would put you in danger by telling you…and I would put you in danger…if I let you take me back to the village."

"Are you putting me in danger or are you afraid that your family will see you?" she asked, folding her arms over her chest. Maybe she'd just talk to him until he lost consciousness again. Pip knew how to kneel, and she had dragged full-grown deer across a horse's back before. A man wouldn't be much different, she reasoned.

"Both," he answered quietly.

"What if they don't see you?"

He blinked and looked at her questioningly.

"What if I keep it a secret?" she rephrased. "Keep you a secret." Even as she said it, she wasn't sure how – her mother would be back from the pasture on the morrow, but that was a problem for tomorrow. Right now, she needed to convince Rhys to let her finish saving his life.

"You would do that?" he asked quietly.

"Yes," she answered without hesitation. "If it'll get you to stop being a stubborn ass, yes."

That half-grin flashed across his face. "I've been told my stubbornness…is a good thing."

She noticed his struggle to speak. "Here. Drink a bit of water, and then I'll get you on Pip. I won't let you fall," she told him.

"Best rider…in the village," he said with another, weaker smile as he took the water skin in his good hand.

"That was you, until you left," she said. She pulled the strap of her quiver over her head and set it aside, the arrows rattling against each other. "Here." She unclasped her cloak. "It'll be short on you, but that won't matter much while we're riding. The hood will hide your face."

He didn't argue. She took that as a sign to get moving – when the fight went out of a stubborn person, they were drawing closer to the cliff that marked departure from life, her mother always warned. She stood, slung her quiver and bow over her shoulder, and caught Pip's halter, bringing the mare as close as she could to where Rhys lay. She tapped the mare's foreleg, a signal she'd been taught when she was a foal, and Pip carefully knelt.

"She looks like one of the warhorses that are taught to kneel for their knight-masters, eh?" Gwyneth said proudly. She turned back to Rhys and found him trying to push himself to his feet, his left arm held against his wounded side protectively. He managed to walk the small distance to Pip. The mare snorted as he leaned against her, breathing heavily. Gwyneth hurriedly stuffed everything back into her healing satchel.

Rhys swung his leg over Pip's back, and she mounted behind him. She felt a feverish heat radiating from his muscular body as she reached around him to grab a fistful of Pip's mane and the reins of the halter. She clucked to the mare, her heart in her throat as the horse lumbered upright again. Rhys made a little breathless sound as the motion jolted them. She wrapped an arm securely around his waist, afraid that if he started sliding she wouldn't be strong enough to keep her promise.

"Home, Pip," she said, squeezing her knees against the mare's side. Pip twitched an ear and then set off through the forest. Gwyneth felt very aware of every movement, even though she could have walked faster than the mare picked her way through the forest. She didn't dare tell Pip to go faster, though, because she felt Rhys shudder against her every so often. She knew that a more urgent speed would hurt him more, but her heart sank. It would take them hours to get home at this leisurely pace.

Rhys seemed to understand what she was thinking. "Do it," he said. "I'll…manage."

Gwyneth swallowed. She wrapped the cloak around Rhys and shifted her grip around his waist. He looked over his shoulder and tried to smile reassuringly, but it looked more like a grimace. "I won't let you fall," she said again, and she asked Pip for more speed. The mare snorted and found a narrow game trail, still walking but very nearly trotting. When the forest thinned out and the moor stretched before them, Gwyneth clucked her tongue. Pip obligingly broke into a trot and then a canter. Rhys clung grimly to a handful of Pip's mane, but she felt him begin to shake. He was taller than her and she had to lean around him every so often to check the path ahead, but she trusted Pip. The mare knew her way home.

When they passed the stone marker that pointed to the village road, Gwyneth pulled the hood of her cloak around Rhys' face. Anyone who saw them would still be curious, but at least she'd be able to tell some sort of story if they asked. Without being told, Pip slowed to a trot as they picked up the road. Through a stroke of luck, they encountered no one – it was nearly sunset, Gwyneth realized with a jolt. Most of the village would be returning to their hearths after the day's work, sitting down to the evening meal. Not for the first time, she was grateful that her mother and father had chosen to build their home on the outskirts of the village rather than in the village proper.

She glanced at her aunt and uncle's house as they passed. Smoke rose from the chimney, but no one opened the door to greet the passersby as they often did. Something felt strange about the stillness, but Rhys listed to one side alarmingly and Gwyneth turned her attention to keeping him from falling. She gritted her teeth and hauled at his limp weight as Pip ambled toward the mounting-stump. If she let him go now, he'd dash his head on the stump and all her work would be for nothing.

"Steady, Pip," she said to the horse, and she pulled at Rhys, getting him somewhat upright and then shifting her grip as she quickly slid from Pip's back onto the stump. She grabbed Rhys and pulled him toward her; Pip shied and sidestepped away from Gwyneth, and with a curse Gwyneth leapt forward to catch Rhys. Her right foot came down wrong as she jumped from the stump, and then she was staggering under Rhys' weight. She gasped at the starburst of pain in her ankle, but she lunged forward, toward the door of the house. If she let Rhys fall all the way to the ground, she would have to drag him, and she didn't want to hurt him.

Somehow, she made it through the door of the house without bashing Rhys' head or falling. Her ankle throbbed. She ignored it, lowering Rhys down to the floor a small distance from the hearth. Somehow the hood of the cloak had stayed up during the whole ordeal. She checked his heartbeat, breathed a small sigh of relief, and then went outside, pulling the halter from Pip's head and patting the horse's warm neck in thanks. Pip blew a warm, grass-scented breath into Gwyneth's face and then wandered over to her favorite grazing spot in the little paddock.

Gwyneth gazed at the spectacular colors of the sunset for a moment, and then she walked back into the house, drawing the latch on the door behind her. She quickly stoked the fire and spread a blanket on the floor, shifting Rhys onto it. He was very pale, his lips a little blue, and she checked the bandage worriedly. It was almost soaked through with blood. Chewing her lip, she cut the bandages and put the copper kettle over the new flames of the fire. The yarrow should have helped clot the blood. Perhaps she hadn't used enough of it. She stood and unhooked a tied bunch of dried yarrow stems from the crossbeam, pushing down the anxiety that nibbled at her thoughts.

A few hours later, she sat back on her heels and brushed a tendril of hair away from her forehead with the back of one hand. She'd stopped the bleeding after several highly concentrated poultices, but she didn't know if she'd stopped it in time. She hadn't ever seen a wound that refused to clot so stubbornly, and the fever that had begun to grip Rhys in the forest now burned hot through his body.

"Feverfew and vervain," she said to herself, finding the dried herbs and crushing them to a powder. Rhys opened his fever-bright eyes when she roused him to drink the resulting tincture that she hoped would reduce his fever. He looked up at her in confusion and hissed in pain when she lifted his shoulders so that he could drink, but he managed to swallow most of the tepid concoction.

Soon, he began to shiver more violently. The movement rattled the sword in the scabbard at his waist. Gwyneth gingerly unbuckled the sword belt. Rhys didn't awaken as she pulled the scabbard way from his side and tucked several heavy woolen blankets about him. She set the sword on the table and fetched the round, smooth fever stones, setting them close to the fire to heat. She'd pack the heated stones by his side to help sweat out the fever.

Gwyneth stood and took a deep breath against the dizziness that assaulted her. She realized that she hadn't eaten anything after her quick lunch of bread and cheese by the brook. She didn't remember feeling hungry at all. With a glance at Rhys, she decided that she could afford to take a moment to eat. She slipped out into the coolness of the night without a lantern, the full moon overhead lighting her well-known path as she walked around the house to the root cellar. The goat bleated at her sleepily. The rabbits she'd killed that morning – had it really only been that morning? – were cool and stiff, their legs stretched long and their little tails gleaming white in the darkness. Perhaps if she made a good stew, she could entice Rhys to eat, she thought as she shut the door of the root cellar. He would need his strength to heal. He'd lost so much blood…

She stiffened when she saw the door to the house ajar. She was sure she'd shut it behind her. Drawing her dagger from her belt, she toed the door open, the blade held before her and the rabbits at the ready to bludgeon the intruder. Sliding into the room, she heard two high voices chattering in a language she didn't immediately recognize. Her eyes searched the room but there was no one there – no one except for two brightly glowing balls of light hovering over Rhys. She stepped forward without quite knowing what she was going to do.

"Get away from him," she said as one of the glows dipped down toward her unconscious charge. She brandished the blade and the two glows zipped up to the thatch, whirling around one another in dizzying circles, rather like two startled little birds. She spared a glance behind her to shut the door and latch it, and then she advanced until she stood protectively beside Rhys. She pointed the dagger up at the two glows, her hand steady even though her mind whirled. What *were* they? They looked somehow familiar, though she was sure she would have remembered seeing such astonishing creatures.

"Who are you and what are you doing here?" she asked.

The glows leaned toward each other. She made out the outline of their bodies, humanoid but with wings sprouting from their back, neither of them taller than her longest finger. She raised her dagger a little higher, even though she felt a little ridiculous at threatening such small creatures. What harm could they do?

"It isn't a difficult question," she said. "You are in my home. Tell me your names and what brings you here."

The small beings whispered together for another moment and then one turned to Gwyneth.

"I am Togha, and this is my brother Caonach," the creature said. Gwyneth thought it was female.

"Flower and Moss," she murmured at the words in the old language. She knew enough of it to understand it when someone spoke, but just as the old ways were dying, so was the old language.

Togha bowed from the waist, her aura dimming and flickering around her. "Aye, my lady." She straightened and looked down at Rhys. "We are here because the trees told us that a Paladin had been gravely wounded."

Gwyneth lowered her dagger and sheathed it. Perhaps she was hallucinating – perhaps she was really lying on the ground beside Rhys, asleep and dreaming. But her mind brushed aside those thoughts. She knew with a calm clarity that these small creatures were real. "I should be alarmed," she murmured to herself.

Caonach flew closer. "Why should you be alarmed?" He hovered at eye level, and Gwyneth got the sense that he was inspecting her with just as much interest as she gazed at him. He wore a little tunic and breeches, a small feather tucked jauntily behind his ear. His wings flickered with iridescent colors, and his small face was pointed and mischievous.

"The *aos sí*," Gwyneth said. She swallowed. "That's what you are."

"Yes," said Caonach, nodding. The feather behind his ear rippled with the motion. "Though we are Glasidhe."

"Glasidhe," Gwyneth repeated.

"Yes," said Caonach. He turned and drifted toward Rhys.

"Did you see the creature that wounded him?" Gwyneth said, laying the rabbits on the cutting board and moving the fever stones to heat by the hearth again. She brushed a hand against Rhys' forehead: his skin still felt hot to the touch, and he was soaked in sweat. She dampened a cloth and laid it on his brow. He shifted and mumbled something nonsensical.

"One of the nymphs told us," said Togha. "A *baobhan sith*, she said."

Now a creeping feeling of certainty wound its way up Gwyneth's spine like a vine. She wordlessly went to the cutting board, skinning the rabbits with ruthless efficiency and buying herself time to think. After she butchered the meat, she put an empty pot over the fire.

"I have to fetch some water," she murmured.

"One of us will go with you," Togha announced, brandishing a sword the length of a sewing needle.

Gwyneth didn't have the strength to argue. She didn't wonder what would happen if someone from the village spied them. Somehow, she knew that the Glasidhe were only seen by those they chose to let see them. She glanced at Rhys and then at Caonach. "Watch over him while I'm gone."

"Aye, my lady," Caonach said gravely, giving her a little salute.

Numbly, she picked up the water bucket and pushed the door open, the Glasidhe's aura lighting her way as she walked toward the well. She wondered what strange world had opened to her, split neatly in half like a shelled walnut; but then she thought that perhaps all of it had been in the shadows around her all along, just waiting to be revealed.

Chapter 4

"I thought I was dreaming," Gwyneth said, the cold water from the well sloshing over the side of the bucket as she tried to walk too fast. She grimaced and slowed slightly. "When I saw you before, I mean. I thought…I thought it was a dream."

"We were curious, my lady," Togha said, her bright voice cutting through the velvet darkness of the night.

"Curious?" Gwyneth shifted the heavy wooden bucket to her other hand. She should have brought two just to even the load on both sides of her body.

"Yes," Togha said simply. She flitted from one side of the dirt road to the other, peering down into the darkness fiercely with her diminutive blade raised at the ready.

"What were you curious about?" Gwyneth said. She stumbled on a rut in the road and cursed as more water sloshed onto her leg and the pain in her ankle flared.

"You," Togha replied, whirling to face her and executing an elaborate bow that involved twirling her sword in a very complicated pattern.

Gwyneth blinked. She checked the amount of water in the bucket; at this rate, if she spilled any more she'd have to make a second trip back to the well. Her ankle ached as she started forward again. She'd make herself a poultice for her ankle when she got back to the house, she decided. She'd nearly forgotten it along with her hunger. "Why were you curious about *me*?"

Togha chuckled, as though the question were amusing. Gwyneth raised her eyes from the path long enough to frown at the Glasidhe. She decided not to push her luck with her ankle, pausing and setting down her bucket. When Togha saw Gwyneth's expression, she hovered so closely to Gwyneth's face that she felt the breeze of her dragonfly wings. The Glasidhe dimmed her aura, and Gwyneth saw her eyes widen.

"You do not know?" the little *aos sí* said, almost in a whisper.

Gwyneth tried to understand what the Glasidhe might mean. "I know that there's a story in my family that we are descended from Tlachtga, daughter of the druid Mug Ruil." She shrugged. "But it may be just a story."

"Just a story," whispered Togha, more shocked than amused now. "You do not *know*?"

"Know *what*?" Gwyneth said. She felt her patience slipping away from her. Her head ached, her ankle pulsed with a steady pain, and her stomach felt empty and hollow. Worry for Rhys pressed down on her. "Rhys hasn't answered any of my questions. I would appreciate it if you would just tell me what you mean."

"Oh," said Togha, her aura flickering. "I do not know. . .that is, my lady. . .I do not know whether *I* should be the one to tell you."

"Fine," Gwyneth said irritably. "Keep your secrets." She picked up the bucket and lugged it the last of the path back to the house. When she opened the door, Caonach stood from where he'd settled himself by Rhys' head.

"He still sweats with fever," the Glasidhe pronounced.

Gwyneth nodded. "I know. Hopefully it will break by morning." She took the pot, added water and the butchered carcasses of the two rabbits along with a few handfuls of herbs. Setting the pot back over the fire, she poured some of the remaining water in a bowl and took the cloth from Rhys' forehead. Gods, he was burning up. She pulled aside the cocoon of blankets. Blood soaked the bandage at his side again. Gwyneth felt tears welling up in her eyes. She was going to fail. This strange wound was going to kill him.

Togha made a concerned sound, hovering just behind Gwyneth's shoulder.

"Maybe I should cauterize it," Gwyneth said. Sometimes speaking ideas aloud helped her sort through the best options. "It just won't stop bleeding – I thought it had clotted with the yarrow, but…"

"Wounds from the claws of the *baobhan sith* do not heal easily," Togha said. She cocked her head to one side. "Actually, they usually leave no survivors."

"That is not helpful," Gwyneth said through gritted teeth as she pulled down yet another bunch of yarrow from the crossbeam. After a moment, she added comfrey and coltsfoot as well as some nettle and meadowsweet. At this point, she was grasping at anything.

"They drink the blood of their victims," Togha continued, as though Gwyneth hadn't said anything.

"Drink the blood…" Gwyneth frowned "…so it would make sense that any wound they give wouldn't clot. There has to be some kind of poison still in the wound." She'd examined the deep cuts and they'd looked clean enough, but of course she wouldn't be able to see venom. She wished with a sudden, deep intensity that her mother hadn't gone to the pastures this night – she thought for a moment about taking Pip and galloping off to find her mother, but that was pure idiocy. She took a deep breath. She was the one here. She had to handle this.

"Is there a cure for the venom?" she asked the Glasidhe, not really expecting an answer. She eyed the bottle of whiskey on the shelf, thinking about how much she'd need to use for the disinfectant.

"Hawthorn ash," Caonach said with immediate confidence and a casual air that made Gwyneth think this was common knowledge among his kind.

She stared at him. "You didn't think of telling me this earlier?"

"You seemed to have the situation in hand, my lady," the Glasidhe said meekly. "I thought perhaps you had already applied it."

Gwyneth rubbed her temples. "We don't have our Beltane branch yet – I should have gotten it anyway," she said despairingly.

"I saw one in the village," Togha piped. "It was quite pretty, blossoms and little bits of ribbon…"

"How much hawthorn ash is needed?" Gwyneth demanded, looking at Caonach.

"No more than a thimbleful," he answered, and then he drew himself up. "We will go fetch a piece of the Beltane branch."

"Thank you," she replied, relieved that she didn't need to ask. She felt badly for being angry at the small aos sí, but she couldn't believe that they hadn't told her the cure for the baobhan sith venom from the first. For that matter, why hadn't Rhys told her? Perhaps he didn't know. She pushed the question aside as she stood and opened the door for the Glasidhe. They zoomed out into the night, Togha hissing at her brother in the melodic language that Gwyneth couldn't understand.

While she waited, she put the kettle over the fire next to the bubbling pot. The scent of the cooking broth wafted up from the pot. Gwyneth busied herself by fetching a few vegetables from the cellar, chopping them up and adding them to the broth. Rhys lay pale and sweating, the slashes on his side a vivid, ugly red. She dipped another cloth in the cool water and wiped his face, wondering if she should fetch his mother and sister. He had two younger brothers as well, she remembered. Her stomach clenched as she thought about how she'd feel if he died without his family having the chance to say goodbye, without even knowing that he lay dying just a few moments' walk from their own house.

She dipped the cloth in the cool water again and wrung it out a bit. When she turned to put it on his forehead, his eyes were open, glimmering in the light of the fire. He closed them briefly as she arranged the damp cloth. Then he licked his fever-cracked lips.

"Don't try to speak," Gwyneth said. She knew she should try to sound soothing, but her voice just sounded tear-choked and miserable. "The Glasidhe went to fetch hawthorn."

He raised one eyebrow in question.

"Apparently hawthorn ash is the cure for the venom of the *baobhan sith*," she said. "Your wounds won't stop bleeding. There's some sort of poison that my herbs didn't draw out."

Rhys swallowed and nodded. Gwyneth didn't know if that meant he agreed with the Glasidhe in their choice of cure or if he was just acknowledging that his was no ordinary wound. His words to her in the forest echoed in her mind: *I don't fear death.*

"You aren't a student in Dublin," she said quietly, sponging at his neck and shoulders with the damp cloth.

He smiled a little and shook his head.

She glanced over her shoulder at the sword on the table. "You've trained with that blade."

He nodded.

"You hunted the *baobhan sith* intentionally."

He nodded again.

Gwyneth sat back on her heels. She felt exhaustion pressing in on her, fraying the edges of her awareness, but she also felt a thrumming sort of intensity, an excitement at getting closer to the truth of what had happened on this strange day...and maybe the truth about herself.

"You called yourself..." She tried to remember the word.

Rhys swallowed. She had to lean close as he whispered, "Paladin."

"Paladin," she said. She shook her head. "I don't know what that is."

He took another breath and swallowed again. She leaned close to hear him. "Protectors."

"Protectors," she repeated quietly. She paused and then gathered her courage. "You work with the *aos sí*."

He looked at her for a long moment and then nodded.

"I knew it," she said under her breath. She didn't feel any happiness – it was more a sense of validation, a sense that her belief in the *aos sí* meant something after all. But if the *aos sí* were real, then that meant… "I really am a druid's daughter," she said quietly.

Rhys raised his eyebrow and smiled faintly as though she'd said something amusing. He tried to speak and instead coughed, an alarming sound that made his face twist in pain. Gwyneth hurriedly fetched the cold tea from the table and helped him swallow some. When he caught his breath, he said hoarsely, "You…are more."

"More?" she repeated dumbly. Then she understood he was talking about what she'd last said. "More than…a druid's daughter?" She shook her head. "I don't understand."

"I didn't…either," he rasped. A ghost of his self-assured grin stretched his pale, cracked lips. "At first."

A tapping at the door drew Gwyneth's attention. She touched Rhys' shoulder briefly and then stood, unlatching the door and opening it just far enough for the Glasidhe to fly through, bearing a substantial branch of hawthorn between them. A few bits of colored ribbon still fluttered from some of the twigs. Gwyneth shut the door and latched it again, beyond caring about the Beltane branch that the Glasidhe had cut into pieces. A man's life was at stake, and that was far more important than a Beltane branch.

"Put it on the table," she said. The Glasidhe followed her instruction as she fetched the stone bowl that her mother used to burn herbs for medicinal smoke. She drew her dagger and hacked a few twigs the size of her finger from the branch. "Do I need to add anything else?"

Caonach said, "No, my lady."

She carried the bowl over to the fire. Rhys watched her with half-closed eyes. After a few attempts, she got one of the longer twigs to catch a spark, and she blew on it carefully as she added it back to the bowl. Soon, a little flame danced in the stone bowl. She fed it more twigs, eyeing the amount of white ash beneath the flames. "The ash goes directly onto the wound?"

"Yes," Caonach said. "As soon after the flame touches it as possible."

Gwyneth nodded. She poured water over the little flame and mixed it quickly with the ash, feeling the heat still rising from the bowl. Rhys braced himself as she knelt by his side. He gave her a small nod and clenched his jaw. She applied the ash quickly, trying not to listen to the sounds emerging through his gritted teeth. Her hands shook as she finished and set the bowl aside. She took the cloth from his forehead and wiped his face, pretending that she didn't notice the tracks of tears down his cheeks. "There," she said in a trembling voice. "It's done."

He didn't respond, staring up at the thatch overhead with glazed eyes.

"Drink the rest of the tea," she said, regaining some composure. "It will help with the pain."

Rhys obediently drank the whole cup of tea – she'd brewed it with comfrey and willow bark – and then sank back onto his blankets. He closed his eyes and sighed, going still. For a terrible moment, Gwyneth thought that he'd just breathed his last and she'd killed him with that hot ash, but then his chest rose and fell again, and she realized he had fallen into an exhausted sleep. She rubbed her eyes, feeling her own tiredness rise up like a storm cloud on the horizon.

"Here," piped a small voice.

Gwyneth started. She'd fallen asleep slumped against one of the chairs from the table. In panic, she looked at Rhys. The steady rise and fall of his chest reassured her. She looked down and found a teacup of stew and a wooden spoon by her knee.

"The bowls were too large for us," Togha said apologetically.

"You finished cooking the stew," murmured Gwyneth.

"You were tending to the Paladin," said Caonach, patting her knee.

"I...thank you," Gwyneth said, touched. She grabbed the cup and spoon, barely waiting for the first mouthful to cool. The rabbit stew tasted delicious. Togha glided over to Rhys and settled cross-legged on his good shoulder, watching him breathe with steady, silent focus.

Gwyneth ate two more cups of stew and checked Rhys' wounds. The cooling ash had begun to flake from his side, but she saw no new blood. She touched his forehead and found that his fever had broken. The relief that washed over her was dizzying in its intensity.

"You should sleep," Caonach said with a paternal air. "We will watch over him."

"And you," added Togha.

Gwyneth nodded wearily. She took one of the blankets, spread it on the floor a small distance from Rhys, and fell instantly asleep as soon as she lay down.

A piercing war cry jolted her awake what felt like moments later. Gwyneth scrambled up from the floor, her hand finding her dagger. The fire had burned down to embers and she blinked in the darkness, her heart pounding. The auras of the Glasidhe flared, illuminating a shimmering white snake that reared up and bared glistening fangs at them. Togha darted toward the snake, her small sword aiming for its eye, and it dodged her blow with fearsome speed. Gwyneth's insides turned to ice. This was no ordinary creature, for there were no snakes in Eire – she had only seen sketches of them and heard tales. She unsheathed her dagger and placed herself between the snake and Rhys.

The white snake whipped its tail and struck Togha, sending the small *aos sí* hurtling into the wall with a sickening crunch. Caonach dove at it with another ear-rending war cry, wielding two short blades. As he arrowed down at the snake, it shifted and changed, lengthening and becoming taller, arms and legs emerging, until a beautiful naked woman knelt where the snake had slithered just a moment before, her eyes still that soulless black, her skin the same shimmering white. Her feet were the cloven hooves of a goat. She reached out a hand and plucked Caonach from the air, baring her fangs at him before tossing him over her shoulder with no more ceremony than tossing a bone away.

A forked black tongue flickered from between the woman's sensual lips, tasting the air. Gwyneth's skin crawled with revulsion. This, then, was a *baobhan sith.* One of them had tracked Rhys here. She fought the urge to be sick and raised her dagger. The beautiful woman smiled at Gwyneth. Her eyes were wholly black. It was like staring into a starless sky, a cold void where no light survived. Her scarlet hair coiled and shimmered, dancing like flames, and her alabaster skin emanated its own light. She was the most beautiful thing that Gwyneth had ever seen.

Gwyneth found her voice. "No further." She leveled the point of her dagger at the woman's bare chest.

The *baobhan sith* moved so fast that Gwyneth didn't see her. She just felt hands upon her shoulders, talons digging through the cloth of her shirt, and then she crashed into the table with bone-jarring force. The world went dark for a moment. She struggled to open her eyes, blinking away the spots at the edge of her vision. Her back and shoulder hurt with bright pain where she'd hit the table, but she took a breath and pushed the hurt away.

The *baobhan sith* knelt over Rhys, running one clawed finger down his cheek. He stared up at her and bared his teeth in defiance.

"You killed my sister," said the woman in a low, hissing voice, the words sensuous, sliding silken through the shadows.

Gwyneth struggled to her knees, searching for her dagger. Her hand closed around its hilt as the *baoban sith* lowered her head toward Rhys. The beautiful woman kissed him, and Gwyneth saw his body relax, his clenched fists melting into limp hands. She took a breath and lunged at the *baoban sith,* sinking her bronze dagger into the alabaster woman's flesh. The *baoban sith* jerked back and hissed. Gwyneth scrambled backward on her hands and rear. She gathered herself for another attack but saw in horror that the black blood of the *baobhan sith* bubbled on her dagger, melting the blade as though it were candle wax. Her other hand swept across the floor and found one of the fever stones, knocked aside by Rhys as the *baobhan sith* attacked.

Then the *baobhan sith*'s clawed hands closed around her throat. Gwyneth choked and tried to hit the monstrous creature with the fever stone, but her blow glanced off the *baobhan sith*'s shoulder harmlessly.

"Stupid girl," hissed the beautiful woman, tightening her grip. Stars exploded behind Gwyneth's eyes and she bucked desperately, but the monster pinned her down with a cold and terrifyingly heavy body. One of the Glasidhe dove at her but she brushed aside the small *aos sí* as though swatting away an insect.

This, then, is how I die, Gwyneth thought as she began to lose her grip on consciousness. She saw savage delight in the *baobhan sith*'s eyes, but even with her darkening vision she saw the sudden look of surprise that froze the beautiful woman's face, her luscious mouth open in a moue of astonishment as she looked down at the gleaming point of the sword protruding from her chest.

White smoke poured from the mouth of the *baobhan sith*, as though a fire were devouring her from the inside out. Her grip around Gwyneth's throat finally slackened, and she drew in a ragged breath, coughing convulsively. The white smoke smelled like burning flesh and that strange hot-iron scent that she'd smelled on Rhys. When the cloud of smoke dissipated, the *baobhan sith* was gone, leaving only Rhys, who was leaning precariously on his sword. He grinned at Gwyneth.

"You'd make…a fine Paladin," he said.

She stared at him, gasping, unable to speak yet. Her throat throbbed with the ghost of the *baobhan sith*'s deadly grip. She pushed herself up onto her elbows.

"Are you hurt?" Rhys asked.

She almost laughed. Instead, she pointed to the rumpled nest of blankets by the fire.

"Giving orders again," Rhys said, but he turned and staggered over to the blankets. He set his sword carefully aside as he lowered himself, breathing hard.

"Togha?" Gwyneth croaked, looking for the little warrior as she remembered the terrible sound the Glasidhe had made as she hit the wall.

"A broken arm and a broken wing," Caonach said, his voice trembling a bit. "But she will live."

"Take what you need," Gwyneth said, gesturing to the herbs hanging from the crossbeam. Her back and side ached, but there was no sharp pain when she moved. Her throat felt like she'd swallowed hot coals, but that was to be expected after being nearly strangled. She managed to drink some of the willow-bark tea, and then she lowered herself back to her blanket by Rhys. As she fell asleep, she felt him touch her shoulder.

"Thank you," he said quietly.

She wanted to tell him that *he* had been the one to save her life this time, but instead she fell into sleep, the smell of the *baobhan sith*'s death-smoke lingering in the air around them, her hand clutching the hilt of her ruined dagger.

Chapter 5

Knocking at the door roused Gwyneth from sleep. She rolled over and her hand brushed against warm, bare skin. Had she gone to sleep in Siobhan's room? They hadn't shared a pallet in years…and why did her back and side ache? She blinked groggily and winced as she swallowed. Was she sick?

Then recent memory rushed back to her, along with awareness that her hand was splayed against Rhys' muscular chest. She froze, feeling a strange sort of shiver play down her skin. It wasn't unpleasant, but she'd never felt it before, and it tugged at something low in her belly that she hadn't known existed. She stared at Rhys, his face smooth in sleep, lips slightly parted and chestnut hair curling over his forehead. She found that she wanted to touch the stubble on his square jaw, and before her hand could act of its own accord, she snatched it away, curling it to her chest as though burned. Rhys took a deep breath and shifted.

The knock at the door came again, reminding Gwyneth of why she'd awoken. Rhys stirred, and she put a quieting hand on his shoulder as his eyes opened. She didn't want him to tear his wounds open again with any sudden movements; he'd been lucky last night in the fight against the *baobhan sith*, and she didn't want to test the bounds of his good fortune. She stood and hurriedly untied her braid, combing her fingers through her hair and plaiting it again nimbly. Tugging on a vest over her rumpled shirt, she pulled her boots onto her feet and walked toward the door, hoping that those small measures would make it look like she hadn't just awoken.

She glanced around the room: the overturned table, a broken earthenware bowl and the chair on its side with one leg dangling at an angle like a broken bone. Tugha and Caonach must have gone into hiding, because she didn't see their glowing auras. All the same, she unlatched the door and quickly slid outside, blinking at the bright sunlight. A glance at the sun told her it was early afternoon.

"Gwyneth," her aunt said, taking a step backward. Her eyes widened.

Gwyneth realized belatedly that there must be bruises around her throat from the *baobhan sith*'s grip. She gritted her teeth at her mistake. "Aunt Maud," she said hoarsely, acting as though nothing was wrong.

"Are you all right?" Siobhan's mother asked. She was related to Gwyneth through her husband, who was Gwyneth's father's brother, and so she looked much older than Gwyneth's own mother. Sometimes, it startled Gwyneth to see the signs of age in her aunt, and today, in the bright clear sunlight of the spring afternoon, Maud looked especially haggard.

"I'm fine, aunt," Gwyneth answered dutifully. Aunt Maud stared at her throat for a moment and then blinked. That was another difference between her mother and her aunt. Brigit would have demanded to know what had happened; Maud merely wanted to know if Gwyneth was in trouble, and then let the matter lie.

Her aunt twisted her hands in her apron and said, "Is your mother home?"

Gwyneth shook her head. "She rode to the pasture yesterday and she hasn't yet returned. She said she would most likely return tonight." She swallowed. Speaking so much felt like shoving daggers down her throat.

"I...understand," Maud said, bobbing her head and wringing her hands.

"What's wrong, Aunt?" Gwyneth asked, looking over her aunt's shoulder across the road to the other stone house that held memories of her childhood. Something fluttered against the door, scarlet as blood. Gwyneth's stomach clenched. She looked sharply at her aunt, who flinched back from her gaze.

"We don't have any paint for the door, so your uncle said the strip of cloth would do as a warning," her aunt said in a small, weary voice.

"Who is sick, Aunt?" Gwyneth's insides contracted in icy fear. The elders in the village spoke about the terrible scourge of the Black Death, the worst of which had swept through the world in *their* grandparents' time. There were still cases every now and again, though mostly in travelers that had come from the trading cities. The red cloth warned others to keep out of the house – some painted crosses on their doors, if they followed the new English faith.

"Siobhan," her aunt whispered. "It is not the Black Death, not that we can tell..." She shook her head. "I think perhaps it is the sweating sickness, but I am not a healer like your mother."

"I'll get my healing kit," Gwyneth said, turning back to the door.

"No," Maud said with vehemence, gripping Gwyneth's arm with sudden strength. "I cannot allow you to come into the house." The pain in her aunt's eyes made Gwyneth's chest ache. How good of a woman, to refuse to let her niece try to save her own daughter because of the threat of contagion.

"But you would let my mother come into the house?" Gwyneth replied. Her voice sounded different, older. She wondered if the boundary between childhood and womanhood was like a line drawn in the dirt. She had surely stepped over it yesterday if that were the case.

"Your mother has trained as a healer her entire life," Maud replied. "And it would be her decision to allow you to come. Since she is not here, I make that choice for her."

"I am not a child," Gwyneth said. "I will get my kit."

Her aunt's eyes lingered on Gwyneth's throat again. "You are dealing with some other matter." She shook her head. "I will not let you in the house, and neither will your uncle. Give me the herbs and tell me how to use them."

Gwyneth stood for a moment in indecision, emotions clotting in her chest: fear for Siobhan, anger at her aunt's insistence that she was still a child, and a strange and cutting relief that she would not be asked to enter a sick house. Finally, she nodded, and her aunt released her arm. "Wait here," she said, and she slipped back inside, shutting the door behind her.

Her shoulder and side ached with sharp pain that blended with the turmoil churning in her gut. Gwyneth swallowed hard and pushed it all down, walking toward the herbs hanging from the crossbeam. She retrieved a small basket and began gathering basics for fever and cough. Rhys looked up at her questioningly, but she shook her head wordlessly and he held his silence. Gwyneth stepped around the table and broken chair, opened the door and slid back outside. The bright sunlight slapped her in the face. How could the sun bear to shine so brightly when her cousin could be dying at this very moment? She took a deep, steadying breath, turned to her aunt and explained the uses of the herbs: two for a tea, two for a poultice to ease breathing and fever. Maud dutifully repeated the instructions and then took the basket.

Gwyneth grasped her aunt's hand. "Why did you not come sooner?" she asked, her throat tight.

"I knocked, but no one answered," Maud replied with a tired smile. "You were out hunting, I think."

Gwyneth's aunt squeezed her hand and turned, crossing the road and entering the house with the scarlet cloth nailed to its door. For a moment, Gwyneth thought of running after her, pushing her way into the house regardless of her aunt's decision, but she didn't. She turned and slipped back into the safe confines of her own home.

Slowly, with a care for her sore body, she righted the table and picked up the broken chair. Her father would be able to put another leg on it when he returned from his trading.

"Gwyneth?" Rhys said quietly, a gentle question in his voice.

She knelt to pick up the shards of the earthen bowl. She'd have to sweep, but her mother did not hold with laying out rushes like some households in town, so at least she wouldn't have to find long grasses and dry them for the floor.

"Gwyneth," Rhys said again. Movement from his direction made her look over at him; he pushed himself to his feet and walked over to her, his legs a bit unsteady.

She looked at him dully. "You shouldn't be up."

He knelt next to her. "What happened?"

She doggedly picked up another piece of pottery, and he covered her hands with his large, calloused ones.

"What happened?" he repeated.

"My cousin," she heard herself say. "She's taken ill. And my aunt will not let me go to her."

Rhys sighed. "She is protecting you."

"I should be able to make my own choice," she muttered, but her cheeks colored in shame as the sharp-edged relief surfaced again. In her years as an apprentice, they had been fortunate not to encounter any truly horrific contagions, though her mother always made her wait outside while she verified that the illness was not one that could be spread through the vapors in the air.

She looked down and realized that Rhys still held her hands. She looked over at him, that strange tingling feeling making the hairs on her arms stand on end. Did he feel it, too? He brushed one thumb over the back of her hand and then released her, picking up the last shards of the shattered bowl from the floor.

"Sometimes others make choices for us," he said. He glanced at her. "Like when you chose to save my life."

She stared at him. "That was no choice."

"There is always a choice." He shrugged. "You could have shot me. You could have run away. You could have let the *baobhan sith* kill me last night."

"Those are not choices," she insisted, shaking her head.

"Perhaps not in the light of day," he admitted. "But cowardice and self-preservation sometimes make the choices in heated moments." He tilted his head. "You possess an uncommon calm in those heated moments, Gwyneth."

Somehow the way he said her name sparked that strange little pull low in her belly. She shook off the feeling. "Well, I'm apprenticed to my mother. She's the best healer for leagues. Everyone knows that."

He didn't reply, peering at her intently with those perceptive eyes, now more gray than blue in the shadows. She held out her hand for the other shards of the bowl, and he placed them gently in her palm as though they were golden coins. She placed them in a smaller bowl. Sometimes her mother liked to put broken things back together – she was a healer, after all. She placed the bowl on the table and then turned back to Rhys. "You should lie down."

"I feel much improved," he said with that cocky half-grin.

She raised her eyebrows and pointed to the chair. "Then at least sit down. I'll bandage your side and then you can eat something."

He obediently sat in the remaining chair that had survived the onslaught of the *baobhan sith*. Her father's favorite stool had thankfully been tucked away in a corner, as her mother always put it carefully away when her father was traveling. Gwyneth hadn't ever understood the habit, but she was grateful for it now.

"Caonach didn't say how long to leave the hawthorn ash," she said, half to herself. "But if you're this improved, I'd say it can be washed off."

Rhys went still. "Caonach?"

"One of the Glasidhe who were here last night," Gwyneth replied as she carried a log over to the fire to awaken the embers. She glanced over her shoulder as Rhys cursed softly. "If it weren't for them, you'd probably be dead."

"I thought it was a fever-dream," Rhys said, running one hand through his hair. The gesture made the muscles of his back and arm ripple in the light of the new fire. Gwyneth blinked and paid attention to stoking the flame. She didn't need a burn to add to her trove of bruises.

"Caonach was the one who told me about the hawthorn," she said.

"What else did he tell you?" Rhys asked tightly.

"That you are a Paladin," Gwyneth said. She watched Rhys' reaction. "You said that once before, you know. In the forest. And you spoke of it last night, when I put the ash on your side."

Rhys looked at her despairingly. "I did?"

Gwyneth raised her eyebrows. "I think the exact words you used in the forest were 'worst Paladin ever.'"

"That may well be," he muttered, shaking his head.

"You said you were a protector," she continued. She needed something to keep her mind off Siobhan. "You work with the *aos sí* and you hunt…creatures."

He nodded, his handsome face still miserable. "We are bound to secrecy."

"You were delirious with fever," Gwyneth said. She flushed. "I was wrong to question you in such a state."

"You saved my life," he replied. "And if anyone deserves to know…"

She frowned. "Why do you say that?"

He pressed his lips together. "Gwyneth…we spoke of your family, didn't we?"

"Yes." She nodded and then turned to put the kettle over the fire. The pot of stew still hung on its hook, and despite the newness of the flames, it was nearly warm enough to eat already. As she picked up the washbasin and a clean cloth, she recalled Rhys' feverish words the night before. "You told me that I was more than a druid's daughter."

"You *are* a druid's daughter," said Rhys softly as she set the basin on the table and soaked a corner of the cloth in the cool water. He reached out and took the cloth from her, wincing as he pressed it to the remnants of the hawthorn ash clinging to his wounds.

"How can I be *more* than that?" Gwyneth pulled down a few stalks of herbs. With this much improvement, she need not make anything too strong. Better to conserve their stores for those who might badly need them – like Siobhan. She shuddered and forced her mind away from her cousin.

"By rights I should not tell you this," Rhys said, rinsing the cloth in the water and dabbing at his side again. "But you believed in the *aos sí* and the Glasidhe revealed themselves to you." He pressed his mouth into a thin line as blood tinged the water in the basin.

"Careful," warned Gwyneth, tugging the cloth from his fingers. "Let me."

He leaned on the table as she finished cleaning his wounds.

"Are the Glasidhe part of the *siabhra*?" she asked, trying to distract him from the discomfort.

He glanced at her and smiled a little. "They can be mischievous, but they are loyal and fierce."

"And the *aos sí,*" continued Gwyneth. "What are they like?" She'd often tried to envision the *aos sí*, but she was sure she hadn't been able to paint them accurately in her mind.

"They are beautiful and terrifying," Rhys murmured. "Their Queens are powerful beyond measure."

"Queens?"

"Titania is the Queen of the Seelie Court," Rhys said. "Mab rules the Unseelie Court."

"Day and night," Gwyneth said.

"Summer and winter," Rhys said, nodding in approval of her knowledge. He tensed and clenched his hands into fists as she carefully cleaned the deepest part of the slashes across his ribs.

"I could stitch you up," Gwyneth said conversationally as she rinsed the cloth, "but the hawthorn seemed to speed the healing."

"Something other than the hawthorn speeds the healing as well,"

Rhys said almost grudgingly. She raised her eyebrows in question. He sighed. "My oath as a Paladin. It...helps."

She didn't understand how an oath could help, but she nodded anyway. "Good."

He sat very still as she applied a hot poultice and bandaged his ribs, their breath mingling. He smelled like the forest. She cleared her throat as she tied off the bandage and surveyed her handiwork. "Put a shirt on and eat something."

Rhys said something that sound suspiciously like, "Giving orders," but he said it with a smile. As she ladled a bowl of the rabbit stew, Gwyneth realized that Rhys' shirt was bloodied and shredded. It would take dedicated washing and mending to make it wearable again; she glanced at him and decided that he would fit into one of her father's shirts. While he was occupied with the utter destruction of the bowl of stew – she surveyed his appetite with a healer's satisfaction – she turned and walked into the room that her father and mother shared. It felt like trespassing, but she quickly found one of her father's plainest shirts and pulled it from the neat pile by their bed.

"Don't make yourself sick," she chided gently as she saw that the bowl was empty. Rhys smiled at her boyishly with full cheeks as he devoured the last of the stew. She exchanged his empty bowl for the clean shirt, and he gingerly pulled it over his head as she fetched him more stew.

She was halfway through her own modest helping, standing by the side of the table, when he dropped his spoon into his bowl with a sigh of contentment. He leaned back for a moment and then said, "I'll be leaving at dusk."

Gwyneth frowned at him even as she tried to ignore how her heart sank. Why did she feel such emptiness at the thought of him leaving? "Why?"

"I've already tarried too long."

"You were wounded. *Are* wounded," she pointed out.

"But able to make my way...back, now," he said.

"Why do you keep doing that?" Gwyneth set down her spoon.

"Doing what?" He tried to look innocent.

"Stopping yourself before you tell me anything more."

He sighed. "Because you should not know anything at all. Because I've put you in danger by being here, as you saw last night." He shook his head.

"Why can't I know?" she said, her voice strong and insistent. "You told me you're a Paladin. You told me you work with the *aos sí* as a protector. You told me you hunt creatures in this world. *Why can't I know more?*"

He looked at her, opened his mouth and closed it again, sitting up straighter in his chair. His eyes widened as he looked over her shoulder. She spun to find the door standing wide open – the door that had been latched. Gwyneth blinked against the bright sunlight. A woman stood silhouetted in the doorway. Rhys pushed himself to his feet and *bowed* as the woman strode across the threshold.

Gwyneth stared at the woman. She recognized a hint of her mother in the woman's features, some similarities in the nose and mouth and the brilliant green eyes. This woman was tall, her legs and arms muscled, clad in breeches, a plain white shirt and a vest intricately embroidered in gold. The hilt of a sword emerged from over the woman's shoulder. She carried with her a sense of wildness, a strange scent that swirled through the room, something sharp and cold like the air before a storm.

"It is not his place to tell you more," said the woman. She wore authority like a cloak. Gwyneth found herself wanting to bow as well, though that was ridiculous. The woman smiled a little, as though she knew Gwyneth had just resisted the urge to genuflect to her. "It is *my* place."

Gwyneth opened her mouth to ask this strange woman who somehow looked familiar her name, but Rhys spoke first, in a tone so different from his usual voice that she looked at him sharply.

"It is an honor," he said reverently, "Lady Bearer."

Chapter 6

The tall woman acknowledged Rhys with a small nod. "It is good to see you are not dead, Paladin." She turned her brilliant eyes to Gwyneth, who felt naked before their searching gaze. "That is your doing, is it not?"

Gwyneth found her voice. "Yes."

The woman nodded. She stood silently for a long moment. Gwyneth glanced back at Rhys, who tilted his head toward the table.

"Please," Gwyneth said, her cheeks coloring as she realized she'd forgotten all courtesy. "Sit at my table and be welcome." She gestured to the one chair.

The woman that Rhys had called Lady Bearer inclined her head in acceptance, and Gwyneth turned to the fire to put the kettle on for tea. She noticed that Rhys had picked up his belt and scabbard, fastening his belt around his hips once more. When she turned from stoking the fire, she asked, "We have just eaten. Will you take some stew?"

The Bearer smiled serenely from her seat at the table. "No, thank you. It was not a long journey." Her eyes shifted to Rhys, who stood very straight, drawing back his shoulders. "You killed a *baobhan sith*."

"Yes, Lady Bearer."

Her impenetrable eyes betrayed nothing. "You were wounded, and Gwyneth found you in the forest."

A prickle of unease swept down Gwyneth's back. She had not introduced herself to the tall woman.

"Yes, Lady Bearer," Rhys answered again.

"And you led a *baobhan sith* here, to this house. To a house of the Blood." The woman did not raise her voice, but hardness entered her words.

"Yes, Lady Bearer," Rhys said. To his credit, his voice did not shake, but Gwyneth saw his hands begin to tremble. She wondered whether it was from fatigue and pain, or fear of the tall woman sitting at the table.

The Bearer looked at Rhys for a long moment. He stood very still, but cast his eyes down as though awaiting judgment. Finally, the Bearer stood and motioned to the chair. "Sit down before you fall down, Paladin."

Rhys looked up as though startled, but he recovered his stoic expression and obeyed without a word. Gwyneth busied herself fetching teacups. When she turned to put the cups on the table, she found the Bearer perched with one hip on the table quite casually, watching her. Gwyneth waited for a question, but none came, so she continued preparing tea. After she'd finished pouring the tea, she set out a little pot of wild honey and with a nod to the stranger, excused herself and fetched some cream from the cellar. She thought she heard Rhys and the woman talking as she rounded the house again, but the goat bleated and Pip snorted at her, ending any chance at eavesdropping.

"Are you sure you are not hungry, my lady?" Gwyneth asked as she set the cream on the table. She blinked at the honorific: she hadn't thought to say it. It had just *happened*, as though something deep within her recognized this woman.

"No, thank you, Gwyneth." The woman picked up her cup of tea and tipped a small amount of cream into it, as well as a generous dollop of honey.

"You know my name," Gwyneth blurted, the words tumbling out of her. "How do you know my name?"

The Bearer chuckled. "I had thought you were going to ask *my* name." She sipped her tea. Rhys watched the two of them as though he were watching two wolves circling one another. Gwyneth wondered why he wore such an expression of awe when looking at the tall woman.

"I do not know you," Gwyneth said honestly, "but you look...you look like my mother, and you know my name."

"It would perhaps be more properly said that your mother looks like me," the woman said, raising one eyebrow as she took another swallow of tea. "This honey is excellent."

"I...gathered it myself," Gwyneth replied, blinking. "Wait, why would...I don't understand."

"Of course you do not, hidden away like this," the Bearer said, almost gently. She set aside her teacup and stood to her full height. Gwyneth thought that this woman might be as tall as her father. Rhys leaned forward slightly and caught his breath. The Bearer looked at Gwyneth and said, "Your mother looks like me because she is the granddaughter of my own granddaughter."

The floor tilted beneath Gwyneth's feet. She put a hand on the table to steady herself. "If my mother is the granddaughter of your granddaughter...then that would make you..."

"Your great-great-grandmother, I believe," said the tall woman.

Gwyneth took a deep breath. Her stomach coiled and clenched. "That sounds..."

"Impossible," finished the woman with a small smile. "It does, doesn't it? But so also do the Glasidhe and *baobhan sith* and our young Paladin here, and you have seen them all with your own eyes."

Rhys blushed furiously when the Bearer gestured to him. Gwyneth leaned on the table and watched as the golden-haired woman bent down and plucked the pitted hilt of Gwyneth's ruined dagger from the floor.

"You helped to kill a *baobhan sith*," said the Bearer, holding up the hilt on the flat of her palm. "That is no small thing."

Gwyneth touched her throat. "It was going to kill us."

The Bearer nodded. "Yes. It would have." She set the dagger hilt on the table and held her hands out to Gwyneth. "Let me see your bruises."

Gwyneth swallowed and stepped toward the tall woman, still turning her words over and over in her mind like a coin flipped between fingers. She tried to estimate the woman's age and gave up, her mind too stunned to properly think.

The Bearer raised her hands and placed them gently on either side of Gwyneth's throat. For a moment, Gwyneth tensed, the feel of the *baobhan sith*'s grip surging to the forefront of her memory; but the Bearer said quietly, "It is all right, blood of my blood."

Later when Gwyneth tried to put words to the sensation, she fell short. She only knew that the Bearer's hands at her throat heated slightly and then cooled, and something flowed *into* her, sweeping away the ache of the bruises at her throat, rushing down into her shoulder and back and side, all the hurt inflicted by the vicious strength of the *baobhan sith* enveloped by the shifting force emanating from the palms of the Bearer. She felt her eyes close, and when the sensation faded, she opened them and caught a glimpse of white fire fading from the Bearer's hands.

"There," said the woman, a note of satisfaction in her voice.

Gwyneth touched two fingers to her throat. She knew without looking in the bit of mirror that the bruise had vanished. Pressing a hand to her side, she looked at the Bearer in wonder when no pain lanced through her ribs. What a skill that would be, to heal with just a touch of the hands! It was nothing short of...magical. Then she looked at Rhys. "Will you heal him, my lady?"

The Bearer did not answer right away. Then she said, "No." She held up a hand at Gwyneth's half-formed protest. "I do not often explain myself, but I understand that you have no knowledge of the world in which the Paladin and I live." Her green eyes caught Gwyneth's, and she shivered at the intensity within them. "You are the blood of my blood, and so healing you is simple. That is one reason, but not the only reason. The Paladins are protectors. They swear on their souls and their swords to defend both worlds from darkness. Pain and scars are two of their best teachers."

Gwyneth shook her head. "That is…harsh."

The Bearer smiled humorlessly. "The worlds are harsh, Gwyneth, and you would do well not to forget it." She pressed her lips together. "Perhaps I should not have healed you. I thought it would help you understand what I am – what *you* are."

"I do not mean to seem ungrateful," Gwyneth said, staring at the woman. Something thrilled within her, some insatiable curiosity that thirsted to *know*. "I'm sorry, I do not understand what…what I am."

"You need not offer any apology," said the Bearer. She tilted her head. "It is your mother who made the choice for you."

Gwyneth felt the air leave her lungs as though the woman had just punched her in the stomach. "My…mother?"

"Yes. Brigit. She was always a willful girl," said the Bearer.

"You…know her?"

"We have met," said the woman with a regal nod.

"How was it my mother's choice? Please explain," Gwyneth said. "I want to know." She leaned on the table again, feeling suddenly dizzy.

"You should sit," Rhys said, standing and guiding her into the chair. Gwyneth allowed it, taking deep breaths. She felt as though she'd just been spun about blindfolded.

"I will tell you," said the Bearer. Her voice shifted to the timbre of the storyteller. "I am Rionach, daughter of Damhnait, daughter of Macha, who was herself the daughter of Tlachtga and sister to Cumma and Doirb."

"Muach," said Gwyneth, even though she knew she shouldn't interrupt. "Legend tells that Tlachtga had three sons. Cumma, Doirb and Muach."

"One of those sons was truly a daughter," said Rionach. "Tlachtga understood too well the dangers of being a woman in this world, and her daughter was hidden on her instructions. It was told to the Mug Ruith and his counselors that she had borne three sons."

"He was a powerful druid," said Gwyneth quietly. "How did he not know the truth?"

"Tlachtga was more powerful," said Rionach firmly. "And she was punished for it."

Gwyneth winced: the legend of Tlachtga told that her father's counselors had raped her, jealous that her power had surpassed their own.

"Do not shy away from the brutal truths of our world," Rionach said. "You cannot see the world for what it is with your eyes closed."

Gwyneth swallowed and nodded. "You are the great-granddaughter of Tlachtga."

"Aye," said Rionach gravely. "I bore three daughters and two sons. Your mother is descended from my eldest daughter Eimear." Her eyes shifted suddenly to Rhys. "And your Paladin is descended from my youngest son, Ailill."

Rhys bowed his head. He didn't look surprised. Gwyneth tried not to feel pleased that Rionach had called Rhys *her* Paladin – that was ridiculous.

"Then *you* are a druid?" she ventured.

"Of a sort, yes," Rionach said. "I am the Bearer of the Caedbranr." She lifted one hand and touched the hilt of the sword over her shoulder. The emerald in its pommel flashed and rolled as surely as the eye of a man who had just awoken. Gwyneth shivered as she felt the pulse of an otherworldly power humming through the air. "Only one of our blood can truly bear this weapon, Gwyneth. Just as the Paladins are protectors, so are we. We stand between the light and the dark. We stand between the two worlds. We keep the balance between them."

"The two worlds," Gwyneth repeated softly. "Tir Na Nog?"

"Faeortalam," replied the Bearer. "Tir Na Nog is part of legend."

"Tlachtga is part of legend," countered Gwyneth.

Rionach smiled at her. "That is true."

Gwyneth sat back in her chair. She looked at the table and touched her forgotten tea. It was still warm, so she stirred in a spoonful of honey and took a contemplative sip. "None of this explains why you are here."

She heard Rhys let out his breath again in a despairing sigh at her abruptness.

"Indeed, it does not." Rionach stood and walked about the room. "You see, Gwyneth, the eldest daughters of houses of the Blood are bequeathed to the Bearer. The Bearer trains them, and when the time comes, she chooses a new Bearer from among them. Her successor." She touched one of the dried bunches of herbs hanging from the crossbeam. "When Macha passed the Sword to me, she bid me choose my successor well. The farther our land drifts from the old ways, the more difficult it will be to hold the two worlds in balance. There will come a time when choices must be made."

"You have been the Bearer for...centuries," Gwyneth said softly, gazing at the tall, strong figure outlined by the light of the fire. She understood now why Rhys looked at the Bearer with such respect.

"I have lived many lives," said Rionach in agreement.

"You must have many descendants from which to choose," Gwyneth said.

"I do," Rionach agreed without any other explanation. She turned her back on Gwyneth and Rhys, looking down into the flames. The battered sheath on her back did not look like it held a weapon of Fae power, Gwyneth thought. The emerald in the pommel *looked* at her, as though it had heard her silent musings.

Gwyneth stared down into her teacup, swirling the liquid as she thought. Why had the Bearer not come before, if the firstborn daughters of the bloodline were her right? Her hands stilled. Of course. She was not the firstborn daughter, though she had thought until this moment that she was now the only surviving daughter. Her memory flickered. "You took my sister."

"She came willingly," said Rionach, still looking into the fire.

"If I come with you, will I see her again?" Gwyneth said in a rush. She didn't remember much at all about her sister, and most of it had faded in the years since she'd died – no, since she'd disappeared, Gwyneth corrected herself. Beneath the almost-painful hope, she felt a little spark of anger at her mother. How could she let everyone mourn a child who was alive, even if that child had been spirited away to the land of the *aos sí*?

"She is dead," said Rionach in a quiet voice.

The strange hope left Gwyneth in a rush. "Oh."

"But even if she were still alive," said Rionach, "I would still have come for you."

"Why?" Gwyneth asked, her voice almost a whisper.

"The past, the present and the future," said Rionach. "All twined together, all whirling around us. I see enough, though I still know little." She turned back to Gwyneth, and there was something like anger written across her face. Gwyneth pressed back against her chair involuntarily. "Your mother hid you through your ignorance. Once you encountered the Paladin, that protection began to fade."

"Protection?"

"Why do you think we take the women of our blood to train in Faeortalam?" said Rionach, lifting an eyebrow. "The world is a dangerous place, Gwyneth, especially for those of our blood."

"But you said that my ignorance was a protection," Gwyneth said, trying to understand.

"In a way," said Rionach. "Your mother tried to hide you in plain sight, and it worked for a while." She paused. "But you knew, did you not?"

"I thought it was childish," admitted Gwyneth. "I thought that perhaps I would forget my dreams once I grew into a woman."

"And you well might have. But you saved the life of a Paladin and you helped him slay a *baobhan sith*." The Bearer nodded. "Now you know that what you felt was the truth. Now you may face it, with your eyes open."

Gwyneth blinked. "Yes. Thank you." She bowed her head respectfully, as she would do before an elder – after all, the Bearer was her great-great-grandmother. She tried to think of something else to say.

Rionach inclined her head. "Much has changed in the past day for you, Gwyneth."

Gwyneth nodded numbly. Then she found her tongue. "Does this mean that I can come with you?"

"Yes," Rionach replied simply. Then she said, "I would like to visit your goat. My grandmother was especially fond of goats. Perhaps take the chance to speak with your Paladin."

Gwyneth had nearly forgotten that Rhys was in the room, he'd been so silent. Rionach swept out of the room, the door closing on its own accord behind her. Gwyneth stood. "Here," she said to Rhys. "You can have your seat back."

"It's your house and your chair," pointed out Rhys.

"It's my mother and father's house," countered Gwyneth in a murmur. She poured more tea into her cup.

Rhys cleared his throat. "And…I am not *your* Paladin."

She looked at him sharply, feeling the blood rushing to her face. "I never said…"

"No, but the Bearer did, and I didn't want…" Two spots of color burned high on his cheekbones.

"Of course," she said. "I understand."

"But you did save my life, and I'm indebted to you," Rhys continued.

"No." Gwyneth shook her head. "I'm in *your* debt. I'm a healer – an apprentice, anyway. I couldn't just leave you to die. There is no debt there. But you saved me from the *baobhan sith*…"

"Which was going to kill me, until you stabbed it with your wee dagger and distracted it," Rhys interjected almost cheerfully.

"You saved me from the *baobhan sith*," Gwyneth repeated doggedly, glaring at him for interrupting. "And you told me…enough. You told me enough to break whatever *spell* my mother thought to hold over me."

"I think it was the Glasidhe who did that," Rhys pointed out.

She shook her head in irritation at him, and then she paused. "Where did they go? Togha and Caonach. They disappeared."

"Glasidhe come and go as they please," Rhys said. "They're beholden to no Court."

"Togha was injured in the fight with the *baobhan sith*," Gwyneth said, frowning.

"Truly, the Glasidhe are masters of slipping about unseen," said Rhys. He smiled. "I can find out where they are, if it would ease your mind."

"It would," she replied in relief.

"After we return to Faeortalam," said Rhys with a nod.

Gwyneth swallowed. She looked at the stone walls of her home, the herbs hanging from the crossbeam and the fire in the hearth; the copper kettle with its dent where she'd dropped it years ago, and her father's favorite stool. "Your family still thinks you are alive, but you can't see them?"

Rhys sighed. "My Paladin blood is from my father. He thought it easier for my mother and sisters if I were to study in Dublin for a few years, and then die of some illness there."

Gwyneth pressed her lips together. "Don't you think it's cruel?"

"Of course," he replied in a quiet voice. "But their ignorance protects them. I cannot protect them all the time."

"You hunted the *baobhan sith* because it was close to the village?"

Rhys shifted. "I follow the orders of my commander."

"How many Paladins *are* there?" Gwyneth had envisioned only a handful, but the way that Rhys spoke of his commander, she shifted her thinking to an army.

"Fourscore or so, right now," he replied.

"Well," Gwyneth said after a moment of silence. "You are about to be made an uncle again, did you know? Your sister Moira."

"Ah, she stayed an O'Connor," said Rhys, smiling. "Married a cousin from the west." Then he straightened. "An uncle *again*?"

"Yes," replied Gwyneth. She felt a pang of sorrow for Rhys. "This is her third child. She already has a hale boy and girl."

Rhys looked down; she couldn't see his face.

"Callan and Cecily, they're named," she said.

He chuckled. "Cecily. What a dreary name for the poor girl."

Gwyneth smiled. "She is a bonny little lass and will not suffer for it."

"That is the hardest part," said Rhys quietly. "The...not knowing."

"Surely you can glean news of your family when you venture into this world," Gwyneth said.

"And reveal myself not to be studying in Dublin?" Rhys shook his head. "No. It cannot be. My father will receive a letter saying that I am dead, perhaps this year, perhaps next." He shrugged his muscled shoulders. "It is better that way." He met her eyes. "Could you imagine what that monster would have done if I'd staggered home instead of being found by you?"

Gwyneth sucked in a breath as she imagined the *baobhan sith*'s claws tearing into Moira O'Connor's plump, angelic little children. Her horror must have showed on her face, because Rhys sighed.

"I do not mean to be harsh, Gwyneth. I just want you to understand. It may be different for you, since you are of the Bearer's blood, and your ma already knows, but..." He shrugged.

"What's it like?" she asked. "Faeortalam."

"It's...magnificent," said Rhys with his half-grin. "Absolutely magnificent."

"So you'd do it again? Leave your family and go train to serve the *aos sí?*"

Rhys nodded. "If you decide to walk this path, you'll see that there's darkness in both worlds, Gwyneth. It's my honor to stand between evil and the innocent."

He said it with such conviction that Gwyneth felt goose flesh rise on her arms. "That's very noble."

"Aye, but it's also a very bloody business," he replied grimly. "I didn't die yesterday, but I may die tomorrow, so my Da may not be lying." He shrugged. "But I'd choose it all again."

The door opened. Rionach walked into the room. "Your goat is quite charming."

"I – thank you?" Gwyneth heard herself say somewhat questioningly.

The Bearer tilted her head slightly, as though she were listening to something that Gwyneth couldn't hear. The Sword thrummed on her back like a plucked string. "Ah. Brigit is nearly here."

Gwyneth's stomach twisted yet again. "You are going to speak to my mother?"

"Of course," Rionach said implacably. "We have much to discuss, she and I."

Gwyneth looked at Rhys. "Should we hide him?"

Rionach chuckled. "No, no. Brigit needs to see your Paladin. She needs to understand that there is no turning back."

"I thought I had a choice," Gwyneth said.

The Bearer looked at her and said, "You have already made it. I can feel it."

And Gwyneth realized with a jolt that the Bearer was right. It was as though her great-great grandmother had peeled aside Gwyneth's skin and bones and stared into her beating heart, which clenched almost painfully with joy at the prospect of traveling to the land of the *aos sí*.

Gwyneth nodded. "You are right. I have."

She squared her shoulders and tried to imitate the Bearer's indomitable posture and expression, wondering whether she would be able to bear the onslaught of her mother's anger and sorrow.

Chapter 7

Brigit showed no surprise as she opened the door of the house. For an instant, she stood silhouetted against the light of day, and then she stepped across the threshold, shutting the door behind her. She smelled of horse and sheep and the long grass of the pastures. As the door closed, her keen gaze traveled around the room, taking in Rhys standing by the fire, Rionach tall and steady as an oak tree by the table, and finally settling on Gwyneth. Gwyneth resisted the urge to look away when her mother's eyes fastened upon her. She couldn't decipher the expression on her mother's face. It may have been anger or sorrow, or perhaps both.

For a long moment, the crackling of the flames that danced on the log in the hearth underscored the silence. Gwyneth felt the air in the room draw tight, like a bowstring with an arrow nocked to it.

"Gwyneth," Brigit said finally, her voice hard. "What have you done, foolish girl?"

Gwyneth swallowed and raised her chin. "I came upon Rhys in the forest yesterday while out hunting. He was wounded, and I brought him here." She held her mother's gaze unflinchingly.

Brigit shifted her attention to the Bearer. Fury crystallized her handsome features into a countenance unfamiliar to Gwyneth. She felt like she looked at a stranger rather than her own mother. Brigit took a step toward Rionach, her body taut. "You have no right to her."

Rionach smiled humorlessly. "You know as well as I that I have rights to all daughters of the Blood."

"You took my firstborn," said Brigit with hard rage.

"She came willingly," replied the Bearer, unmoved.

Brigit gestured to Gwyneth. "She does not know her own mind. She knows not the perils of *your* world."

The Bearer turned her head and looked at Gwyneth. Rhys did not look at her; he kept his eyes on Brigit, one hand resting casually on the hilt of his sword, as though he expected Gwyneth's mother to attack them.

Gwyneth drew back her shoulders. She picked up the pitted hilt of her dagger from the table and held it out for her mother's inspection. "I helped to kill a *baobhan sith*."

Her mother's face drew tighter, paling further. "And you endanger her," she hissed at Rhys.

"She chose her path," Rhys replied with steady certainty. He raised one dark eyebrow. "I told her to leave me to die, actually."

"You must see that I couldn't do that, Mother," Gwyneth said quietly.

"I told you," Brigit said, rounding on her, "I *told* you not to speak to any strangers – to come to *me* if anything happened…"

"He would have died," Gwyneth said. "And that is counter to everything that you have taught me." She lifted one shoulder in a shrug. "Rhys is no stranger to me. I did not think your warning applied to him."

Brigit turned to Rionach again. "You sent a Paladin from this village, one that my daughter *knew*, to lure her into your trap!"

The Bearer said nothing. Gwyneth wondered with a horrible clutching sensation if that was true – she glanced at Rhys, and thought she saw a flicker of uncertainty in his eyes, still trained on her mother. That, at least, gave her hope that if there *had* been some plot, he hadn't been fully aware of it. But all of that mattered little. She drew back her shoulders.

"It does not matter how it came about, Mother," she said. "All that matters now is that I have made my decision."

"You are a child," Brigit spat. "You cannot choose such a thing."

Gwyneth had never before seen her mother so emotional. Brigit carried the reputation of the calm, steadfast healer, the quiet, knowledgeable woman who did not give in to vapors and fits of passion. Now she thought she glimpsed the edge of panic in the widening of her mother's eyes. "Mother," she said, as gently as she could. "I am not a child. I cannot forget what I now know. I would not change the choice I made yesterday."

"You can still choose to stay here," Brigit said, almost desperately. "I know runes to conceal and hide…"

"Do not misrepresent your own small abilities, Brigit," the Bearer said in the tone of an elder correcting a child telling tales.

Brigit went whiter still, staring at Rionach in mute fury. Gwyneth couldn't remember the last time that anyone had questioned her mother's authority.

"Your runes did not even conceal your daughter from the Glasidhe," said Rionach with a small shake of her head.

"The Small Folk do have a will of their own," said Rhys, tilting his head slightly and smiling.

"I thought they were dreams, and nothing more," Gwyneth said. She gathered her courage. "Why have you hidden the truth of things from me, Mother?" She almost asked if her mother was truly going to tell her the truth, as she'd said before she departed for the pastures, but she decided against it.

"To protect you," her mother said with colorless lips. "I did not want to lose you, too."

"That is the way of life, isn't it?" Gwyneth shook her head. "You have always told me that death walks beside us each day. Sometimes we can stave him off with our knowledge, and sometimes we cannot." She took a deep breath. "I understand that you were trying to protect me. But I do not understand why you took away my choice."

"You are a *child*," repeated her mother in a low voice.

"I am not," Gwyneth replied firmly.

"You realize," Brigit said with the air of a woman clawing at any thread of hope, "that you will have to leave forever. You realize that it is banishment. It is cruel and heartless, to rip children from their families." Her face softened. "Do you love me so little?"

Gwyneth tried to sort through her own emotions as she stared at her mother. "You know I love you, Mother, but you knew that there would come a time when I would leave this house and begin my own life."

"In the village," Brigit replied quickly, "with a suitable young man, once you had finished your apprenticeship with me and I could teach you nothing more. We...we would still be able to see each other...and you would bear children..."

Gwyneth swallowed down the distaste that rose in her whenever her mother mentioned future grandchildren. "Life does not give us our dreams."

Except now, she realized. *Except for mine.* A little thrill of excitement ran through her again at the thought of traveling with the Bearer and Paladin into Faeortalam.

"You seek to hide away a daughter of the Blood who may become the Bearer of the Iron Sword," said Rionach, suddenly seeming even taller, shadows gathering in the corners of the room as though she drew all light into herself.

"I seek to save my daughter's life," Brigit replied defiantly.

"Or to control it," intoned Rionach solemnly. "This does not become you. You are a daughter of Tlachtga, Brigit O'Dogherty. Remember yourself."

"I remember that my daughter has been taken and my son dead," Brigit said.

Gwyneth realized with a pang that her mother didn't know of her eldest daughter's death. She held her tongue, watching Rionach.

"As Gwyneth said, death walks alongside all of us," Rionach said almost gently. Then the shadows darkened, and a strange hum emanated from the scabbard on her back. "Remember yourself, daughter, and do not disgrace yourself further."

Brigit stared at Rionach as though the Bearer had spoken in tongues. Gwyneth tried to hold back the tide of thoughts rushing through her mind as she absorbed the words of both the Bearer and her mother. She felt a keen, piercing sorrow at the thought of never seeing her mother and father again; and then her aunt and uncle, and Siobhan – she gasped as she remembered.

"Aunt Maud said that Siobhan had taken ill. She wouldn't let me into the house to see to her," she said.

Brigit nodded once, curtly. "I saw the scarlet mark on the door." Her mouth pressed into a harsh line. "You were too occupied with the Paladin."

"I did not know," protested Gwyneth, the sting of her mother's words bright and sharp. "I gave Aunt Maud some herbs and told her what to do..."

Her mother said nothing, staring at Rionach and then at Rhys. "I hope you're happy, boy," she said bitterly to Rhys, derision in her voice.

"Mother!" Gwyneth said in shock. She would have never suspected that this spiteful woman existed within the calm, steady healer.

"You should tend to your niece, Brigit," Rionach said. It sounded more like a suggestion than a command.

Brigit did not reply, but she stalked forward and retrieved her healing satchel, pulling the strap over her head and settling it against her hip. She wordlessly pulled her stool out from under the table, stepped up and selected a few dried herbs, and walked toward the door. She paused and turned, her face a strange mask. "When I return, I expect my home to be empty."

Confusion swirled like smoke within Gwyneth's head. She hadn't thought the departure to be so imminent and her mother so intractable, but before she could think of something to say, her mother opened the door and was gone. Some of the tension left Rhys' shoulders, and he let his hand slide away from the hilt of his sword.

"Let us go, then," the Bearer said.

Gwyneth swallowed. "I...didn't think it would be *now*."

"If not now, then when?" The tall, powerful woman looked at her with a sort of mild curiosity.

"I...I thought I would have time to say goodbye," Gwyneth replied. "My father is traveling, and he should be home in a few days – and Siobhan is sick, I must speak to her before I go..." She stopped as Rionach shook her head.

"Gwyneth," said the Bearer in that strange, almost-kind voice, "leaving is never easy, whether it is the journey of life or the journey of death. If we allow ourselves, we will delay setting out endlessly, and that is how all the days of one's life slip away uncounted."

"I just wanted to say goodbye," Gwyneth said.

"You have," Rionach replied simply. "Did you not bid your father a good journey before he left? Did you not bid good night to your cousin when you parted last?"

Gwyneth felt her cheeks heat in shame and remorse.

"There are a thousand different small farewells that we make every day, and the dawn is never guaranteed," continued the Bearer with her unshakeable serenity.

"It is not so bad as you think it will be," Rhys said to her in a low voice. "At first, it hurts. But soon you'll be so busy with training that you will have no extra energy to feel homesick." He half-grinned.

The spark of desire and curiosity at Rhys' words helped Gwyneth push down the grief threatening to overwhelm her. She nodded, trying to imitate the Bearer's calm mien.

"You need not pack anything," said the Bearer, as though she'd read Gwyneth's mind. Perhaps she had. "Just a cloak and your bow, if you wish to take it."

Gwyneth nodded, turning to walk into her chamber. The Bearer turned to Rhys. "Provisions for the journey to the Gate, Paladin, and payment for them," Gwyneth heard her say.

Gwyneth didn't linger long in her room, because she somehow knew that if she delayed, she'd lose her courage. She was leaving her village and her family forever to follow two strangers into another world – into the world of the *aos sí*. She stifled the urge to chuckle at how incredibly ridiculous that sounded, even in her head, but everything had changed in the past two days. Her world had shifted on its axis, layers of shadow and blood peeled away, revealing the bone-deep truth that she'd somehow known all along. She fastened her cloak around her shoulders and picked up her bow and quiver. On a whim, she opened her small jewelry box. Her father had returned from his last long trading trip with an extravagant gift for her: a necklace of wrought silver, a circular pendant with the great Tree of Life stretching its branches to the sky and its roots into the ground. She slid the chain over her head and felt the pendant nestle in the hollow of her throat.

When she emerged into the common room, Rhys tied the top of a small cloth sack and slung it over his shoulder: their provisions, she guessed. He counted out three silver coins from his belt purse and left them on the table. It was a sum far too princely for the foodstuffs in the sack – it would have bought their entire house and the animals too, Gwyneth thought, but she said nothing. A treacherous part of her heart wanted to see her mother's reaction to the silver coins. Would she sweep them from the table in an uncharacteristic fit of rage, or would she store them away primly to buy more sheep or more silk thread for her embroidery?

"I cannot wait until my cousin is out of danger?" Gwyneth heard herself say, the hope in her voice pitiable.

"No," said the Bearer steadily. "Come."

Gwyneth tried to push away the feeling of dizziness, taking deep breaths as her feet carried her toward the door. She looked over her shoulder and memorized the look of the room: the herbs hanging from the cross beam, the well-made table, her mother's skillful embroidery decorating the stone walls, the tidy hearth and the copper kettle gleaming over the flames. Her heart stuttered as she thought of her father returning home to find that she'd disappeared without a trace. What would her mother tell him? How much did he already know?

Rhys touched her arm, jolting her out of her thoughts. The heat of his large, calloused hand burned through her shirt. "It does no good to dwell on it," he said quietly, just for her ears.

Gwyneth nodded. She shifted her bow on her shoulder, turned and walked over the threshold, stepping into the bright spring sunlight beyond.

Chapter 8

Somehow, Gwyneth had expected her mother to find them in the forest, to give chase and heal the sting of her last words...a ridiculous, childish thought, but she felt it all the same. Rionach set a punishing pace, her long legs striding over the ground at a speed that nearly forced Gwyneth to jog to keep up. She kept glancing at Rhys as the day wore on and the sun slanted golden through the trees, stretching long shadows across their path.

"Stop eyeing me like I'm about to fall over," Rhys said to her in an undertone as they climbed over a huge fallen tree.

"You almost died two days ago," she replied, clambering down through the branches of the tree and finally putting her feet on solid ground again.

"But I didn't," he said. "Come on, we can't fall behind."

Rionach spared them little attention as they traveled, and Gwyneth had quickly learned that the Bearer kept her pace no matter whether Gwyneth and Rhys were on her heels or barely able to see her through the trees. A few times, it had only been the glint of sunlight on the Bearer's golden hair that saved them from losing her entirely. Gwyneth felt the exertion in her legs, but she found that she enjoyed the challenge. At least Rionach didn't treat them like children.

Despite his assertion that he was fine, Rhys didn't have any breath to spare for conversation, leaving Gwyneth alone with her own thoughts. In the hours of that first day of travel, she replayed the conversation with her mother over and over again in her mind. She asked herself what she could have said differently, what she could have done differently. Perhaps if she'd met her mother at the door or in front of the house and had a chance to explain before Brigit stepped over the threshold...perhaps if she'd said straightaway about Siobhan...perhaps if she hadn't gotten angry about her mother treating her like a child...

Her thoughts wove a snarled tangle. As dusk fell, she decided that there really wasn't anything else that she could have done. Her mother had made her decision, and Gwyneth had made hers. The realization made her chest ache, and for a brief moment a treacherous part of her mind whispered that it wasn't too late. She could turn and navigate her way back to her village, to everything she had known and loved for her entire life. Her steps slowed. Then Rhys turned and looked at her over his shoulder, his eyes inquiring; and she darted after him with renewed energy.

The ache in her chest intensified when they stopped to rest for the night. Her body suddenly seemed to understand that they'd been traveling at a brisk pace all day, and her legs tightened uncomfortably as she sat on the gnarled root of a large tree.

"Gwyneth, you will take the first watch. Wake the Paladin when the moon has risen above the trees. And then, Paladin, wake me a few hours before dawn," Rionach instructed.

Rhys accepted the instructions without a word. Gwyneth adjusted the strap of her quiver on her shoulder where it had begun to chafe at the hard travel, and she wondered what exactly she was intended to guard against. Then she remembered the shining white snake coiling across the floor, its liquid eyes fixed malevolently on Rhys, and she shivered.

"If anything is amiss," Rhys said to her in a low voice, "just wake us." He handed her a small packet of food: a piece of day-old bread, some hard cheese and dried meat that Gwyneth recognized from her father's last trading trip during the winter months.

Gwyneth nodded. The darkness of the forest pressed around them, the silvery light of dusk fading from the sky. She ate the bread and cheese, enjoying the plain fare despite herself. Her father had always said that a day of hard travel was the best salt for any meal. She felt the coolness of the ground seeping up into her legs.

"I feel like I should be weeping," she said quietly to Rhys. "I left ...everything behind me."

He finished his food and considered her words. "You left behind what you've known, but you're stepping into an adventure bigger than you can imagine." His half-grin flashed white in the shadows.

"Did you...did you feel this way?" she asked. Somehow the question felt too personal, too raw, despite the fact that in the scant time they'd become reacquainted in this new truth, her hands had been covered in Rhys' blood and she'd taken him into her home. Few things were more personal than healing someone, seeing them at their most vulnerable, but somehow Gwyneth felt differently about Rhys. Maybe Rionach was right: scars and pain were part of a Paladin's lot. They were no ordinary people.

Rhys took a breath, considering her question. "I was glad," he said with an air of admission. "This, to me, is better than anything my other life could have afforded me."

"But you didn't know that then," Gwyneth whispered. She wrapped her arms around herself, pulling her cloak tighter around her shoulders.

"But I did," said Rhys. She saw him nod in the fading light. "And you do, too."

Gwyneth settled herself against the trunk of the tree. Rhys wrapped himself in his cloak and promptly fell asleep. Rionach sat against a tree a few strides away from Gwyneth, and Gwyneth thought she saw the glimmer of the Bearer's eyes in the darkness, but she wasn't entirely sure, and she wasn't foolish enough to ask. Her legs stiffened and every ache in her body intensified as she sat the watch, her eyelids growing heavy as she struggled to stay awake. Exhaustion weighed on her, dragging at her mind with the heavy weight of her homesickness and her questions. Had she done the right thing, leaving with Siobhan sick and her mother angry? Would she ever see her family again? How long of a journey was it to the world of the *aos sí*? And what would happen to her if she weren't truly meant to be a Paladin or the Bearer?

Gwyneth pinched her arms to keep herself awake. She stood and stretched, leaning back against the tree, searching the shadows for anything strange. Something rustled in the underbrush. Her awareness sharpened almost painfully, a rush of alertness sweeping over her as she heard the rustle again. She slid her bow off her shoulder, her hands clumsy with the early-spring cold, but she nocked an arrow and sighted down its length toward the quivering brush. The noise intensified. Rhys stirred, and she drew back her arrow, stepping in front of him to place herself between him and the unknown creature.

A rabbit, unusually fat for so early in the year, hopped out of the brush. Gwyneth let out a breath of relief, lowering her bow. The rabbit looked at her with its shining black-button eyes, nose quivering, and then it unconcernedly bounced into another patch of underbrush.

"Should've shot it," said Rhys with a yawn behind her.

Gwyneth managed not to squeak in surprise, pasting a scowl on her face instead as she turned to look at him.

"Rabbit for breakfast," he said. He ran a hand through his unruly hair and stretched, prodding at his side gingerly. Then he nodded to Gwyneth. "Right. Get some sleep."

"Is it time for my watch to be over?" she replied, sliding her arrow back into her quiver and peering up through the branches of the trees, trying to glimpse the moon.

"Near enough, and I'm not going back to sleep," he replied with a shrug. His teeth gleamed as he grinned. "Good thing you defended us against that vicious fluffy bunny."

Even though he couldn't see her, Gwyneth rolled her eyes. She found that she was too tired to come up with a witty reply. Hopefully by morning she'd think of something properly scathing. She found a spot in the roots of the tree that seemed a likely place to get some decent sleep and rolled herself in her cloak. She propped her bow and quiver close at hand, and then she fell promptly asleep.

"But Paladin, if the young one is worried, should we not wake her to tell her that we are all right?"

The small, bright voice wormed its way into Gwyneth's slumber more effectively than a ray of daylight. She could tell that the speaker was trying to keep his voice down, but his words carried nonetheless.

"You woke me already," Rhys replied in a low voice. "And I say you should not wake her earlier than necessary. We had a long day of travel yesterday."

"And a long day ahead of you today," piped a different bright voice.

Gwyneth blinked as she recognized the voices. She bit back a groan as she shifted, her body aching sharply in protest. For all that she climbed trees, hunted, rode horseback and helped with all the myriad tasks of keeping a household clothed and fed, she realized that she was nowhere near as conditioned as Rhys to withstand fast, hard travel on foot. She sucked in a breath and pushed herself to a sitting position. The cold morning air slid icy hands into her loosened cloak. She blinked and put a hand up to her tousled hair.

"But she is already awake!" said the first voice with joyous full volume now.

Gwyneth tried not to wince at the piercing exclamation. She pulled her hair out of its braid and combed through it with her fingers as two glows zoomed toward her in the silvery light of the predawn forest.

"Lady Gwyneth!"

"Caonach," Gwyneth replied in greeting as she plaited her hair. The Glasidhe made her an elegant bow. "It is good to see you." She glanced over to where Rionach had sat against the tree, but the Bearer was nowhere to be seen. Rhys seemed unconcerned about the Bearer's absence. Togha sat on his shoulder, dangling her feet jauntily.

"We meant no insult by leaving," Caonach said, wings fluttering.

"It took me by surprise," Gwyneth said, tying off the end of her braid. "Especially after the fight with the *baobhan sith*...I was worried about you."

Caonach's aura swirled and sparked with a flush of color. Gwyneth realized that was the Glasidhe's equivalent of a blush, and she smiled even as her stomach rumbled.

"You have a good heart, Lady Gwyneth," Caonach said to her seriously, still hovering.

"Better than any other of the girls of the Blood all twittering in the White City like useless little sparrows," said Togha in an undertone.

"You would do well not to speak of the Blood in such a way," said Rionach, appearing suddenly and cleanly out of the dusky morning shadows without any warning at all. She spoke mildly, but Togha flinched and bowed from the waist. Rhys put up a hand to catch her as she nearly lost her balance on his shoulder.

"I beg forgiveness, Lady Bearer," Togha said with uncharacteristic gravity. "I did not think."

"You came to the Paladin and to the daughter of the Blood when they needed you," Rionach said. "It is forgiven many times over, but do not take that as liberty to behave badly." She arched an eyebrow.

"Of course not, Lady Bearer," Togha replied, but she'd recovered enough from the rebuke to flash a cheeky grin.

Rionach held up a plump rabbit by the scruff of its neck. It was still alive – its black button eyes wide and panicked, and its nose twitching with frenzied breath; but it didn't struggle. Gwyneth had never felt squeamish about hunting before, but she had a sneaking suspicion that this was the rabbit she had let hop away in the early hours of the dark morning. Her stomach clenched. To hunt was one thing, but to kill a creature held still by magic? She glanced at Rhys.

"Do not look to the Paladin," Rionach said. She held out the rabbit to Gwyneth by the scruff of its neck.

Gwyneth swallowed and clenched her jaw. How had the Bearer found the rabbit that had escaped her arrow? She took a breath and obediently took the creature from Rionach. Its breath warmed her hand as she shifted her grip. She stared ahead into the ghostly gray trees of the forest just before dawn, the Glasidhe's auras cutting sharp edges into the shadows around them. Gwyneth knew both Rionach and Rhys were watching her: she could feel their eyes on her just as surely as the soft living weight of the rabbit in her hands. With a sharp motion, she broke the rabbit's neck. Its body went limp and only then did she dare to look at it, its once-bright eyes now dull with death.

"Paladin, let us see your skill with a smokeless fire," Rionach said. She unbuckled the sheath of a short dagger from the belt at her waist and held it out to Gwyneth. "Skin the rabbit."

Gwyneth accepted the blade from the Bearer without a second thought, though she noted Caonach and Togha whispering something between them as she unsheathed the small, finely made weapon. She paused as she realized that the silver dagger was worth more than her father made in an entire trading trip – it was finely wrought, and as she examined it in the scant light she saw with a jolt the jewels set into the handle, blue and green stones that glimmered like the scales of some fantastic beast. Surely there must have been some mistake – Rionach could not intend for her to skin a rabbit with such a princely blade.

"It would do you well to learn not to stare with your mouth agape," Rionach said, not unkindly. "You will soon see things much more wondrous and rare, and there will be others watching you when you do."

Gwyneth blinked and forced her hands to move. She had skinned rabbits so often that the blade moved through the motions almost without thought. As she slid the red, naked carcass out of its fur casing, she asked, "What do you mean, my lady, when you say others will be watching me?"

"You will find out soon enough," said Rionach, but then after a moment of silence, she spoke again. "You are not the only daughter of the Blood with hopes of being the Bearer."

Gwyneth shivered and hoped Rionach hadn't noticed. There had only been a handful of girls in the village near her own age, and she'd always been viewed as somewhat odd, with her penchant for hunting and climbing trees, and her willingness to learn the messy, difficult trade of healing. She had accompanied her father on a few trading trips when she'd well and truly been just a child, before her monthly courses had started. She hadn't understood then why the jauntily dressed girls in the larger towns had laughed at her and whispered behind their hands as she rode through town perched atop her father's cart, eagerly gazing at the world beyond their small village. A few years later, she'd realized with burning shame that the girls had been mocking her – she'd been a wild-haired little girl wearing boys' clothes, since her mother thought it safer for her on the road with her father and besides, she was whip-thin still, flat-chested as a boy anyway.

When Gwyneth finished butchering the rabbit, she didn't bother to bury the offal since they'd be sleeping somewhere further on in the forest that night. Rhys crouched near a little fire, the pale blue flames twisting over three silver sticks balanced neatly against one another. Gwyneth found a sturdy stick of green wood, stripped it of its bark and sharpened one end for a spit, sliding the carcass of the rabbit onto it. When she turned back to the fire, Rhys had produced two more silver sticks, forked at the ends to hold her spit. The small blue fire, though it was only a little bigger than Gwyneth's fist, threw off a tremendous amount of heat. She balanced the spit on the forks and then sank down onto her haunches next to Rhys. The heat of the fire felt quite good against the biting morning chill.

Caonach and Togha took it upon themselves to man the spit; Gwyneth glanced at Rhys, who smiled slightly and shrugged. The Glasidhe clearly claimed whatever task caught their fancy at the moment, and they applied themselves quite seriously to it. Rionach had disappeared again. Gwyneth cleaned the dagger thoroughly and slid it back into its sheath.

"It isn't often the Bearer gives a blade to one of the daughters of the Blood," Rhys said quietly. She felt a little jolt as his gray eyes met her own. "It is a sign of high favor."

Gwyneth blinked. "High favor? But I haven't *done* anything."

Rhys raised his eyebrows. "You saved my life. I'd say that's something."

"And you helped to kill the *baobhan sith*," piped Togha as she and Caonach turned the rabbit on the spit with dogged determination. The meat gleamed and sizzled. Gwyneth's stomach growled.

"Well, yes," admitted Gwyneth. "But...both of those things...what else could I have done?"

"You could have left me in the woods to die," said Rhys.

"You could have screamed and cowered before the *baobhan sith*," contributed Caonach.

"I couldn't have done either of those things," protested Gwyneth. She realized she felt much different now – as the daughter of a healer, she'd always been aware of life and death, but now that she'd had a hand in it, in the killing of a creature and the saving of a man, she felt profoundly changed. She felt much older than her years.

"And that is why the Bearer gave you a blade," Rhys said in satisfaction.

"We will reach the Gate this evening," pronounced Rionach, emerging noiselessly from behind a tree. Gwyneth wondered if she'd learn to move as silently as the Bearer. A small smile appeared on the older woman's face. "Goddess willing, my successor will surpass me in all skills," Rionach said. She ignored Gwyneth's narrowed eyes. "Half an hour more, and then we must be on our way."

"Aye, Lady Bearer," said Rhys with the firm air of someone used to taking orders. He tested the rabbit with his dagger and extinguished the blue flames with a twist of his hand, his forehead creasing in concentration. When he cut the meat and went to give Rionach her portion, the Bearer had once again disappeared.

"Is she always like this?" Gwyneth asked in an undertone, searching the shadows.

"I haven't had the honor of traveling with the Bearer before," said Rhys, two spots of color appearing high on his cheeks. He concentrated on butchering the meat. "I have only been a Paladin for a handful of years, and to accompany the Bearer on a mission is also a sign of high favor."

He handed her a portion of rabbit. The meat was still hot, but it wasn't so hot that it burned her fingers; she waited for a few moments despite her grumbling stomach and watering mouth. When she finally ate it, she thought that it could have used a little salt, but other than that was one of the finer meals that she'd had recently. After a long winter of salted and dried meat and lean game, the first taste of spring-fat meat always seemed richer than she remembered. Caonach and Togha cut their portions from the remaining third of the rabbit with their own small blades, whirring away to sit in the crook of an oak tree and chatter to each other while eating. Gwyneth paused in licking her fingers and looked at Rhys in alarm when he began to split the remaining rabbit in two. "But that's Rionach's portion," she protested.

Rhys chuckled. "The older ones barely eat at all."

"Older ones?"

"The oldest Paladins and, of course, the Bearer," said Rhys. He held out half of the remaining rabbit to Gwyneth. "The Bearer is actually quite good at remembering that we need to eat. Sometimes Orla and Aedan forget entirely. Or they're just trying to toughen us up."

"Orla and Aedan?" Gwyneth relented and took the rest of the

meat from Rhys. Something told her that if she didn't eat her portion, he would.

"Our instructors," said Rhys through a mouthful of rabbit. "Part of the Council. Most senior Paladins."

Gwyneth chewed contemplatively and swallowed. "When you say old...how old do you mean?"

"Oh, centuries," replied Rhys casually. "Paladins are usually killed in the line of duty – they say that an old Paladin is either very dangerous or very cowardly."

"I'm guessing that Orla and Aedan are the dangerous sort." Somehow, she didn't think that the Paladins would allow cowards to instruct their young.

"They could kill you before you knew what was happening," said Rhys with a savage grin. Gwyneth thought of the knife scars on his chest. She wondered if they were from training or from actual fights.

"We'd better get ready to move," Rhys said. He sucked the last bit of meat from one of the rabbit bones and tossed it to the forest floor for the scavengers. After touching one silver stick with the pad of a finger – to make sure it was cool enough, Gwyneth realized – he scooped the three silver sticks that had been at the heart of his small blue fire and deposited them in his belt pouch. Gwyneth cleaned her hands as best she could, wishing briefly for a stream to wash her hands and face, and then picked up her quiver, hiding a wince as the strap settled against skin raw from their breakneck pace the previous day. Soft, she chided herself. She couldn't be so soft if she wanted to survive in the new world for which she'd given up everything she'd ever known. She slid the dagger that Rionach had given her onto her belt, and the weight of it at her hip pleased her in an unexpected way.

Rionach appeared, looked at them both silently, and then turned on her heel, sliding into the forest with effortless speed. Rhys squared his shoulders and leapt after her, Gwyneth following close behind him. Caonach and Togha flew overhead, weaving through the branches of the trees and singing a bright, fierce song that lifted

Gwyneth's spirits even though she couldn't understand the words. Despite the protest of her sore muscles as they leapt over logs and dodged around trees, straining to keep the Bearer in sight, Gwyneth smiled as they ran through the forest. She would watch the sun set below the horizon of a different world, and that prospect sent sparks of excitement crackling through her. She had never felt more alive.

She grinned and passed Rhys with a burst of speed, catching the expression of surprise that passed over his face. Then, with an answering grin, he matched her pace, and they hurtled together toward the Gate that would lead them into the realm of the Fae.

Chapter 9

"Siabhra, rouse your lazy bones!"

Gwyneth stifled her groan at the banging on her door and instead focused on shifting her sore body into an upright position. She'd thought that traveling through the forest at the Bearer's breakneck pace had left her weary, but now, after beginning her training at the Hall of the Inionacha, she thought longingly of a whole day running through the forest.

They had passed through the Gate in the gloaming of twilight on the second day of travel, the silvery light painting the forest around them in delicate hues. Something had felt different to Gwyneth, something that she could not quite describe, a sensation just beyond her ken, one she had never before experienced.

"Liminal times," Rhys had said in an undertone to her as Rionach had stepped forward, her green eyes gleaming in the scant light. "The veil between the worlds is always thinnest at dawn and dusk, and on the days we celebrate: Samhain and Beltane, summer and winter solstice..."

A sudden uncertainty had gripped Gwyneth. She'd had to resist the urge to reach out and take Rhys' hand – more because she felt as scared as a child, not because she wished to feel the heavy heat of his calloused hand, she told herself. "Will I see you again, after we cross over?" she'd asked in something like a whisper.

"The Paladins and the Inionacha train together sometimes," he had replied.

"Inionacha," she repeated. Daughters. All the other girls whose mothers had been borne from the daughters of Rionach.

"But I am not in training anymore," he had admitted, not meeting her eyes.

"You are the only one I know in this new world," she'd said, hating the thread of desperation in her voice.

"There are many others," he'd replied enigmatically. Rionach had begun chanting, a low and measured song that thrummed through the air like a drumbeat.

"I saved your life," she pointed out. "Surely you can promise me that you'll not leave me alone in the Fae world."

"I cannot make any promises," Rhys replied with his half-grin.

She had pushed away the urge to yell at him or cry; she hadn't been sure which impulse ruled the other. How could he be so callous?

"Try not to worry so much," he had said, almost gently. "I am a Paladin, and my life is not my own. That is why I cannot make any promises."

She had swallowed and nodded. As the forest shivered around them and the air tightened like a bowstring with the power of Rionach's voice, Rhys had reached over and twined his fingers through hers. His touch, more than anything, had let her watch the shining outline of the Gate trace through the air, a doorway of fire, without looking away or shivering in apprehension. Her hand had felt cold when he'd slipped his hand out of her grip, and then Rionach had beckoned her with a look, and she had stepped through the Gate into the wondrous and terrifying confusion of the ether between the worlds.

They had emerged into a golden morning, the sunlight gleaming on smooth white flagstones in a magnificent courtyard. Gwyneth felt distinctly travel-worn as she took in the jewel-like colors of this new world. Even the sky overhead looked a richer and truer blue than she had ever seen. She took a deep breath of the cool, fresh air. It tasted different than the air she had breathed her entire life, sweeter and wilder, though before that moment she would have sworn that the breezes among the green hills of Eire were the best balm to any soul. A strange, leaping excitement overpowered her apprehension. She shifted her bow and quiver on her shoulder.

"Do you wish me to escort Gwyneth to the quarters of the Inionacha, my lady?" asked Rhys with a small bow from the waist.

"I shall take her myself," Rionach replied. She inclined her head. "You may go, Paladin."

Something had twisted in Gwyneth's chest as Rhys had turned to her and bowed in proper, formal farewell. She hadn't known if she'd imagined the regret that flashed through his gray eyes for an instant before he turned away and strode down one of the white-paved paths stretching away from the courtyard.

"Come," Rionach had said simply. Gwyneth had followed her down the shining pathways of the city built of white stone, every building larger and more magnificent than the last, beautiful statues adorning the columns and alcoves, glimmering mother-of-pearl inlays creating patterns that drew Gwyneth's eye and held them captive even when she wanted to look away. She had felt breathless with wonder, but remembering Rionach's advice, she had tried to school her face into an expression of polite approval. She modeled her expression after the look that her aunt had worn when Gwyneth had asked her to look over her needlework: too courteous to express her true opinion. Her aunt had been raised in Dublin before venturing to the north to marry her husband, and Gwyneth suddenly wished that she'd paid more attention to the small differences in her aunt's well-bred manners, despite the fact that her own mother had waved a hand in dismissal at any kind of suggestion that Gwyneth needed to learn anything other than healing and the most basic courtesy.

She followed a step behind Rionach as the Bearer swept down the gleaming white path, stretching her legs to keep up with the older woman's long-legged stride. They passed no one else as they walked, which Gwyneth thought odd – but then again, this was a city, and she had no experience with cities. Did its inhabitants have to rise at dawn? She saw no livestock, no cows or pigs or chickens; she realized with a jolt that it was possible they did not even *have* cows or pigs or chickens in this world.

Rionach halted before a tall, long building. Gwyneth quickly counted the small square windows: there were at least three floors to the structure, and perhaps a dozen rooms at the on each floor, if her estimation was any good at all. The front doors were made of some gleaming dark wood, arched and wrought with silver. Without a touch from any visible hand, the doors swung inward noiselessly, and Rionach walked through, Gwyneth hurriedly following.

After Gwyneth's eyes adjusted to the dimmer light in the hall beyond the doors, she caught herself with her mouth agape and quickly closed it. The large building was a house, grander than any she'd ever entered even on her trading trips with her father, the entry hall lined with beautiful glass globes that hung suspended in midair and contained a whirling bit of the same blue fire that Rhys had conjured in the forest. At least a dozen smaller doors lined the hall at intervals.

Just as the doors shut behind them, one of the smaller doors opened. A woman almost as tall as Rionach glided into the hall with cat-like grace. She wore her dark hair in a simple plait down her back, and she was clad in a simple silvery-gray gown, but she was still the most beautiful woman that Gwyneth had ever seen.

The dark-haired woman stopped and curtseyed elegantly. "Lady Bearer. You honor us. Do you wish to see the Inionacha, my lady?"

"No," Rionach answered with her usual candor. She gestured toward Gwyneth with one hand. "I wish you to take this one and train her."

The dark-haired woman stepped closer to Gwyneth, who forced herself to stand tall and meet her piercing gaze. She saw that the woman's ears were pointed, and with a thrill she knew that the woman was Sidhe.

"It will be difficult," said the woman finally. "She is twice the age of most."

"She is not a first daughter," said Rionach, "so I did not have rights to her until her sister died."

"Ah," said the Sidhe woman.

Gwyneth bit her tongue to keep herself from asking if the woman had known her sister.

"Ava," came a mellifluous voice as one of the doors on the other side of the hall opened, "you did not tell me you were going *straight* to the entry hall – ah, Rionach, so good to see you!"

A slender woman with golden hair grinned unabashedly at the Bearer. To Gwyneth's surprise, an answering grin appeared on Rionach's lips.

"Cara, it is good to see you as well," Rionach said.

A disapproving look crossed dark-haired Ava's beautiful face as Cara embraced the Bearer heartily. Cara wore a white shirt and blue breeches, and her golden hair tumbled loose down her back.

"You brought another one for us," said Cara, stepping back from Rionach and turning to Gwyneth. "What's your name, dove?"

"Gwyneth, my lady." Gwyneth's lips formed the words more from reflex than actual thought.

"Well, Gwyneth, the first thing you must learn is that here, you will only address the Bearer as 'my lady,'" said Cara.

Gwyneth found that the rebuke stung despite Cara's kind voice.

"Or the Queens," added Ava, arching one delicate dark brow.

Cara laughed brightly. "As though any of our doves would meet the Queens," she said, shaking her head, her eyes sparkling as though it were a merry joke. Gwyneth thought that Cara's eyes were a more vivid blue than the sky.

"I trust you will be able to train her quickly," Rionach said. She looked at Gwyneth with consideration in her eyes. "Three years, I think. Perhaps four."

"Three years?" repeated Cara, her brilliant eyes widening.

How long did training usually take? Gwyneth had wondered, feeling the edges of both wonder and panic. She'd known that there would be training, yes, and the chance of being the Bearer, though she didn't even rightly know what that meant yet, but she hadn't fully grasped that these other girls had been in this world for most of their lives.

"You will be starting at a very distinct disadvantage, Gwyneth," said Ava, her dark eyes fixed on Gwyneth's face as though to measure her reaction.

Gwyneth raised her chin. "Yes."

"And this does not make you want to turn aside from this path?"

"I have chosen this path," Gwyneth said, trying to keep her voice steady. She felt very small and alone in the huge entryway with these beautiful women scrutinizing her. "I will see it through to the best of my ability."

"She has the spark," said Cara in an undertone to Rionach as though Gwyneth were not standing right in front of them. The golden-haired woman nodded once, a look of consideration on her lovely face.

"There is always a choice," said Ava, as though Cara had not spoken. The dark-haired woman's voice lowered and she leaned closer to Gwyneth. "Remember that, young one."

Gwyneth nodded once in imitation of Cara. She had to learn fast, now that she understood the gravity of her disadvantage. "I will – if I cannot call you 'my lady,' how shall I address you?"

"Instructor will do quite well," said Ava.

Gwyneth nodded. "Yes, Instructor."

"Well, I suppose you cannot join us for the morning meal," Cara said to Rionach.

Gwyneth's heart sank as the Bearer shook her head. Though the tall woman had been inscrutable during the journey, she was still one of the two people that Gwyneth knew in the Fae world, and the Bearer had not been unkind to her.

"No," replied Rionach. "I must speak to Orla and Aedan."

Gwyneth recognized the names – Paladins, she remembered, high-ranking ones, from how Rhys had spoken of them.

The Bearer looked at Gwyneth. "She has rudimentary skills in healing. Ensure that she is placed appropriately in that discipline. Her skill with a bow is satisfactory for one her age, and she understands the basics of knife work."

"Then we aren't starting from absolutely *nothing*," Cara said with a bright grin that lit up the entrance hall.

"We will evaluate her skills, Lady Bearer," said Ava with a nod.

Rionach nodded. "Train her well." Then she addressed Gwyneth directly. "Work hard. Not many are given such a chance so late."

Gwyneth felt goose-flesh rise on her arms at the gravity of the Bearer's voice. "I will, my lady." She swallowed hard and added, "I won't let you down."

The hint of a smile curved one corner of the Bearer's mouth. "See that you don't." Then she nodded to the two instructors, turned, and strode away, her steps echoing in the high-ceilinged hall.

"Well," said Cara, "no use in putting it off. It was dusk when you came through the Gate, was it not?"

"Yes, my l – Instructor," Gwyneth said, pushing down the sudden violent nausea clenching her stomach. Now she was well and truly alone, in a strange world with strangers.

"I will take the morning classes," Ava said to Cara.

"Yes," nodded the golden-haired woman. "It would be best to get my portion of the testing out of the way first, before she is too tired."

They had run all day at Rionach's punishing pace through the forest, pausing only briefly for noon and evening meals, and now her new instructors had tasks for her? Gwyneth took a deep breath. She had saved a Paladin. She had helped to kill a *baobhan sith*. She had been brought into the Fae world by the Bearer. Whatever tasks the instructors set before her, she would perform to the best of her ability.

"Yes, that's it," murmured Cara. "Good spirit, there." Louder, she continued, "Follow me. If you see any of the others, you are not to speak to them until you are done with our evaluation."

"Yes, Instructor," Gwyneth said. She tried not to think of her tired, sore body as she followed her new taskmaster.

The tasks of the evaluation had been numerous and varied. Some were straightforward, and some Gwyneth couldn't understand their purpose at all. First, Cara had brought her to a small courtyard. There had been five shining blades laid out on a dark cloak on the ground, each weapon as long as Gwyneth's forearm. They had looked identical at first, but as Gwyneth neared them she began to *feel* the differences between them. It was almost as if the blades were *speaking* to her, though they used no words and she could not rightly say she actually *heard* anything. Gwyneth thought that it was much like the feeling she'd gotten in the forest sometimes, a feeling that there were words just out of her reach, a feeling that there were living beings with whom she could not speak.

"Choose one blade," Cara said, even though Gwyneth had somehow already known that she had to choose. "The first one you touch shall be your choice. There is no way to change your choice once you have touched a blade."

Cara said nothing more, watching Gwyneth with her brilliant blue gaze. Gwyneth felt something stir within her chest as she stepped closer to the silver weapons. Though they all looked to be crafted in the same style, they each felt different – which made sense, because what choice would there be if all of the blades were as similar as they looked?

Gwyneth took a deep breath and tried to listen, straining her ears. The silence in the courtyard roared around her. She gritted her teeth, reaching with all of her senses, staring and listening and clasping her hands behind her back to counter the urge to touch the blades. She tasted something faintly metallic in the air, something faintly reminiscent of the scent left by the *baobhan sith*. That strange sensation in her chest intensified. She stopped resisting it, and it was as though a hawk unfurled its wings behind her ribs. Suddenly the humming just beyond her hearing clarified, and she could *hear* the swords. She stepped back at the sudden assault on this new, tender sense of hearing beyond hearing. After a deep breath, she closed the distance again and untangled the sibilant whispers of the blades, gazing at each in turn.

I will give you victory in battle, hissed the first blade, a hint of scarlet flashing down its blade as though the blood of conquered enemies ran down its edge. Gwyneth shivered and shifted her eyes to the next weapon quickly.

I will give you strength, promised the second blade, a thrill of energy crossing the air between the weapon and Gwyneth, filling her with an exhilarating sense of unconquerable physical strength. She leaned toward the sword. Cara tilted her head slightly, watching. Gwyneth clenched her hands and moved to the next blade. At the very least, she had to understand what each blade offered before making her choice.

The third blade in the center of the array remained silent. Gwyneth waited for a moment, but when it did not say anything, she moved on to the next choice.

I will give you beauty, murmured the fourth blade, showing her a reflection in its silver length: a woman even more beautiful than the two Sidhe instructors, a woman that Gwyneth somehow knew was her; but even as she wondered at the radiance of the woman in the reflection, the newfound power in her chest beat its wings in protest. Such beauty would be hollow, and what good was beauty against the ravages of disease and war? Though her fingers itched to touch the fourth sword and part of her thought that if she chose that blade, perhaps Rhys would not leave her alone in this new world...Gwyneth moved to the fourth sword.

I will give you wisdom, said the fifth blade in a rich, resonant voice-beyond-a-voice. It showed her a dizzying number of leather-bound tomes, all their knowledge whirling and funneling into Gwyneth's head. She had never been a scholar, she thought in despair; she had only been taught to read so that she could decipher recipes for healing ointments and teas sent with her father and other traders from the midwives and healers of other villages. Perhaps this blade would be the best choice, because how else could she learn everything quickly enough not to disappoint Rionach?

But why had the third blade not promised her anything? The thought interrupted the grip of the fifth sword, and Gwyneth turned her attention back to the sword in the center of the cloak. She directed her thoughts at it, trying to speak in the same manner that the blades spoke to her.

Why did you make no promises? she asked the third sword.

Because I promise nothing, the third sword replied, the words shimmering into her mind. *I will give you a sharp edge, a weapon in your hand. I am simply what I am, and that will be added to what you are.*

And then a thought occurred to Gwyneth: what if the other swords' offers were not truly gifts? What was expected in return for the victory, strength, beauty and wisdom offered by the other silken, persuasive voices?

You will be a blade and nothing more? she asked the third sword.

I cannot say I am nothing more than a blade, but I will promise you nothing and demand nothing in return. I will simply be a weapon in your hand. The third sword glimmered with the light of the morning, but it showed her no vision in the silver of its blade.

The other voices twined about Gwyneth, trying to catch her attention, but she brushed them all away. The newly awakened thing within her chest, the strange creature that was a part of her but separate, spread its wings in approval as she leaned toward the third sword. When she wrapped her fingers around its grip, all the other voices fell away. The blade felt good in her hand, balanced and light for a weapon of its size. She did not hear its anymore, but she felt a strange sense of relief at that realization.

"When you are ready for a sword, that will be your weapon," said Cara. "Until you receive permission, it will hang in your quarters."

Gwyneth had wondered for a moment why the instructors would not lock forbidden weapons away from them, but she had only said, "Will I bring it to my quarters now?"

"No," replied Cara simply, holding out one long-fingered, graceful hand.

Gwyneth gave her the sword. She glanced back to the cloak, but the other blades were gone, and when she looked back to the Sidhe woman, her hands were empty.

The choosing of her blade had been the task that Gwyneth remembered most vividly and thought about the most over the coming days; Cara had expressed neither approval nor disapproval at Gwyneth's choice, and sometimes Gwyneth wondered what would have happened if she had chosen one of the other swords. But the idea of being beholden to an enchanted object didn't sit well with her, even when she wistfully thought of all the work that perhaps could have been avoided with the blades that promised strength or wisdom.

Cara had put her through several other tasks. Gwyneth lost track of time, as they moved through different rooms and the light changed so often that she couldn't be sure if it was still morning, or perhaps it was evening, or maybe even the next day altogether. Time seemed a fluid thing in this world, or perhaps it was only in the presence of the Sidhe instructors.

Though Cara had cautioned her not to acknowledge the other inhabitants of the building if she saw them, Gwyneth had no cause to follow the instructor's warning. She stopped wondering about time and eventually stopped thinking about how tired and hungry she was, focusing instead on completing the next evaluation. Her own stubbornness and the newly awakened power in her chest drove her onward. She couldn't put into words the new feeling that thrummed through her veins. If forced, she would have probably said that it felt like fire swirling through her chest, but a fire that was a part of her and would not harm her.

The evaluation seemed to be endless. Cara had Gwyneth shoot arrows first at stationary targets, which she hit easily; and then at clay targets thrown into the air by an unseen force. Once Gwyneth stopped goggling at the sorcery she hit those too. Then they progressed to brass rings which twisted through the air, trying to avoid the shots Gwyneth aimed; and then finally there were globes of fire that Gwyneth did not *want* to hit at first because she thought they might explode, but she steeled herself and tried anyway.

The tasks that Ava set were harder for Gwyneth to understand. Some of them seemed downright useless, like when Ava instructed Gwyneth to sit on a stool in the middle of a plain room and then left her there for what felt like hours without a word. When Gwyneth finally stood, she stretched and then explored the circular room, but she could not even find a door in the strangely smooth walls. After a while, panic bubbled up – what if she was supposed to find her way out of the room by some magical means? But then Gwyneth found that she still had one of the packets of food from their journey in her belt pouch, so she sat cross-legged on the smooth, cool floor and ate the stale bread, cheese and dried meat. She felt much better after that. She stretched for a while, decided against going to sleep, and then took out her whetting-stone, examining the edge on the dagger that Rionach had given to her with a critical eye. When Ava opened the invisible door, Gwyneth looked up from sharpening the blade, silently put away the dagger and whetting-stone, and followed Ava to the next task.

The two Sidhe instructors tested her on identification of herbs and gave her a wooden sword to fight a nebulous silver opponent;

they had her patch a hole in her trousers with a silver thread and needle and asked her to start a fire without any flint or even two sticks to rub together. They asked her what she saw in a blue glass mirror and had her test the weight of different feathers in her hands. Gwyneth stopped trying to remember everything that they told her to do, but she tried her best at everything. And then, finally, the two Sidhe women had looked at each other and nodded.

"Follow me," Ava said, and Gwyneth numbly pointed her feet after the dark-haired woman. But rather than lead her to another room with another task, Ava led her through one of the doors in the entrance hall marked with a silver circle, up a winding staircase, and down a long hall with differently colored doors. She stopped at a door painted a bright robin's-egg blue. "This will be your room. You will find everything you need within it." She paused. "You will not wear anything other than what we give you. Do you understand?"

Gwyneth dully realized that meant her belt-pouch and the dagger from Rionach. She was too tired to feel anything properly, so she'd nodded. "Yes, Instructor."

Ava nodded. "Tomorrow you will begin your training with the other Inionacha."

Gwyneth felt a vague stab of nervousness, then was surprised that she had the energy to feel even that.

Then Ava had turned and left her, and Gwyneth had pressed a hand to the door, staring at it in mute exhaustion. It had swung inward silently, revealing a small room appointed with well-made but spare furnishings: a bed, neatly made with a gray quilt; a small table and two chairs; and a tall wardrobe in the corner. A handsome chest sat at the foot of the bed, the only object in the room providing any color with its deep scarlet wood and gleaming brass hinges. The sword that Gwyneth had chosen in the first task hung by its guard on the wall.

After standing in the open door for a moment, Gwyneth stepped inside the room, closed the door behind her and promptly sloughed off her boots and clothes, and fell onto the bed. Sleep claimed her without fanfare.

The next days were even more exhausting than those first tasks set by Ava and Cara. Gwyneth had found out quickly that not all the young women in the house took kindly to another descendant of Rionach being added to their ranks. Some of the Inionacha, Gwyneth learned, viewed all the others as competition, rivals to be conquered and nothing more. She found it difficult to keep track of all the others, as she struggled to keep up with her own lessons – the fighting she found easy, even if it was tiring, it was the incessant *reading* set by Ava that took her hours each night. But by the end of the first week, she estimated that there were about forty other Inionacha around her own age, a number far higher than she'd initially expected.

It was Mary, a tall and coldly beautiful girl born in London, who gave Gwyneth the sneering nickname Siabhra, after one of the old names for the small Fae – it meant mischievous, but also tiny and inconsequential. In the old tales, the *siabhra* were the part of the host of the *aos si* who were not particularly a threat. They were an annoyance, nothing more.

Mary collected a group of girls about her who were alternately beautiful and cruel, ambitious and insecure; one of her cronies unfailingly yelled at Gwyneth's door every morning as they passed on their way downstairs before the morning bell. At first, this had annoyed Gwyneth, since she wanted to soak up every minute of sleep before the rousing bell, but she'd learned to ignore it after a few weeks.

"Liking your time with the *children*, Siabhra?" Mary said loftily as the older girls passed through the courtyard on their way to another lesson.

"She noticed you enough to give you a nickname," whispered one of the younger girls to Gwyneth with a grin as they practiced their patterns with blunt wooden blades. The youngest girls, who were no more than five or six, spent much of their time learning to read in one of the libraries, watched over by one of the instructors or the young women who must have been nearing twenty-one or twenty-two. The little ones slept in a common dormitory, and Gwyneth suspected that Ava or Cara slept in the dormitory as well, as though to guard the youngest Inionacha – though she couldn't understand what threat would be able to penetrate this building in the heart of the White City.

Once the Inionacha reached the age of eight, they were divided into different classes and each girl progressed individually, based on their skills. Gwyneth had started in the youngest class in history and geography, but she had applied herself with almost maniacal fervor and now she was with girls only a few years younger than she. In weapons handling, Cara had placed her with one of the intermediate classes. The ages varied from a few talented ten-year-olds to girls a year or two older than Gwyneth who had trouble grasping certain skills.

"I don't know why they care about me," Gwyneth muttered back to her sparring partner. She gritted her teeth as a quick movement ignited one of her sore muscles.

"Because," the other girl whispered, "you were brought by the *Bearer*."

Gwyneth stared at the other girl long enough for Cara to reprimand her with a light swat to the back of one leg with the thin, flexible wooden rod that the instructors carried during lessons. It alternately served as a pointer, a tool by which they could help cue certain body positions, and a disciplinary method, though Gwyneth had never seen the two Sidhe women use it cruelly.

"Come on then, you're much better than me at this," said the other girl, speaking at normal volume. "Least you could do is help me learn."

Gwyneth blinked and raised her practice blade to the ready position. She had the advantage of reach on the other girl. She didn't remember her name, though they'd been sparring partners more than once in the past week. The other girl was sturdily built and plainer-looking than many of Inionacha, and she had a habit of dropping her guard when a sidestroke caught her off guard. Gwyneth slid her blade through the opening and touched the tip of the wooden sword to the other girl's throat. Gwyneth frowned as she tried to remember her name while they reset.

"Edelinne," the girl said, "but you can call me Ed."

"Ed?" Gwyneth raised her eyebrows.

Edelinne shrugged and grinned. "Don't look much like an Edelinne, do I?"

Gwyneth smiled for what felt like the first time since she'd started lessons with the other Inionacha.

"There, you *can* smile," Edelinne said in satisfaction. They started another point and Gwyneth won handily again. Edelinne stamped her foot. "Oh, bloody hell, I will *never* get to a real blade at this rate."

"I can help," Gwyneth offered before she actually thought about it. Perhaps it was the fact that Edelinne was the first girl to offer anything but disinterested courtesy, wary disapproval or outright hostility.

"*Fantastique,*" said Edelinne with a grin. She shrugged one shoulder as Gwyneth raised her eyebrows again at the French. "I came from Normandy. We cannot all be so lucky to grow up in the land of the druids, eh?"

"I suppose not," said Gwyneth.

"Less talking, more blade work," said Cara, touching the rod to Edelinne's shoulder in subtle remonstrance.

"Yes, Instructor," said Edelinne dutifully.

As Gwyneth raised her blade, she realized she had made her first friend among the Inionacha. The thought made her miss Rhys with a sudden fierce intensity that caught her by surprise. She collected the feeling and tucked it away, focusing instead on Edelinne's blunt wooden blade. It was not even noon yet, and she had a full afternoon of lessons. She couldn't afford to be distracted by such useless emotions, not if her goal was to advance to classes with her peers and even those older than she – because that, she knew, was the only way to show Rionach that she did not take the choice offered to her lightly. She had chosen this path, and it was a choice she would have to make every day, through the relentlessly sore body and exhausted mind, the demanding lessons and the difficult relationships with the older girls, but Gwyneth was determined to do it. She felt it in her bones, though she would never say the words aloud: she was meant to be the next Bearer.

She just had to prove herself worthy.

Chapter 10

"I overheard a few of the older ones at evening meal," Edelinne said.

Gwyneth glanced up from pushing the table in Edelinne's room over to make room for their evening lessons.

"They were saying that it will be no surprise when you are moved up to the next class in blade work. And then I will be left alone again," the Norman girl said sadly, her accent coming through strongly as it always did when she was upset.

"Forms will be in a fortnight," Gwyneth replied. To progress to the next class, the Inionacha had to pass increasingly difficult tests called forms held twice each year, at midsummer and midwinter. "If you have a good showing, then Cara will probably move you up as well."

"I am just too blasted slow," her friend said, nearly wailing.

Gwyneth fought the urge to sigh. While some of the other girls near to her own age had made tentative overtures that were at least something other than outright hostility, Edelinne remained her first and truest friend. She picked up one of the chairs and carried it over to the far side of the room.

"You have not even been here a year," Edelinne continued, swinging her wooden practice blade through the empty air vengefully.

"And already you surpass most of us who have been studying since we were five years old."

"I'm still terrible at writing essays," pointed out Gwyneth – which was true. Her penmanship was nothing short of disastrous, and it took her ages to transcribe anything legibly. "And it took me three weeks before I was able to summon my *taebramh*."

Edelinne stared at her, chin wobbling. "It took me *three years* to find mine, Gwyn, and that was *after* we actually began the classes for it!"

It was a well-known fact that some of the more naturally talented Inionacha had been able to summon their *taebramh* since before they could speak in full sentences. Mary, for one, never let anyone forget it. Gwyneth tried to think of something to say that wouldn't make Edelinne burst into tears. One of the older girls who taught history sometimes, Beatrix, had also taught them classes in anatomy. Gwyneth, of course, had known all of this from her apprenticeship with her mother and couldn't understand why Edelinne and some of the others had turned bright red. But what Gwyneth hadn't truly understood was the volatility of their collective emotions as they steadily grew into women. The anatomy lessons certainly hadn't prepared her for *that*. She didn't have many other friends other than Edelinne, but even the classroom and the sparring courtyard weren't safe from the torrents of tears that overtook some of the girls at seemingly random moments.

Finally, Gwyneth settled for, "Well, we're all different, Ed." It sounded stupid even to her.

Edelinne looked at her with tears swimming in her large brown eyes. "You're right," she said in a trembling voice. "We *are* all different. I'm the most hopeless of us all, and everyone knows that you're probably going to be the next Bearer."

Gwyneth snorted. "Not if Mary and her cronies have anything to do with it."

"They have *nothing* to do with it, don't you see?" Edelinne said, tears spilling down her cheeks now. Gwyneth kept her distance and wondered if this befuddlement was how young men felt when trying to speak to others of her sex. She certainly didn't understand all the caterwauling – there was a time and a place for tears, yes, but she'd made certain that for her part, she cried into her pillow at night those first months, and not in front of any of the other girls.

"I'm not thinking that far ahead," Gwyneth said, trying to sound dismissive but not harsh. She picked up her own practice blade.

"That's a lie, and you know it," Edelinne muttered as she wiped her nose on her sleeve, but there was no anger in her voice.

"Forms in a fortnight," Gwyneth said firmly, stepping to the center of the room and raising her wooden blade.

Edelinne smiled and snuffled. "You know, when I talked to you that first day, I wouldn't have guessed that in less than a year *you'd* be the one helping *me*."

Gwyneth shrugged. "You help me in a lot of different ways. Come on, we need to get started if we're going to get through everything before evening meal."

"I'm already sore from yesterday," grumbled Edelinne, but she raised her practice blade.

Almost two hours later, Edelinne had managed to score two points on Gwyneth; during the last point, she whacked Gwyneth in the ribs hard with the edge of her blade.

"Oh, I'm sorry!" the shorter girl cried as Gwyneth conceded the point with a grimace. "I'm just not used to getting through your guard, I swung too hard – "

"Don't apologize," growled Gwyneth. Edelinne opened her mouth and then closed it soundlessly, watching with wide eyes as Gwyneth prodded at her ribs gingerly. The hit had ignited a burst of pain, but she hadn't felt anything shift or pop. "Nothing broken, I'll just have a great bruise for a while."

"Will you be healed in time for forms?" Edelinne said worriedly.

Gwyneth shrugged. "I'll be fine."

"I could try the cooling spell we learned the other day," Edelinne offered.

"Really," said Gwyneth. "I'll be fine, it's nothing, Ed."

Edelinne watched her walk across the room. "You're certain?"

"I'm certain. Help me move the furniture back before evening meal, or you'll have to do it all on your own."

Gwyneth managed to keep her composure while they moved the table and chairs back to their rightful place, but by the time she got back to her own room to wash before the evening meal, she was sweating as though she'd been running for half an hour. Her blade glinted at her from its place on the wall. "Good thing we weren't sparring with real blades," she said to herself as she stripped out of her clothes to wash. Her ribs smarted, sending lances of pain into her chest every time she took a breath, and a bruise already bloomed down her side. She hadn't felt anything break, she reminded herself as she cleaned up for the evening meal.

A quick little knock sounded on one of the panes of her window as she finished braiding her hair. The windows in the dormitory opened to admit fresh air, a thoroughly enjoyable luxury at which Gwyneth still marveled; but more importantly, it allowed her visits from Caonach and Togha. Cara and Ava had never told her that Glasidhe visitors – or visitors of any kind – were not allowed; but Gwyneth had the feeling that was more because none of the girls *knew* anyone in Faeortalam, unless they had a cousin or brother who was a Paladin. Gwyneth quickly tied off her plait and opened the window. Togha slipped inside, her aura dimmed.

"Lady Gwyneth!" the indomitable Glasidhe piped. She bowed and then flew a quick, excited circuit of the room. "You have grown since last we spoke!"

"Really?" said Gwyneth as she shut the window. "You visited barely a week ago."

"You are growing into a woman," Togha said, nodding sagely.

Gwyneth smiled. In the presence of the small warrior, she almost forgot about her aching ribs. "What brings you here this evening, Togha? Will you be staying?"

"I would very much like to stay, but I do not think *you* will be staying," said Togha slyly.

"I only have a quarter hour until the bell for evening meal, Togha, so I don't have time for riddles tonight." Sometimes the Small Folk's delight in puzzles made a simple conversation take nearly an hour.

Togha fluttered her wings. "Well, if you do not want the Paladin's invitation, then I will simply..."

"What invitation?" Gwyneth said quickly.

Togha produced a small bit of parchment, tied to an object wrapped in cloth. Gwyneth held out a hand and the Glasidhe deposited her burden. The object was the size of an acorn but strangely heavy. "You carried this here?"

"Of course," replied Togha archly, flicking one wing dismissively. "That is nothing."

Gwyneth tugged the message free and unrolled it. Her heart sank as she saw there were only four words written on it: *The white oak, midnight*. What was that supposed to mean? She unrolled the object from the cloth and found herself looking at a small, unremarkable black stone.

"A mirror stone," said Togha, hovering over Gwyneth's hand, her aura sparking in interest. "Well, truly it is a river-stone, but this one is for the mirror. So I call it a mirror stone."

"I've never seen one before," said Gwyneth honestly. She tried to remember if they'd ever covered anything in lessons about mirror stones, but her mind didn't produce anything useful.

"The Paladin like to use them," said Togha. "Rhys must have learned how to make them." She tilted her head to the side. "It's a very complicated rune, you know, well beyond some of the older ones' ken."

"He said he was done with training," Gwyneth said, shaking her head. She'd given up on seeing Rhys months ago, and the first sharp ache had faded to a kind of sullen acceptance. Reason and practicality told her that she'd only known him for a few days anyway, but even telling herself that hadn't helped in the beginning.

"Oh, you are *never* done training," Togha said. "He is considered a full Paladin, yes, but he is still young. Still learning."

Togha especially had seemed to understand Gwyneth's desire to know Rhys' whereabouts. Between her and Caonach, Gwyneth had managed to maintain a rough sketch of Rhys' schedule. She knew when he was assigned a mission and she knew when he returned, though the Glasidhe were sometimes a few days delayed in telling her the news. To her relief, he hadn't suffered any major wounds during the time that she'd been with the Inionacha – though what she could do if he did, she didn't know. She would have to admit to her Glasidhe visitors if she asked Cara or Ava to visit the Paladin. They'd had guest instructors in their blade classes from the Paladins, and her heart had leapt into her throat every time, but each instructor had turned out to be a battle-scarred Paladin with gray and white threading through their hair. The woman Paladin that had come to teach them for three days had been missing an eye, and she hadn't deigned to wear an eye patch, leaving the mass of empty scar tissue exposed for them all to see.

"So, what is a mirror stone?" Gwyneth asked.

"You hold it in your hand and touch a mirror," said Togha, turning a somersault in the air. "It takes you someplace."

"Where?"

"Silly girl, look at the note!" chided Togha with a bright laugh.

Gwyneth waved the note. "It's four words. It doesn't tell me anything other than the white oak at midnight."

"Well, do you need to know anything else?" Togha cocked her head to one side impishly. "It *is* from Rhys, after all."

"Why has he never sent me anything before this?" Gwyneth asked suddenly. It was a question she had never asked out loud, but it had whirled in her head often in the twilight between waking and sleeping.

"You should ask him tonight," the Glasidhe replied.

"You don't know?"

"Just because I know does not mean that I will tell you," Togha returned cheekily.

Gwyneth chuckled despite herself. She winced at the nauseating wave of pain from her ribs.

"I think it is because he did not want to jeopardize anything," the Glasidhe said in a quieter, serious voice.

"How would sending me a message jeopardize anything?"

"Perhaps he does not want you to choose to be a Paladin simply because he is a Paladin," replied Togha.

"Most Inionacha who choose to be Paladin don't make that decision until they're at least twenty," protested Gwyneth.

"But you are not any ordinary Inionacha," returned the Glasidhe. She flew over to the blade on the wall as she often did, hovering silently before it, her aura reflected in its gleaming silver length.

"I'm not even allowed to train with a real sword yet," muttered Gwyneth.

"You are not any ordinary Inionacha," repeated Togha firmly. She swept a hand through her blue-tinged hair and then whirled over to Gwyneth again.

A knock sounded at the door of the room. "Gwyn, ready for evening meal?" came Edelinne's voice.

Gwyneth had always felt a vague twinge of guilt that she hadn't ever told Edelinne about her visits from the Glasidhe, but she'd always reasoned that it was for her friend's protection. If the instructors ever found out and punished Gwyneth, Edelinne at least would not bear any of the blame. "Just a moment," she called, hastily stashing the mirror stone and note in her wardrobe in one of her boots and opening the window for Togha.

"I will return with a quarter hour to midnight. Wear something green! It sets off your eyes and hair," Togha told her, patting Gwyneth's ear before whirring out of the window into the dusk, nearly invisible without her aura.

Gwyneth shut the window and walked quickly over to the door. "Just finishing my hair," she told Edelinne, stepping out into the hallway.

Edelinne narrowed her eyes. "It takes you less than a minute to braid your hair. You wear it the same way every single day."

For a moment, Gwyneth debated with herself. Should she tell Edelinne about the invitation and the mirror stone? But then she'd have to admit to receiving Glasidhe visitors, and she'd already made her decision about that…

"Looking more dazed than usual, Siabhra," remarked Mary as she swept by down the corridor. Two of her friends, dark-haired twins with gray eyes and prettily snub noses, sniggered as they followed her.

Edelinne scowled after them as she always did. Mary glanced over her shoulder, flipping her waist-length white-blonde braid with one hand. "And you really shouldn't wrinkle your face like that," the tall, beautiful girl added, directing her words at Edelinne. She hadn't lost any of her aristocratic English accent during her time in the Fae world. "It makes you even uglier than you already are."

"Oh, go suck an egg," Edelinne said crossly. Mary smiled, her blue eyes glinting, and the twins tittered as they disappeared down the stairwell.

"You're only giving her satisfaction, Ed," Gwyneth said.

"She might be beautiful on the outside but she's ugly as a toad on the inside," said Edelinne, crossing her arms over her chest.

"Wonder if there's a spell to reverse the two," said Gwyneth thoughtfully.

That surprised a laugh out of Edelinne as they both conjured the mental image of Mary turned into a toad. "Oh, could you imagine? Come on, there's the bell, let's not be late…" They stared down the hallway toward the stairs. "Do you think she'd be a *gigantic* toad, or a small one?"

"Or perhaps a gigantic toad that doesn't *know* it's a toad, and still walks about like a pretty, stuck-up girl from London?" suggested Gwyneth, grinning.

Edelinne laughed so loudly that a few of the other girls on the staircase turned to look at them, but Edelinne didn't bother to try to quiet her mirth. Gwyneth's cheeks hurt from smiling, as happened often when she spent time with her best friend.

They entered the dining hall and found two seats at the long table. Though they weren't separated by age, most girls of the same classes stuck together. Friendships and personalities created a natural hierarchy, with the oldest girls sitting at the far end of the table. The young ones ate earlier, because they went to bed at dusk. Edelinne had told Gwyneth stories of when they were all young. Ed remembered when every girl had been brought to the training hall, and she could recite most of each girl's lineage as well.

"You aren't a first daughter," she'd told Gwyneth, "so I hadn't thought to see you here." And then she'd closed her mouth quickly. No one had spoken to Gwyneth about her older sister – the one who had died. Gwyneth found that she didn't have much of a desire to ask about her sister, either, contrary to what she'd first thought. It felt like a kind of betrayal, but she was satisfied with being given the chance to train with the Inionacha and prove her worth to the Bearer.

The meals at the hall were hearty but plain fare: that night's meal was venison stew with more vegetables than meat, and a roasted potato for each girl that wished to have one.

"Don't understand why some of the others don't eat everything," said Gwyneth in an undertone to Edelinne as her friend passed the large wooden bowl of potatoes.

"Well," said Ed, coloring, "maybe some of them just aren't as hungry."

Gwyneth split open the potato and dressed it with a generous dollop of fresh butter, watching it melt with ravenous satisfaction. She glanced at Ed, the tone of her friend's voice different than the jocular mood of just the moment prior and realized with a sinking feeling that Ed had only taken half a portion of stew and no potato at all. "I…well, that's all right then, if they really aren't hungry," she said, trying to make light of it.

Ed didn't say anything, poking at her stew without any enthusiasm.

"Or maybe some little cows just need to eat less," said a voice with a London accent behind them.

Redness flooded Edelinne's face. Neither of them turned to look, because they both knew it was Mary who'd spoken. Sometimes the older girl circled the table like a roving wolf with her little pack of followers, waiting until the very last moment to claim their seats because their territory was well known and no one else dared sit there.

Gwyneth clenched her jaw. "Hm. I don't know, Ed, did you just hear something? Thought I heard something like a toad croaking…"

Edelinne, though her eyes were still downcast, pressed her lips together and sat up straighter.

"Though I think that to call you a toad would be an insult to honest toads everywhere," Gwyneth continued, turning to look Mary squarely in the eye. She heard the collective gasp and then the rush of whispers around them as the other girls watched the confrontation.

"Oh, Siabhra," said Mary with a small, cold smile. "You think your little attempts at insults are even close to anything that would sting me?" She laughed, a high bright sound like chimes, but Gwyneth saw the darkening glint in the older girl's blue eyes.

"It's not an insult," said Gwyneth in a calm, clear voice, letting herself smile a little as she looked up at Mary. "It's just the truth. I'm just saying out loud what everyone else thinks. You're ugly as a toad on the inside."

Whispers flowed around them again, like they were rocks in a stream. This time the girls sounded more excited, and there were a few giggles mixed in with the whispering. Gwyneth didn't take her eyes from Mary. She felt the air tighten between them and she noted the spots of color high on Mary's pretty cheeks. Ah, so she'd gotten to the older girl. Good.

Ed touched Gwyneth's leg. "Just stop, Gwyn, pay her no mind, like you always say."

"You'd do well to listen to the fat little cow," said Mary, raising one white-gold eyebrow.

"Fat little cow," snickered one of the dark-haired twins.

Gwyneth stood. She noted in faint surprise that she *had* grown – her eyes were even with Mary's, whereas the other girl had been taller than her by half a head only a year ago.

"Seats, everyone," called Beatrix from the other end of the table, the informal warning that they used to ensure all the Inionacha were properly seated before Ava and Cara joined them for the meal. Breaches of courtesy in the dining hall were not tolerated.

"You heard Beatrix," said Gwyneth. She felt her *taebramh* unfolding its wings behind her breastbone, and she didn't stop it. The air began to vibrate around her. She leaned closer to Mary, whose beautiful face registered a hint of confusion. "Run along now and find your seats," she said to the older girl and her posse, flicking her hand at them dismissively.

Mary opened her rosebud mouth to reply, her eyes narrowing in outrage, but the dark-haired twins had already deserted her, walking quickly toward their seats. Gwyneth tilted her head and made another shooing motion with her hand. Mary pressed her mouth together and then spun on her heel as the chimes of the last dinner bell sounded. A low snigger ran through the younger girls as they watched her try to maintain some sort of dignity as she scurried to her seat. A few of the shorter girls even stood to watch. Gwyneth savored the rush of victory. She felt *powerful.*

Ed tugged at her sleeve urgently. "Sit down," she hissed.

Gwyneth obeyed her friend. A few of the girls around them grinned at her and one clapped softly. Apparently, she and Edelinne had not been the only ones to suffer at the barbed tongues of Mary and her cronies. Gwyneth saw Ava look at Mary sharply. The Unseelie Instructor took her seat at one end of the table and the Seelie Instructor took the other, and they motioned for the girls to begin their meal.

Gwyneth ate her meal hungrily. Somehow the stew and potato tasted much better than she'd expected. Perhaps triumph was a better seasoning than hunger or hard work, she thought as she served herself more stew.

"Why so quiet, Ed?" she asked as she started on her second helping. Some of the others were starting to leave the dining hall. A few of the older girls sat with Cara, discussing the finer points of archery; and at Ava's end of the table, two of the girls in Gwyneth's history class sat near the Unseelie woman, though Gwyneth wasn't sure if that was of their own volition or if they had been assigned some sort of punishment. She couldn't rightly tell, from the looks on their faces.

"You shouldn't have done that," Ed said, almost sadly.

"What, stood up to Mary?" Gwyneth glanced over to where Mary and her cronies typically sat. They had all left. Gwyneth grinned, feeling another heady rush of victory. "I should have done that sooner."

Edelinne just sighed again. "It might be well and good for you. You're handy with *taebramh* and fighting. Even if you're not chosen, the Paladin will certainly want you." She paused. "I'm just a sodden lump of failure."

"First of all, you're not a 'sodden lump of failure," Gwyneth said, turning to look at her friend and setting down her fork. "You've improved threefold in bladework alone in the past few months. And second of all, I thought you'd be pleased that we stood up to Mary. Maybe she'll leave us alone now."

"*We* didn't stand up to Mary, Gwyn," Edelinne replied, her brown eyes huge in her face. "*You* stood up to Mary. Maybe it'll be better for *you* now." She shrugged and sucked her lips over her teeth, like she did when she was trying not to cry.

"I – but you're my friend, Ed," Gwyneth said. "I'll do whatever I can to help you."

Edelinne sighed and stood. "Maybe it would be better if you found a better best friend."

Gwyneth glanced longingly at her unfinished stew but stood as well. "Ed, stop talking nonsense."

"It's not nonsense," said Ed stubbornly, walking toward the door that led to their dormitory stairwell.

Gwyneth found herself at a loss for words. She opened her mouth and closed it again in frustration.

"See?" Edelinne turned at the bottom of the stairwell. "You don't know what to say."

"I don't," admitted Gwyneth. "I don't know why you're always so harsh with yourself, Ed." She held up a hand as Edelinne started to speak. "I know, I know, you're a year older than me and you're still in the second-level intermediate blade class, you're not as fast or as strong as most of us, and you hate your hair." She shrugged. "What does any of that have to do with you and I being friends? We help each other."

"*You* help *me*," said Edelinne.

"You help me with my essays," pointed out Gwyneth. A few girls passed them and gave them curious looks, but another few girls grinned at Gwyneth over their shoulders. Gwyneth felt a little spark of pride.

"Right," said Edelinne. "And even that's less and less lately. You learn fast, Gwyn, and you don't need me anymore."

"Being friends isn't about *needing* each other," retorted Gwyneth. She had the strangely sinking feeling that she was losing this argument. Why did Ed have to choose tonight to do this? Why couldn't they both revel in her victory over Mary?

A redheaded girl who had never spoken to Gwyneth directly touched her shoulder. "Heard about what you said to Mary. Good riddance, I say." Her words rang with an Irish accent that reminded

Gwyneth sharply of Rhys and the river-stone waiting up in her room. But the redhead was at least a year older than her, if not two, and common courtesy dictated that Gwyneth reply. Edelinne nudged her in the ribs, apparently forgetting that she'd hit Gwyneth very hard with the edge of a practice blade.

Gwyneth shrugged, trying not to grimace at the tendril of pain threading through her side. "Just said what was on my mind."

"Well, there's precious few who'll do such when it comes to her," said the redhead with a smile. She dipped her head. "I'm Aine."

"Gwyneth," she replied.

"There's a few of us that practice for forms out in the courtyard after dinner," said Aine. "Would you like to join us? I've heard you're fair with a blade."

Despite the fact that her ribs still ached, Gwyneth found herself nodding. "Fair with a *practice* blade," she said with a grin.

Aine chuckled. "Well, all of us use practice blades for these sessions, of course, so we'll see your skills." She winked one vibrantly green eye. "See you in a few minutes, Siabhra."

Coming from Aine, the dismissive nickname became warm and teasing. Gwyneth found that she didn't mind it at all. She turned to ask Ed if she wanted to join, but Edelinne had disappeared during her conversation with Aine. Gwyneth started up the stairs. She knocked on Edelinne's door, but there was no answer, so she shrugged and went back to her own room to retrieve her practice blade. She'd thought about catching a few hours of sleep before using the river-stone, but she pushed that aside. She hadn't realized how badly she'd wanted to be accepted by the other Inionacha until Aine's bright-eyed, approving invitation. Still flush with her triumph in the dining hall, she slid her practice scabbard onto her belt and changed into the shirt she'd worn during her lessons with Ed, practicality winning out.

All in all, it was shaping up to be a very interesting day, Gwyneth thought as she closed her chamber door behind her and headed toward the courtyard. Her heart quickened as she thought of seeing

Rhys again, and she smiled as she saw the half-dozen older girls gathered in the courtyard. She was the youngest, though two of the girls she recognized from the history class that met in the classroom the hour before hers.

"I thought Gwyneth deserved an invite after her duel with Mary in the dining hall tonight," said Aine with a bright grin.

A few of the young women chuckled.

"Well, let's get to it then," said Aine with a flourish of her blade. She turned her vibrant eyes to Gwyneth. "Siabhra, you're with me for the first round."

Gwyneth smiled and drew her practice blade from its scabbard.

Chapter 11

The practice session with Aine and the other girls left Gwyneth so exhausted that she fell asleep despite her excitement over the mirror stone. She woke to an insistent tapping on the window and jolted out of her bed with a start. If Togha was here already, that meant it was almost midnight! Gwyneth lit the candle by her bed with a spark of *taebramh* and hurried over to the window.

"It's five minutes until midnight!" hissed Togha as soon as she slipped inside.

Gwyneth swore and shed her clothes without any thought to modesty, pulling on a new green shirt and black breeches, stuffing her feet into her good boots and then cursing as she remembered that she'd stashed the river-stone in the bottom of the same boot.

"Hurry, hurry," chanted the Glasidhe, whirring in a circle around her head.

Gwyneth grabbed her cloak and then on a whim threw open the chest at the bottom of her bed, casting about the bottom until she found the dagger that the Bearer had given to her.

"The stone will not work past its appointed time!" said Togha urgently.

"That would have been helpful to know beforehand," Gwyneth said. She put a hand to her hair but Togha grabbed one sleeve and tugged her toward the door.

"Where is the mirror?" Togha said. "No time, no time!"

For a terrible moment, Gwyneth couldn't remember the location of the nearest mirror, though she'd specifically walked past it when returning to her room from the sparring session with Aine.

"Down in the hallway," she said. It was a small mirror, but it was placed conveniently for all the girls to use before they entered the dining hall or made their way to classes. Their instructors placed a high value on personal neatness, but real mirrors were a luxury that they did not afford their students. Gwyneth had decided after a few weeks that their instructors forced all the girls in the hall to use the same mirror to teach teamwork and to discourage personal vanity…though she suspected that Mary had a mirror of her own in her room, because the older girl was the vainest of them all and never spent any time in front of that particular mirror.

Togha spun in circles around Gwyneth's head as she fastened her cloak around her shoulders and hurried to the door of her chambers, the river-stone warming in her hand. A little flutter of excitement whirred through Gwyneth's belly. Oddly enough, she didn't feel apprehensive at all about using the river-stone. Rhys had sent it to her. Togha had carried it herself. She trusted them both: after all, they'd saved each others' lives in the mortal world, what seemed like years ago now.

Gwyneth slipped out into the darkened hallway and shut her door carefully behind her. She walked down the hallway with precise, quiet steps, her booted feet silent on the wooden floorboards. She wove an intricate path around the spots where she knew the floorboards creaked, and she breathed a small sigh of relief when she reached the top of the stairs. Then she stopped abruptly. Togha landed on her shoulder.

"What is it?" the Glasidhe whispered into her ear.

"How will I get back?" she replied, barely breathing any sound at all into the words. The darkness pressed around her, the silence like a quilt wrapped about her shoulders. The hall felt very different when all its occupants were sleeping.

"The same river-stone will bring you back after four hours precisely," Togha replied, her breath tickling Gwyneth's ear.

That was good enough for Gwyneth. She sped down the stairs as fast as she dared without making any noise, reaching the glinting bit of mirror just as Togha grabbed her earlobe and said urgently, *"Touch the mirror!"*

Gwyneth held up the river-stone, which had begun to warm in her palm, watching in fascination as swirls of silver began to coalesce on its smooth surface. Togha made a sound of frustration and swooped down, grabbing Gwyneth's left hand and pulling it with fierce determination toward the mirror, managing to lift it only about as high as Gwyneth's waist. Gwyneth remembered herself and moved her hand toward the mirror. She felt Togha's small hands wrapped around one of her fingers, and then her hand touched the mirror.

The mirror rippled. Afterward, Gwyneth struggled to describe it. She wasn't sure whether the mirror had expanded, or she had shrunk, but her hand sunk into the silver surface as though it were a pool of still water. The river-stone suddenly felt like a small bird in her hand, trembling and warm, and she almost let go of it in surprise, but instead she tried to hold it delicately, and the mirror swallowed her whole.

For an instant, she spun through a place that was both bright and dark, bright colors suspended in colorful clouds and stars of many hues stippling the fantastic vista. Gwyneth wondered if there was a name for the place. She didn't remember seeing it when she traveled through the Gate with Rionach and Rhys, but perhaps her mind had simply been too stunned to fully recognize its magnificence.

Then, without any warning, her feet were on solid ground again, and she stumbled. Twigs crunched under her boots and she blinked, trying to gain any sense of her surroundings in the darkness. After a moment, her eyes adjusted. She stood at the edge of a forest, the trees tall and dark in the moonlight, a cold breeze making the branches sway, shadows dancing.

Togha released her grip on Gwyneth's finger and somersaulted into the air, her aura sparking back into brightness, swirling with dark blue and silver. Gwyneth rubbed her thumb across the river stone and slipped it back into her belt pouch. She stood gazing at the forest: for the first time since she had been brought to the hall of the Inionacha, she was someplace she had never been in Faeortalam, without one of her Instructors or an older girl as an escort. She shivered as the breeze slipped beneath her cloak.

"The white oak. Midnight," she murmured to herself. Would it have been *that* difficult for Rhys to include legible instructions?

Then she drew her shoulders back and touched the hilt of the dagger at her belt. Never mind that the river-stone had not come with any other directions. She was a daughter of the Blood, and the Bearer herself had brought her to Faeortalam.

"Come on," Togha said, ignoring Gwyneth's hesitation.

Gwyneth grinned as she suddenly understood. Rhys had not sent any other *written* directions with the river-stone, but he'd sent the river-stone via Togha. How silly of Gwyneth to think that the Glasidhe messenger was not somehow tasked to ensure her safe arrival. "You've been here before?" she asked Togha quietly. Her voice still sounded very loud as she started into the forest. Togha's aura lit the way surer than a lantern.

"No," Togha replied cheerily, her bright response entirely at odds with the dark, forbidding forest.

Gwyneth tripped over a root and stumbled. She bit down on a curse and wondered if this had been such a good idea after all. It had been well and good to dream about meeting Rhys again in the warmth and safety of her own chambers at the hall, but now, stumbling about in a cold, unknown forest, her enthusiasm wavered.

"But I know the way," Togha continued.

"Did – Rhys tell you?" Gwyneth asked, narrowly avoiding smashing her face into a low-hanging branch that she swore had not been there the prior moment.

"Oh, careful, the nymphs get possessive sometimes," Togha advised.

"Nymphs? *Possessive*?"

"The Paladins spend much of their time in the forest. The nymphs become quite fond of them."

Gwyneth tripped over another root and a thornbush appeared where she reached to steady herself. She snatched her hand away and chose to fall to one knee instead. "I didn't know I'd be trekking through a spiteful forest," she muttered.

The branches of the trees rustled, though there wasn't any wind. Gwyneth wasn't sure if the nymphs were laughing at her or warning her.

"They are mischievous, but they would not truly harm you," Togha said. "At least that is what Rhys said."

A little spark of warmth kindled in Gwyneth's chest when she thought of Rhys planning to send her the river-stone and assuring Togha that the nymphs would allow Gwyneth safe passage.

"Any guest of the Paladins will arrive safely," added the Glasidhe scout.

Gwyneth sighed. Of course they would. It was nothing special that Rhys had arranged safe passage for her.

But it is *something special that he invited you in the first place*, a small voice said within a corner of her mind.

"Do the Paladins invite many of the Inionacha to these...gatherings?" she asked Togha as she carefully navigated around a patch of vines that seemed to be waiting for her to step into them. She kept an eye on the vines until she was well past, half expecting them to twist to life and wrap around her ankles.

"I do not keep tally of the comings and goings of those in favor with the Paladins," replied Togha, weaving around a tree with dizzying speed.

"But you run messages for them."

"I run messages for a *few* of them who are in favor with *me*," Togha corrected her archly.

Gwyneth chuckled despite the looming trees and cold darkness. She wondered how much longer it would take them to reach the white oak, but then she remembered the headlong run through the woods when she and Rhys followed Rionach for the entire day with nary a rest. She would not complain like an untested child. A shiver worked its way up her spine regardless of her resolution.

"Young Paladins do not send messengers often," Togha said.

"Why?" Gwyneth dodged another branch that swung into her path. The trees were not even trying to hide it anymore.

Togha didn't answer her. Gwyneth threaded her way through the forest, trying to stay nimble and alert, though her limbs were beginning to ache with the cold. Was it winter in the mortal world as well? Would they be lighting the fires and painting their faces for Samhain soon? She wondered briefly how her mother and father were handling her absence. Homesickness pierced her with its sharp ache. She took a deep breath. She had learned how to keep it at bay in the familiar confines of the hall, but now, in these dark woods so like those in which she'd learned to hunt as a child, longing for her village rose up again in her.

A branch hit her shoulder. Gwyneth sidestepped and paused, watching the trees around her warily. Perhaps these woods were *not* so similar to those around her home, she thought as she rubbed her shoulder. The tree hadn't hit her hard enough to bruise, but it still stung.

"The more you show a reaction, the more they'll pester you," advised Togha, hovering just in front of Gwyneth.

A sharp retort rose to Gwyneth's lips – something like, *Is cutting off the next branch that hits me a reaction?* But she swallowed the words and reminded herself that nymphs were creatures of Faeortalam just as Togha was, and as an Inionacha she was charged with according all of them respect…even when they were being difficult, so she just nodded and set off again after Togha.

After what seemed like another hour hiking through the woods – and two more stinging little slaps by the trees – Togha pronounced, "We are here!"

The white oak did not stand dramatically in a meadow, shining in the moonlight. It was almost hidden in the shadows, its branches tangled with those of its neighbors, and it was not magnificent or imposing as Gwyneth had imagined.

"You thought to find something more striking?"

Gwyneth whirled at the voice. It sounded like rain pattering on leaves woven into words. A nymph stood barely an arm's length away from her, and Gwyneth took a step backward involuntarily before she realized how rude that would seem.

The nymph's skin was the same white-and-gray pattern as the bark of the white oak. Under the light of Togha's aura, the nymph's hair shone glossy brown as an acorn, and her eyes glinted the pale, tender green of new spring leaves.

"More striking? No, not necessarily," said Gwyneth carefully. The nymph tilted her head. She was not as tall as Gwyneth, and she was built sturdily like the trunk of her tree. "I have just never had the privilege to speak with a nymph before," Gwyneth continued honestly.

The nymph chuckled. "You know how to speak prettily, for one so young," she said.

"Thank you," Gwyneth said. She paused, wondering if it would seem very rude to ask the location of the Paladin. Would Rhys appear through the trees? Was there another portal?

As if in answer, the nymph held out what looked to Gwyneth like a strip of black cloth. When she took it from the nymph's grasp, Gwyneth saw that it was a simple mask, two holes cut in the black cloth. She peered more closely at it and picked out faint runes swimming beneath the surface of the weft and weave.

"Don your mask and enter the ball," said the nymph.

Gwyneth blinked. "I . . . what?"

But the nymph had vanished neatly, a few leaves swirling down in a spiral where she had stood.

Togha hummed in excitement. "A *masquerade*, how exciting!"

"Masquerade?" Gwyneth repeated, uncomprehending as she stared down at the plain cloth in her hands. She had heard of the magnificent costumed balls held in Italy and France – Edelinne had said that she thought she remembered her mother, a lady-in-waiting to one or another of the French royalty, telling stories of them. But who had ever heard of a masquerade with simple black masks in the middle of a dark, cold forest?

"You are entirely too unimaginative," scolded Togha. "Have you not seen the wondrous things of this world? Put on your mask!"

Gwyneth felt utterly foolish as she raised the strip of black cloth to her face. She shut her eyes as she tied the cloth snugly at the back of her head. A curious feeling rippled over her, like soft, slick fabric whirling over skin. When she opened her eyes, she started in surprise: she no longer wore her plain green shirt, but a flowing, silken emerald tunic that reached nearly to her knees, over an undershirt that gleamed silver. Velvet breeches had replaced her plain black ones, and whatever spell inhabited the mask had polished her boots to a mirror-like sheen.

Togha hovered before her, head cocked to one side. "It gave you a bird of some sort, I think, with scarlet feathers. Sets off your hair nicely." She nodded in approval.

Gwyneth blinked. "A bird?"

"Your *masque,* silly girl!"

She reached up toward her face: she didn't feel anything other than the plain, light cloth of the simple mask she had tied on just a moment ago.

"You won't be able to feel it, but you'll see others," Togha said. "Or perhaps they will have mirrors."

"Don't I need a mirror to return?" Gwyneth asked, latching onto that small, practical aspect. It was easier not to be overwhelmed when she had something like that to think about.

"No," replied Togha. "Only the mirror you came from. That is your return point."

"Oh." Gwyneth stopped and listened. Strains of music reached her ears. She turned and stepped past the white oak, and found herself at the edge of a large, circular clearing. In the center of the meadow stood another white oak, its branches spreading higher and farther than any other tree Gwyneth had ever seen. She took in a breath, marveling at its beauty, and she thought she heard the echo of a chuckle from behind her. When she looked over her shoulder, no one was there. She turned back to the clearing.

Dozens of figures moved gracefully about the clearing, all in strange and magnificent masques. *Taebramh* lights floated among the branches of the stately tree like stars captured and hung amid its dignified arms. Gwyneth glimpsed a dance floor that looked like a perfectly frozen lake, a ring where two figures dueled each other to the cheers of those watching, and a woman playing a golden harp nearly as tall as she. She felt breathless with the sudden magnificence of the lavish masquerade, and though she knew no one could see her face, she was suddenly hesitant. After all, her Instructors had warned them about their own people – warned them about the Sidhe. The Seelie and Unseelie were very different, Ava and Cara had said, but they were alike in that some viewed mortals – even Inionacha – as playthings. Gwyneth had thought to herself that it seemed unlikely any of the Sidhe would risk the wrath of the Bearer by toying with a daughter of the Blood...but now she wasn't so sure. Now she thought that perhaps stepping over the threshold into this strange and beautiful ball in the midnight woods would be tantamount to giving them her permission to bewitch her.

Don't be ridiculous, the practical voice in her head retorted. *Even if there are Sidhe here, they shan't* bewitch *you unless you lose your head. Find Rhys.*

But how was she to find Rhys among all the splendid masques? she wondered despairingly. She looked for Togha and saw the tail of the Glasidhe's aura as she streaked toward a knot of Glasidhe holding their own festivities up among the branches of the great oak. She took a hesitant step into the clearing. The air warmed considerably. With another step, she felt as though it was a pleasant spring day, and she unfastened her cloak – to which the runes of the mask had added a lining of plush sable fur.

A robe shimmering with silvery, fluid runes floated toward her. She watched it in confusion, wondering why the mask had given her such beautiful clothing if she was now going to don a long, black robe. No one *else* that she had glimpsed was wearing a robe, but perhaps there was some sort of protocol she didn't know. But the robe stopped, a silvery mist floating above its collar and at its cuffs – like a head and hands, she realized. The robe bowed, and held out one arm. When she stared at it, uncomprehending, it motioned at her cloak.

"I thought to find you and explain the Tower Servants before one presented itself to you," said a man wearing a gleaming red fox masque.

Relief and some other, hotter emotion flooded through Gwyneth. She recognized Rhys' voice as though she had just spoken to him yesterday rather than over a year past.

The Tower Servant, as Rhys had named it, gestured more insistently toward Gwyneth's cloak.

"You must let them be courteous and take your cloak," Rhys said, his gray eyes glinting from within the shimmering red fur of the fox. "Otherwise they become quite irritated."

"Oh," Gwyneth said. She laid her cloak over the Tower Servant's outstretched robe sleeve. It bowed gracefully and sped away. She turned back to Rhys, her heart suddenly beating as fast as though she'd just sparred with Aine.

"The hawk is an interesting choice," said Rhys. He took a step closer, but Gwyneth thought that perhaps he was feeling just as nervous as she, because he seemed to lose his voice and paused.

"Why do you say that?" she managed.

"I thought that you would be a wolf or a pard," he said. "Some sleek and deadly creature."

Gwyneth was suddenly very glad of the mask. Otherwise Rhys might have seen the hot blush that rushed to her cheeks at his words, which thrummed a chord deep within her, though she was not entirely sure if it was his words or just his voice.

"Well, you are a fast and clever creature," she countered.

He chuckled. "Yes, though sometimes I am neither fast enough nor clever enough to save myself trouble."

She grinned. He offered her his arm and she took it as they began walking toward the great oak tree.

"This is quite magnificent," she said.

"Which part?" he asked.

"All of it," she said, shaking her head slightly in wonder as her eyes traveled over each new, unique sight. She drew back her shoulders. "It almost convinces me to forgive you for barely speaking to me for an entire year."

"It did not mean I did not *wish* to speak to you," he said.

"And why did you not?" Part of Gwyneth wanted to simply soak in the lavish masquerade and revel in Rhys' closeness, but it was not the greatest part of her.

"You know that there are Inionacha who become Paladins?"

"Yes."

"Then you know why."

She shook her head. "If you think I would choose to become a Paladin simply because you are one, then you must think me incredibly weak-willed."

"That is not what I think at all," he replied.

A Tower Servant glided by with a silver tray of goblets balanced on the silver mist that served as its hands. Rhys deftly passed her one of the goblets and took one for himself as well.

"Then what *do* you think?" Gwyneth countered.

Rhys took a swallow of the liquid in the goblet and turned to face her. "I thought that you might be glad to see me again."

"I *am* glad," Gwyneth said. Her irritation drained away. "Truly, I am."

He smiled. Somehow, he was still handsome wearing the artfully rune-crafted masque. "I am glad to hear that."

"I am glad that you are glad to hear that," Gwyneth countered with an answering smile, taking a sip from her own goblet. Lush, heady wine filled her mouth, and warmth spread into her chest as she swallowed.

"Then it is quite settled that we are both glad to be glad," Rhys said, his smile widening to a grin.

"I've worried about you," Gwyneth blurted, the words somehow summoned by the warmth of the wine, even though she'd barely sipped at her goblet.

"I do not wish for you to worry," Rhys said, his smile fading, "but it would be silly of me to simply tell you not to worry." He lifted his shoulder in his characteristic half-shrug. "I am a Paladin, after all."

Gwyneth swallowed hard and then turned her head to survey the festivities. "Is everyone here a Paladin?"

"There are the Paladins and their guests," said Rhys. "It is the Samhain celebration, after all."

"This is much different than any Samhain that I've seen," said Gwyneth. "Perhaps this is more like how they celebrate Samhain in Normandy?"

Rhys chuckled. "Perhaps, but it makes it no less enjoyable. Would you like to dance?" He offered her his arm again.

"Perhaps I'd prefer to duel," she replied, thinking doubtfully of her lack of innate talent in the few dancing lessons that they'd had at the hall.

Rhys laughed again. "That could also be arranged."

Gwyneth blushed again. "I am sure everyone here far surpasses me in skill."

"At this celebration, it is not necessarily about displaying skill as enjoying oneself."

"You keep saying that," she said, suddenly very aware that she felt the heat of his body next to hers as they walked toward the dueling-circle.

"Being a Paladin is dangerous," he replied quietly. "It teaches us very quickly that we must seize every day and wring from it what pleasure we can."

"That could make for a very hedonistic life," Gwyneth said.

"Hedonistic," he repeated with a warm chuckle. "You are certainly different than the girl who saved my life in the forest."

"I'm not so different than I was," she replied, a little defensively. "I've just been reading books, is all."

"And there is nothing at all wrong with that," he said, smiling. "Do you think you can delay your judgment of our philosophy until you've experienced it, at least for a few hours?"

Her cheeks warmed yet again. She wondered if that would ever stop when she was near Rhys. Then she found her voice and replied, "I do believe I can manage that."

His eyes flashed silver within the fox masque as he raised her hand and kissed it, a courtly gesture that seemed completely appropriate within the elegance of the masquerade. "I am glad."

Gwyneth smiled and tucked away her worries, determined to hold true to her word. The *taebramh* lights hovered like captive stars above them and the ethereal music twined through the shadows as they joined the lovely creatures created just for the Samhain celebration, the shimmer of runes giving them all the sheen of beautiful transience.

Chapter 12

True to her word, Gwyneth enjoyed the Samhain celebration. It was as though the rest of the world had fallen away, and all that existed was encapsulated within the enchanted meadow. The *taebramh* lights shone in the branches of the great tree and the Glasidhe painted colorful patterns with their jewel-toned auras above the dance floor and the dueling ring. Tower Servants moved silently through the festivities with silver trays, and Gwyneth tasted all manner of sweet and savory foods that she was sure she had never eaten before and probably would never eat again. The goblets of wine refilled themselves, and she set hers aside once she realized it.

"You don't like the wine?" Rhys asked, his brow creasing in concern.

"I like it *too* much," Gwyneth replied with a giddy grin. She felt little sparks bubbling through her cheeks and fingers, and she pressed her lips together to make sure that they were still under her command.

Time slowed but the night whirled past them with glittering magnificence. Rhys brought Gwyneth over to the dueling ring and a woman wearing the sleek face of a whiskered white cat grinned at them, her canines glinting in the shifting light. Gwyneth found herself grinning back, and then the hilt of a blade was pressed into her hand. She didn't stop to think as she stepped into the ring, quickly evaluating the other woman. They were of about the same height, but the woman moved with an elegant grace that belied reflexes and training. Gwyneth had learned quickly that beauty often hid deadly skill, especially in Faeortalam.

The slim dueling blades glittered like shards of ice as they raised them in salute to one another. The cat-masked woman wore a tight black bodice with silver lace spilling from the neck and wrists, black velvet breeches that left nothing at all to the imagination, and red boots with silver toecaps. Gwyneth wondered briefly why the mask had given the other woman a *white* cat to wear, as she seemed very fond of dramatic colors.

The murmur of the onlookers swirled around them like water around rocks in a stream. Gwyneth narrowed her focus to the blade in the other woman's hand. The woman stepped delicately, the silver on her boots flashing. Gwyneth ignored everything except the sword, slipping into that quiet place where the beating of her heart slowed and her mind settled into her limbs, ready to react without any hesitation. They circled each other for a moment, and then the woman grinned and leaped forward, her sword becoming nothing more than a blur in her hand.

Gwyneth leapt to the side and met the woman's blade with her own, the shock of the blow vibrating through the hilt into her palm. She angled her sword and slid her opponent's blade to the side, darting forward to dare an attack of her own. The woman took two quick steps away, making Gwyneth feel slow, but she raised her eyebrows and the whiskers of the cat masque twitched in consideration. They circled each other again. The woman feinted but Gwyneth kept her focus, prompting another grin.

Gwyneth bristled at the condescension in the woman's slow circling and smiling. She felt her *taebramh* stirring, spreading its wings behind her collarbone. The woman tossed her sword to her left hand and swung it in a beautiful crescent arc that would have made

Gwyneth's blade instructor nod in curt approval. Gwyneth blocked the blow and spun away before the woman could catch her blade in a lock. She was beginning to think that her opponent was Sidhe rather than Paladin, though she could not in good conscience say that she'd ever sparred either.

Her *taebramh* beat its wings once in her chest, infusing her limbs with a rush of strength. Gwyneth executed her own feint, committing so convincingly that her opponent actually began to move her sword in that direction of the expected blow; and then Gwyneth reversed her direction, spinning to the other side, her blade arcing blindly toward what she knew would be the other fighter's vulnerability, if she'd taken the bait of the feint.

Instead, her blade clashed jarringly with the other woman's sword, arresting Gwyneth's momentum painfully. Her ribs reminded her of the earlier abuse they'd suffered with a piercing ache, but she pushed the discomfort aside over a rising respect for the difficult reversal and counter executed gracefully by her opponent. She quickly stepped to the side, creating distance between them, but the cat-faced woman pressed toward her relentlessly, her blade flashing from one side to the other.

Gwyneth felt her arm moving, felt her sword blocking the flurry of blows without any conscious thought. Her *taebramh* spread its powerful wings again, raising its fierce head and fixing her opponent with one savage, predatory eye. In the back of her mind, Gwyneth knew that her body would hurt later, that this new speed and strength did not come without some price, but she welcomed it. Her world had narrowed to outsmarting this smiling feline woman.

The speed of their blows sparked louder murmurs from the spectators, but they meant nothing to Gwyneth. She felt her blade moving and she gritted her teeth, giving her body to her *taebramh*, allowing it to push her past what she thought were her limits. She had never felt her arms move so fast or her legs propel her forward with such strength. Her opponent responded in kind, her smile widening to a grin again and her eyes glinting blue from within the white-cat masque.

There was a suspended moment in which time slowed, the space between each heartbeat long and crystalline. Gwyneth sensed the opening before she saw it, her sword already moving, and her *taebramh* surged triumphantly. At the last possible instant, Gwyneth fought to soften her blow, the tip of her sword shearing a handful of lace from the neck of the cat-faced woman's bodice and scoring a line against her opponent's translucently white skin. A drop of dark blood welled from the scratch, and the sight of it hit Gwyneth like a blow.

She dropped her sword, her *taebramh* folding its wings and regarding the shallow cut just above the other woman's collarbone with a hard satisfaction. For a heartbeat, her opponent's face darkened thunderously, but then the woman straightened and pressed two fingers to her collarbone, looking with interest at the smear of blood.

"I apologize," said Gwyneth huskily. "I should have exercised more control."

The woman licked her own blood from her fingers, her tongue pink and darting. "On the contrary, Lady Hawk, you exercised admirable control. I pushed you past what I thought you should have been able to counter, and you kept pace."

Gwyneth bowed her head at the compliment. She felt her legs trembling.

"Lord Fox, you have brought us a most interesting guest," said the cat-faced woman, smiling her feline smile at Rhys. She bent gracefully, her movements as precise as though she had not just fought a duel so intense that it had left Gwyneth with legs weak as a new calf's. The woman picked up the bit of lace that Gwyneth's blade had shorn from her bodice and stepped delicately over to Rhys, leaning close to tuck the token into the collar of his shirt. Gwyneth heard Rhys draw in his breath. She swallowed hard.

Then the woman spun into the center of the ring like a dancer. "And now who shall be next with the blades?" She grinned at

Gwyneth. "Though I think Lady Hawk holds the luck, for she has both a quick blade *and* a handsome suitor!"

Suitor. The word slid past Gwyneth's defenses with more silent speed than her opponent's blade. She looked at Rhys and saw him grinning, so she managed a smile of her own as well, as though they both enjoyed the cat-faced woman's wit. Chuckles ran through the knot of onlookers.

"I think perhaps he will have some competition now that Lady Hawk has displayed her skill," purred the feline-masked woman, her eyes glinting as she looked pointedly at a few of the men around the dueling ring. A few of them smiled, and one, a tall man with broad shoulders wearing a wolf masque, replied in an accented voice, "Perhaps Lord Fox surpasses all of us with his skill with a blade." He raised one eyebrow. Gwyneth knew that he wasn't talking about an actual sword, and she was grateful again for the concealment of the masque.

"Perhaps," allowed the woman with a smile, her whiskers twitching, "but methinks that demonstration is not appropriate for the dueling ring."

The wolf-masked man laughed a loud, booming laugh that overran the other sounds of merriment from the other onlookers. Rhys grinned his inscrutable grin. Gwyneth wondered suddenly if they were all laughing at her expense. She was, after all, still young, despite the fact that her year in Faeortalam had made her feel much older than her actual age.

"Ah, no need to ruffle your feathers, Lady Hawk," the cat-faced woman said in a lower voice that was almost kind. "But take care to understand what kind of duel you are truly stepping into before you enter the ring."

Then the woman saluted her with a flourish and handed her sword to one of the men who had stepped into the ring. Rhys appeared by Gwyneth's side just as the wolf-faced man stepped forward, his large hand extended. For a moment, Gwyneth stared at him, confused.

"Your blade, Lady Hawk, nothing more," the imposing man said in a low, rumbling voice that somehow sounded quite comforting.

Gwyneth smiled in thanks and handed him the blade. She felt Rhys' hand on her elbow, guiding her away from the ring. The crowd parted for them, some smiling or nodding to Gwyneth.

"I did not think your opponent would press so hard," Rhys said, a hint of an apology in his voice.

"And I did not think she would give you her favor," Gwyneth returned, an edge to her voice.

He chuckled. "Such things are commonplace."

"Perhaps to *you*," she muttered.

"You dueled magnificently," he continued, as though he hadn't heard her.

"I am glad you think so," she returned, a bit stiffly.

He stopped and turned to face her, pulling the bit of lace from his collar. "Does it truly vex you that she gave me this?"

"I don't quite know what it *means*, her giving you that, but…yes," Gwyneth admitted. Her legs were beginning to feel a bit more stable and her ribs had stopped aching. She wondered briefly how much longer they had until she had to use the river-stone to return to the hall of the Inionacha.

"Why does it vex you if you don't know what it means?"

"I don't know," she returned, narrowing her eyes. "Don't mock me."

He held the lace in the palm of his hand. "Court etiquette is complicated, Gwyneth. A lady's favor can mean many different things." He grinned his half-grin. "In this case, coupled with what the lady said before she gave this to me, she was expressing her approval that I had chosen you to bring to the masque."

"Oh." Gwyneth felt suddenly foolish, but she was grateful that Rhys had explained. "In Doendhtalam, favors are much more…straightforward."

He nodded. "That is true." He tilted his head slightly to one side. "I would not have accepted this, if it meant that I was accepting her favor in *that* respect."

"She did seem a bit too dangerous for you," Gwyneth said lightly, smiling despite the sudden butterflies in her stomach.

Rhys stepped closer. "You think it is not dangerous to invite an Inionacha to the Samhain celebration?"

"I…don't know," she said, feeling suddenly breathless.

"Well," he said, his gray eyes intent, "it's worth every bit of the risk."

Gwyneth felt some strange force pulling them closer, and she succumbed to it, but then Rhys stepped back, breaking the spell. A Tower Servant glided to a stop next to him, and he lifted two silver goblets from the tray.

"Not wine," he said to Gwyneth with a smile.

She took the goblet gratefully and found it to be blessedly cool water, flavored with just a hint of sweet fruit that reminded her of strawberries. She drank her fill and felt immediately better.

"Thank you," she said belatedly to Rhys.

He just smiled and offered her his arm. They walked at a leisurely pace around the meadow and watched the revelers on the silver dance floor for a while. The music was alternately slow and sweet, and then with a shift it became strange and wild, the dancers' movements changing accordingly.

"*This* is what I remember of Samhain," murmured Gwyneth as they watched one of the wild dances. Rhys made a wordless sound of agreement. She glanced at him, wishing that she could see his face rather than the fox masque. "Do you miss home?"

"This is our home," he replied.

"You know what I mean," she said softly.

"You asked me nearly that exact question before you chose to follow the Bearer into Faeortalam," said Rhys.

"Yes."

"There are moments," he said in a low voice. "When you told me of my sister's children, I wished I could go to see them. They will never know me. To them, I am dead."

Gwyneth shivered. Had her mother and father told the rest of the village that she had died? Was she now dead to all those who had known her?

"But that is the cost of being a protector," he continued with quiet conviction. "We are what stand between our world and the darkness. We are the guardians of this world and Doendhtalam. Even if those we once loved are unaware, we protect them still."

Gwyneth took a long, deep breath of the spring-like air. She let it out slowly and finally she nodded. "And who protects the protectors?"

He smiled. "We like to think we don't often need protecting, but sometimes the Bearer steps in for a particularly concerning threat. And in my case...you."

She tried to hide her pleasure at his words by taking a draught from her silver goblet. The music shifted to a slow, haunting melody. A Tower Servant appeared as though summoned by thought itself, raising its empty tray. She placed her goblet on the tray and turned to Rhys. "Shall we dance?"

"Of course, Lady Hawk," he said gallantly, offering his arm.

They danced for far longer than Gwyneth originally thought that her tired legs could stand but being near Rhys had a strange effect on her. After dancing, they walked about the great oak, gazing up at the constellations of *taebramh* lights in its branches and watching the Glasidhe compete to create the most dazzling pattern of their aura against the dark sky.

"Have you enjoyed yourself?" Rhys asked softly.

"More than any other celebration that I can remember," Gwyneth replied truthfully. She felt as though the night had been at once an eternity and the blink of an eye. Her stomach sank as she knew that soon she would have to return to the hall. "I don't want to go back," she confessed. They were standing close enough that she could feel the strong curve of his arm against her own.

Rhys sighed. "This is why I did not extend any invitations until now. I did not want you to become enamored of this false image of the life of a Paladin."

She shook her head. "No. I am not enamored of the celebration." She turned toward him, feeling very daring, as though she were walking along the edge of a cliff.

"You are Inionacha," he said quietly.

"I am Inionacha, not a nun," she retorted, thinking of the dour-faced women who had once walked through their village with their hair covered by dark cloth.

He chuckled. "You are correct in that."

They stared at each other for a long moment. Gwyneth felt the river-stone shift in her belt pouch.

"It's time for you to return," said Rhys.

"Will you take off your masque?" she asked, her voice barely more than a whisper. "I'd like…to see your face."

Rhys lowered his head for a moment and then nodded. "We will both need to untie our masks at the same time and stay in contact to ensure that the runes do not place us on opposite sides of the forest." He reached one hand up to the back of his head and she mirrored him, her heart suddenly jumping. Rhys held out his free hand, and she twined her fingers through his, the feeling of his skin upon hers headier than the wine. She worked her knot loose, holding the mask tight to her face with just her fingers.

"Now," Rhys said, and she let the mask fall away. His grip on her hand tightened as the forest dissolved around them, the bright colors of the Glasidhe and the captured stars of the *taebramh* lights whirling into the true darkness of the night woods. Gwyneth felt her sumptuous clothes return to their former plainness, and the weight of her cloak settled neatly about her shoulders. The warmth of Rhys' hand remained constant as they were wrapped in dark silence. The river-stone quivered again.

"Only a moment left," Rhys murmured. With a deft twist of his fingers, he wove a small ball of *taebramh* and tossed it into the air above them.

"Thank you," Gwyneth said sincerely, though she wasn't sure if she was simply thanking him for the invitation or something more. She found herself drinking in the sight of him, his strong jaw and sharp cheekbones illuminated by the small, softly pulsing globe of light.

"I was not sure you would accept my invitation," Rhys replied. He looked down. "I left you quite alone after you saved my life."

"It was what you thought was best," Gwyneth said, and she found that she believed her words. She smiled. "Just perhaps try to send a message every now and again?"

"I will," he said with his half-grin.

"Be safe," she said earnestly as she opened her belt purse.

"Safety is never guaranteed," he replied. He leaned toward her. "But I will always do my best to keep myself in one piece."

She smiled, and then he was very close, and she tipped her head up. His lips met hers, warmth rushing through her body. He cupped her cheek gently with one large, calloused hand and drew back. Two spots of color burned high on his cheeks.

"Be well," he told her, and she slipped her hand into her belt pouch. He dropped his hand as she curled her fingers around the river-stone, and the forest melted away.

Chapter 13

The whirl through the varicolored ether felt less jarring to Gwyneth on the return trip, but perhaps that was because her cheeks were still glowing from Rhys' kiss. She slid through the mirror on the landing in the hall, the sounds of a scuffle enveloping her. After regaining her footing and blinking against the darkness, she made out a tangle of limbs and hair at the bottom of the staircase. She moved forward and stumbled, her feet tangling in a length of cloth that she recognized as one of the bed sheets from their rooms. After quickly disentangling herself, she turned her attention back to the scuffle and found Edelinne sitting triumphantly on top of one of Mary's cronies, a pale-haired girl with startling lavender eyes.

"Try to wriggle away again and I'll hit you right in your pretty face," Edelinne said firmly.

"Ed!" Gwyneth said in surprise. She felt a little breathless – the transition itself had not been half so jarring now that she knew what to expect, but the night of revelry and her parting with Rhys had left her dizzy. A spike of fear pierced through the haze in her head – what if Edelinne did something that couldn't be explained away in the morning? Gwyneth couldn't bear the thought of Ed being punished after *she'd* been the one to enjoy the night of revelry with the Paladins.

Ed lowered her face toward the pale-haired girl, speaking in a furious whisper. "Tell Mary next time she should come herself to do her dirty work instead of sending someone so *small*." She sat back, and the girl grimaced. "I'm going to let you up now, and you're going to run along back to your room and not mention a word of this to anyone." Ed paused thoughtfully. The girl squeaked. "Well, except Mary, of course," Ed said finally with a hint of a grin. "You can tell *her* all about it. Got it?"

The pale-haired girl nodded. Edelinne stood and the girl scrambled away, gathering up the sheet and stumbling back up the stairs. Ed watched her go, muttering to herself in French as she climbed the stairs.

"We'd better go," she whispered to Gwyneth. "Margery made a funny sound when I tackled her, and I don't know if my quiet-charm quite worked."

Gwyneth thought it best to follow Edelinne up the stairs, though questions burned in her mind. The shorter girl led Gwyneth back to her room and followed her inside.

"What happened?" asked Gwyneth as the door shut quietly behind them.

"I could ask you the same thing," said Edelinne, crossing her arms over her chest.

"I..." Gwyneth realized that she still clutched the river-stone. There was no hiding it now. She held it out for Edelinne's inspection. "I had an...invitation."

Ed nodded. "To the Paladins' Samhain celebration."

"How did you know...?"

"I listen," Ed replied simply. "I think a few of the older girls went as well."

Gwyneth wondered suddenly if the woman in the white cat masque had been one of the older women. But then she thought that the blood her blade had drawn from her opponent had looked darker than the red of mortal blood.

"You could have told me, you know," Edelinne continued, not meeting Gwyneth's eyes. She stared at the sword on the wall instead.

"I should have," agreed Gwyneth quietly. "I just...I didn't want you to feel..."

"Excluded?" Edelinne raised her eyebrows.

Gwyneth shifted uncomfortably. "I see what you're saying."

"Well." Ed shrugged. "It's all right, I guess. You'll just have to tell me all about it, *oui?*"

"Oui," Gwyneth agreed with a smile. She walked over to her bed and sat down, setting the river-rock on her pillow and then pulling off her boots. "What was Margery doing by the mirror, anyway?"

"Mary sent her to cover it," replied Ed.

Gwyneth blinked. "And what happens when you try to come back through a covered mirror?"

Ed shook her head. "You can't."

"Does it send you back to where you were?"

"If it's a well-made river-stone, yes. If not..." Ed shrugged. "I don't really know." She raised her eyebrows. "You really got under Mary's skin today."

"I suppose I did," murmured Gwyneth.

"But I heard Margery sneaking downstairs. I'd put a little spell on the top stair so that anyone passing by would sound a little bell in my room," Ed said with a hint of pride.

"That's a lot more advanced than anything we've been taught, Ed," Gwyneth said appreciatively.

Edelinne colored. "Well, yes. I'm handy with understanding little things like that, I suppose."

"It's not a *little* thing, Ed! You saved me from either being sent back to the woods or being trapped in the ether. That's not a little thing."

"Well," Ed said after a moment. "That's what friends do for each other, don't they?"

Gwyneth smiled. She stood and gave Edelinne a hug. "Yes. And I'm sorry I didn't tell you."

Ed waved her hand. "Like I said, forgiven. If I'm not going to be invited to these balls, then at least I can hear about them from you." She smiled. "And stand guard over your return mirror."

"How do the older girls do it, I wonder?"

"I hear a few of them have their own mirrors," replied Edelinne.

Gwyneth hummed in contemplation. "I think it will be a while until I travel by river-stone again, but I'll think about that."

"You should get what sleep you can," Ed said, brushing imaginary wrinkles out of her shirt. Gwyneth noticed that she was wearing her sleep-shirt with hastily donned trousers beneath it.

"I'll tell you all about the ball tomorrow," Gwyneth promised, picking up her sleep-shirt.

"Not *all* about it. We've got to make it *last,*" Edelinne replied as she walked to the door.

Gwyneth chuckled. "Whatever you say. Thanks, Ed."

Edelinne smiled and shut the door behind her.

Gwyneth changed into her sleeping clothes and slid into bed. She slipped the river-stone beneath her pillow and fell asleep thinking not of the magnificent masques of the Samhain ball, but of the *taebramh*-light illuminating Rhys' bare face as he leaned toward her and the feel of his lips against hers.

The waking bell came too fast, but Gwyneth counted her tiredness as a well-earned price for attending the Paladins' Samhain celebration. She wasn't sure if she imagined it, but Beatrix looked haggard as she ushered the younger girls to their places at breakfast. Beatrix covered her mouth as she yawned and then saw Gwyneth looking at her; she caught her eye and winked. Gwyneth suppressed her smile. She certainly *hadn't* imagined it.

"Mary looks like someone put a frog in her porridge," Ed whispered as they ate breakfast.

"Or like someone tackled one of her flunkies and foiled her nefarious plot," Gwyneth whispered back. They giggled. It felt good to laugh with Edelinne again, the disagreement from the day before forgotten. Gwyneth wondered if it would always be so easy to forgive as they stepped farther into womanhood.

History class occupied most of the morning, followed by penmanship for those girls who had not yet satisfied Instructor Ava with their handwriting. Edelinne had tested out of the class long ago. She gave Gwyneth a sympathetic look as she pulled the strap of her satchel over her shoulder.

"I'll see you at midday meal," Gwyneth said, trying not to yawn. Her night of revelry had definitely caught up to her during the last hour of history class.

"I'm going to go practice forms," Ed said with a nod.

Gwyneth waved farewell and walked back into the classroom, selecting a roll of parchment from the supplies at the back of the room. She had grown so used to life at the Hall that sometimes she forgot that she had stepped into Faeortalam, but a small detail like the abundance and quality of the parchment they used to *practice* their penmanship jolted her memory. When her mother had taught Gwyneth her letters, she'd practiced first in a flat-swept patch of dirt, sketching the letters into the earth with a sharpened stick; then she had eventually been allowed to use old skins scraped thin and about to be tossed into the refuse pile. Here in the Hall of the Inionacha, they had no lack of supplies for their education. Strange, thought Gwyneth, that a thing so simple as a roll of parchment could make her feel so grateful and yet so out of place.

The other girls assigned to penmanship filtered into the class; one of the young women of Beatrix's age walked into the room and turned over the sandglass at the front table. Gwyneth unrolled her parchment and sharpened her quill. After setting out her inkwell, she opened her history book to a passage that she needed to memorize: penmanship might at the very least help her with another class. Despite her tiredness – of perhaps *because* of it – she settled into that calm, clear space that in her prior life had been reserved for hunting. Everything else fell away other than the scratching of her quill, and she found that she was almost *enjoying* penmanship – something unthinkable on most days. The tedium of it annoyed her, although she tried to see the practical application; but she had often wondered if Rionach had to sit through such ridiculous lessons. Why did the Bearer need to have good penmanship, anyway? Wouldn't she just be able to send a message by her *taebramh* or by the Glasidhe?

But Gwyneth tucked those thoughts away and fell into a nearly meditative state, moving her quill smoothly at just the right speed – quickly enough to guard against inkblots, but not so quick that her haste created skips in the continuous line of the ink. Every word was a different challenge, each letter becoming its own small test. She checked the history book for her next line.

"Gwyneth."

Gwyneth blinked and looked up. She realized that she was the only one in the classroom – when had all the other girls left? The top chamber of the sandglass at the front of the room showed empty. Then her mind finally shook off the last of her contemplative state and she realized that she had just heard Instructor Ava's voice. She stood hastily, knocking over her inkwell.

The Unseelie Instructor caught the inkwell before it spilled ink over Gwyneth's parchment in a fast-as-thought, catlike movement. She raised her dark eyebrows slightly as she set the inkwell back in its proper place.

"Instructor Ava," said Gwyneth, bowing her head respectfully as all Inionacha did when addressing one of their two Sidhe Instructors. "I apologize, I did not hear you approach."

"Nor did you hear the other students leaving for the midday meal," Ava said.

Color rushed to Gwyneth's face as her stomach rumbled audibly.

"But you have not yet missed it, so do not be alarmed," Ava said almost kindly. She tilted her head as she surveyed Gwyneth's parchment. Gwyneth heard her own heartbeat in her ears in the silence as the Instructor slid the parchment toward her with two long, graceful white fingers.

Finally, after what seemed an eternity, the Instructor nodded once. "Well done."

"Thank you, Instructor," Gwyneth managed.

"Do you have any inclination to learn how to Walk, Gwyneth?" Ava continued.

"I...I don't know, Instructor. I haven't tried," Gwyneth admitted.

"I should hope not," the Unseelie woman replied mildly. "Unsupervised Walking is much more dangerous than some realize. But I think you have traveled through the ether already, have you not?"

Gwyneth swallowed hard but raised her chin. "Yes, Instructor."

Ava looked at her silently for a long moment, her beautiful face unreadable. Gwyneth wondered suddenly and irrationally if her Instructor had been the woman in the white-cat masque – but the notion of the Unseelie Instructor wearing that corset with the lace spilling from it seemed patently ridiculous. Gwyneth swallowed again, this time to tamp down the irrational mirth bubbling up her throat as her traitorous imagination gleefully conjured the image of Instructor Ava's disapproving expression if she had encountered the woman in the white-cat masque. *How impractical*, remarked the Instructor in her mind's eye, raising a dark eyebrow as she surveyed the sumptuous and scandalous raiment. Gwyneth bit the inside of her cheek.

"Take care in choosing both your friends and your enemies, Gwyneth," Ava said finally, her voice silken. "Someday that may make all the difference."

"My friends, or my...enemies?" Gwyneth asked. The word seemed too harsh. Surely Mary was not her *enemy*. They disliked each other strongly, but they were both Inionacha. Then she remembered that Mary had sent Margery to cover the mirror – if the river-stone had not sent her back to the Paladin's forest, then perhaps she would still be trapped in the ether. A little shiver slipped down her spine. Maybe Mary *was* her enemy.

"Both deserve your equal attention," replied Ava. "And you must understand that sometimes the line between one and the other is not so sharply drawn as you might think."

Gwyneth opened her mouth and closed it again. She didn't know how to reply, so she just nodded, hoping the Instructor thought that enough.

"We should both be getting to the midday meal," the Unseelie woman said.

"Yes, Instructor." Gwyneth bowed her head respectfully and when she looked up again, Ava was gone. Both their Sidhe Instructors moved about silently like cats. Gwyneth hurriedly put away her supplies, gathered her books and rolled her parchment.

"You're late," whispered Ed as Gwyneth gratefully took the empty seat beside her. The girls had already taken their seats and the food was being passed.

"Instructor Ava," whispered Gwyneth in reply with a little shrug.

"Well," Ed said, louder, "I ladled you out a portion – didn't know you were going to be *this* late."

"Thanks, Ed," she replied as she dug into the meal. It was just this side of cold, but she didn't really care. Food was food. She concentrated on eating quickly.

"And you say that *I* need to slow down," muttered Ed, adding something in French.

Gwyneth pointed her spoon at Ed. "I am adaptable."

"Adaptable," repeated Ed with a snort. They grinned at each other.

Gwyneth pushed away her empty bowl. "You should come practice for forms tonight."

"With Aine and the rest?" Edelinne shook her head. "They invited you, not me."

"They invited me because of what I said to Mary," Gwyneth pointed out. "You've just stood up to her in a much bigger way."

"Nobody knows about *that*," Ed retorted, shaking her head.

"You know better than anyone that the older girls have their ways of knowing things," Gwyneth replied. "And besides, maybe you could teach us the charm you used on the top step of the stair. It sounds handy, and we're certainly not going to learn it in formal lessons."

"I...well, only if you won't be embarrassed to bring me along," Ed said, looking down at her empty bowl.

"Ed," Gwyneth said firmly.

"All right, all right," Edelinne said, putting up her hands.

Gwyneth grinned as they gathered their empty bowls. When she turned, she nearly ran into Beatrix. The young woman stepped gracefully out of the way, moving nearly as quickly as their Sidhe Instructors. "Oh," said Gwyneth quickly. "I apologize..."

"You did not *actually* run into me, so there is no need to apologize for something that *almost* happened," replied Beatrix with a smile.

"I'll take your bowl," said Ed, fairly wrenching the dish from Gwyneth's grasp in her haste.

"I...of course," said Gwyneth.

"I was sent to tell you that you will no longer be taking the penmanship class," Beatrix continued, still smiling. "In its place, you are to report to the Theory classroom on the third floor."

Gwyneth had never even heard of Theory. "I don't know where that is," she confessed.

"It's the one with the blue door," Beatrix said in an undertone, leaning toward her. She stood tall again and gave Gwyneth a nod. Gwyneth watched her go, wondering if she'd ever move with such confidence. Then she shook herself from her thoughts, picked up the strap of her satchel and settled the weight of her books against her hip as she turned her feet toward her afternoon classes.

Chapter 14

"Well, this has certainly been a fortunate week for both of us," Edelinne said at the end of that week as she and Gwyneth worked on an essay for their history class.

"Maybe there was some enchantment at the Paladin's Samhain festival," Gwyneth said with a smile. She found she actually enjoyed history more now that she wasn't copying whole passages for penmanship.

"If it was, then I'll gladly tackle Margery every night for a week," replied Ed cheerfully. Then she shrugged, carefully placing her quill back in its holder so she didn't splatter ink on her parchment. "But I think you're not giving yourself enough credit."

"*I'm* not giving myself enough credit?" Gwyneth raised her eyebrows. They were working in Ed's room, since Ed had laid quiet-charms on the threshold and walls. It felt like a sanctuary.

"We are both not giving ourselves enough credit," Ed corrected with a smile. She grinned. "You in Theory and me graduating from the intermediate blade class – who would have thought?"

"I knew you were going to pass forms," Gwyneth said firmly.

Ed waved her hand with a dismissive noise. "It is easy to say that now that I have."

Gwyneth chuckled. "And you certainly made your presence known with Aine and the others."

"It is not so hard to teach simple charms." Ed shrugged as she inspected the ink on her parchment for dryness.

Rather than argue with her friend, Gwyneth just smiled. She could tell from the pleased curve to Edelinne's mouth that no matter what Ed said, she was rightfully proud of herself.

"Enough about classes," said Ed. "Tell me more about Rhys as I wait for this parchment to dry."

"I've already told you everything," replied Gwyneth in half-hearted protest.

"Then tell me again," Ed said implacably. "Like I said, I'm living vicariously through you." She sighed. "Maybe someday I'll actually meet a man in person."

Gwyneth laughed. "We've had a few men come over to instruct us."

"First of all, they are much too old for us," Edelinne said with an exaggerated expression of disdain. "And second of all, I do not want instruction in blade work." She waggled her eyebrows suggestively.

Gwyneth replaced her quill on its stand. "You should warn me before you say something like that," she said through her laughter. "Otherwise I'll have to redo this entire essay or risk being sent back to penmanship!"

"No going back to penmanship now that Instructor Ava has sucked you into her Theory class," replied Ed with a grin.

"It was taught by one of the Diligent," said Gwyneth, shrugging. "Who knows if Ava will actually ever teach the class herself."

"You're just at the beginning," Ed said. She looked contemplatively at her essay. "Maybe I'll become one of the Diligent."

"But they're all near the end of their time here in the Hall," protested Gwyneth. "Or they would have been, if they hadn't chosen to become instructors. You can't be giving up that easily."

Edelinne smiled at her. "I'm not *giving up*, Gwyneth. I think the Bearer has already made her choice for her successor..."

"Not this again," groaned Gwyneth.

"...which I won't go into now," Ed continued with a pointed look, "but I'm just being realistic. I don't have the bladework to become a Paladin, and I like books but not enough to shut myself away with the Scholars." She shrugged. "Teaching everyone the little charm I made gave me the idea. The Diligent teach the younger classes, and maybe I'm not ready for it now, but..." She let her sentence trail into silence.

"I thought you wanted to talk about Rhys," Gwyneth said in an attempt to turn the conversation back to its original lighthearted topic.

"On the subject of men," continued Ed, "I don't quite think that I'd like to return to Normandy." She made a face. "The idea of having children has never appealed to me."

Every year, there were Inionacha who returned to Doendhtalam after taking a vow of secrecy: they would reveal nothing of Faeortalam to anyone unless that person was of the Blood. Gwyneth had learned that many families of the Blood intermarried for generations, the men becoming Paladins (along with some of the women) and the first daughters sent to the Hall of the Inionacha. She still felt like an outsider during those conversations, and sometimes she wondered again why her mother had tried to hide her.

"You don't have to make any decision right now," she told Edelinne.

"It never hurts to begin thinking of the future," Ed replied with gravity.

"Thinking of the future while we're sorting through the past," Gwyneth replied, looking woefully down at her half-finished history essay. She pressed her lips together. "I think I'll finish this tomorrow."

"You said that last night," pointed out Ed.

"I know, but my brain can only sort through so much Amidalus," said Gwyneth, rubbing her temples for emphasis. "He's brilliant, certainly, but do you think he could use a bit *less* of native languages in his analysis of the Merrow."

"I think their language is beautiful," Ed said, a bit defensively. "And I heard from one of the Diligent that Instructor Ava can speak it fluently."

Gwyneth looked at Edelinne in surprise. "I didn't know that."

"You should ask your Paladin man when the Merrow will be sending their ambassadors," Edelinne said thoughtfully. "I would give my left foot to be able to meet a Merrow in person, much less hear them speak."

"Your left foot?" Gwyneth repeated skeptically. "That seems… extreme."

"Perhaps," Edelinne agreed. "But that's the one that causes all the trouble – I was sick when I was a babe in the cradle, see, and that leg never really healed proper."

"I thought that most Inionacha…" Gwyneth stopped herself.

"My mother knew that a deformity would make me unacceptable to come to the Hall," said Ed. "She spent a lot of time with me as a child, making sure I could walk and run without any trace of a limp."

"She had hopes for you to be the Bearer?"

"She did not want the Bearer to take my sister, I think," Ed said quietly, her accent strong. Then she shrugged. "I should not have said anything. It is nothing."

"I never noticed," Gwyneth replied truthfully, though now her mind raced through all the instances when her friend had stumbled or failed to move fast enough in forms.

"It is close enough to nothing that I barely notice it anymore," said Ed with another shrug.

"When's the end of the time that the Bearer can take the second daughter?" Gwyneth said thoughtfully, leaning back in her chair. They had no classes in the succession of the Blood, which she thought strange, because that was their entire purpose here in Faeortalam, wasn't it? The Hall existed to prepare an Inionacha to assume the mantle of Bearer.

"There's nothing written that I've been able to find," Ed replied, still scratching away at her essay. Gwyneth watched her with a hint of envy – Ed was so good at multitasking when it came to academics. "But I think it probably has something to do with the amount of time that the first daughter spends in the Hall."

"My sister, though," Gwyneth shook her head and squinted. "She must have been here at least seven or eight years."

"It is best not to speak of it," said Ed in a low voice.

Gwyneth pressed her lips together. "Why is it that we aren't supposed to speak about things that have such a direct effect on our lives?"

"Aren't you happy to be here?" Edelinne raised her eyebrows. "You made the choice, Gwyn. It's not as though the Bearer stole you from the cradle and you awoke in a new world."

"You're right," Gwyneth admitted. "I just feel sometimes that I don't fully understand why we are secreted away here."

"You probably won't be much longer," said Ed.

"What?" Gwyneth narrowed her eyes.

"No, I'm not referring to the Bearer choosing her successor," Edelinne replied patiently. "The older girls can't speak of it to us, but I'm sure that they are sent out on missions much like the young Paladins." She tilted her head and inspected her length of parchment.

"I suppose that makes sense, but they do a very good job of keeping it from us," Gwyneth replied. She wondered briefly if Rhys had ever been sent on a mission with one of the older Inionacha. The thought of it sparked some strange, writhing feeling in her belly that felt very close to jealousy.

"Well, they would, wouldn't they? There's a bit of danger involved, and they wouldn't want to send anyone before they are ready."

"But it sounds…exciting." Gwyneth found herself smiling.

"Easy for you to say, you already dealt with a *baobhain sith* before you set foot through the Gate," muttered Ed.

"Do you think they'd send us through into the mortal world?"

"I don't know." Edelinne shrugged. Then she looked up at Gwyneth. "Oh, you've got that look on your face."

"What look?" Gwyneth tried to compose her face into something resembling polite interest.

"That look that says you're going to find a way to get wrapped up in something," said Ed fondly.

"Maybe you shouldn't tell me these things you hear," Gwyneth suggested, her lips curving into a smile again as she began to tidy the desk, wiping the ink from the quill and stoppering the inkwell.

"*Au contraire, mon cher,*" Edelinne replied, her eyes sparkling devilishly. "This is *exactly* why I tell you these things I hear."

Gwyneth laughed.

"Now that I have given you that little bit to chew on," Ed continued, cleaning her quill and then gesturing with it to emphasize her words, "let us return to the original subject. Tell me again how you danced with your Paladin."

"He's not *my* Paladin," protested Gwyneth halfheartedly, her cheeks heating with pleasure at the words. Did she want Rhys to be *her* Paladin? What would that even mean? She shook her head. "There's too much at stake for either of us for that to happen."

Ed pointed the quill at Gwyneth and narrowed her eyes. "Do not try to fool *me, mon cher.*"

"And I am…too young to think of such things." Gwyneth floundered onward with excuses, even as she thought that there were young women married and having children at her age in the village. A strange mixture of curiosity and sorrow flashed through her as she wondered yet again if Siobhan had survived her sickness and perhaps gone on to marry a merchant who could indeed take her to Dublin.

Edelinne muttered something under her breath in French that Gwyneth was reasonably sure echoed her own thoughts.

"We were wearing masques, so I couldn't see his face, but I still knew it was him," Gwyneth said. "His eyes – I knew because of his eyes."

Ed smiled and folded her hands, listening intently as Gwyneth continued describing her fleeting time with Rhys at the Paladins' celebration. Perhaps in a few weeks they would both tire of speaking about it, Gwyneth thought as she tried to explain the music, how it had changed from a beautiful, slow song to a wild and unpredictable melody. Edelinne propped her chin on her hands and let her eyes close as she did when she imagined something.

Perhaps someday they would tire of it, Gwyneth thought, smiling as she continued on, but today was not that day.

Winter settled its grip around the Hall. The days passed slowly but the weeks passed quickly; Gwyneth found herself challenged by her new classes, but not entirely overwhelmed as she'd expected. In fleeting moments of relaxation when she was not occupied with classwork, practicing bladework, or learning whatever new small spell that Ed had invented or improved, Gwyneth wondered if the Paladins held a Solstice celebration, and if she should expect an invitation. She tried not to let herself hope, but she looked at the window sharply every time rain tapped against it, thinking that perhaps she would see the aura of a Glasidhe messenger through the glass.

A fortnight before the Winter Solstice, Gwyneth took her place in the Theory classroom. The interior of the classroom changed between each of their lessons, so she always tried to arrive with a few moments to look at the different artifacts that appeared floating by the high ceiling and on the many shelves that snaked along the walls. Bright winter sunlight streamed through the long, thin windows that reminded Gwyneth of the archer's slits in a castle's turret.

Today, a white fire danced in midair in the center of their circle of chairs. There were no desks in the room like the other classrooms. It still gave Gwyneth a distinct feeling of pleasure to sink into the comfortable cushion of the armchairs in the Theory room. It made her feel very adult, somehow. The white fire gave off a pleasant, shimmering heat as Gwyneth settled into her chair – she was always careful to take the most threadbare, since she was the youngest of all the students in the class, and she thought it best not to push her luck. Besides, she got along well with the other young women in Theory: Aine, for one, who seemed to be skilled at any task set before her; Isabella, a pale-skinned, dark-haired girl from Castile who had a very Unseelie look about her; Brita, who hailed from a village not so far from Gwyneth's own in the north of Eire; Valerie, the counter to Isabella with golden skin and white-gold hair, from Lorraine, whose accent reminded Gwyneth pleasantly of Edelinne; Catherine, an English girl who had been scooped from a life as a street urchin in London; and Audhild, from the far northern lands of the Norsemen, who did not say much at all but fixed the instructor with an intent blue gaze for the entirety of the class, her thick wheat-colored braid trailing over one shoulder.

"I hear we shall attempt to Walk soon," said Brita with a bright smile as she settled into the chair next to Gwyneth.

Gwyneth felt a little thrill at the prospect of venturing into the whirling either with only her own will to guide her. "That will be exciting," she replied, her eyes still roving about the room. A bejeweled egg as large as her head sat on one of the higher shelves, and she wondered what type of creature would have an egg so large as that.

Brita followed Gwyneth's gaze. "I think that is a Merrow egg – after the little one hatched, of course."

Gwyneth realized the egg was not bejeweled at all, as she had initially thought, but the bright metallic color of the shell had defied her expectations of an eggshell. She followed its curve carefully with her eyes and found a nearly imperceptible seam, jagged but very cleverly concealed, all the pieces painstakingly reassembled. "I hear," she said, "that Instructor Ava is fluent in the Merrow tongue."

"She is," agreed Aine, taking the seat on the other side of Brita.

"Merrow shells are among the rarest of magical objects," Brita continued. She was very good at remembering the uses of sundry objects that appeared in the classroom. "A very small piece of Merrow shell can impart great strength and some of the Merrow's abilities. If a Merrow stays in their land-walker form too long, or is greatly weakened by an injury, they will take a piece of their own shell to regain their strength or to teach their bodies how to remember to change."

"So why would a Merrow ever give their own shell away?" Gwyneth wondered aloud. The light from the white fire glistened on the sapphire hues of the Merrow egg. She felt as though she were gazing into a shifting sphere of ocean.

"If a Merrow child dies, it is considered a great honor to receive the shell that bore them," replied Brita in a quiet voice.

Gwyneth shivered. Now she felt as though she were looking at the bones of a child as she contemplated at the shell.

"But there are also times when a pact is sealed by a Merrow leader giving part of their shell to the leader with whom they are creating an alliance," said Brita.

"The Bearer made an alliance with the Merrow," said Aine, taking the seat on the other side of Gwyneth.

"A formal alliance? I thought that the Bearer did not negotiate such things," Valerie said, setting down her satchel. Her white-gold hair fell in a sheet down her back. Gwyneth eyed it and wondered if Valerie used her own *taebramh* on her hair, or if she had just been gifted with natural beauty. It was highly discouraged for them to use their own *taebramh* to change anything at all with their appearances and forbidden for them to change each other. Manipulating living flesh took a high level of skill and control and could go terribly wrong. But Gwyneth thought that perhaps hair would be easier.

"She does when it is necessary, I think," replied Aine with a shrug.

Audhild arrived silently and inspected the seat of her chair, brushing away an invisible speck of dust. The Norse woman sat with a coiled precision that reminded Gwyneth of the Paladins. Isabella took a seat and said something in a quiet, melodious tongue to Audhild, who gave no sign she understood save for a slight softening of her stern expression. Catherine sat in her chair in a distinctly unladylike position, letting her knees splay wide, her blue eyes glittering as she dared any of the others to correct her.

"I don't see why the Bearer would make an alliance with the Merrow," said Valerie, tossing her hair over one shoulder before sitting down. "Their kingdom is in the depths of the ocean, after all."

"And the ocean touches all our shores, does it not?"

At the sound of Instructor Ava's voice, Gwyneth leapt to her feet. The older girls stood up with more composure, but she saw Valerie color slightly.

"Yes, Instructor," Valerie replied in a calm, measured voice.

The Unseelie Instructor glided into the circle of their chairs and nudged the white fire higher with a small motion of one hand. She stood beneath the fire, the light gleaming blue and purple in her midnight-dark hair. "Who first spoke of the Merrow egg?"

Gwyneth felt her mouth go dry. "I did, Instructor." Her voice came out nearly a croak. She felt the Unseelie Instructor's gaze pierce through to her soul, but she took a deep breath and didn't flinch.

"Good," Ava said simply. "That is the subject of today's lesson."

Though the young women tried to contain it, even Gwyneth felt the disappointment that rippled through them.

Instructor Ava arched an eyebrow. "The lesson is not satisfactory for you?"

None of the young women answered until Ava fixed her regard on Brita.

"It is satisfactory, Instructor," Brita said. "It is through my own fault that I allowed myself to hold other expectations."

"And what were these other expectations?" Ava pressed calmly. Gwyneth felt as though she were watching a snake mesmerize a mouse before striking with dizzying speed.

"We – *I* thought that perhaps we might be permitted to Walk soon," Brita replied.

"All in good time," replied Ava after a considered pause during which the only sound was the quiet hiss of the flames twisting above their heads. "But it is important for you to understand the Merrow." She swept her gaze around the circle of young women. "You will be attending the Winter Solstice at the Unseelie Court, and there will most certainly be some of the Merrow delegation present."

Gwyneth felt her heart skip a beat, and she heard Aine actually draw in a sharp breath.

"You have all been placed in this class for a reason," Ava continued, as though she had not just told the Inionacha such a heady piece of news. "The next Bearer will be chosen from among you."

Gwyneth felt as though her heart had stopped entirely. Across the circle, Audhild merely raised her eyebrows, face unreadable; Brita pressed her lips together as though suppressing a smile, and Aine actually *did* smile. Valerie looked like the declaration did not surprise her at all. Catherine dug at dirt beneath her fingernails. Isabella combed three fingers through her thick, dark hair. For a brief moment, Gwyneth felt giddy with triumph: neither Mary nor any of her cronies had been selected to be a part of the Theory class.

"Do not let it go to your heads," Ava continued in her smooth, commanding voice. "I do not yet know when the Bearer will make her choice, but I believe it will be within a handful of years." She looked at each of them in turn. "You have already been told that you are not to speak of anything that occurs in this room, have you not?"

"Yes, Instructor," Gwyneth answered in chorus with the six other young women. She felt her heart beating hard in her chest. Questions whirled in her head. Would she see Rhys at the Winter Solstice? How could they *not* speak of such a thing to anyone else? Could she speak of it to Togha?

"Now," said Instructor Ava, folding her white hands before her. "Let us begin the lesson for today. You may take your seats."

Gwyneth sank back into her chair and took a deep breath, marveling at how quickly the foundations of her world had been shaken yet again. But she drew her attention back to Instructor Ava with fierce focus, determined to absorb as much of the lesson as possible. The six other women in Theory had come to be her friends – some more than others, but none of them were her enemies. Yet now she felt an undercurrent of energy entirely different than friendship. They would all work together, but now they knew that one of the six of them would become Bearer, if what Instructor Ava said were true; and listening to the Unseelie woman, it was difficult to believe that she was capable of being wrong.

One step closer, Gwyneth thought. Her *taebramh* unfolded its wings in her chest approvingly, and she let herself smile slightly.

Chapter 15

Gwyneth sat cross-legged on her bed, breathing deeply as she reached for her *taebramh*. She sank into the quiet space that had become easier for her to reach; now she did not need to be in the forest with an arrow nocked to her bow, on the hunt or investigating the snap of a twig or the creak of a floorboard in the night. While her *taebramh* responded to her no matter the circumstance – a fact she did not think it wise to advertise, since so many Inionacha had such trouble learning to summon it – the breathing exercises helped to refine her control. When she slipped into that silent, meditative trance, she felt as though her *taebramh* responded to her thoughts just as she realized them herself. It was a heady feeling, and she spent more and more time chasing after that satisfaction.

They had not yet been permitted to Walk in Theory class, despite the fact that Instructor Ava slowly expanded the hours that the seven Inionacha spent in the circular room with the blue door. None of the other young women in the Hall remarked on it, though Gwyneth thought it was likely that they just knew well enough to hold their tongue. If any of her acquaintances had simply begun disappearing from history and language classes, she would have certainly noticed.

Gwyneth thought Theory an inadequate name for the class at this point; they had begun by learning the intricate theories behind *taebramh* and the ether, the balance between the worlds and the creatures that inhabited both the mortal and the Fae realms, but now they ventured into the application of theory nearly every day. Instructor Ava taught them herself, and Cara had made a few appearances as well in the fortnight since Ava had announced that the Bearer's successor would be chosen from among them. Time felt fluid. Some days Gwyneth felt as though she had lived a whole year within the hours she spent in the tower room; other days passed quite quickly and pleasantly, reminding her of the sun-drenched days of high summer when she had helped shepherd her family's sheep on the moors.

Even Edelinne had not remarked on Gwyneth's disappearance from the classes they usually shared, but she occasionally caught Gwyneth's eye and winked at her, breaking into a grin when Gwyneth merely raised an eyebrow. Gwyneth thought it safe to assume that her friend recognized what had happened, even if they couldn't speak of it directly. They found other things to talk about, and they still found time to practice bladework with Aine and her group of friends. As the days passed, Gwyneth caught glances from the other young women that she knew they had not intended for her to see: a few envious, some tinged with anger, one or two even mixed with a pity that Gwyneth did not understand. Why would anyone pity her for being chosen as one of the handful of Inionacha from whom the Bearer would choose her successor? Wasn't that the very reason behind their training and their sacrifice? They had all been taken away from their families, from the world of their birth, brought here to the Hall to be raised in the ways of the Inionacha. Why would they not want to be the next Bearer?

For her part, Gwyneth thought it all happening strangely fast – she had been in Faeortalam for barely two years, but somehow, she did not feel unprepared. In the quiet of her own thoughts and the silence of the night's deep darkness, she knew that she had been made for the task set before her. It was not something she would ever say aloud, not even to Edelinne, who would most likely agree wholeheartedly. It was not something she could even properly explain in words to herself, but she just *knew* in her bones that she had been made to carry the Sword. She wondered sometimes if the other six women felt the same way…and if they did, how crushing it would be to find out that such a bone-deep conviction was wrong.

A tapping sound reached Gwyneth's ears. She allowed it to filter through the layers of her awareness, and then she slowly and deliberately climbed out of the silent well of her meditation. The patter at the window came again, more sharply, as she opened her eyes. She smiled as she recognized Togha's aura through the pane of glass. She unfolded her legs, stretching as she stood, and padded across the room barefoot to open the window, the worn wood smooth and cool under her toes.

A swirl of snow spiraled into the room when Gwyneth opened the window, pushing against the winter wind. The frigid air slapped her face and she blinked, brought fully back to awareness. Togha tumbled over the sill, buffeted by a freezing gust. Gwyneth scooped up the Glasidhe as she slid off the sill, her small body alarmingly cold. Pulling the window shut and latching it, Gwyneth hurried over toward the banked fire. The glowing coals still radiated heat, and she held her hands as close as she dared, her skin prickling.

Togha's aura pulsed brighter and the diminutive messenger shook herself thoroughly, flicking melted snow and bits of ice from her wings.

"Togha," Gwyneth said, settling to her knees in front of the fire, careful not to tilt her cupped hands as she moved. "Why did you come out in this storm?"

Togha shook herself again. "To bring you a message, of course." She sat down in Gwyneth's hand and pulled off one of her boots with a squelch, upending it to empty the thimbleful of slush.

"I doubt there's a message important enough for you to freeze to death," Gwyneth said.

Togha flicked a wing dismissively. "This is not the worst storm I've endured. And besides, it's not for me to know the message, so I bring it regardless."

Even as her heart leapt at the prospect of a missive from Rhys, Gwyneth also felt a sinking disappointment that Rhys would send Togha out in such weather.

"Storm was a bit unexpected, too," Togha admitted, pulling off her other boot and adding to the pile of slush on Gwyneth's palm. "Must be some unrest on the Unseelie side of things."

"I thought the White City was not under the control of either Queen," Gwyneth said.

"And what do you think happens to the storms and the summers that the Queens conjure, hmm?" Togha put her hands on her hips, standing barefoot in the middle of Gwyneth's hand, her translucent wings moving slightly like those of a resting dragonfly. "They do not just *vanish* when they reach the borders of their lands, especially when it is already winter."

Gwyneth thought about it for a moment. "I suppose that makes sense."

"Whether it does or does not, that is how it is." Togha fluttered her wings for emphasis.

"What do you mean, *unrest* on the Unseelie side of things?" Gwyneth asked.

"Oh, it could be just as simple as Mab is displeased about something," replied Togha with a shrug as she began shedding the soaked layers of her intricately tailored clothing.

"A storm like this because the Unseelie Queen is irritated?" Gwyneth repeated flatly. The wind howled against the windows. She summoned a thread of *taebramh* and lit one of the small spheres on her table. Edelinne had shown her how to modify the light-globes to throw off heat as well. "Here," she said to Togha. "You can dry out your clothes on the table." She stood, Togha putting one hand on her thumb for balance, and walked over to the table. Togha made a sound of approval and appreciation as she hopped from Gwyneth's palm with her armful of sodden garments.

The Glasidhe messenger shed every stitch of clothing without hesitation, her movements efficient and practical as she arranged her storm-soaked raiment in a half-circle around the light globe. Small wisps of steam began to rise from the cloth, and she nodded in satisfaction. Without so much as a blush of modesty, she turned to Gwyneth, naked as the day she was born – were Glasidhe born or hatched like Merrow? Gwyneth wondered suddenly – and offered her the message tube.

"Thank you," Gwyneth said. Togha bowed in reply and then crouched beside her belt, unsheathing her small daggers and inspecting them in the soft white light of the *taebramh* globe.

Gwyneth broke the wax seal of the small tube with a thumbnail. The Glasidhe took great pains to ensure that their messages always reached their destination intact. Gwyneth had come to respect them greatly for their dedication to their chosen art, and only lately had she realized her fortune in meeting the two Glasidhe in Doendhtalam. Without them, Rhys would have died. The Bearer may have still found the cottage, but the *baobhan sith* might have killed Gwyneth and Rhys before Rionach had stepped foot across the threshold.

"How does Rhys pay you to carry these messages?" she murmured, more to herself than Togha.

The Glasidhe messenger crossed her arms over her bare chest and raised her pointed little chin. "That is quite rude to ask. We never divulge the terms of our contracts." Her wings quivered as if outraged.

"I didn't mean to offend," Gwyneth said quickly, caught off guard by the intensity of Togha's reaction. "I'm just very grateful to have you as both a messenger…and a friend."

Togha's harsh posture softened. She didn't reply, but she muttered something under her breath in the Glasidhe tongue and settled down next to her daggers, producing a miniscule whetting stone from her small belt pouch.

Gwyneth turned her attention back to the message tube, sliding out the tightly rolled parchment. She carefully spread it on the table. Togha pointedly turned her back, leaning intently over her daggers as though she had not sharpened them in months.

Gwyneth stared down at the blank piece of parchment. It was about as large as the palm of her hand, and nothing at all was written on it. She felt a spark of indignation: who would send Togha through a storm with a *blank* message? Then a rune flickered at the corner of the little page, igniting as though a spark had caught the parchment aflame. Gwyneth moved her hand out of instinct, but the flame wasn't actually burning the parchment: it crept across the page with all the movement of real flame, leaving behind charcoal-dark letters written in a close and careful hand that Gwyneth recognized instantly.

It was a much longer message than Rhys had ever sent. He had written to the very edge of the parchment, and there were barely spaces between his words. All the same, Gwyneth began reading his missive with a sudden intense hunger.

Dearest Gwyneth, it began. A warm flame kindled in her chest. *Dearest.*

The Paladins received word that your Instructors have chosen seven Inionacha, from whom the Bearer will choose her successor.

Gwyneth wondered briefly how the Paladins received their information about the happenings within the Hall of the Inionacha. She also wished that she could talk to Rhys face-to-face. Her heart always leapt when he sent her a message, but his written words were so much stiffer than his half-smiling voice, a mischievous spark hidden in the depths of his tone.

I will be at the Solstice celebration. We are told the Seven will attend as well. Send an answer with Togha if you will be among them, though I am confident that your sheer stubbornness is enough to convince the Lady Bearer that you should carry the Sword after her.

Heat rushed to Gwyneth's cheeks. Ed, of course, always hinted that Gwyneth would be the next Bearer, but half of that was in jest – or so she reassured Gwyneth. And now, to have Rhys write such a thing, it seemed to invite retribution for such cockiness. After all, who was she to think that she could step into the role of the powerful, inscrutable Bearer?

Even as her thoughts swirled with doubt, Gwyneth felt her *taebramh* spread its wings in her chest. Ava had told them once that many of those with the strongest *taebramh* experienced their power as another living creature, separate from them but still within them. She had guided them through a few visualizations, but Gwyneth hadn't needed the exercises to know that her *taebramh* took the shape of a hawk, fierce and proud. She had felt it soon after crossing over into Faeortalam, and when she thought hard about it, she'd felt the same sensation of a hawk spreading its wings in her chest many times before she had even put words to her power, before she'd even drawn a glow to her fingertips.

She had known what her *taebramh* had felt like and looked like before she even stepped foot in the Hall, just as she'd known in her bones that she would be the next Bearer before she was chosen as one of the Seven. It seemed like sacrilege to admit it to anyone else. It seemed like speaking it aloud was tantamount to inviting misfortune.

Gwyneth turned her attention back to Rhys' missive. Her *taebramh* folded its wings, settling glossy feathers against its sides. Togha began singing to herself, a wild little tune that reminded Gwyneth of the music at the Paladins' Samhain celebration.

We should speak at the Solstice. I have heard other rumors that caution demands I do not write. Dire warnings aside, I dream of the day your lips touch mine again.

Heat of a different sort rushed through Gwyneth at those words. She brushed her fingertips against her lips, remembering the feel of

Rhys' kiss. The moon had traveled through its phases twice since the Samhain celebration. Since that enchanted night, time had simultaneously slowed and passed at a breakneck pace. She still remembered every detail of the Paladin's wild, beautiful festival with crystal clarity, but her life in the Hall had changed so dramatically in the ensuing days that she knew she was not the same girl who'd used the river-stone.

No matter what the future holds, I will always be...

Ever yours, Rhys

Gwyneth ran her thumb over the signature. The dark ink trembled with the light of the runes still swirling beneath the surface of the parchment. She read the missive in its entirety twice more, committing every word to memory, before finding the rune in the bottom corner that wiped the parchment clean. She laid the bare scrap on the table. Togha daintily walked over and rolled it up, nodding in satisfaction.

"Reusing parchment keeps costs down," she told Gwyneth in a very business-like tone.

Gwyneth smiled. "Anything I can do to help, Togha, you know you just have to say the word."

"I know," the Glasidhe replied simply. She pirouetted back to her clothes, pronouncing after a cursory inspection, "Still not dry."

Gwyneth glanced at the window, watching the large flakes of snow swirl against the glass, gray in the dark of night. "You're welcome to stay here for the night, or until the storm abates."

"A most generous offer," said Togha. She flicked her wings thoughtfully. "If it will not be any great inconvenience to you, I will rest until morning."

"If it wasn't for you and Caonach, Rhys would be dead," Gwyneth said firmly. "And if he had died without helping me kill the *baobhan sith*, I would probably be dead as well."

"You underestimate yourself," Togha replied.

Gwyneth shrugged. "If you say so."

"I do," said the Glasidhe decisively.

Gwyneth smiled and moved toward her wardrobe to fetch an extra blanket for Togha's bed – perhaps one of her soft, clean shirts would do, she thought. "Togha," she said as she selected a neatly folded shirt, "will you be at the Winter Solstice celebration at the Unseelie Court?"

"Of course," replied Togha, absorbed in resheathing her newly sharpened daggers. She stood with her hands on her hips and surveyed her gear, aligning a few items differently before nodding in satisfaction. "There are always many messages to be carried at the celebrations of the Courts."

"I will be going," said Gwyneth. "As will Rhys," she added.

"How fortunate," said Togha with sly delight. She fluttered her wings and bowed in thanks as Gwyneth set the shirt on the table.

"If you would like a blanket or something else, I have those as well," Gwyneth said quickly as Togha inspected the soft cloth of the shirt.

"I am not so demanding as all that," Togha replied loftily. She smiled brilliantly at Gwyneth, taking the sting out of her words.

"I wouldn't view it as demanding," said Gwyneth, smiling. "Like I said, you're my friend. I want to make sure you're comfortable, that's all."

Togha murmured something unintelligible in agreement as she hopped into the shirt and promptly tugged at the cloth to create a little hollow, pulling the fabric this way and that until she had sculpted her nest to her satisfaction. The wind howled against the window, and Gwyneth felt glad that the Glasidhe messenger had agreed to stay for the night.

"You should go to sleep too. The hour is late," said Togha, her voice partially muffled by the folds of cloth now surrounding her. "I am quite warm and will sleep quite well."

As Togha spoke of sleep, Gwyneth felt a tide of tiredness rise up and sweep over her. She thought of Rhys' missive, going over his words one more time in her mind to ensure that she truly remembered them.

"You will not forget," Togha said drowsily. "Do not worry."

With a twist of her wrist, Gwyneth dimmed the light from the *taebramh* globe on the table, leaving its pulsing heat for Togha. She padded over to her bed and slipped under the quilt, its comforting weight settling over her.

Dire warnings aside, I dream of the day your lips touch mine again.

Gwyneth smiled as she closed her eyes. For an instant, her tired mind tried to catch at the dire warning, tried to understand what would make Rhys, so cool and collected in the face of danger, so cautious; but instead, their kiss rose up in her memory like a leaf floating serenely on the surface of a silken pond. No matter what the depths of the future held, no matter the dangers lurking beneath the surface of the calm waters, at least she would always have the feel of his lips upon hers. She sank into sleep as the echoes of the beautiful music from the Samhain celebration whirled in her head, a haunting accompaniment to her dreams.

Chapter 16

"I know you can't talk to me about what exactly goes on in your Theory class," said Edelinne the next morning at breakfast, "but..." She paused and glanced around them in an uncharacteristic show of caution. "Most of us know – or rather, we *suspect* – that the Theory class isn't really a *Theory* class."

Edelinne's words flowed around Gwyneth, her friend's familiar voice comforting in a way but uninteresting. Gwyneth had awoken that morning to a cold draft from her open window. Togha had folded the shirt neatly on the table a safe distance from the heat of the *taebramh* globe. She kept thinking about Rhys' words, and now that she'd had a night of sleep, his warning stood out to her more than his endearments. A strange sensation of uneasiness turned in her stomach. She dug at her porridge with the edge of her spoon, frowning.

"Gwyn," Ed said with more insistence.

Gwyneth blinked and looked at her friend. "What?"

"Did you hear anything I just said?"

"No," Gwyneth admitted.

Ed tucked a strand of errant hair behind her ear, raising an eyebrow. "I *said* that most of us know that your Theory class really isn't a Theory class."

"It is," Gwyneth replied automatically. She took a bite of porridge because she knew she had to eat *something*. The food, simple but usually tasty, just didn't appeal to her this morning. The porridge tasted sodden and lumpy, and she had to force herself to swallow it. She dug her spoon into the bowl again with determination even as her thoughts whirled sickeningly from one possibility to the next. Was Rhys in danger? Was *she* in danger? Why did he have to be so *cryptic*? She shoveled the next spoonful of porridge into her mouth, trying not to wince at the unappetizing texture.

"Gwyneth," Edelinne said firmly.

Gwyneth turned to her friend with a full mouth, raising her eyebrows.

"What happened?" Ed caught Gwyneth's eyes and held her gaze, concern written across her face.

Swallowing the tasteless porridge, Gwyneth said, "I don't know what you mean."

"Do *not* try to play that card with me," Edelinne said, her Norman accent coming through strongly.

"I can't talk about it here," Gwyneth said finally. She shoveled another heaping spoonful of porridge into her mouth, both hoping that Ed would stop asking questions but also wondering if her sharp-witted friend would be helpful in solving the mystery of Rhys' message.

"You cannot talk about anything anymore," muttered Ed, pushing away her empty bowl.

Hurt flashed through the dull panic reverberating within Gwyneth, sharp enough to make her set down her spoon and look at Ed. The other young woman pressed her lips together and sighed, saying something to herself in French and then raising her voice so that Gwyneth could hear her.

"I apologize," she said without meeting Gwyneth's eyes. "That was not kind of me to say."

Gwyneth took a breath. "It may have been unkind," she said

slowly, "but you're not wrong." She felt a sudden sharp loneliness as she realized just how wide the chasm between her and Edelinne – between all the Inionacha who were not one of the Seven – had become. A lump formed in her throat and she swallowed thickly. "Everything is changing," she said, just loud enough for Ed to hear.

"Yes," Ed agreed. She took a deep breath. "Are you going to eat anymore? If not, we can go to my room. We have a bit of time before classes."

Gwyneth knew she'd regret her half-eaten breakfast later, but she couldn't stomach the thought of forcing down any more porridge. None of the food on the table looked appealing to her. She nodded and they stood, garnering a few curious glances from the other young women only halfway through their morning meals.

"All right," said Ed, shutting the door to her chambers behind her and tapping the silencing rune she'd carved neatly into the wood. It glowed with a spark of her *taebramh*. "You don't *have* to talk to me, Gwyn, I hope you know that, but I'm just…concerned."

Pacing the edges of Ed's room, Gwyneth couldn't find her usual comfort in the familiar surroundings. "I appreciate your concern, Ed, I do, but I just…I don't know what I'm allowed to tell anyone anymore."

"Even if we weren't chosen as one of the Seven, that doesn't make the rest of us dullards," Ed said, softening her words with an arched eyebrow and a smile. Gwyneth thought the smile looked forced, and it made her feel even worse. "But that isn't what's upset you. You've been in Theory since just after Samhain, but something happened within the past day."

"I got a message last night," Gwyneth admitted, crossing her arms over her chest.

"From Rhys?" Ed guessed, her smile gaining an edge of wickedness.

"Yes," Gwyneth replied shortly.

Edelinne tilted her head to one side. "I gather it wasn't an invitation to another tryst in the forest."

"It wasn't a *tryst*, there were other people there," Gwyneth muttered. "Lots of other people." She shook her head. "He was trying to warn me about something, but he didn't exactly say what."

"Two minds are better than one to work on a puzzle," Ed said, sitting down in one of the chairs by her table.

For an instant, Gwyneth hesitated. Then she gave in to the hint of relief that washed through her at the thought of Edelinne applying her sharp mind to the mystery. "Rhys said that there's a danger coming, but he didn't name it. There were no specifics."

"Obviously he thought it important enough to send a messenger," said Edelinne, squinting in thought. "What did he say, exactly?"

Gwyneth closed her eyes as she recited Rhys' words. "He wrote, 'We should speak at the Solstice. I have heard other rumors that caution demands I do not write.' That was the most important part of the message."

"No, it wasn't," Ed said, peering at Gwyneth with sharply perceptive eyes. "The most important part of the message was when he wrote of his undying devotion or somesuch."

Gwyneth felt color rushing to her cheeks. "The most *worrying* part of the message, then," she amended.

"If you don't mind, it might be best if I hear the whole thing," Ed said seriously.

"I'm certain he didn't intend for anyone else to read it," Gwyneth hedged, feeling the heat radiating from her face.

"All right then, be secretive," Ed said lightly with a wave of her hand. "As long as he didn't mention anything else that might be important."

"The Paladins know about the Seven," Gwyneth said. After the words left her mouth, she wondered suddenly and sharply if Edelinne cared that she hadn't been chosen.

"You can put away your pity for someone who deserves it," Ed told her decisively.

"How did you know that was what I was thinking?" Gwyneth asked, distracted momentarily from the whirl of worry in her gut.

"Apparently I'm a late bloomer," said Edelinne. "Beatrix told me last week it's likely I have a touch of the Sight, but mine surfaces specifically with other people, not with the future."

"You have visions of what people will feel or do?"

"No." Ed shook her head. "It's more like I can just feel what they're feeling. Maybe it's not the Sight at all. But they don't have another word for it yet."

"That's...interesting."

"It's not the most glamorous of gifts," Ed replied with a hint of dismissal in her voice. "Nor is it particularly useful."

"Except for when I'm trying to dodge your questions," pointed out Gwyneth.

"Except then," Ed agreed cheerfully. She sobered. "That's why I thought perhaps I could be a Diligent. I think I could be a very good instructor if I know when a student is frustrated or feeling lost."

"I think you would be a good instructor no matter if you used your Sight or not," replied Gwyneth.

Ed waved her hand again. "Enough about me." She settled into her thoughtful pose, squinting and propping her elbow on her knee, her chin balanced on her hand. "I have heard other rumors that caution demands I do not write," she murmured in a low voice.

"Rhys is not a very *cautious* person," Gwyneth said, folding her arms over her chest and resuming her pacing.

Ed chewed her lip. "It's not much to go on at all, but he wanted you to be aware that there's *something*. Perhaps he thinks this danger poses a threat to the Inionacha." She stilled, her eyes narrowing. "The Paladins know of the Seven. Perhaps this threat knows of you, too."

"But who would want to harm the Inionacha? Or the Seven?" Gwyneth shook her head.

"The very reason the Paladin exist is to fight alongside the Sidhe to protect this world and the mortal world," Ed said.

"I know that," said Gwyneth.

"Yes, but have you ever truly thought about *what* they fight? It cannot all be so simple as a *baobhan sith*."

Gwyneth tasted the faint metallic tang of the *baobhan sith*'s death-smoke in the back of her mouth as she remembered the terrifying creature.

"Rhys was – *is* – a young Paladin, Gwyn. They wouldn't have sent him after the *baobhan sith* unless that is considered a relatively minor threat," Ed continued with her inexorable logic.

"It almost killed him," Gwyneth said quietly. The memory of the day she had found Rhys in the forest felt so distant. It seemed like years ago, like another lifetime. If someone had told her she had actually heard about it as a well-told tale from a traveling minstrel, she might have believed it. But then she remembered the immediacy of it, the urgency thrumming through her as she fought to save the life of the young stranger who had told her to let him die. She swallowed hard.

"But it didn't kill him," said Ed firmly. "Paladins live by the sword, Gwyn. That's their life, just as preparing to bear the Sword is ours." She paused. "*Was* mine. Is still yours."

Hearing Ed separate them so logically made Gwyneth uneasy. "I don't like it when you say things like that."

Ed shrugged. "Doesn't make it any less true." She sank back into her thinking pose. "You're right, he gave you precious little."

"He said he'd be at the Solstice celebration," Gwyneth said. "That we'd talk then."

"He doesn't want to write anything in a message and he wants to speak in person," murmured Ed. She pressed her lips together. "Must be something downright terrifying, if he doesn't trust your messenger."

"That's what worries me," agreed Gwyneth. It was almost a relief to hear steady, logical Edelinne say out loud what she'd been thinking since she'd awakened that morning.

"Worry isn't a solution," said Ed. "Just keep an eye out for anything unusual, and I'll keep my ear to the ground." She stood and regarded Gwyneth solemnly. "Be careful when you go to the Solstice, Gwyn. The Seven may be a target."

"Instructor Ava will be coming with us, I think, and perhaps even the Bearer," said Gwyneth. She tried to tell herself that no creature would be able to overpower their skilled instructor and the indomitable Bearer, but a tentacle of something that might have been fear still writhed in her belly.

The bells calling them to class echoed through the Hall.

"Don't let it distract you," Ed told Gwyneth earnestly. "The best thing you can do is to learn everything Ava is teaching you up in that tower room. If the Paladins know about something dangerous, it's a good bet that the Instructors do, too."

"Or maybe they don't," said Gwyneth.

"Even if they don't, learn everything she teaches you," repeated Ed firmly.

"Practice tonight in the courtyard?" Gwyneth asked as they headed for the door and Edelinne deactivated her silencing rune.

"Of course, if you do not have other obligations," replied Edelinne.

Gwyneth felt a small measure of comfort as she walked down the corridor, stopping at her own room to collect her satchel of books and writing instruments. She hoped that she'd find a way to preserve her friendship with Edelinne, even when she became the Bearer. Her *taebramh* stirred at the thought, ruffling its feathers approvingly at the certainty in her mind. She climbed the spiral staircase of the tower and pushed the blue door open, finding that she was the last to arrive.

"The Instructor is not here yet," Audhild reassured her in her heavily accented voice, even giving Gwyneth a small smile.

Gwyneth settled into the chair beside Audhild, smiling in reply to the taciturn Norse woman.

"I think the Instructor should send us out on missions with the Paladin," said Brita. It always seemed to be Brita pushing the boundaries, seeing what sparked a response in the other women in the moments they were without an Instructor.

"Seems like a dullard thing to do," said Catherine in her broad accent, raising one eyebrow. Gwyneth felt a kind of kinship with Catherine: she, too, had not known of her heritage until the Bearer had appeared to spirit her away into Faeortalam. But the snub-nosed young woman from London rarely talked about her past. It wasn't that she avoided it – it was simply that few young women were brave enough to ask her directly about it.

"And why do you think that?" Brita asked, catching the thread of the disagreement and tugging at it with bright interest in her eyes.

"We're not as expendable as they are," replied Catherine with a shrug.

Gwyneth felt her face flush hot as she thought of anyone calling Rhys *expendable*.

"But only one of us will be the Bearer," said Brita, tossing her hair over her shoulder. She smiled a catlike smile that wasn't entirely friendly. "By the odds, it will be me or Gwyneth."

"And how do you figure that?" drawled Catherine unconcernedly, raising one eyebrow.

"The First Bearer was from Eire, and so is Rionach," said Brita with a logical air.

"We are all of the Blood," said beautiful dark-haired Isabella in her delicately accented voice. "No matter if we were raised in the land of the Bearer's birth."

Brita settled back in her chair. Gwyneth watched the door, hoping that the Instructor arrived soon to put an end to Brita wallowing in the argument of her own creation.

"I suppose we will all have our own thoughts on the *purity* of our lineage," Brita said.

"That's patently ridiculous, Brita, and you know it," replied Aine, sounding bored.

"I just don't think that the Inionacha should accept any girl with a trace of any Blood," said Brita. She shrugged. "Better off sending *those* to the Paladins for cannon fodder."

"The Paladin are honorable warriors who protect all of us," Gwyneth heard herself say in a steely voice. Heat rushed to her face as the eyes of the other six women turned to her.

"Oh, yes," purred Brita. "Gwyneth with her Paladin lover."

Gwyneth opened her mouth to tell Brita that Rhys wasn't her *lover* – they'd only kissed, after all – but then she realized that her protest would only fuel the other woman's appetite for stirring up trouble.

"Pay her no mind," Audhild said in a low voice, her Norse accent suddenly sounding very regal and slightly threatening.

Brita turned her glittering eyes to Audhild. "Are you sure the Instructors are not bringing you to the Solstice feast to hand you off to the *ulfdrengr*? I hear they are just as civilized as their animals."

Audhild gave Brita a cold, wolfish grin. "If I am ever chosen to be *ulfdrengr*, no concealment spells will hide you."

Brita sat up straighter in her chair. "Is that a threat, Northwoman?" Her voice slid through the air with silken, serpentine grace.

Gwyneth found herself tensing, and she caught Aine's eye across the circle of chairs. The other young woman shook her head slightly. Whatever conflict this was, they did not interfere, Aine seemed to be willing her to understand. Isabella watched the exchange with a slightly bored air. Valerie combed her fingers through the ends of her white-gold hair, one eyebrow raised slightly, and Catherine slouched in her chair, inspecting her fingernails while she pointedly ignored the rest of them.

Audhild's cold, sharp smile never faltered and her ice-blue eyes remained fixed on Brita. "It is not a threat. It is merely a statement of fact." She waved a hand in dismissal. "If you are so faint of heart to waver at such a thing, then you are not strong enough to be Bearer."

Brita leaned forward. "If you are so thick of head to think a mongrel like you could be chosen – "

"Brita," said Aine sharply.

But Brita was on her feet and then Audhild rose as well, steady and unwavering, and the movement rippled through the circle of young women. Gwyneth glanced desperately at the tower door: why was the Instructor so late, especially when now it seemed Brita's hatemongering might come to blows? It was not the first disagreement that Brita had brokered, nor would it be the last, but the air felt different this time.

Isabella tried to interject in her musical Castilian accent. "Let us stop and speak reasonably."

"There was no reason ever in this one's head," Audhild said steadily.

Brita's face twisted into an ugly mask. Gwyneth shivered as a cold draft whirled through the room. Something felt different – something felt *wrong*. She glanced at the other women and met Catherine's eyes. To her surprise, the London woman had stood as well rather than lounging in indifference, her face sharpened by keen readiness.

"Brita," said Aine loudly and clearly, "you are not yourself."

"She is herself," said Valerie, her beautiful face darkening. "She has always looked down upon those of us not born in her precious Eire."

Brita seemed not to hear anyone. She thrust out a clawed hand toward Audhild. "You are not *worthy*."

"Something is wrong," Gwyneth said, more to herself than anyone else. The air in the room thickened and the shadows lengthened. Brita grew taller, her fingers lengthening, her eyes retreating into her skull until there were only pools of darkness where her disdainful glance had glittered.

Gwyneth's hand went to her hip, where the hilt of her practice blade usually rested – but they brought no weapons to the Tower, and a practice blade would be useless against any real threat anyway. Her breath caught in her throat. This was not Brita. This was some monster that had taken Brita's body, and now peeled away her skin to reveal its true form.

The thing that had been Brita licked sharpened teeth. "This one thought she was worthy," it said in a voice that pierced Gwyneth's skull like shards of ice.

Isabella ran for the door. The thing just watched her, eerie flames now flickering in its cavernous eye sockets. Shreds of Brita's bright red curls still hung from the back of its skull. Bile rose in the back of Gwyneth's throat. Isabella grabbed the door handle and fell back with a cry, her hand smoking, the sickening smell of burning flesh filling the room.

"She was willing to sell her soul to be the Bearer," continued the creature wearing Brita's body. Its smile peeled more flesh from its face. Gwyneth swallowed down the sour taste in the back of her throat. She felt paralyzed – what were they to do, locked in this room with a creature that had evaded their Instructors and the defenses of the Hall?

Audhild faced down the creature with cool, immovable grace. Behind the creature, Gwyneth saw Valerie sliding noiselessly toward the wall. A short blade rested on a shelf too high to reach, but Gwyneth thought that if anyone could climb to it, Valerie might.

"And what are you, soul-eater? What claim do you have to us?" Audhild asked, her voice steady.

"It is not my claim but my master's claim," said the creature.

Gwyneth slid behind her chair, giving in to the instinct to put some sort of shield between her body and this monster. The creature's burning dark eyes shifted to her. Its tongue flicked out from between its teeth like a snake tasting the air.

"I can taste your fear," it said almost appreciatively. "You are the youngest." It took a step toward Gwyneth, moving with the slow deliberation of a predator whose prey has been cornered.

Gwyneth felt her legs trembling and her heart beating wildly in her chest. She took a deep breath, trying to force the fear down.

The creature wearing what was left of Brita's body drew in a long breath and hissed appreciatively, clacking together the exposed bones in its fingers. "Young fear tastes so much…brighter."

Behind the creature, Valerie had almost reached the shelves, but then she would have to climb. Gwyneth reached for her *taebramh*, though she could think of no spell that she had been taught to counter the likes of this terrifying being.

"You are *syivhalla*," Audhild said suddenly, drawing the thing's attention back to her.

It tilted its head slightly to one side, a motion made sickening by the crunch of bone.

"You are a demon my people have fought before," Audhild continued steadily.

Gwyneth tried to catch her breath, tried to slow her heart. Every time she reached for her *taebramh*, it slipped from her fingers like a spinning coil of rope. She couldn't think. She couldn't breathe. They were all going to die here in this room, slaughtered by a spirit clever enough to use one of them as its disguise.

"You will not die here," Audhild said, taking her eyes from the creature for just an instant to look at Gwyneth.

The creature laughed, a sound that crawled across Gwyneth's skin and set her teeth on edge. In the instant of silence after the creature's laugh, she thought she heard dull thuds from the other side of the Tower door. In that same instant of silence, a book fell from a shelf, nudged from its place by Valerie's foot as she strained upward, her fingers reaching for the sword.

The *syivhalla* snarled, whirling toward Valerie. Audhild picked up her chair and smashed it across the creature's back. The wood splintered, and the creature didn't even falter. Aine put herself in the *syivhalla*'s path, her hands glowing with her *taebramh*. She sketched quick runes in the air, her face a mask of concentration even as the creature advanced on her. Gwyneth's chest tightened with nameless fear. Audhild picked up two of the splintered chair legs and ran after the creature.

Aine sent a crackling, writhing ball of *taebramh* at the creature. It stepped aside with boneless speed and the fireball crashed into the shelves behind them. Books and sundry objects crashed down to the floor; the cacophony snapped through the clawed hold of terror on Gwyneth's body. As Aine called up another fireball, her face white as the creature lunged at her, Audhild launched herself at the *syivhalla*'s back. Catherine tackled Aine, pushing her out of the monster's path. The *syivhalla*'s clawed hand caught Catherine's arm and the London girl screamed.

Audhild drove the splintered ends of her makeshift weapons into the *syivhalla*'s back with savage force, enough to make the creature release its hold on Catherine. Aine dragged Catherine toward the wall, leaving a pool of blood on the floor.

You will not die here.

Audhild's words echoed in Gwyneth's head. The space between one heartbeat and the next lengthened. She felt her fear recede and her *taebramh* rear its head, its fierce eye fixing on the *syivhalla.* Valerie reached the sword. The *syivhalla* threw Audhild off its back and swiped at her. The Norsewoman leapt aside. Gwyneth felt her *taebramh* filling her as it had never done before; she ripped away all limitations, giving herself over fully to the power. It filled her bones and the edges of her vision went white.

The *syivhalla* caught Audhild by the throat and threw her across the room. Valerie leapt down from the shelves, sword flashing. The creature spun with inhuman speed and sent Valerie crashing over a table, the sword skidding from her grasp. Gwyneth held out a hand, her motions not her own now, the wings of her *taebramh* spreading outside her chest, its fierce sharp beak giving her courage. The blade sang as it soared through the air, the handle fitting neatly into her hand. She did not feel any surprise. There was no time to feel surprise. Her *taebramh* raced down the blade. It felt like an extension of her arm as she advanced on the *syivhalla.*

There was no room for fear or doubt beneath the raging fire of her *taebramh.* At the edge of her awareness, she heard the other women screaming, shouting from the other side of the door, a louder boom and the stones shaking beneath their feet.

"And it is the youngest with the power," hissed the *syivhalla*. "Interesting, indeed."

Gwyneth leapt forward as the monster brought up an arm to block her blade, the shock running through Gwyneth's arm painfully as though she had just driven her sword against rock. Her *taebramh* burned through the creature's flesh, blackening it, peeling it away, licking at it like true fire until the creature pulled its arm away with a screech.

"I will still kill you all the same," it snarled, the flames in its eyes brightening.

Gwyneth gripped the blade in both hands. "Come and try." Her voice did not sound like her own. Her *taebramh* raged through her, so hot that she thought she would be incinerated – but not until after she destroyed this foul creature. Not until she had done what she could to protect the other Inionacha.

The Tower shook again with another explosion. Gwyneth swung at the creature and it blocked the sword again, growling as more of her *taebramh* leapt onto its flesh. She quickly withdrew her blade and thrust at its chest; it slid to the side, sinuous as a shadow, sparks of her *taebramh* still crawling over its skin. It swiped at her with a clawed hand and she jumped back, but not quite fast enough: its talons ripped through her left sleeve and scored lines of fire down her arm. She felt blood sliding down her arm, but still she was smiling. Her *taebramh* beat its wings and let out a shrill cry within her chest that reverberated through her bones. She feinted to the left and then swung right, the edge of her blade biting into the creature's side, sliding between its ribs. The fire of her *taebramh* roared into the *syivhalla*, melting its bones and burning its flesh. As if from a distance, Gwyneth felt her own heart slowing, as though the rushing *taebramh* was her own blood pouring out of her. The creature shrieked. She gritted her teeth and kept her grip on the blade.

Then there was no more flesh and bone for her *taebramh* to burn, but the *syivhalla* was not gone. Her blade still lodged in its side,

Gwyneth stared up at the demonic visage of the creature, its flesh made from writhing snakes of darkness, her *taebramh* licking over its form with no effect. Dimly she heard shouting and a sound like breaking rocks. The *syivhalla* flinched, twisting its body to look at the door.

Gwyneth felt suddenly boneless as her hands slipped from the hilt of the blade. She felt someone grab her and drag her – she wanted to tell them to stop jerking so roughly – and then there were other voices and the air hummed with power. The rush of her *taebramh* receded like…like the ocean pulling away from the shore. She had never seen the ocean, she thought dizzily, her vision clearing enough for her to see that she was staring up at the dome of the Tower.

The *syivhalla* snarled. Gwyneth struggled onto her elbows. Her entire body hurt as though she'd fallen from Pip's back a thousand times in a row. A man and a woman she didn't know stood with swords drawn on either side of the *syivhalla*. With perfect choreography, as though they'd killed creatures as terrifying as this a thousand times, the man and woman chanted a low song in a language Gwyneth did not understand. The *syivhalla* swiped at the woman and she danced away.

There were other people coming through the doorway: Instructor Ava and Instructor Cara, Beatrix, and then the faces became a blur. Gwyneth watched as the man and woman walked in a slow circle around the *syivhalla*. The pitch of the creature's snarls changed, taking on the timbre of a trapped animal. Gwyneth couldn't stop watching. She *wanted* to see the thing die.

It was over in an instant. The man held the creature's attention with an attack and then the woman leapt forward, driving her sword through the creature's chest and shouting a word that made the air tremble. As the creature howled, she twisted her blade and yanked it from the *syivhalla*'s chest. A burned and shriveled knot of shadow remained on her blade – the creature's heart, Gwyneth realized. She wasn't sure how she knew.

The man withdrew a glass orb from the bandolier across his chest and held it toward the writhing knot of shadow, now condensing into itself. The sphere glowed and drew the remnants of the *syivhalla* into it like a chimney channeling smoke. The woman took out a cloth and cleaned the black sludge from her blade with efficient strokes, glancing up every few seconds to watch the progress of the glowing orb in capturing the remnants of the *syivhalla*.

Her body pulsing with pain, Gwyneth pushed herself up to a seated position. Her head spun. The room slid in and out of focus. Someone said something close to her, but she couldn't make out the words. Everything blended together. She heard her own breath rushing in and out of her lungs. The voice sound again, right in her ear, sharp and urgent.

"Gwyneth. Are you hurt?"

She didn't know if it was Beatrix or Cara. She shook her head numbly. There were pools of blood on the floor, shining darkly against the wooden floorboards. Catherine lay against the far wall, her face gray and her shirt soaked with blood, panting as Aine pressed a bloodied hand against the wound. Gwyneth's eyes traveled across the floor until her gaze caught on the still form with white-gold hair. Two other figures bent over Audhild, working feverishly. When one of them moved, Gwyneth glimpsed the gleaming bone and red flesh where the side of Audhild's face had been. She rolled to her knees and vomited. Someone knelt by her and pulled back her hair, laying a cool hand on her brow.

Her left arm buckled as her stomach gave one last heave; she glanced at her arm and saw in surprise that the sleeve was in tatters. She'd forgotten that the *syivhalla* had caught her in its claws. A strong arm snaked across her chest and kept her from falling onto her face. She felt vaguely grateful.

"Easy, now," said the man who'd fought the *syivhalla*, helping Gwyneth sit back. He kept one arm around her shoulders and she found herself leaning into him gratefully. She felt…empty. "Long, slow breaths," he instructed her.

"You killed it," she said, her voice hoarse. "I tried...but I didn't..."

Her eyes wandered over to where she knew Audhild lay, but the man caught her chin in a warm hand. "I need you to keep your focus here," he said, his voice kind but firm. She met the man's eyes: they were green at the edges, gold in the center, flecks of brown sprinkled throughout.

"That's it," he said reassuringly. "Right here."

Another set of hands pushed up her sleeve and turned her arm. Gwyneth thought that she probably should have felt some kind of pain, but she didn't. She just felt tired. And cold. She shivered.

"What is your name?" the man asked. He had long golden lashes, and a scar that threaded through his left eyebrow.

"What's yours?" she responded.

He smiled. "Aedan."

Gwyneth felt a prickle of familiarity at the name, but she was too tired to place it. "Gwyneth."

She thought she saw recognition in his eyes for an instant, but she wasn't entirely sure.

"She overextended herself, but the wound itself is not grave," said a woman's voice at her side. Gwyneth didn't turn her head to look, instead contemplating the gold in the center of Aedan's eyes. He'd told her to look at him.

"I couldn't kill it," she said. Her lips felt numb and the words came out slurred.

"You held it off for long enough," said Aedan with warm reassurance.

She blinked slowly. There were people moaning and sobbing. Who had been hurt? Her thoughts kept skittering away from her.

The woman passed a steaming mug into Aedan's hand. He held it to her lips. "Drink, Gwyneth."

She stiffened. She didn't want to slide into sleep, because the *syivhalla* would be waiting.

"You will not dream," he said quietly. "Your body needs to rest and heal."

She didn't know whether she imagined the concern in his voice, but she put her lips to the mug. The tea tasted faintly of mint. Warmth spread through her limbs. As her eyes closed, she felt Aedan shift his arms and pick her up. His chest felt warm and comforting against her. As her consciousness faded, Gwyneth thought that she never again wanted to see the Tower room after it had been painted with the blood of the Seven.

Chapter 17

Gwyneth awoke with a jerk, her heart pounding so hard that she thought her chest would split open with the force of her fear. Panic choked her, closing her throat; she gasped, her hands clutching at the bedclothes of an unfamiliar bed. It was dark, and she couldn't see, but she knew she wasn't in her own room, and she didn't know why she felt such fear.

Then she remembered, and another wave of terror crashed down on her. She had been so *helpless*. The other women had fought the monster that had taken Brita's body while she'd stared dumbly, frozen in place by indecision and fear.

"You said she wouldn't dream," said a voice, a familiar voice that cut through the suffocating layers of panic with its sharp bossiness.

"She isn't dreaming," a second voice replied patiently. "She is awake."

Gwyneth opened her eyes.

"Gwyn," said Edelinne, her face appearing at the edge of Gwyneth's blurred vision. Ed's hand covered hers, squeezing her fingers reassuringly. "I'm here. You're safe."

"Long, slow breaths," said the second voice. The phrase struck another chord of memory. She shifted her eyes and recognized the man who had fought the *syivhalla*. His presence reassured her in a way that even Ed couldn't: if another creature appeared, there was someone who knew what to do.

"That's it," Ed said, patting Gwyneth's hand as her breathing slowed.

It took effort to calm her racing heart and convince herself that she was in no immediate danger when all her instincts screamed at her that the next monster was lurking in the shadows nearby. Gwyneth felt the prickles of sweat on her skin. She grimaced and started to push herself up into a sitting position in the bed. A flash of pain through her left arm arrested her movement.

"Easy," said Aedan. He stood at the foot of the bed, not too close that she felt uncomfortable but close enough that she felt secure. She wondered how many times he'd watched over wounded companions. He seemed to know exactly what to do and say in every moment.

"Do you want something for the pain?" Ed asked quickly.

Gwyneth shook her head and swallowed thickly. "I don't want to go back to sleep," she rasped. Her throat felt dry as a creek bed during a drought. She grimaced and took the cup Ed offered with her good hand. After a few swallows of cool water, she said, "How long was I asleep?"

The water restored some of her self-awareness. She looked around, taking in the curtains around the bed and the plain bedside table.

"You're in the healing ward," Ed said, as though she hadn't heard Gwyneth's question.

Gwyneth nodded and took another sip of water. Ed shifted uncomfortably in her chair. Directing her question toward Aedan, Gwyneth asked again, "How long was I asleep?"

He held her gaze steadily. "Almost three days."

She swallowed down the alarm that blossomed in her chest. "I wasn't wounded that gravely."

"No," he replied, "but you used your *taebramh* in a way that you had never used it before. That few *can* use it," he added, almost as an afterthought.

"I had to do something," Gwyneth said. The memories of the attack flashed rapidly through her mind, the colors bright and garish. She remembered Audhild throwing the chair at the creature, Isabella's hand charred by the door, Valerie climbing the shelves to get to the blade, Aine calling up a fireball of her *taebramh*, Catherine pushing Aine out of the path of the creature's claws. She shivered as their screams echoed in her head. Then she shivered again as dread sank its claws into her heart. "Did...did all the Seven survive?"

She had meant to ask if any of the other women had died, but even to utter the word felt like a betrayal, felt like she had already accepted their death. Ed wouldn't meet her eyes, so she looked at Aedan.

"Tell me," she said, her voice hardening.

"Isabella lost her hand to the curse on the door," said Aedan in a level voice. "Catherine died shortly after the attack. She lost too much blood."

Gwyneth felt a little pulse of shock: she'd seen the *syivhalla* sink its claws into Catherine, but she had thought the wound survivable.

"Aine and Valerie should both recover," Aedan continued.

"Audhild?" Gwyneth asked numbly.

"She is still alive," he replied, "but her wounds are grave."

"Are they all in the healing ward?" Gwyneth asked, pushing herself up to a seated position with her right arm. Her head swam but she gritted her teeth.

"Yes," Aedan replied simply.

"You shouldn't be up yet," Ed said worriedly.

"It's only a few scratches on my arm," Gwyneth snapped even as dizziness stole her breath. She shifted her eyes to Aedan, anger bubbling up at his calm recitation of the decimation of the Seven. Some small logical part of her mind told her that it didn't make sense to be angry at him, but she felt it all the same.

"I do not know them as you do," said Aedan almost gently, "so you must forgive my dispassionate statement of their fates."

Gwyneth took a shuddering breath and nodded. "I understand," she managed. Then she tilted her head. "Why are you still here?"

"Why would I not be here?" Aedan asked.

She narrowed her eyes as she remembered where she'd heard his name: Rhys. "You're a Paladin. An important one."

He smiled. "I do not know whether I would put myself in that category."

"I would have thought false modesty beneath you," Gwyneth said.

"Gwyn," Ed said in an undertone, a note of reproach in her voice.

"Your convalescence certainly hasn't dulled your wit," Aedan said, almost to himself.

"You heard about my wit?" Gwyneth returned, raising an eyebrow.

Ed sighed forbearingly at her bedside.

"I am a Paladin," said Aedan, with a nod of his head. "I oversee the training of the younger Paladin, much like your Instructors here." He nodded. "I should have known that you would know of me from Rhys."

Heat flashed through Gwyneth.

"I do not say that to embarrass you," Aedan continued, again in that half-gentle voice. "But you must realize that when a young Paladin's life is saved by a daughter of the Blood, that is cause enough for us to know her name; it is even more cause still when the Bearer herself escorts the two of them back into Faeortalam."

"Was Rhys...punished?" she asked, her mouth dry. She hadn't thought of that possibility.

"There are consequences to every choice," Aedan replied. His expression gave her no hint.

Gwyneth took another swallow of water to soothe her parched throat. She felt suddenly tired. "Consequences like Brita accepting the *syivhalla*." As much as she wanted to ask more about Rhys, she did not want this capable and cryptic Paladin to use her words against him.

"A Paladin had been tracking this *syivhalla*," Aedan said. "He sent a message to us yesterday that the creature had avoided capture and he thought it was headed in the direction of the White City."

"It seems as though it would be counter to a creature's instincts to go near the White City," said Edelinne. "There are Paladins here, Guards and Knights from both Courts, and often the Bearer herself."

"But the *syivhalla* knew it could avoid them all if it only entrapped one of the Inionacha," Gwyneth said quietly, her voice nearly a whisper. She swallowed and looked down into her nearly empty cup. "Brita was the ultimate prize. One of the Seven."

"Perhaps she was taken by force," Edelinne suggested almost hopefully.

Aedan shook his head. "There are always choices," he said.

"And consequences to every choice," Gwyneth said bitterly. Her weariness felt bone deep.

"Do you think you could eat some broth?" Edelinne asked, standing and brushing invisible specks of dust from her breeches.

Gwyneth nodded silently. Ed disappeared through the curtains. Gwyneth wondered if her friend had been searching for an excuse to leave.

"The only ones who truly know what happened up in the Tower are those who were there," said Aedan, moving around the bed. He pulled the chair that Edelinne had occupied backward a small distance and then sat down. "Your friend loves you and sometimes does not know what to say. It will pass in time."

"Was Orla the woman who fought the *syivhalla* with you?" Gwyneth asked, done talking about the emotional tangle surrounding the events in the Tower. She'd unsnarl it herself somehow, or cut it away entirely like a burr in sheared wool.

"Yes," Aedan replied.

"Is she your partner when you hunt as a Paladin?"

"She is my partner in all things," Aedan said, a surprising warmth entering his voice.

Gwyneth cleared her throat. "Is that how it…how it usually is, with Paladins?"

"You are still recovering," Aedan said. "There is no need to raise up any specters from mere shadows."

"I don't know what you mean," muttered Gwyneth. She knew she sounded like a petulant child. She sighed and gathered her thoughts before saying anything else. "Thank you," she said finally, "for saving us. For fighting the *syivhalla*. For…staying here."

"The Bearer asked, and I cannot refuse a request from Rionach," Aedan replied.

"Does she think there is still danger?" Gwyneth hated the tremor in her voice. She clenched her fists. Fissures of pain shot through her left arm. She welcomed the sharp, bright sensation; it cut through the dull dread suddenly curdling her stomach.

"As far as we understand, there is no other specific threat," Aedan said.

The careful precision of his words didn't escape Gwyneth. She suddenly missed home – not her room in the Hall of the Inionacha, but her room in the small stone cottage in the village in the Eire moors – with a fierce, heart-piercing intensity. She closed her eyes against the whirl of homesickness, waiting for it to pass.

"You miss your home," said Aedan.

"Why do you keep doing that?" she said without opening her eyes.

"It is part of our skills to read emotions," replied the Paladin.

"I don't need anyone else to interpret what I'm feeling," Gwyneth said, not caring that her words sounded dangerously close to a reprimand, and she was speaking to a senior Paladin.

"Danger is present in every world, whether we know of it or not," Aedan said steadily.

"Sounds like something the Bearer would say," she said. She wasn't sure if she meant that as a compliment or an accusation. That strange anger curled like smoke within her chest again. The words came without conscious thought. "We thought we were protected. We thought *you* protected us. How could you let this happen?"

The pools of blood gleaming on the floor of the Tower flashed through her mind. She wished she had said something to gray-faced Catherine in the last moments of her life. She wondered if Aine had found the right words. Traitorous tears sprang up in her eyes. "Why wasn't there an Instructor or a Diligent in the room?" Her voice sounded ragged.

"Their presence may not have changed anything," Aedan said quietly.

"*Then why are they here?*" Gwyneth's voice rose.

"They are here to teach you and protect you," Aedan replied, his green-gold eyes fixed on her face. His face blurred as tears filled her eyes. "But just as your mother tried to protect you from this world, so too are your Instructors limited. We are all limited."

"Don't speak of my mother," Gwyneth ground out.

"Why not?" Aedan asked immovably.

"Because I am beginning to think she was right in trying to hide me," said Gwyneth. Hot tears spilled onto her cheeks. She didn't bother to wipe them away.

"She could not have hidden you forever," Aedan said. "Just as your Instructors cannot protect you forever."

"But we weren't…we weren't *ready*," whispered Gwyneth, grief closing her throat as she thought of Catherine lying cold and still, Isabella awakening to a stump where her graceful hand had once been, Audhild fighting to survive her terrible wounds.

"Life seldom waits until you are ready, Gwyneth."

She looked at Aedan, drained of her anger, now feeling only sorrow. He looked at her as her uncle had once looked at her, with both fondness and sadness. It was the look of an elder who had to watch their young charge suffer to learn the lessons of life. She nodded to show that she understood, and she hoped that he knew she was not angry at *him*. Well…she *was*, but they both knew it was misplaced.

Aedan echoed her motion with his own nod, and she felt that at least she hadn't offended him with the wild swing of her emotions.

"I...perhaps I shouldn't ask, but..." She gathered her courage. "Does Rhys know? Should I...should I send a message, or would it only distract him?" She chewed her lip, her face heating at her admission. She'd changed the subject from Rhys but now she brought him up herself; Aedan was bound to think her a simpleton or a sop.

But he merely said, "You must write to him yourself. I do not know if he has received any word, but if anyone outside these walls knows what has happened, word has not been passed through me. It is not my place to speak of what happens within the Hall of the Inionacha."

She nodded again, wondering whether the Instructors would allow Togha into the healing ward, or if Edelinne could summon a Glasidhe messenger.

"I – *we* – we are grateful," she said, knowing that she was repeating herself but unable to help herself. "If you hadn't broken the curse on the door when you did, we'd all probably be dead."

"It was Orla who broke the curse," said Aedan. "She is much more skilled in that arena than I."

"Is she still here?" Gwyneth asked, feeling a sudden curiosity about the woman Paladin.

"Yes," he replied.

"Perhaps I will be able to meet her before she leaves," she said, unable to bring herself to ask Aedan if his partner would visit her. She already despised being an invalid in a bed in the healing ward: it made her feel small and childlike, not being able to do the simplest thing for herself.

"I believe you have already met," Aedan replied.

Before Gwyneth could ask his meaning, Edelinne swept back through the curtains. "I didn't know what kind of broth you'd like, or if you wanted some actual soup, so I got three kinds of broth and then stew and then soup with dumplings," she announced as she heaved the laden tray onto the bedside table.

"It smells good," Gwyneth said in surprise. Her stomach growled.

"I'll leave you to your meal," Aedan said with an elegant half-bow as he stood. "If it is all right with you, Gwyneth, I'll return this evening."

"If it is not an inconvenience," she said. She didn't want to say out loud that he made her feel safe.

"Not at all," he said, and then he slipped through the curtains silent as a shadow. Gwyneth stared after him, wondering when she had met Orla. She thought back to the woman who had fought the *syivhalla*, trying to remember her face. Her impression of Orla had been a pointed face, feline and fierce. She blinked, remembering the cat-masked woman at the Samhain celebration.

"Now, which would you like to start with?" Ed asked, surveying the steaming bowls.

"Whichever you think is best," Gwyneth replied, resolving that she would not let her unpredictable emotions overwhelm her again at the cost of her friend. She accepted the bowl in her right hand and balanced it atop the blankets in her lap, using her left hand to cradle it. "Thank you, Ed."

"No matter," Ed said, taking her seat again with a flourish. She sobered as Gwyneth swallowed her first spoonful of broth. "We were all…shocked. And worried."

Gwyneth spooned more broth toward her mouth, trying not to spill.

"It was just so unexpected – oh, here, let me help," Ed said, rescuing the bowl and spoon from Gwyneth's unsteady grip.

"You always seem to end up with the most glamorous tasks, Ed," Gwyneth said fondly as her friend pulled her chair right up to the edge of the bed. Ed began feeding Gwyneth with industrious precision, not a drop of broth spilled.

"Well, someone has to make sure you don't get into *too* much trouble," Ed said lightly, but there was a tremor in her voice and Gwyneth saw the tears gathering at the corners of Ed's eyes. She reached out with her good hand and touched Ed's knee. Ed set the spoon into the bowl and covered Gwyneth's hand with her own. They sat like that for a while, and then Ed gave a great sniffle and picked up the spoon again.

At some urging from Ed, Gwyneth finished two of the bowls of broth and promised to eat some stew after she rested awhile. Ed stacked the empty bowls and disappeared. When she opened the curtain, Gwyneth heard for an instant a swell of voices, murmurs meant to be quiet but loud through the sheer number of voices speaking. It sounded to her like all the Inionacha were hovering outside the healing ward, but she was too tired to feel self-conscious. Her eyelids heavy, she wondered just how much the events in the Tower had changed all of them, and if that change was for the better or for the worse. Her thoughts provided no clear answer, and she gave in to the weariness tugging at her mind, sliding into sleep despite the possibility of dreams.

Chapter 18

When Gwyneth awoke again, she knew instantly that something was different – something had happened, something important – but it took a moment for her sleep-wrapped mind to put the pieces of the past days back together into a coherent picture. She closed her eyes for a moment against the tide of sorrow that washed over her, grief piercing her to her bones as she remembered that Catherine was dead, Isabella had lost her hand, and Audhild was still fighting for her life. She swallowed hard, trying to keep her head above the storm of sadness. It felt like fighting against a wind-whipped sea, every current trying to drag her down into its cold, crushing depths.

When Gwyneth opened her eyes again, her throat tight, she realized that she was alone. She heard voices outside the curtains, but no one sat by her bedside. She drew in a shuddering breath, pushing down the urge to stare into each shadow, waiting for the next monster to appear.

"You will not cower in fear," she whispered to herself. There was a pitcher of water and a cup on her bedside table. The pitcher felt like it was carved out of rock, heavy in her hand, but she gritted her teeth and poured a cup of water, the pitcher shaking by the end. She managed to set it down without spilling it entirely. Drinking the cup of water seemed to distract her mind enough for the last of the storm of uncertainty and fear to abate.

Gwyneth moved the fingers of her left hand experimentally. Her arm still responded with a flash of pain, but it was not the bone-deep, biting pain that she remembered last. Her stomach growled. She wished that the bowls of stew and soup had not been cleared away from the bedside table – she would have gladly eaten them cold. She wondered about Ed, and then felt vaguely guilty that she had assumed her friend had nothing better to do than to sit by her bedside for hours upon end. Her stomach rumbled and then curled into a knot.

Gwyneth shifted in the bed and took stock of the rest of her body: her legs responded to her commands, and all in all she felt much better than when she had last awakened. She wore only a long shift, and her face burned as she wondered who had undressed her while she lay senseless, even as the logical part of her knew that it would have been one of the Diligent or a Healer. The murmur of voices outside the curtain rose and fell. An urge to be a part of whatever conversation was happening struck her with unwavering intensity. Perhaps if she could partake of the normal daily rhythms of the Hall, she would be able to forget the gleaming pools of blood on the floorboards of the Tower.

She pushed the quilt to the side and swung her legs off the side of the bed. The cool stone floor of the healing ward shocked her bare feet, but a little shiver of unexpected pleasure ran up her spine at the sensation. Her feet felt tender and new, as though she'd never run barefoot down dirt roads or through fields peppered with thistle and thorn vines; but she embraced the exquisite sensitivity as she took one step and then another, curling her toes and uncurling them on the flagstones.

Trailing her fingers on the bedside table to ensure that her balance had awoken as well, Gwyneth spied the breeches and shirt laid across the back of the chair by the foot of her bed. A dull, throbbing ache took up residence in her left arm as she moved it from where it had been carefully positioned while she slept. She stepped carefully toward the chair and perched on the edge of the bed, deciding that discretion was the better part of valor when it came to pulling on pants for the first time since the battle in the Tower. Raising the shift over her head ignited new sparks of pain in her left arm as she lifted it above her head, but she pressed her lips together and waited out the discomfort. She caught a glimpse of yellowed, healing bruises spread across her ribs as she carefully pulled on the clean shirt. Strange, she thought, she didn't particularly remember getting those bruises.

There were boots set neatly by the chair, but Gwyneth decided that she liked the feel of the flagstones under her bare feet. With concentrated effort, she combed through her hair with the fingers of her right hand and then braided it efficiently, forcing herself to use her left hand despite the discomfort. Then she paused: laid on the seat of the chair was the short sword that she had used to hold off the *syivhalla*. It was sheathed in plain dark leather, but she recognized the hilt instantly, the palm of her sword hand tingling in recognition. She gave in to the impulse and touched the hilt, wrapping her hand around it. Familiarity washed over her, even as she remembered the feeling of her *taebramh* raging through her, the scent of burning flesh and the *syivhalla*'s inhuman, cavernous gaze as her *taebramh* ate away the last of Brita's body.

The memory seized her with its merciless detail: the pointed teeth of the *syivhalla,* the bones of its fingers gleaming as it clacked them together in pleasure at the smell of her fear, the small desperate sounds of Catherine, Aine and Valerie in the background, the floor shaking as the Paladin broke through the curse on the Tower door. Without thinking about her wound, she grasped the sheath in her left hand, the pain distant in the throes of the memory. She slid the blade a hand's-breadth out of the sheath, the silvery sound twining around her.

For the first time since the battle in the Tower room, Gwyneth felt her *taebramh* stir, as though it had been slumbering with its head tucked down against its feathered breast. She tilted the blade and glimpsed a reflection of a woman with sharp cheekbones and hard, glittering green eyes with shadows imprinted beneath them. For a moment, she watched the woman, wondering if the sword had some strange ability to reach into the past or the future, then thinking that perhaps she had some touch of the Sight brought forth by the battle with the *syivhalla*. Sometimes it happened that way, powers manifesting only after grave danger.

The moment stretched long as she watched the image of the woman in the sword. She looked tough, but also haunted, as though her green eyes had seen death and chaos. Gwyneth felt a kinship with her and tilted her head. The woman in the reflection tilted her head as well. A little burst of shock rippled through Gwyneth as she realized that she was not looking at a vision, but her own reflection. She felt an instant of foolishness, followed by a surge of fascination.

She reexamined herself in the reflection. She had never considered herself a vain girl – no, *woman*, she corrected herself. The image in the sword contained no remaining trace of girlishness. She remembered how when she had first seen Rhys, he had looked much older than his true age; now she understood that the same had happened to her. It was logical. She looked far older than her sixteen years. She felt far older now, too. Perhaps Faeortalam merely made one's experiences manifest in appearance – but then, why did Rionach not look like an old woman? She tucked away that question, stared at herself for one more heartbeat, and then slid the sword back into its sheath, picking it up and threading it onto the belt coiled neatly beneath it. Its weight against her left hip felt nearly as comforting as Aedan's presence.

Still barefoot, Gwyneth padded toward the curtain encircling the bed. Soft light emanated from *taebramh* globes hovering near the ceiling. She pushed aside the heavy cloth and stepped out into a sort of passageway, a corridor for the healers and visitors to walk down the row of curtained beds in the healing ward. Resting her right hand on the hilt of her sword, she walked down the corridor toward the door out of the healing ward, resisting the urge to pull aside each curtain until she found Audhild and Isabella. The ward seemed strangely empty, though she heard a muted conversation from within one of the curtained rooms.

Her *taebramh* shifted its wings and cocked its head within her breast, blinking the fierce eye turned toward the emptiness of the healing hall. She thought that the eyes in her reflection looked much more like the fierce eyes of the hawk that lived within her, outlined in white fire between her ribs and beneath her breastbone. The thought bolstered her as she approached the door and the hum of voices grew louder, even with the silencing runes that slid slickly beneath the surface of the wood door, surfacing and disappearing like small white fish in the dark of a deep pond.

The elegant brass handle of the door felt warm beneath her hand. She pulled it open, its well-oiled hinges making no sound, and stepped into the pool of light beyond it. As she shut the door behind her, the thrum of voices faded to silence and then swelled again as the occupants of the room recognized her. Gwyneth fought the urge to flee back into the quiet of the healing ward as she realized that there was at least a score of women – and a few men, she saw in surprise – occupying the sundry chairs and stools of the large chamber, some with cups of tea and food on the small tables before them, others with books or sketchpads.

Heads turned toward her, and the silence took on an expectant quality. What did they expect from her? Gwyneth felt her face heat and she became keenly aware of her ridiculously bare feet. She tried to tuck her toes beneath the hem of her loose trousers, but only succeeded in drawing more attention to her lack of boots. At least she had made an attempt to neaten her hair. She should have washed her face as well, she thought, suddenly convinced that there was probably still some remnant of sleep on her face and resisting the urge to wipe her palms across her skin.

Aine stood from one of the closer tables, her red hair bound back in a sober bun. She lacked her usual grin, and her face looked paler and thinner than Gwyneth remembered. "Gwyneth," she said, dredging up a smile. "Would you like to come sit with me?"

"Yes," Gwyneth managed. The word came out a croak and dropped ungracefully into the silence.

Aine swept the rest of the room with a pointed look as Gwyneth walked toward the small table. The two other women that sat with Aine – ones who had practiced swordsmanship with Aine and Gwyneth in the courtyard – quietly stood and melted away into a different part of the room.

"I should have said they didn't have to leave," Aine said, sliding back into her chair, "but courtesy requires energy I just don't have right now." She sighed.

Gwyneth took the chair across the small table, turning her back on most of the other occupants of the room. She still felt their stares like pinpricks on her shoulders.

"It's good to see you out of the healing ward," Aine continued in a steady, quiet voice, as though Gwyneth were a young horse that would spook at loud noises. Her blue eyes flickered to the hilt of the sword at Gwyneth's hip, but her expression did not change.

"It's good to be out of the healing ward," Gwyneth said truthfully. She felt suddenly very thirsty, as though she'd just completed a full afternoon of sword practice out in the heat of a summer afternoon.

"Oh, would you like tea or something cold?" Aine said. She motioned, and Gwyneth nearly fell out of her chair when a robe suspended in midair glided over to the table, silver mist hovering where its face and hands should have been.

"What are the Paladins' servants doing here in the Hall?" she managed when she swallowed her heart back down from where it had leapt into her throat.

"Well, there are Paladins here," replied Aine with a slight shrug. "They just...appeared, and they're happy to help us."

The Paladin servant tucked its silver-mist hands into the sleeves of its robe and bowed to them, as though agreeing with Aine.

"I...all right," Gwyneth said. "I'd like some cold water, please, and whatever the cooks have in the kitchen – bread or meat or stew, it doesn't matter to me."

The servant bowed again and glided away.

"He's going to bring back a feast," Aine said. She shrugged one shoulder. "It will all be eaten, one way or another."

"Why...why are there so many people here?" Gwyneth asked, curling her toes over the stretcher of her chair. The smooth wood of the dowel felt good under her feet.

"Different reasons," Aine replied. "Some just want to be nearer to us because of what we experienced. A few, I think, want to try to protect us. And then others just want to be where everyone else is gathering." She took a sip of her tea. "It makes them feel safer."

"What we experienced?" Gwyneth repeated blankly. The hum of conversation had begun to rise around them again as the others realized that Gwyneth wasn't going to make a grand speech or break down in tears.

Aine pressed her lips into a thin line. "I think the best way to explain it is that some of our fellow Inionacha are jealous that we faced the *syivhalla*."

Gwyneth stared at Aine. It took her mind several heartbeats to comprehend what she had just said. "Jealous," she repeated, almost to herself. She shook her head.

"I know," Aine said softly. "No one should be jealous of what we experienced."

"Are they jealous that they didn't die like Catherine or lose a hand like Isabella?" Gwyneth said cuttingly, her voice coming out louder than she'd intended. Silence followed for a moment, but Gwyneth didn't care that everyone had heard her harsh statement. Let them think she was unforgiving toward their stupidity. She shifted in her chair as her *taebramh* unfolded its wings and then resettled them, turning its head left and right.

"It is not an easy thing," Aine said finally, staring down into her cup of tea.

"No," said Gwyneth, leaning back. She felt tired. "I suppose it isn't." She wanted to ask Aine if she had found the right words to speak to Catherine as the young woman from London had lain bleeding on the Tower floor. She wanted to ask Aine if she was suddenly thrust into vivid memories of those terrifying moments, if she could smell the burning flesh and the sweet scent of blood and the metallic, hair-raising odor of the *syivhalla* as it peeled away the flesh that had once been Brita.

Gwyneth settled for one of the less thorny questions. "Why did Brita do it?"

Aine shook her head. "I didn't understand her while she was alive, so I won't pretend to understand her after she's dead."

"After she died betraying us," Gwyneth said.

"Don't mistake me, I have no sympathy for her," said Aine, "but I have done some research on *syivhalla*. They can be very seductive and persuasive. It's possible that Brita thought that the *syivhalla* would not harm us."

Gwyneth snorted. "It wouldn't take an expert in dark sorcery to understand that nothing good would come of selling your soul to such a creature."

"It is easy to say such things now," Aine replied.

The Paladin servant floated serenely over to their table, bearing a small tray packed with different food offerings, a tall earthenware pitcher, and a steaming mug of tea. Gwyneth found herself distracted by the levitating tray, which the servant placed on their table without so much as a drop spilled.

"Thank you," she said with honest gratitude. Her stomach rumbled loudly at the smell of the steaming bowl of stew and the fresh-baked bread on the tray.

The Paladin servant bowed and then whirled away.

"Do you think we could make some of our own?" Gwyneth said, watching the floating robe disappear around a corner.

"The Paladins guard that secret very closely," Aine said, raising one eyebrow.

Gwyneth smiled before she realized what her lips were doing. She froze and carefully rearranged her lips. What right had she to smile so soon after the horrible events in the Tower? She was sure Aine had noticed, but the other woman said nothing.

"Can you tell me what else has happened since I've been in the healing ward?" Gwyneth said, pouring water from the pitcher into the empty earthenware mug. She gestured to Aine, inviting her to take some food. Aine picked up her cup of tea and leaned back in her chair as Gwyneth pulled the bowl of stew toward her. As Gwyneth ate, Aine spoke.

"After the attack, they took all of us to the healing ward, even me. Valerie fractured her wrist and a few ribs, but she has been out of the ward for a few days now. Catherine…" Aine paused for a moment and swallowed visibly. When she spoke again, her voice sounded tight with emotion. "Catherine died just after they broke through the curse on the door. They thought they had lost Audhild as well, but she proved tougher than they thought."

"That's no surprise," said Gwyneth around a mouthful of buttered bread. The food tasted amazing, every flavor magnified and enhanced by her hunger and her convalescence.

"It isn't," Aine agreed. She hesitated. "They thought they might lose you too, for the first day. I heard Orla and Aedan saying that you used too much *taebramh*."

"I had to do something," Gwyneth muttered, cheeks heating.

"I know," replied Aine with a nod. "I am just telling you what I heard them say."

Gwyneth stopped herself from saying anything else ridiculous by stuffing her mouth full of food.

"They only made me stay overnight in the healing ward," continued Aine, her eyes distant. "Valerie and I shared a room, actually, since neither of us needed much of the healers' attention. I think the Bearer was here, but I'm not entirely sure. They may have wanted us all in the healing ward for better security."

Gwyneth shoved another spoonful of stew into her mouth to cut off the comment she wanted to make about *that*.

"When I was allowed to go back to my own room...it was strange. There were Diligent checking in on me at all hours. I think one of them spent the night outside my door. I told them in the morning that I'd already strengthened the runes on the door and there wasn't any need." Aine took a sip of tea. "Instructor Ava isn't teaching us classes right now, especially not in the Tower, so I decided to take my books and spend time down here, in case I could be useful." Aine shrugged.

Gwyneth felt a sudden fierce kinship with Aine. "Has Valerie spent time down here as well?"

"She has," Aine said, "but she has also been sleeping most of her days."

Gwyneth set her empty stew bowl aside and started on the meat pie, savoring the first bite.

"It would have been strange having Theory with just the two of us," said Aine with a shrug. "And I do not know if we will even have Theory again."

"Why not?" Gwyneth asked sharply through a half-chewed bite of pie.

Aine nodded to the sword at Gwyneth's hip. "It's rather clear to us who is meant to be the next Bearer."

Gwyneth choked on a swallow of water and had to take a moment to cough and clear her throat, even as her *taebramh* swelled its chest and beat its wings in agreement with Aine. Finally, she was able to talk again. "I..." She leaned forward over the table and lowered her voice. "Aine, you can't think that this is *the* Sword?"

"No, of course not," Aine replied calmly. "But there aren't many who can use their *taebramh* as you did. You used a plain blade to hold off a *syivhalla*. That means something, Gwyneth."

"All it means is that I did what I thought could make a difference," Gwyneth said.

"You did make a difference." Aine nodded. "You saved us."

"You threw fireballs at it," Gwyneth pointed out.

"All I did was distract it for a moment," said Aine, shaking her head. "I owe my life to you and Audhild."

"Audhild was the bravest of us." Gwyneth said the words firmly, almost hoping for Aine to contradict her. "And we all owe our lives to Orla and Aedan."

"You might have killed it, if they hadn't come through the door," said Aine.

Gwyneth took the last bite of the meat pie rather than argue.

"There are rumors that Rionach may begin to disband the Inionacha," Aine continued, swirling the dregs of her tea in its cup.

"What?" Gwyneth sat up straight in her seat. "*Why?*"

"Because she has chosen the next Bearer," Aine said, a note of patience entering her voice. "That is the way of it. The Hall is not used all the time, not when there is a young Bearer. Not like this, anyway."

"What if the Bearer was killed?" Gwyneth asked, shaking her head. "I thought there were always Inionacha."

"If the Bearer were killed without an Inionacha nearby…we do not rightly know what would happen," Aine said slowly.

"What do you *think* would happen?" Gwyneth asked. Her mind shied away from the type of creature that would be able to kill the Bearer.

"Perhaps the Sword would somehow hide itself," Aine said thoughtfully. She reached out and took one of the small pastries from the last remaining plate of food on the tray, biting into it contemplatively.

"Or perhaps the power would pass to the closest daughter of the Blood?" Gwyneth guessed.

"It would take something earth-shattering for the Bearer not to fulfill her duty," said Aine, shaking her head as she finished the pastry and reached for another.

For all that they had been training to become the Bearer, Gwyneth realized that they knew precious little about the actual mechanics of the transfer. "Well," she said, "I hope that the rumor is not true. I would hate to see the Hall disbanded."

"It will happen eventually," said Aine with serene conviction.

Gwyneth took a bite of the pastry and chewed appreciatively. She'd developed a taste for chocolate in the past few months; it had been an expensive luxury in her village, and even here in the Hall it was not entirely common.

"Oh, Gwyneth, you're up!"

Gwyneth turned at the sound of Ed's voice, another traitorous smile forming on her lips. Ed pushed her way through the room, even jabbing an elbow into one Paladin who didn't realize she was attempting to pass him.

"And you've eaten," Ed continued, surveying the empty tray with approval. "I was just coming to, ahem, visit you."

"Well, pull up a seat," Aine said, gesturing to the empty chair.

"Thank you," Ed said, hopping up into the seat and plucking the last pastry from the plate. She leaned toward Gwyneth and said just loud enough for her to hear: "Rhys is here." Louder, she said, "Gwyn, if there's not a healer posted by your bed here in the healing ward, I think that means you're free to go back to your own room." She emphasized the last three words just enough for Gwyneth to catch it.

Gwyneth felt suddenly dizzy. Rhys, here in the Hall? Why? Had he heard about the attack? Had Aedan sent for him? Would he be reprimanded for his attachment to her?

"I do feel a bit tired," she said, her voice wavering just enough to make it believable. "I'll go fetch my boots from the ward and then go rest, I think."

"The other door at the end of the corridor in the healing ward leads out to the main hall," Aine said helpfully.

The Paladin servant reappeared, removed the untouched tea from the tray and whisked away everything else.

"You can have the tea if you'd like, Ed, or if you'd like more, Aine," Gwyneth said, her stomach turning somersaults as she slid down from her chair. She looked at Aine. "Would it be all right if I visited you in your room later?"

"I could come to your room," Aine offered.

"No, I'd like to keep stretching my legs," replied Gwyneth. "I can't lay about in bed all day again."

"Do you think he would bring us more pastries?" Ed asked, eyeing the Paladin servant as he cleared away another tray from a different table.

"I'm sure," Aine replied.

"They always seem to listen to you. How do you summon them?" Ed continued, eyes bright with interest as she drew Aine's attention away from Gwyneth.

Gwyneth didn't waste the opportunity, stealing away from the table. The silence of the healing ward enveloped her beyond the door. She padded quickly down the corridor and pulled on her boots, mouth dry, barely pausing before walking to the door at the opposite end of the ward. She wasn't sure she'd understood Ed correctly...but if she had, she'd see Rhys in moments. Her heart thundered in her chest and she took a deep breath, gripping the banister as she started up the stairs toward her chambers.

Chapter 19

She knew he was in the room before she even opened the door; she felt his presence as surely as if she'd seen him. Her hands shook as she sketched the combination of runes to unlock the quieting charms on the door, and then the locking rune. The only other Inionacha who knew the combination to her door, of course, was Ed – though an Instructor or a Diligent could command the door to open in dire need. Gwyneth felt a rush of gratitude toward her friend, wondering yet again what she had done to deserve such a stalwart ally who seemed to know what Gwyneth needed even when Gwyneth did not.

Her skin prickled as she slid through the open door, shutting it quickly behind her. For some reason, her eyes stayed trained on the floor just in front of her boots, even as her heart pounded in her chest like a drumbeat. She heard him draw in a breath.

"Gwyneth."

It was the first time she'd heard his voice since the masquerade, which felt like years ago though she knew it had only been a few moons. A thrill ran through her, and she raised her eyes. He stood before the hearth, flames crackling on the log in the grate, the light silhouetting his muscular frame. His eyes gleamed, more blue than gray as their gazes met.

"Your hair is longer," she said, her eyes traveling over his chestnut curls.

He chuckled, but his smile was strained. "I should have guessed you would act as though nothing were wrong."

She took two steps forward as he turned fully toward her. With some surprise, she saw the shadows beneath his eyes. "You look…tired."

He didn't reply, looking at her silently for a long moment, and then he closed the distance between them with two long strides. Gwyneth stiffened as he gathered her into his arms – she had been poked and prodded and touched entirely too much in the healing ward. She felt him pause and then begin to draw away, and all her reservation left her in a rush. She pressed her face into his warm, muscled chest and looped her arms around his waist, ignoring the sparks of pain from her wound. His arms tightened around her.

For the first time since Brita's eyes had transformed into the cavernous stare of the *syivhalla*, Gwyneth felt truly, unquestionably, peacefully safe. Warmth flowed through her as she felt Rhys stroke her hair gently with one large, calloused hand.

"How did you know?" she asked, her voice muffled by his chest.

"I didn't," he replied, his voice rumbling through her cheek. "Not until Ed sent me a message."

Warmth at Ed's steadfast, practical actions flickered like a candle flame in her chest. "How did you find your way here?"

"You mean, how did I get permission?" Rhys replied. He seemed perfectly content to conduct the conversation with her burrowed into his chest. "I volunteered to take messages to Aedan and Orla."

"They know you're here." Gwyneth felt a prickle of concern for him, drawing back enough to peer up at his face.

"I could not keep myself hidden from them," he replied, raising one dark eyebrow. "And my affection for you is no great secret."

Somehow that kindled even greater warmth in her chest. His eyes soft with concern, he brushed one calloused thumb gently down her cheek. Then he held her at arm's length, plainly inspecting her. She held up her left arm helpfully. He pressed his lips together into a thin line as she pulled up her sleeve to reveal the bandages.

"Not nearly as bad as the wound you took in the forest," she said, trying for a casual tone and failing.

"A *baobhan sith* and a *syivhalla* are not nearly the same thing," he said, his fingers warm on the skin at her wrist. She wondered if he could feel her heart fluttering like a sparrow's wings.

"Is that what you were trying to warn me about?" she asked. Their words filled the space between them. She knew that if they stopped talking, other things would happen...and the thought of those other things ignited a curl of heat low in her belly.

"I had heard whispers," he replied, his eyes darkening. "At first, I thought them nothing more than spiteful threats in the last words of the creatures that I hunt. But..." He shook his head, gazing at the fire as though he couldn't meet her eyes. "I should have done more."

She couldn't stand the heaviness in his voice and the guilt written in the set of his jaw. Before she properly thought about it, she reached up and caught his chin with her good hand, turning his face toward her. "You cannot protect me from all the evil of this world, Rhys," she said in a low voice.

"That doesn't mean I don't want to," he said huskily. "Gods, Gwyneth, when I got that message..."

Gwyneth wondered briefly what Ed had wrote, but she tucked the question away. She brushed her fingers against the stubble on Rhys' jaw. "I'm sorry you had to find out like that."

"I'm just glad I found out at all."

For a moment, Gwyneth wanted to point out that *she* never received messages when he fought and killed dangerous creatures or left on missions into the wilds of Faeortalam and Doendhtalam. But the air between them heated, the space between them contracted, and then Rhys gently brushed his lips against hers, sending a jolt of heat through her and extinguishing all conscious thought. She tilted her head back and he slid one hand lightly behind her neck, sending a shiver down her spine. He cradled her as though he was afraid of breaking her, as though she were made of glass and rough handling might shatter her.

She wanted to be shattered.

Heat spiraled through her as she gave in to the nameless hunger, pressing closer to Rhys. The memory of the *syivhalla*'s soulless eyes flashed through her mind for an instant, reminding her that she had very nearly died without experiencing the full measure of womanhood. She boldly deepened the chaste kiss, parting his lips with her tongue; Rhys drew back slightly for an instant in surprise and then returned her ardor in full measure, giving a little growl that only stoked the fire racing through her body. His fingers slid through her hair as she slipped her hand beneath his shirt, delighting in the feel of his warm skin and the hard, muscular planes of his abdomen.

She traced her fingers over the smooth ridges of the scars on his side and poured herself into the kiss, only pausing to gasp for air when he released her long enough to pull her firmly against him. They fit neatly together, she thought through the haze of desire. She wanted to know if they fit so perfectly in all ways, and a rush of excitement and dizzying need coursed through her. His other hand echoed her motion, finding the hem of her shirt. The roughness of his callouses against the tenderness of her days-old bruises only spurred her hunger. She heard herself making small sounds, little breathy moans that disappeared into his mouth.

They existed outside of time. They existed outside of reason. When his mouth was on hers and his hands touched her body, everything else fell away, wrapping her in a whirling cocoon of desire. She wanted more. She felt his hard length pressed against her belly; the evidence of his desire for her added to her excitement. Raking her nails gently down his chest, she reached for him, but as she brushed her fingers against him, Rhys caught her wrist.

Gwyneth blinked up at him in hazy confusion. Didn't he want

her the same way that she wanted him? She bit her kiss-swollen lip uncertainly.

Rhys groaned. "Gods, Gwyneth." He took a deep breath and gently disentangled himself.

"Did I do something wrong?" she asked, the whirlwind of desire fading. She blinked again, starting to feel very foolish and small.

"No," he said quickly, brushing her cheek with his knuckles. "No, not at all." He looked down at himself ruefully. "I'd say you are doing everything very well."

"But you don't want to…?" She let the question trail off, her cheeks burning now as she decided not to speak aloud the very explicit thoughts that had occupied her mind only moments before.

Rhys gave her that devastating half-smile, his eyes darkening. "Oh, how I want to." His grin faded. "I just want to be sure that you are not reacting to what you just experienced."

"It's not only that," she said in protest, her flush deepening. How had he known that she'd thought about the fact that she'd nearly died a few days ago?

He gave her a brief, gentle kiss. "Don't you think that Paladins have brushes with death?"

"I try not to think about it too much," she answered truthfully. Her arm began to throb with a dull, insistent pain. She shifted uncomfortably.

"Would you like to sit?" Rhys asked perceptively. "Or perhaps I should go and let you rest."

"No," she said immediately. "I mean…I would like you to stay, if you are able." She looked up at him keenly. "Will you be punished if Aedan and Orla find out you are here?"

"Your runes on the door are quite effective," he said. "I checked them myself."

"You didn't answer my question," Gwyneth pointed out. A lance of pain shot through her arm and she flinched.

Rhys' lips curled upward slightly. "Don't worry about me, Gwyneth."

"But you're allowed to be worried about me?" she countered.

"Will *you* be punished if your Instructors find me here?" he asked, raising one eyebrow.

"I don't know," she answered truthfully. "They've never expressly forbade visitors, but they haven't encouraged it either."

"Suitably vague," he commented. Then his face softened. "I won't be needed for a few hours yet, I think. Come."

He took her hand and led her toward the bed, seated her on the edge of it and gently pulled her boots off her feet. Something about the tenderness of his rough hands made tears prick at the corners of her eyes. His nimble fingers found the buckle at her waist, and he hung her new blade by the belt over one of the bedposts within easy reach.

"I've only been up a few hours and I'm already tired," Gwyneth said, sighing. It wasn't quite a complaint – she wasn't dead, after all. But she still didn't understand why her body felt so heavy. One moment she was losing herself in the fire of Rhys' kiss, and the next she felt ready to sleep for the rest of the day. How annoying. "I don't want to sleep," she said in quiet protest as Rhys pulled off his own boots.

"Then just rest," Rhys said, lowering himself onto the bed beside her.

She felt a little spark of excitement, quickly doused by her exhaustion. How doubly annoying. She'd dreamt of something very close to this scenario countless times, and now she was too tired to even fully enjoy it. Rhys angled himself so that her head was pillowed on his arm and she could feel the comforting warmth of his body, but they weren't pressed tightly against one another.

"Just rest," Rhys repeated, brushing his other hand over her head.

Gwyneth felt the tug of exhaustion. With the warmth of Rhys at her back, sleep swallowed her whole. It was not a silken slide into slumber; the instant her eyes closed, the blackness enveloped her, and she was powerless to resist.

For a short time, or maybe it was a great while, she did not dream. In the hazy way of thinking while asleep, Gwyneth wondered if this was what death was like: warm darkness, a dropping away of the self, and then oblivion. Even as a child, she had not rightly believed in any of the tales of an afterlife. She had always questioned, but she had *wanted* to believe.

Folk believe what they must to survive this harsh life, her mother had told her after the first death that Gwyneth had witnessed: a young woman not much more than a girl, newly taken to wife and birthing her first child. The babe had not come smoothly, and the woman had died panting and sweating, moaning and delirious with pain. The babe had died as well despite all the skill of Gwyneth's mother. The husband had not paid them at all, but he was not wild in his grief as Gwyneth had expected. He had only nodded once in resignation, his mouth twisting.

Gwyneth had wondered many things after that. She had wondered why women had drawn the lot of bearing children; she knew that the Christians had their story of Eve, but she did not believe in their stories. She had wondered why the goddess with three faces – Maiden, Mother and Wise Woman – allowed women to suffer so, and die these bloody, gasping deaths trying to bring forth new life.

The shred of awareness she retained in the darkness of her deep sleep curled like smoke through the blackness, drifting and dissipating, coalescing and dispersing again. If death was anything like this, Gwyneth thought in her dream-self, then perhaps it would not be so terrible. The darkness did not judge, did not inflict pain. It simply *was.*

And then something changed. Gwyneth felt herself wrenched from the comforting darkness, though she was not awakening: a dream took hold, inexorable and insistent, the terrible face of the *syivhalla* appearing out of the shadows, Brita's face bleached white as bone, her flesh torn and hanging ghoulishly from her skull, the fire of the creature burning through her eyes until caverns stared at Gwyneth, filled with the dancing flame of the creature's malevolent spirit.

Gwyneth tried to scream, but in this dream she could not move. She could not speak. She could not summon her *taebramh*. She stood mute and powerless as the *syivhalla* turned its head with the crunch of bone. Audhild stood before the monster, teeth bared in defiance, *taebramh* glowing at her hands.

The creature caught Audhild in its clawed hands and snapped her neck, tossing the Northwoman aside like a rag doll. Gwyneth felt the rage and sorrow raging in her chest, but she could not make a sound. She could not move. She watched in mute terror and rage as the *syivhalla* killed first Aine and then Isabella, their bodies joining Audhild in a heap of bloodied limbs and death-glossed eyes. The grief and anger spiraled into a storm within Gwyneth. The *syivhalla* dragged Valerie toward its sharp teeth with a fistful of Valerie's long white-gold hair. Valerie screamed and fought, her beautiful face wild with mingled courage and terror. A bloody ribbon of hair tore free from her scalp and Valerie fell back, her movements quick and cat-like even in the mind-dulling vortex of fear.

But the *syivhalla* just flicked its blackened tongue between its teeth and reached for Valerie again. Gwyneth fought the bonds of the dream. Where were Orla and Aedan? Where were the Instructors and the Diligent? Why could she not hear the dull boom of the curse-breaking at the door?

There is no door, whispered a sibilant voice, neither the *syivhalla* nor Gwyneth. *You are trapped here. You will watch.*

Fear coursed through Gwyneth. Was she going mad? Would she be trapped in this nightmare forever, witnessing the deaths of the other Inionacha?

You cannot escape, the voice crooned with wicked satisfaction.

And then it was not just the Seven before the claws of the *syivhalla*. Ed appeared, her face at first frightened and then determined as she began sketching complex runes in the air, lips moving with difficult incantations that few other Inionacha understood.

No, Gwyneth screamed silently. She fought against the invisible bonds holding her captive in the nightmare. She would not let the creature kill Ed. Ed, who had protected her from Mary's malice, who had helped her believe in herself when she first arrived at the Hall, who had not let jealousy poison their friendship.

But she could not move. She could not speak. The *syivhalla* brushed aside one of Ed's runes, a glowing pinwheel of fire, as though it were merely an insect flitting annoyingly through the air. Ed conjured a flaming dragon that spread its wings like a shield before her, lashing its tail and bellowing its fury at the *syivhalla*. For a heartbeat, the creature paused, regarding Ed's creation with something akin to interest, tilting its head slightly to one side. Then it raised a clawed hand and split a seam down the center of the dragon, the protective spell collapsing in a swirl of sparks.

No. Gwyneth strained against the stricture of the nightmare. She felt something give, something tear, something she had never felt before – and before the creature sank its claws into Ed, Gwyneth awoke.

Or she thought she awoke. But when she pushed herself up in the bed, she felt a curious lightness, a peeling away that felt like shedding a weighted pack. Looking down at her hands, she saw her own skin glowing faintly with a strange luminescence. For a moment, she panicked: had she just died? Was *this* what death was? Had she torn herself from life with the strength of her struggle against the strange, powerful nightmare?

But then she looked back and saw herself sleeping peacefully, no outward sign of the terrifying nightmare in her measured breathing and half-parted lips. Rhys slept beside her, one hand still touching her hair. She watched for a long moment, riding out a strange sense of vertigo at looking down at her own body. Rhys looked so young without the weight of his Paladin experience in his eyes. He had thrown off the quilt, the hem of his shirt riding up to reveal a sliver of his smooth skin and the sharp curve of his hipbone. Gwyneth couldn't help herself; she reached out and touched the crescent of skin, tracing the pearly edge of a thread-thin scar that she had never seen.

A shiver rippled through Rhys. Rather than drawing back, she leaned closer. He stirred and opened hazy gray eyes. His brows knitted together for an instant as he blinked, his long dark lashes stark against the white of his skin. Then he yawned, his pink tongue and white teeth putting her in mind of a hunting hound; and he said to her almost lazily, "Why did you not tell me you could Walk?"

Shock rippled through Gwyneth, followed closely by a flush of embarrassment. Of course. Walking. How could she have been such a dullard?

"I – did not know I could," she answered, her voice shivering through the air as though she were underwater.

Rhys pushed himself onto one elbow. "You did not *mean* to Walk?"

Gwyneth slid over him and stood. The wood floor did not feel cold under her feet. She wondered if she would feel the cold of winter – she glided over to the window and pressed a palm against the glass, her fingers translucent in the gray pearl light of early dawn. She felt a strange sensation of slick smoothness, but it was different than cold. It was different than anything she'd ever felt. She narrowed her eyes and pressed her hand to the glass again, and her fingers passed through it. It was snowing; she felt the snowflakes pass through her hand with small, shivering shocks of something-different-than-cold.

"Gwyneth," Rhys said, sliding out from the bed.

"No," she answered, her voice dreamy. "I did not mean to Walk." She turned to him with a smile on her face. Here in this translucent form, the pain of her physical body faded and the edges of her grief for the death and injury of Catherine, Isabella and Audhild felt blunted. It was as though in separating from her body, she separated from the immediacy of the past days.

She decided that if she could not have the fire of Rhys' touch, this strange but not unpleasant detachment would do quite nicely.

"It is dangerous to Walk without being properly taught," Rhys said, his voice tightly controlled now.

She turned away from the window toward him. "Why? If I could do it without being taught, then it must not be so difficult."

"I forget that I cannot measure you against any ordinary standard," said Rhys, almost to himself. He ran one hand through his sleep-mussed hair. Gwyneth turned back toward the window, passing one finger and then another through the glass again, memorizing the feel of making her Walker-form solid enough to touch the window and then making herself spirit-thin, her outline shimmering as she slid her whole hand out the window. She smiled, feeling the snow pass through her palm.

"It takes even the most skilled Paladin extensive training to do what you have done in your first moments of Walking," Rhys said carefully.

Something was different in his voice. She turned back to him, and before he smoothed his expression she saw the flash of reverence and something that might have been fear. But in her Walker-form, she did not feel regret or uncertainty as she might have. She glanced at her sleeping body, still and silent beneath the quilt.

"Perhaps you should rest," Rhys said, "and speak to your Instructors about this when the sun has fully risen."

"No," she replied simply, tracing through the frost on the window with one fingertip.

"Gwyneth," he said.

She looked over her shoulder. In her Walker-form, she shed the uncertainty and childishness of her body. "No. Don't presume that you may tell me what to do."

"I just want you to heal," he said in a low voice, the same voice that Gwyneth would have used in Doendhtalam to approach a skittish colt.

"This will help me heal," she said.

"From what I have read and what I have been told," Rhys said carefully, "you feel less emotion when Walking. I can understand why it would feel better than your body right now."

"You don't understand," Gwyneth said quietly. Part of her was shocked that she was speaking to Rhys in such a way – shouldn't she be giddy with his presence, the flame in her belly coaxing her to touch him, her lips hot with his kiss and her blood singing at the feel of his skin upon hers?

But in her Walker-form, she had no flesh to burn with passion. She did not feel her heart pounding in her ears. She felt her love for him, yes, but it did not mean she could not see him clearly now, without the distraction of her body.

"You weren't there," she continued. The chill of the nightmare rippled through her, but she brushed it away.

"I wasn't," he agreed.

"Then you don't know how it feels," she said quietly. Outside the window, the sky lightened, turned a silken dove gray, the smooth sheets of snow-clouds covering the color of the dawn.

"You're right," Rhys said. "I don't know how you feel. But I *have* seen friends die, Gwyneth. I have been a full Paladin for only a few years, but I have seen my share of death at the hands of evil creatures."

If she had been in her body, she might have raged at him; she might have challenged him to tell her which of his dead companions he had trained with as she had trained with the Seven; she might have growled at him that it was entirely different, that he could not compare armed Paladins hunting creatures against Inionacha waiting for lessons and attacked by surprise, by the treachery of one of their own.

But in her Walker-form, she felt all these things as though from a distance. She did not answer him, staring out the window and watching the dawn. She heard him sigh and walk over to the hearth, prodding the banked fire to life with a scrape of the poker. Time slipped around her like water around a stone in a stream. She felt strangely content, watching the daylight illuminate the courtyard outside her window, the cold silent beauty of the snow a balm upon the now-distant terror of the nightmare.

Gwyneth felt herself enter a kind of trance. She did not need to breathe in her Walker-form, so it was easy to sink into complete stillness. She contemplated death again, this time without the beat of her heart and the rise and fall of her own chest to remind her that she was alive. She heard Rhys say something, but his words meant nothing to her. Then there was silence: he had left her.

She pressed both hands to the smooth glass of the window, and then passed them through into the silken air beyond. The snowflakes now were larger, falling faster. She felt them pass through her and thought that perhaps it was good that Rhys had left. They would all leave her, eventually, passing through her life as quickly as one of the delicately spun snowflakes, beautiful but transient.

She stood at the window and watched the sky darken as the snow swirled into a storm, the translucent lines of her Walker-form wavering in the fading light.

Chapter 20

"Gwyneth, this behavior does not become you."

The voice broke through the stillness surrounding Gwyneth. She did not know how long she had stood at the window, watching the snowstorm. She did not care. The light had changed from silken dove gray to the dark of a storm. It could have been night. She did not know. But somehow the voice reached her through the cocoon of silence that surrounded her with such comfort.

She turned from the window. Aedan stood by the door of her chamber, flanked by Instructor Ava. Rhys stood in the shadows to one side. She felt a flicker of something close to anger at his betrayal. Why could he not simply let her be? Why did he have to bring a Paladin and an Instructor into the privacy of her chambers?

Aedan saw that he had broken through her trance. He strode forward with silent, sure steps. "Walking for too long will drain your *taebramh*," he said in a nearly gentle voice.

"I have *taebramh* to spare," Gwyneth replied dismissively. She saw disapproval flash through Instructor Ava's eyes at her reply to the Paladin, but she could not bring herself to care.

"Be that as it may," Aedan continued, "it does not help your companions if you drain yourself like this."

Gwyneth drew back her shoulders. "You did not arrive in time to save them."

Heaviness entered Aedan's gold-green eyes. "No. I did not."

"I could not save them," she said. She felt the edges of grief again, sharp as a knife, and she pressed a hand to the window.

"Let yourself feel it," said Aedan, his voice calm and certain.

Instructor Ava's hands were moving, twisting through the air, but Aedan drew her attention away from the Unseelie Instructor.

"Just as your physical wound healed, this will heal as well," Aedan continued, his smooth voice catching her awareness. She stepped away from the window even as she knew that this was some sort of Paladin craft, this honeyed smoothness of the voice that both soothed her and compelled her. "But you cannot help those who survived in this way, Gwyneth. You must understand that."

"How can I help them? I could not help them in the Tower," Gwyneth said, ragged raw sorrow beginning to catch at her, pull her back toward her slumbering body. Or perhaps that was Instructor Ava, now close to the bed, her hands still moving.

"You were a healer once," said Aedan, a note of approval in his voice. "You could be so again."

"I am not more skilled than the healers trained here in Faeortalam," Gwyneth said. Speaking of all of it made her tired. She felt a pull toward her body.

"Perhaps not," agreed Aedan, "but you can help heal them all the same."

"If I can, I will," Gwyneth said. She was drifting across the floor now, some invisible current bearing her toward her body. She knew this was trickery, but the early relief of Walking had faded. Perhaps they were right. Perhaps she needed to rest. She felt a prickle of unease: she had never Walked, so she had never returned to her body after Walking. What if she did not know how?

"We will help you," Aedan said, and she knew he was speaking of both returning to her body and healing the other Inionacha. His smooth, steady voice wrapped her with its certainty. "Let us help you."

Gwyneth stood at the side of the bed now, staring down at her body. Her face looked paler, her cheeks more sunken, than what she remembered when she had awoken in her Walker form. "I do not want to dream," she said almost desperately.

"You are stronger than the nightmares," Aedan told her with his quiet confidence. She looked at his eyes, the honeyed center of his gaze filling her with calm.

She nodded, Instructor Ava touched her body's forehead, and Gwyneth snapped back into her body with a suddenness like breaking bone. She gasped at the heaviness and pain, the clumsy flesh enveloping her spirit like a shroud, like a tomb.

"Just breathe," said Aedan into her ear, and she tried. She felt another touch on her forehead, and a rippling wave of energy passed through her, washing away some of the pain.

"That is all I can do," came Instructor Ava's cool voice, speaking over her to Aedan.

It took all her focus to open her eyes. She blinked up at them, her gaze unfocused.

"You must rest," said Aedan.

She licked her dry lips and tried to speak, but no sound came from her throat.

"We will stay," said the Paladin. "Do not fear."

And, miraculously, she did not. Gwyneth stopped fighting the heaviness of her body and for a second time let sleep overtake her.

It was only when she woke again that she realized that she had not dreamed. Her body ached, but it was more of the soreness from after a long few days of training in the practice yard with Ed and the other young women. She heard a quiet conversation over by the fire, and as she came fully back to awareness, she recognized the voices: Ed and Aedan. She blinked at that unexpected combination and pushed herself up with her good arm out of habit, even though it took her a moment of searching to find any discomfort from her injury. Her mouth tasted like mint and honey, though she didn't remember drinking any draught. She wrinkled her nose in suspicion.

"You woke for a few moments twice," Ed said, walking over to the bed. "Enough to drink something, though I'm guessing you don't remember it."

"No," Gwyneth said. Thankfully, her voice didn't come out like a frog's croak. Small mercies. Her eyes searched the room. The remnants of a simple meal lay on the small table near the hearth, and her two chairs had been pulled close to the fire's warmth. Aedan uncoiled himself from the second chair.

Though she knew it would be painfully obvious, Gwyneth couldn't stop her eyes from searching the rest of the room.

"He isn't here," said Ed quietly. "He's on duty, I think, or perhaps carrying a message."

"I see," Gwyneth said, even though her heart contracted with disappointment.

"You caused some alarm, Gwyneth," Aedan said, his graceful gait bringing him closer to the bed, but not as close as Ed.

Gwyneth winced as she remembered Walking. "I didn't intend to," she said, even as her cheeks heated at her childish reply.

Aedan did not chastise her, and that was somehow worse than if he had reprimanded her for her excuse. He only gazed at her silently with those gold-green eyes, as though he were waiting for her next words.

"How long did I…Walk?" It sounded too generous to name her sulking by the window Walking. She'd been barely a dozen paces away from her body the entire time, incorporeal form or no.

"Nearly eight hours, which is quite long for a novice," said Aedan.

Ed gave a very unladylike snort at his words. "Gwyneth rarely acts like a novice at anything."

Gwyneth looked sharply at Ed's face; there was both fondness and fear written across her friend's expression.

"I'm sorry," she said honestly, because it seemed like the only thing left to say.

Ed perched on the edge of the bed. "The *syivhalla* nearly killed you, and you want to finish the job by wasting away without your spirit." She shook her head. "Typical."

Gwyneth felt her dry lips stretch in something like a smile. "You say that like almost being killed by a *syivhalla* is a weekly occurrence for me."

"Maybe not weekly, but you're certainly prone to both danger and excitement," said Ed.

Gwyneth sat up straighter against the headboard and tucked an errant strand of hair behind her ears. She looked at Aedan. "Did…how did you know to come?"

"How do you think we knew?" he said, raising his eyebrows this time.

She felt her cheeks burn. "Rhys." Mixed with that strange embarrassment was a prickle of betrayal again.

"And if he had not had the good sense to come and get me, you might be dead by now," said Aedan very matter-of-factly.

"Thank you again," Gwyneth said. Her words felt inadequate. She plucked at a seam on the quilt, wishing she had another way to thank the Paladin for saving her life a second time.

"I am merely doing my duty," Aedan replied.

"You must have more important things to do," Gwyneth said, shifting uncomfortably. She didn't like the feeling of being indebted, even it was to the steady, likeable Paladin.

"No," he said evenly.

"You're important," Ed said firmly, looking down at Gwyneth with such earnestness blazing on her face that Gwyneth felt unworthy of it.

She didn't know how to reply, so she said nothing. Then she frowned as a thought struck her. "The Bearer didn't come?"

"No," Aedan said again in that same calm voice.

Ed cleared her throat. "You must be hungry. I'll get some food – do you think you can manage solids, or would you like soup again?"

"I'll eat anything you bring," said Gwyneth truthfully. Her body felt hollow and aching, and she belatedly recognized part of it as hunger pangs. She didn't want Ed to leave, but they both knew that they couldn't ask the Paladin to fetch food. Even though he said he didn't have other important tasks, *that* would certainly be a step too far.

The corner of Aedan's mouth twitched upward into a hint of a smile, as though he had heard Gwyneth's thoughts. As the door closed behind Ed, Gwyneth gazed keenly at him.

"Can you hear my thoughts?" she asked boldly.

"No," he answered. "We have had some version of this conversation before, daughter of Rionach."

Gwyneth shifted underneath the quilt, feeling the soft coolness of the finely spun sheets against her skin as though for the first time. All her senses, she realized, felt heightened after her return to her body, like the almost-painful sensitivity of a newly healed patch of skin. She shivered, and then immediately hoped that Aedan hadn't noticed. She did not want him to think her any weaker than he already did.

"You do not need to hold up your shield here in the privacy of your own chamber," Aedan said, almost gently.

"When you say things like that," Gwyneth muttered, "it makes me think that you are not entirely telling the whole truth about hearing thoughts."

Aedan chuckled, the sound low and comforting. Gwyneth glanced up at him in surprise.

"Paladins are trained in many things, Gwyneth, because we face so many different dangers. We do not know which skill may save our life or the lives of those we protect," he said, a bit of an instructional tone entering his voice. Gwyneth found she didn't mind. "Still," he continued, "some of us have our particular talents, and one of mine is the ability to read people very well."

"So well that it seems as though you hear their thoughts," Gwyneth said. Her mouth felt strange and stretched. She realized that she was smiling. The movement felt foreign, like she was moving a limb that had long been held immobile.

"Yes," agreed Aedan. His gold-green eyes sparkled with good humor, as though they'd been talking about something much more entertaining than his uncanny skill at inferring her thoughts.

"Can I…May I ask some questions about the Paladins?" Gwyneth asked. She felt the edges of that dark, consuming grief rippling at the border of her heartbeat, and she did not want to give it any purchase. Perhaps if she talked about something else, she could avoid those ink-black waves that washed over her with such despair.

"Yes," Aedan replied simply. He tilted his head. "We should sit by the fire. I have the feeling you have many questions about the Paladins."

Gwyneth's face heated. "I just have not had the opportunity to speak with a senior Paladin and thought I would take advantage of your kindness."

"As you should," Aedan said. She wasn't sure if she imagined the approval in his voice. He gestured to the glowing coals of the fire in the hearth, walking toward one of the chairs with an unhurried, graceful stride. Gwyneth felt oddly grateful that he did not look over his shoulder or wait for her. His confidence in her sent a curl of strength rippling through her body. She pushed back the quilt and stretched with luxurious concentration, feeling the muscles of her legs and back contract with exquisite tenderness. It was not pain exactly, but something close to it.

The soles of her feet felt bruised and newly made as she pressed them to the smooth wooden floorboards, but she walked over to the empty chair with deliberate strides, refusing to wince. She still wore the loose shirt and breeches that she'd pulled on before visiting the room outside the healing ward, and again she felt that vague gratitude that no one had changed her into a sleeping shift. Her privacy had been invaded too much, on the whole, in the past days, and she took it as a sign that she was healing that she truly minded now.

Gwyneth settled into the seat beside Aedan, gazing into the glowing coals of the fire. The warmth lapped pleasurably against her legs. A copper kettle gleamed on its hook over the hearth, steam curling from its spout.

"Would you like some tea while we wait for Edelinne to return with more hearty fare?" Aedan asked.

"I should serve the tea to *you*," Gwyneth managed. Her awareness of his status as a senior Paladin ebbed and flowed, coming painfully to the front of her mind now.

"Nonsense," he said firmly, standing with languid grace and retrieving the kettle. There were a few mugs over on the table, sturdy earthenware that could endure being dropped on the wooden floors with perhaps only a chip or a crack. Gwyneth wondered how many mugs of tea Ed and Aedan and Rhys had drank while watching her sleep. She clenched her jaw and stared into the fire. The longer she was awake, the more ridiculous she felt about refusing to return to her body after Walking. There were others who had been injured much worse than her during the attack in the Tower, and here she was taking up the time of one of the Paladins who had saved their lives. She felt a piercing sense of shame.

Rather than give in to the tide of roiling emotions beginning to swirl within her chest, she stood and wrapped her fingers around the handle of the poker. The metal, warmed by the ambient heat of the fire, felt like smooth skin beneath her palm. She prodded at the cherry-red coals, evoking a flurry of sparks that spiraled through the air. Gwyneth wondered how the sparks would feel in her Walker-form, remembering the sensation of the snowflakes passing through her hand. She thrust the thought away and slid the poker back into its place standing upright beside the hearth, picking up a piece of the firewood stacked in a neat pile against the wall.

Sparks exploded with crackling, hissing fury as the bark of the wood came into contact with the red-hot coals. Newborn white flame licked at the pale flesh of the firewood. Gwyneth blinked. Dread clawed at her throat suddenly. The flames of the fire became the malevolent blue flames in the cavernous eyes of the *syivhalla*. She felt her body clench, her fingers curling into fists, her nails digging into her tender palms. Gooseflesh rippled along her arms as a curl of smoke reached her nose, becoming the acrid stench of burning flesh as the *syivhalla* peeled away what had once been Brita's smug, pretty face. As if from a distance, she heard Aedan speaking quietly.

"Do not let the memories control you," he said in his mesmerizing, honey-smooth voice. His words slipped into her consciousness easily, parallel to the sensations gripping her tightly with fear and dread. "It is natural to feel these things. It is natural for certain sights or sounds or smells to bring up your experience, and it is also natural for you to remember it without any of these."

Gwyneth felt her heart slowing at the calm cadence of his voice.

"Breathe and allow yourself to feel the memory but remind yourself that it is just that: a memory. It is not happening to you now. It happened to you in the past, and it will not control your future."

"It will not control my future," Gwyneth said quietly. It was as though she had found an anchor against the current of memory and sensation. She still felt their tug, the cold fear spurring her heart and the heavy dread souring her stomach, but she blinked and repeated the words again, and the flames were simply flames licking at a log. The smoke lost its sharp burnt-flesh scent. She drew in a shuddering breath and stepped back from the hearth, stumbling as her leg hit the chair behind her.

Aedan's warm hand steadied her, his touch gentle but firm on her shoulder. She sat in the chair and accepted the hot mug of tea he pressed into her hands, the thick earthenware warm and solid.

"Establishing your daily routine again also helps," Aedan continued, settling into the other chair, "as does choosing a few trusted friends to share your memories."

Gwyneth frowned at that, pressing her lips together.

Aedan raised one eyebrow, his eyes glinting knowingly. "They will not have been through the actual experience with you, no, but your friends here have also had their own trials, Gwyneth. It is a bit arrogant to think that you are the only one who has ever felt suffering and grief such as this, is it not?"

He said the words calmly, unladen with any judgment. Gwyneth took a breath and nodded. "Yes. I understand what you are saying."

She thought of Edelinne and her troubled childhood, her illness that had left her impaired, her mother demanding perfection all the same out of the fear that the Inionacha would demand another child other than her unloved eldest. She thought of Rhys, the pain in his eyes when she spoke of his family and knew more than he did, the acceptance and heaviness when he had told her that he had seen companions die fighting the Dark creatures the Paladins hunted. She thought of Audhild, disfigured for the rest of her life, forced to bear outward scars of the terrible attack in the Tower. Her thoughts even turned to Instructor Ava and Instructor Cara, and the guilt they must feel at the loss of Inionacha entrusted to their care by the Bearer.

Gwyneth took a sip of her tea, finding it much sweeter than she normally liked, but now it was comforting. She took another sip. "How long do Paladins train?"

Aedan stretched his legs toward the fire, crossing them at the ankles. His boots were well worn but impeccably clean. "All our lives. But if you are asking how long one must apprentice before taking the Oath, then the answer is a bit more complex." He settled back in his chair and took a swallow of his own tea. "Just like here with the Inionacha, we receive young ones of various ages, not necessarily children, but sometimes. Much of the time they are relations of current Paladins. More often they are nieces and nephews of those of the Blood."

"And it is the same Blood as the Inionacha, yes, but just from the male line?" Gwyneth asked. She still wasn't sure if she liked the idea of being deemed suitable just because of one's heritage. It smacked too much of something like the English monarchy. In Ireland, at least, chieftains proved themselves on the field of battle or in negotiations between clans.

"I can see that some of our reality might offend your Irish mettle," said Aedan with a grin. "That is not a bad thing at all." He sipped at his tea again. "Yes, you have the idea mostly right. Even Inionacha may become Paladins, if they so choose, but the half-century or so before the passing of the Sword is always a time fraught with danger for the Blood, especially the women of the Bearer's line."

"Why?" The simple question passed Gwyneth's lips before she could think better of it.

"There are forces in this world and others that would like nothing more than to possess the Caedbranr," replied Aedan. "And one of the most likely ways for that to happen would be for the Bearer to be killed with no successor able to take up the Sword, and an enemy close by to take possession of it."

"But the descendants of the Bearer are numerous," said Gwyneth, her brow creased in thought. "Any of the Inionacha could be the next Bearer."

"Though theoretically that may be true, it is well known that the Caedbranr is not just a weapon to be wielded by any of the Blood who happen to grasp it. It helps to choose the next Bearer as well, do you see?"

"No," Gwyneth answered truthfully. Another mouthful of tea travelled warmly into her stomach. She felt much better already, the conversation and the warmth of the fire and the tea building her defenses against the dark tides of despair still lapping at the edges of her consciousness.

"To put it bluntly, the Caedbranr has a mind of its own, Gwyneth," Aedan said.

"I…did not expect that," Gwyneth said. She wondered why Rionach had never spoken of it, and then immediately felt foolish. She couldn't imagine the tall, impenetrable Bearer explaining the intricacies of her relationship with the Sword to anyone at all, not even her successor.

"I do not think it is as strange as you may think," Aedan said. "But we should turn the conversation back to its original subject, I think. What else would you like to know about the Paladins?"

Gwyneth regained focus on her many questions about the Paladins, and she unabashedly used the opportunity to gain answers from Aedan. Rhys had always been so tight-lipped about the particularities of Paladin life, and she suspected that it had been so that she did not worry as Aedan revealed the bloody, struggling existence of the warriors sworn to protect both Faeortalam and Doendhtalam from the creatures of Darkness.

"But where do the creatures come from?" she asked. "Why not simply find their source and destroy it?"

"Where do pestilence and plague and sorrow in the mortal world come from, and why can we not eliminate those as well?" Aedan replied.

"I see," said Gwyneth, though the answer didn't quite satisfy her. "Who determines what missions the Paladins are assigned?"

"We have our own ways of knowing when and where there will be threats, and how serious they may be," Aedan answered. "We assign different Paladins, single or in teams, to the threats. There is a particularly useful map that one of our forebears created which tells us many of these things, and also tells us of the status of our Paladins in the field. It's quite magnificent."

Gwyneth thought that the map must be awe-inspiring for Aedan to say so; she didn't think he would be easily impressed. And then another thought struck her. "So, if a Paladin is wounded," she said slowly, "will that show on the map?"

"Sometimes," Aedan answered carefully. "In particular parts of Doendhtalam, other forces obscure the map's ability to track our Paladins. Eire is one of those places, because it is the convergence of many ancient powers."

Gwyneth swallowed the last of her tea, trying to think of how to phrase her question, but Aedan answered it for her anyway.

"We did not know Rhys had been wounded," he said. "The map did not show it to us."

"Those missions are more dangerous, aren't they?" Gwyneth asked quietly. "The ones where you can't see them."

"In a way," Aedan answered. "But we cannot always rush to the aid of a wounded Paladin. We are all taught to be self-sufficient, because there is always the possibility that no others will come to our aid. There are too few Paladins, and too many dangers. Sometimes there are none to rescue because they are all on their own missions."

Gwyneth thought of the Inionacha, studying and practicing swordsmanship and runes within the safety of the Hall while Paladins of their same age were hunting Dark creatures on their own. She swirled the dregs of her tea in her mug contemplatively.

The door opened, and Ed breathlessly bore a tray laden with food to the table. She set it down and whirled to face Gwyneth, her cheeks pink with exertion and excitement. "I just heard on the way back from the kitchens, Gwyneth. Audhild is awake!"

"I'll go to see her," Gwyneth said immediately, standing. She caught the edge of the look that passed between Aedan and Ed: gentle reproach from Aedan, and slight embarrassment from Ed in response.

"I should have waited to tell you that," Ed muttered, tugging at the end of her braid. "You should eat first."

"I should go see Audhild," Gwyneth said, shaking her head as she pulled on her boots. Aedan gave her a silent look. She remembered his words and took a deep breath. "But you're right, Ed. Thank you for bringing the food. I'll eat before I go down to see her."

"Good." Ed smiled.

They sat down at the table together, all three of them, and ate a quick but companionable meal. Gwyneth sensed Aedan's quiet approval, and she found herself happier for winning it. In the short time she'd known him, Aedan had won a place usually reserved for trusted Instructors and friends. They finished their meal and Ed brushed the crumbs from her hands.

"Let me braid your hair, and then we'll be off," she said.

Gwyneth nodded.

Aedan smiled. "I'll take my leave of you, ladies. I will find you later, Gwyneth, and we may continue our conversation, if you like."

"Thank you," Gwyneth said, and she was sure he understood the many layers of her thanks.

"Paladins do not forget it when someone saves one of their own," Aedan replied. He inclined his head to them, and then silently left the room.

"There," pronounced Ed in satisfaction. "Your clothes look perfectly fine – I tested a no-wrinkle rune on them, by the way, and it's worked quite well. You're presentable."

"You're the best, Ed," Gwyneth said, and she meant that too. She walked over to the bed and picked up her sword belt, buckling it about her waist.

"I know," Ed replied simply. "Come on then, let's go visit our fierce Northwoman."

Gwyneth smiled as they stepped into the hallway and Ed turned to sketch the closing runes on Gwyneth's door. They walked together down the hallway in companionable silence, the slight touch of their shoulders every few steps words enough for them both.

Chapter 21

Gwyneth heard the murmur in the room outside the healing ward before they entered. She braced herself as Ed opened the door and plunged into the sound with determined steps, her Norman accent strong as she issued commands to the knots of young women clogging the path to the door of the healing ward.

"Let us through, now, no need to crowd," Ed said, scattering a group of younger girls with a fierce look. Gwyneth realized the younger ones were staring at *her*, and that became its own problem as one after another turned to whisper to a companion and froze, wide-eyed, when they saw Gwyneth.

"She's one of us just as you are, so go on," said Ed, clucking her tongue and waving one arm at a clump of girls as though she were herding geese. Faced with Ed's authoritative onslaught, the young Inionacha scattered just as haphazardly as startled geese, too. Gwyneth found herself biting her cheek to keep from laughing, but then they were at the door to the healing ward, Ed shot one more stern look over her shoulder, and in the hush that followed they slipped into the cool dimness of the ward. Gwyneth instantly sobered as the smell of the healing ward enveloped them: the sharp scent of healing herbs mixed with wafts of steam from boiling water and the smell of freshly laundered bandages that Gwyneth had always found so difficult to describe. A sharp burst of homesickness pierced her chest, as it always did when the scents of her mother's healing embraced her as her mother never again would.

"Steady," murmured Ed.

"Gwyneth," said the Diligent who also served as the head healer. She had a broad, honest face that Gwyneth had instinctually trusted, with black hair that curled in wisps about her temples even when the rest was braided neatly or pinned in a bun at the nape of her neck. She nodded to Gwyneth, and then to Ed. "Edelinne. I thought I would see you two before the day was out."

"Martha," greeted Ed.

"Can we…how is she?" Gwyneth asked, feeling suddenly tongue-tied; then she remembered Audhild's bravery, her flashing eyes as she wielded a broken chair leg against the *syivhalla*. Taking a slow, steady breath, she drew back her shoulders. If Audhild could face that monster with nothing in her hands but a piece of wood, then Gwyneth could face whatever heart-wrenching sight awaited her.

"She still has a long road ahead of her," said Martha. "This soon after waking, I would not normally allow visitors, but she has asked for you, Gwyneth." The healer paused. "It seems that she wants to see you with her own eyes to be convinced that you survived."

Gwyneth nodded.

"As I said," continued Martha in a lower, softer voice, "it is still a long road."

"Even with healing runes?" Ed asked, frowning.

Martha looked at Ed in reproach. "Healing runes take a measure of *taebramh* from the person to whom they are applied. You know this, Edelinne."

Edelinne had known it, but Gwyneth knew from the look on Ed's face that she hadn't asked the question for her own benefit. She remembered her own dismissive words to Rhys as she stood at her window in her Walker-form. Even though her mouth went dry, she said the words again. "I have *taebramh* to spare."

"I cannot sanction you giving *taebramh* to another so soon after your own injury," Martha said firmly, shaking her head.

Gwyneth opened her mouth and then closed it as she saw the gleam in Ed's eyes. "I…understand." A little thrill coursed through her as Martha nodded, satisfied. The healer turned, and they followed her down the main aisle of the healing ward, passing several unused beds, the curtains at the front of the partition drawn back neatly to emphasize the beds' clean, well-pressed emptiness. Gwyneth couldn't remember which bed had been hers. It felt like a week since she had left the healing ward, even though it had barely been two days.

Martha led them to the last curtained room in the healing ward. There had been three other closed curtains, all on the other side, all nearer to the main entrance.

"I'd like Ed to come in with me," Gwyneth said quietly. "Just in case…I feel faint, or…"

"Nonsense," said Martha, shaking her head. "I'll come in, of course."

Gwyneth slid her eyes to Ed when Martha turned to pass through the curtain, catching the minute shake of Ed's head. They would work through the problem, Ed was saying. Gwyneth stepped through the curtain after Martha.

A novice healer, one of the younger girls who had chosen to apprentice recently, stood in one corner of the small curtained chamber, hands clasped in front of her.

"You may go, Nadia," Martha said with quiet authority. The girl bowed her flaxen head and slipped silently away.

Gwyneth knew from the set of Martha's shoulders and Ed's small intake of breath that it was bad. She steeled herself and stepped around Ed, gaining a clear view of the bed.

Bandages still covered a good portion of Audhild's face and neck, but Gwyneth saw enough to know that the Inionacha's scars would be beyond the skill of even rune-healers. The claws of the *syivhalla* had savaged the Northwoman's visage with that single blow: an angry wound, still stitched in some places, bisected Audhild's nose and drew the visible side of her mouth downward into an involuntary frown. Her left eye was covered by a neat roll of bandage, and Gwyneth knew with her healer's instinct that the eye may yet be lost. Another cut had laid open the brow above Audhild's undamaged eye, the healing wound already puckering her eyebrow. Bandages wrapped her throat and left ear. Gwyneth looked questioningly at Martha, but the other woman gave no sign that she understood Gwyneth's silent question. Ed motioned back toward the bed.

Gwyneth turned back to Audhild and found her awake, regarding Gwyneth with one glittering eye. The side of her savaged mouth turned up in something like a smile. Gwyneth stepped closer, to the edge of the bed.

"It's good to see you awake," Gwyneth said lamely after a long moment of silence.

Audhild swallowed visibly and said hoarsely, "It does not feel so good." Her eye flashed with her dry humor.

Gwyneth pushed down a sudden rush of emotion. Who was she to be feeling sorry for herself and wallowing in misery when Audhild could still make jokes from what might have been her deathbed? "I'm sure you'll be up and about in no time."

Audhild's mouth turned upward again. Her eye traveled to Martha. "A moment alone?" she rasped.

Somehow Martha seemed more willing to consider the request when it came from Audhild. The healer said finally, "A few moments, no more."

Ed made a show of turning to leave. Gwyneth winced at the effort it cost Audhild to say hoarsely, "Not you. Stay."

Martha disappeared outside the curtain. Ed sketched a quick rune in the air and then turned efficiently toward Audhild. "We can help heal you."

"That is not…why," Audhild said, but her eye gleamed with a feverish light.

"We'll do the healing rune first," said Ed in a whisper, bending close to both Audhild and Gwyneth, "and then you can tell us whatever it is you need to tell us." She shook her head as Audhild took a breath. "We know you're not strong enough yet for the healing rune on your own. That's why Gwyneth is here."

"I've never done this before," said Gwyneth, matching Ed's whisper. She felt compelled to say it aloud.

"You never Walked before yesterday either," fired back Ed. "Do you want to help or not?"

Gwyneth nodded. With an effort, Audhild held up one hand; Gwyneth grasped it with her own, Audhild's skin surprisingly cool to the touch.

"It should be fairly simple," Ed said in that same efficient whisper, her fingers already twitching as though she were rehearsing her runes. She withdrew a small, delicate glass jar from her belt purse. Gwyneth tried not to stare: when and where had her friend acquired such a fine little object? She knew Ed would explain later, though, so she turned her attention back to Ed's words. "Gwyn, you'll call up your *taebramh*. Audhild, you'll need to as well, in order to accept what Gwyneth is going to give you. Can you do that?"

Audhild gave a long, deliberate blink that Ed accepted to mean yes. She pulled the stopper from the small glass jar. "And then I'll put the runes on you with salve – it's more effective than just sketching skin-to-skin, I've done some experiments. Gwyn, you'll need to keep giving *taebramh* to her until I tell you, all right?"

Gwyneth gave a tight nod. She found herself transfixed by Audhild's gaze, her single ice-blue eye pale and wolfish in the dim light of the healing ward. She squeezed Audhild's hand, took a deep breath, and called up her *taebramh*. The hawk within her chest spread its wings and raised its head, fixing one sharp, predatory eye on Audhild. The fire of Gwyneth's *taebramh* flowed down her arm and into their joined hands.

"Call up your own, Audhild," said Ed sternly, her voice still not above a whisper.

The injured woman gasped and clenched her teeth, and Gwyneth felt answering warmth in Audhild's hand, flickering like a candle flame. Her own *taebramh* surged into it with something like delight. Audhild swallowed a sound that might have been of pain or pleasure. The edges of Gwyneth's vision went white with the fire of her *taebramh* and she fought to focus, the stare of Audhild's eye anchoring her. The moment stretched and swayed around them, long and bright and unbroken. Gwyneth felt Ed moving around her, movements quick and darting as a hummingbird, inking a rune on the visible patch of skin on Audhild's forehead and then another one on her throat, pulling down the neck of Audhild's shift to sketch yet another on the flat expanse of white skin below Audhild's collarbone.

When the runes activated, it took little effort to push *taebramh* into Audhild: Gwyneth felt something like a current pulling the *taebramh* from her body, but it did not worry her. Let Audhild take what was needed. She felt a measure of control that she hadn't known she possessed; she kept a firm grip on the shining rope of *taebramh* passing through her arm and meeting the faint flicker of Audhild's power. The wounded woman arched from the bed, her eye still locked upon Gwyneth's gaze, and Gwyneth added her own will to Ed's runes, telling Audhild to be healed, telling the lines assembled with masterful strokes to knit Audhild's flesh and ease her pain. Tiny white sparks flickered along the seam of the wound on Audhild's brow; the stitches fell away in black flecks of knotted thread as the cut sealed closed. Little curls of steam escaped from the edges of the bandages, as though the *taebramh* and the runes were healing Audhild by searing her torn flesh, cauterizing it with their power.

The hawk within Gwyneth's chest opened and closed its sharply curved beak, observing Audhild as it turned its head from side to side. Then Audhild shuddered and the runes on her forehead and neck flared brightly, then disappeared; the current pulling Gwyneth's *taebramh* vanished at the same instant, and then something hit her hand as Audhild's eye rolled back.

"Let go, let go," Ed hissed, nearly pushing Gwyneth off her feet.

Gwyneth raised both her hands to show Ed that she had, indeed, let go of her grip on Audhild's hand. A laugh bubbled up out of her unexpectedly. Ed rolled her eyes and turned back to Audhild, checking the injured woman's heartbeat and breathing.

"Didn't expect her to lose consciousness," she said matter-of-factly, tucking the glass jar back into her belt purse.

Gwyneth didn't need to ask whether it had worked. Ed brushed away the little knotted clumps of the discarded stitches, and as her fingers touched Audhild's face, the other woman awoke with a little gasp, her eye flaring wide.

"How do you feel?" Ed asked gently. Gwyneth heard an undercurrent of hunger in Ed's voice and saw it in the way that Ed leaned closer.

"Better," said Audhild in a much stronger voice. She paused, seeming to be evaluating her wounds. Gwyneth knew the feeling; she found herself flexing the fingers of her injured arm, assessing the tenderness of her own new scar.

Audhild took a deep breath and blinked several times. Then she pushed herself up to a sitting position in the bed. Ed smiled and looked at Gwyneth with triumph shining in her brown eyes. Gwyneth found herself smiling in return.

Then Ed's rune in the air by the curtain shimmered with a soft chime like a bell and dissipated. Ed quickly stepped back from the bed, taking up a position somewhere behind Gwyneth as though she were just an observer as she'd said she would be.

"Thank you for coming to see me," Audhild said to Gwyneth as Martha stepped through the curtain.

Gwyneth felt the tension as the healer paused, but she didn't look over her shoulder. That would be tantamount to admitting they had done something…but why did they have to hide what they'd just done? The question entered her mind and she just as quickly dismissed it.

"Of course," she answered Audhild. "I'll be back tonight, if you'd like."

"This afternoon?" Audhild said, a thread of hope and hunger in her voice.

"This afternoon," Gwyneth said with a nod.

"I think Audhild should rest now," Martha said in a cool voice. It was clear the healer had her suspicions, but she said nothing as she led them back to the door of the healing ward. She regarded them both for a moment and then spoke to Gwyneth. "It seems you do not need an observer after all. I expect you will come alone this afternoon."

Gwyneth nodded even as her cheeks flushed in anger for Ed at the callous dismissal, but Ed touched her elbow and they left the healing ward. The room beyond the door was nearly empty. Gwyneth wondered whether Martha had banished all of those Inionacha, too, but Ed simply said, "Noon meal." She touched Gwyneth's elbow again. "Come on."

As soon as the door of Gwyneth's chambers shut behind them and the runes flared to life before fading again, Ed turned to Gwyneth with a luminescent grin. "*C'est magnifique,* Gwyn! *Incroyable!*" She seized Gwyneth in a hard hug and then just as quickly released her, pacing about the room with feverish intensity. "I thought it would work, but I've never had the opportunity – I needed someone with a talent, with such a huge amount of *taebramh* that they could sustain the runes within *another person*!"

"You were just waiting for me to wake up, then?" Gwyneth asked dryly, raising an eyebrow.

"Well, not *exactly*," Ed answered guilelessly, "I was thinking of asking Aedan but I didn't think he'd approve. Orla seems to be the one of the two willing to take more risks, but she hasn't been seen much since she helped put down the *syivhalla*."

Gwyneth cleared her throat and pressed her lips together. She felt strangely put out that Ed had used her like a tool. Shouldn't she be grateful to her friend for helping Audhild?

"Gwyn, you should be *excited*," Ed said with that gleaming grin. "We just shortened Audhild's healing time by at least a *fortnight*. And the scars should be a bit less serious as well."

"Thank you for helping her," Gwyneth managed. She didn't understand her own reaction.

Ed paused and tilted her head to one side. "If I didn't know you better, Gwyn, I'd say that you were *jealous* that my runes worked." She smiled, really just some of her leftover grin spilling onto her lips again, but it lessened the sting of her words.

"No," Gwyneth said. She wasn't sure if she was lying. "I'm just…a bit tired." *That*, at least, wasn't a lie. She felt the dull-edged beginning of a headache behind her eyes. With an effort, she managed an answering smile. "I'm glad it worked. Really, I am. I'm just still…working through things."

Ed certainly couldn't argue with *that*, so her friend nodded, brown curls bouncing. "Understandable." She wrinkled her nose and turned, looking at the fire with a critical eye. The cold light of the winter noon sun filtered through the window, painting the room in icy hues.

"It's fine," Gwyneth said tiredly, even as Ed strode purposefully over to the fire and stacked two logs onto the coals, poking at it until little flames licked at the wood.

"Do you want to rest?" Ed asked, crossing her arms over her chest.

"I don't want to sleep," Gwyneth answered honestly. She had the feeling that her tiredness was not a great enough exhaustion to ward off nightmares.

"Well, then I'll make some tea. Are you hungry?" Ed busied herself with the kettle.

"There's enough left over from what you brought up," Gwyneth said, rousing herself enough to walk over to the table and make herself a plate of bread, cheese and meat.

"I avoid the dining hall as much as possible nowadays," Ed said. She turned to catch Gwyneth's eye. "You'll never guess who tried to talk to me the other day."

Gwyneth raised her eyebrows in silent question, her mouth full of her first bite.

"Mary." Ed shook her head as she said the name of their one-time archenemy.

Gwyneth nearly choked with laughter as she swallowed. "You look like you found a toad in your porridge."

"No, I just had to listen to one croak at me for the better part of evening meal two days ago," Ed replied in disgust.

"What did she want?" Gwyneth tried to imagine haughty Mary speaking to Ed of her own free will and failed. She realized, though, that their feud with Mary felt like it was years in the past, her memories of it overlaid with a childish sheen. Every insult had seemed sharper then, every barbed word penetrating more deeply without the hard carapace of confidence that eventually grew to be their protection.

Ed shrugged. "Wanted to somehow cozy up to me, I think." She glanced at Gwyneth. "Probably because she thought I was the easiest way to get to you."

Gwyneth snorted and took another bite.

"No, really," Ed said. "Like I said, you're important."

"What did you say to her?"

"I told her she was still a toad." Ed tried to suppress her grin and failed, hiding it instead by busying herself with building a sandwich from her bread and meat.

Gwyneth made sure to swallow this time before allowing herself to laugh. The sound startled her at first, but then she relaxed. A shadow fell away from the back of her mind. She could still laugh, even though she mourned. The two were not mutually exclusive.

"Let me know how Audhild feels after you go to visit her this afternoon?" The kettle whistled, and Ed hopped to her feet.

"I can get that, you know," Gwyneth said.

"I know," Ed replied, making no move to relinquish the task as she retrieved the kettle and inspected the mugs on the table with a critical eye.

"Ed," Gwyneth said quietly. Her friend turned at the softness of Gwyneth's voice. "Thank you for helping Audhild. It means a lot to her and it also means a lot to me." She paused and looked into Ed's brown eyes, willing her to understand. "You keep saying I'm important, and I want you to know this. *You're* important. To me."

Two spots of color appeared high on Ed's freckled cheeks.

"No matter what happens," Gwyneth continued, "you'll always be like a sister to me, Ed."

Uncertainty flickered in Ed's eyes, just enough for Gwyneth to see. But then Ed smiled. "I know," she said brightly, turning back to pour the tea.

They finished their meal in silence, and sat drinking their tea, watching the fire crackle in the hearth and the shadows lengthen.

"I should go," said Ed finally. "I told Aine I'd practice silencing runes with her tonight."

"And I should go visit Audhild again," said Gwyneth.

They looked at each other for a long moment. Then Ed nodded briskly and set out for the door. She was gone before Gwyneth could think of anything to say. As she pulled on her boots, she wondered why it was so difficult sometimes to understand if something was ending or beginning.

Chapter 22

A familiar tapping at the windowpane brought Gwyneth out of her thoughts. She unfolded her legs and stood, taking a deep breath and stretching before padding over to the window. Moonlight silvered the snow blanketing the roof of the Hall and turrets of the Tower visible beyond the window. Gwyneth saw with a little jolt of surprised pleasure not one but two Glasidhe auras shimmering on the sill.

Togha and Caonach slipped into the room on the heels of a wintry chill. Gwyneth pulled the window closed behind them, the cold air running fingers up her arm. The two Glasidhe wore tiny fur-lined capes, open at the back to allow for their wings, the hoods drawn up over their heads.

"It is always a fine line between dressing too heavily and enduring the cold," pronounced Caonach, flicking a bit of melting snow from his wings. Togha pushed back the hood of her cape and combed her fingers through her hair with tiny, dexterous fingers.

"Come and warm yourselves by the fire," Gwyneth said. "It's good to see you."

She held out a flat hand to the two Glasidhe, as was only polite after their flight through the icy night to visit her. They stepped onto her palm, the soles of their boots little shocks of cold against her skin.

"We would have visited earlier," said Caonach, "after we heard about the attack, but we also heard that you survived, and we were busy with messages for the Solstice."

"And we heard Rhys was already here," Togha added with a devilish grin.

"He was," said Gwyneth. "Or rather, he still is, but they've been keeping him busy as well."

She rested her hand on the seat of the second chair by the fire, and the two Glasidhe stepped daintily from her palm.

"Dark business, the deaths of Inionacha," said Caonach, shaking out his cloak and then shedding it with particular care for his wings.

Gwyneth pressed her lips together as she sat down in her own chair. A spark of anger flared in her chest, struck by the flint of Caonach's words against her grief. But rather than let it burgeon into a flame, she took a breath and said quietly, "I still feel very sad about it."

"As you should, as you should," said Togha, leaping over with barely a flutter of her wings to land on Gwyneth's knee.

The slight weight of the loyal Glasidhe comforted Gwyneth and helped smother the spark of anger.

"Do you have a message for me?" Gwyneth asked, just to say something.

"No," said Caonach, shaking his head.

"We came to visit *you*," said Togha, walking delicately across Gwyneth's thigh to touch her arm.

"I…thank you," said Gwyneth. "That means a lot to me, it really does."

"We will always extend our friendship to you, Lady Gwyneth," said Caonach, his voice solemn. "No matter what the future brings, we will always be your loyal friends."

Togha pressed both hands to Gwyneth's bare skin and nodded.

"Thank you," Gwyneth said automatically. Then she straightened. "Why did you just call me *Lady*? You've known me since before I came to the Hall. You helped me save Rhys' life. There's no need for that."

"You are the next Bearer," Togha said, patting her arm. "It is only right we show you respect."

"Not when it's just us," Gwyneth said firmly. "If we are among others, then I understand, but not when we're alone, all right?" She felt as though she were standing on the edge of a precipice, staring down at roiling unknown waters.

"As you wish," Caonach said gracefully.

They sat in silence for a few moments. Gwyneth watched the firelight reflect in iridescent fractals on the Glasidhe's beautiful dragonfly wings.

"I'm forgetting myself," she said finally, remembering her manners. "You must be hungry after your flight."

"We could perhaps eat a small morsel," Togha said with delicate courtesy, but Gwyneth didn't miss the way that they both straightened at the possibility of food.

In a gesture that was so familiar as to be nearly unconscious, Gwyneth put out a hand to Togha and gently transferred the Glasidhe to her shoulder. Togha grasped the curve of Gwyneth's ear for balance as Gwyneth stood and made her way over to the table. She was glad of the habit she'd developed of keeping enough food for two meals in her chamber, encouraged by her near-constant visitors. Her room did not entirely feel like her own any more, but Gwyneth supposed that was better than feeling alone.

She set out a small portion of bread, a small jar of honey and some cheese. "I don't have any sweets, but I could go fetch some," she said, thinking of the Glasidhe's fondness for any type of pastry or candy.

"This will do quite well, thank you," Caonach said, landing gracefully on the table and wasting no time in untying the bit of twine that held in place the cloth over the honey jar. Togha hopped from her shoulder and began cutting small, precise squares from a piece of bread.

Gwyneth watched the small Fae begin their concentrated destruction of a good portion of the food. They ate with focused intent, wings quivering every now and again with pleasure. The sight brought a slight smile to Gwyneth's face, but she knew it was rude to stare at them, though her friends likely wouldn't reprimand her. Instead, she fetched one of the chairs from near the hearth, drawing it to a small distance from the table.

"One of the Seven who was injured, Audhild, she told me something very strange yesterday," she said into the silence. She hadn't even spoken to Ed about Audhild's words, and Rhys was nowhere to be found.

"She is awake?" said Caonach, pausing in his single-minded consumption. "That is good."

"Yes," agreed Gwyneth. "Ed and I…well, mostly Ed…we helped heal her with some runes."

"You are always looking to help," said Togha approvingly.

"It takes no small skill to heal with runes," added Caonach. "But why two of you? Usually it is just one healer who applies the runes."

"Well, neither of us are healers, really – I mean, I know what I learned from my mother in Doendhtalam, of course, but everything is different here." Gwyneth paused. "Audhild did not have enough *taebramh* of her own to sustain the runes, and Ed thought that I could give her enough of my own *taebramh* for the runes to work."

Caonach gazed up at her solemnly. "That takes no small skill, either," he repeated.

"But we are not surprised," said Togha with half a shrug and a grin. She flicked one wing as she looked at her brother. "Or at least, *I* am not. You are singular, Gwyneth, and that is why you are the next Bearer."

Gwyneth felt her face heat. "Does everyone know this?"

"Not *everyone*," said Togha. "The *ulfdrengr* probably do not, and perhaps not the Merrow as well."

"So all the Sidhe know?" Gwyneth felt a pit opening in her stomach. Why was it that she was the last to be told such things?

"The Queens have a way of knowing such things, and then their Three know, and then those close to the Three, and so on," Caonach explained in a helpful tone.

Gwyneth sighed. "I see."

"But tell us these important words from your companion," Caonach continued.

Gwyneth sat back in her chair. "Audhild told me that the others of the Seven...that *she* thinks they were simply the strongest of the rest of the Inionacha, placed around me to protect me."

Both Glasidhe stopped eating, turning to face her. Togha folded her legs and sat with her hands on her knees, and Caonach folded his arms over his chest.

"If that's true," Gwyneth continued quietly, "I think that means that the Bearer and the Instructors suspected that there would be an attack." She couldn't bring herself to say that they *knew* about it. *That* betrayal would be a dagger in her heart. As it was, the idea that Brita, Catherine, Aine, Isabella, Valerie and Audhild were simply drawn around Gwyneth to protect her, to die in her place if necessary...she felt bile rising in her throat. "The thought of it makes me sick," she managed, her words choked. "Catherine and Brita are *dead.* Isabella lost a hand. Audhild may still lose an eye, and even if she doesn't, her life will never be the same."

"Did the others know?" Caonach asked softly. "The other women."

"I don't know," Gwyneth admitted. "Audhild said that she and Aine had their suspicions." A terrible thought occurred to her. "If...if they *did* know, if they'd already been told that I was Rionach's successor, then Brita would have seen the *syivhalla* as her only opportunity to become the Bearer." She paused, swallowing against another wave of nausea.

"Whatever they knew, and whatever they were told, it is not your fault, Gwyneth," Togha said, leaping from the table to Gwyneth's shoulder and touching her ear with both hands. "It is not your fault," the fierce little Glasidhe repeated, urgency in her voice.

"Why didn't they have the Paladins here, if they thought there would be an attack?" Gwyneth said through numb lips. She wanted to ask Rhys how much he'd known. She felt as though everyone except her had been told of this danger.

"They did," Caonach replied seriously. "Aedan and Orla do not just make social calls to the Hall of the Inionacha."

"You cannot change what has happened," Togha said, her voice laced with sadness. "No matter how you wish it, you cannot change the past."

"Catherine will still be dead, and Brita remembered as a traitor, and Isabella learning to use her other hand." Gwyneth heard the savage bitterness in her voice and did not care at all.

"Yes," said Caonach unflinchingly.

"They should have told me," Gwyneth growled.

"Why?" Caonach asked.

"Because if people are going to risk their lives for me, I should know of it," Gwyneth said, standing. Togha grabbed her ear for balance. "Sorry," she apologized for the sudden movement, receiving a forgiving pat on the ear in return.

"It still would not have changed anything, except perhaps your own actions," said Caonach.

"I feel like I'm hitting my head against a wall," Gwyneth said, crossing her arms over her chest. "It doesn't…it doesn't *feel* right."

"When you are the Bearer," said Caonach, "you will be a protector. You are a protector now, Gwyneth, though it is hard for you to see. Perhaps you should think of it a different way. You saved the lives of all the other Inionacha by holding the *syivhalla* at bay until Paladin Orla broke through the curse on the Tower door, did you not?"

"How do you know that?"

"It is our profession to know many things about many people," replied Togha.

"The deaths would have been greater in number if you had not been there, Gwyneth," pressed Caonach.

"The attack would not have happened at all if I had not been there," countered Gwyneth.

"The creature did not know its target," said Caonach with his unflappable calm. "It attacked blindly until it fixed its sights on you, because you were the strongest. *Are* the strongest."

"That means there was no way to stop it," said Gwyneth slowly. She paced in front of the fire, its warmth dancing against one side of the body and then the other as she turned.

"There will always be Dark creatures seeking to destroy the good and strong, in this world and in all others," said Togha.

"It feels like being defeated before I've even had a chance to fight." Gwyneth felt unexpected tears prickling at the corners of her eyes.

"No," Togha said into her ear fiercely. "You won against that creature, Gwyneth. You did not let it kill you, and you did not let it kill the others, once it turned its attention to you. That is a *victory*."

"No victory comes without cost," said Togha gravely.

Gwyneth sighed and sat down in the chair by the hearth, careful this time not to jar Togha. "If everyone knows that I am the next Bearer, then why still have the Hall of the Inionacha?"

Her *taebramh* spread its wings beneath her collarbone. Despite her sorrow, a hard sense of pride and determination filled her chest. *She was the next Bearer.* She had known it in her bones since leaving Doendhtalam, but it was another thing altogether to hear it spoken with such a casual ring of truth by those she trusted.

"Soon there may not be a Hall of the Inionacha," said Caonach almost gently.

"Change will take hold," said Togha, her voice nearly dreamlike. "With a new Bearer always comes change."

"It is always a cause for great celebration," added Caonach.

"For being the next Bearer, I don't know much about how it happens," mused Gwyneth.

"Lady Rionach will pass the Caedbranr to you," replied Togha.

"You make it sound very simple."

"In a way, it is," she said.

"But..." said Gwyneth slowly. "What will happen to Rionach?"

"She will return to the stars," said Togha with a sigh.

"She will...you mean she'll *die*?"

"There cannot be *two* Bearers," pointed out Caonach with a sensible air.

"Well, no, I understand that," said Gwyneth, "but...she'll die right after passing the Sword to me?"

"We have not seen the ceremony ourselves, so we do not rightly know," confessed Togha. "But that is the story of the last passing of the Sword."

"Lady Rionach has held the Sword for nigh on five centuries," said Caonach. "It is many years for one soul to endure. She may look forward to the peace of her rest."

"I haven't thought of it quite in that way," admitted Gwyneth.

"It is difficult to think beyond the edge of your own destiny," replied the diminutive messenger.

"Neither of you were alive when the Sword was passed to Rionach?"

Togha laughed, a sound that rippled over Gwyneth like a cascade of small bells ringing. Caonach chuckled, his mirth closer to the sound of a brook chattering over smooth rocks.

"Sometimes we forget that you have only known of this world for barely two full years," Togha said with indulgent affection.

"It feels like I've been here longer," Gwyneth replied, staring into the hearth. "When I first saw Rhys, I didn't recognize him at first because he seemed so much *older*. I didn't believe he'd only been gone for the handful of years he'd been away from the village." She shifted in her chair, feeling the ache of her still-healing arm. "Now I understand. I feel older."

"You have learned much," said Caonach.

"And you have *done* much," chimed Togha.

"But that's just it," said Gwyneth. She felt the lull of sleep settling over her shoulders again like a mantle, urging her eyes to close. With an effort, she stood and paced before the fire. "I haven't really *done* anything. Until the *syivhalla*, all I've done is study here in the Hall. I've learned swordsmanship and history, theory and runecraft and geography, but I haven't really *done* anything at all."

Togha clicked her tongue against her teeth. "Nonsense," she chirped. "These are all very important things! How is one to be Bearer if one does not know how to handle a sword?"

Togha's laugh sounded different to Gwyneth – forced, she realized. She looked over to the Glasidhe. Caonach stood in a thoughtful pose, arms folded over his chest, wings rotating slowly in the way that Glasidhe often moved when deep in contemplation.

"This isn't the true Faeortalam," Gwyneth continued, forging into her thoughts with renewed vigor because Caonach had not contradicted her. "Yes, I'm *in* Faeortalam, I've *learned* of Faeortalam, but I haven't truly experienced it. Except for the Paladins' Samhain celebration."

The memory brought a small smile to her lips despite the gravity of the conversation. She wondered briefly if Orla would humor her and grant her another match, blade against blade.

"But the Inionacha must be protected," said Togha in half-hearted protest, looking to her brother for support and fluttering her wings in agitation when he remained silent.

"How is keeping us away from the world protecting us?" said Gwyneth, shaking her head. "And how is training dozens of girls away from their families doing any sort of good when apparently the Bearer can pluck a second daughter to be the next Bearer anyway?"

"It is...*tradition*," replied Togha, somewhat weakly.

"I see more sense in the Paladin way of life than I do the Inionacha," said Gwyneth firmly, lifting her chin against the tremble of doubt in her chest. Who was she to question the traditions that Rionach had built over her centuries as the Bearer of the Sword?

"If all daughters of the Blood were to take up the blade of a Paladin, then perhaps there would be none left to bear the Caedbranr," pointed out Caonach.

Gwyneth recognized his tone from Instructor Ava's classes: Instructor Ava often opined on viewpoints that were actually contradictory to her own true beliefs, solely to force her students to articulate the reasons behind their own stances.

"There are countless daughters of the Blood, at this point," Gwyneth said, almost dismissively.

"That will change very soon," murmured Caonach.

Gwyneth frowned. "What do you mean? There will still be many of the Blood, even when I…when I become Bearer." It was the first time she'd actually spoken the words aloud.

"The Sword calls most strongly to direct descendants of the Bearer," said Togha.

It took a long moment for the meaning of Togha's words to seep into Gwyneth's understanding. A little shiver ran through her, and then she straightened her shoulders. "Well," she said. "There are many women my own age in my village who have had two or three children by now."

She wondered with brief and excruciating clarity if her mother had midwifed any of the births, and if any of the mothers or babes had died. Experience told her that at least three or four out of every dozen births went badly for the mother or babe.

"It will be easier for you," said Togha, drifting through the air to land on Gwyneth's shoulder again. She patted Gwyneth's ear. "The Caedbranr eases the way for the child, and the Sidhe consider it a great honor to assist the Bearer in the birth of one of her children."

"What if I don't have any daughters?" Gwyneth asked, even as she imagined a little girl with her golden hair and Rhys' gray eyes, her lips curved in an innocent version of Rhys' half-smile. A thrill of warmth ran through her at the thought of bearing Rhys' children, even as a parallel current of something like panic rippled down her limbs.

"You will have daughters," said Caonach with such conviction that Gwyneth nearly asked him if the Glasidhe were ever gifted with the Sight.

"This is certainly much to think about," said Togha.

"Yes," agreed Gwyneth, running one hand down her braid.

"Perhaps you should return to sleep," suggested Caonach.

"We will watch over you," Togha piped.

"There are runes on the door," said Gwyneth with a small shrug. She poked at the embers of the fire and settled another log atop the coals, watching until new flames licked the curls of bark. "No need to set a watch."

She padded back to the window to check that she'd latched it after opening it for the Glasidhe, and then she gratefully slid back into her bed. Togha leapt neatly from her shoulder as she wriggled under the quilt. Most of the warmth had seeped away, but she didn't mind the coolness of the bed sheets against her skin.

"You're welcome to stay as long as you'd like," she said, a yawn marbling her words. She'd long ago ceased to worry about any rules about visitors set by the Instructors.

"We may stay until the snow abates," said Caonach, hovering by the window.

Gwyneth laid her head down on her pillow. She felt Togha's small hands stroke her hair.

"We are very proud to be counted among your friends," murmured the Glasidhe, so softly that Gwyneth thought she might have imagined it as she slid into sleep's welcoming, warm darkness.

Chapter 23

To Gwyneth's surprise and delight, Togha and Caonach announced the next morning that they would be staying a sennight, perhaps longer.

"There are always messages to be taken," said Togha with a flick of her wing, "but there are always other messengers willing to take them."

"We would like to help you prepare for your journey," said Caonach in his solemn way.

"Journey?" repeated Gwyneth through a mouthful of bread and jam. Despite the tangle of conflicting emotions that still roiled her chest every so often – anger, grief, frustration, impatience – her appetite had returned full force. Her body seemed to be trying to compensate for her time spent Walking and her missed meals; she'd have to begin practicing her bladework with real intensity again soon, she thought, or risk losing her strength and skill amid this prodigious new appetite.

"To the Unseelie celebration of the Midwinter Solstice," said Togha as she zipped in a dizzying circle around Gwyneth's head.

Finishing her slice of bread, Gwyneth checked the kettle and found it hot enough. She brought it over to the table carefully, setting it on the small woven mat that kept it from scorching the table.

"What makes you think," she said as she poured the hot water into the teapot that had mysteriously appeared on her table during her convalescence, "that I'm still going to the Solstice? It's in what, ten days?"

"Nine," replied Togha cheerfully.

Gwyneth shook her head. "I don't think so. Wouldn't Rionach have sent word if that was her intention? Especially after the attack..."

She glanced up as she heard footsteps in the hallway outside her door, and the soft clicking sound that indicated someone drawing the unlocking runes on the door. As she finished pouring a second cup of tea, Edelinne burst into the room.

"Good morning, Ed," Gwyneth said, pushing the mug toward her friend.

"Knew you'd have tea ready," Ed said in satisfaction. She held out a sealed square of parchment toward Gwyneth. "Just arrived for you. Oh good, there's jam and bread, too. Hello, Togha, Caonach."

The Glasidhe exchanged greetings with Ed as Gwyneth examined the wax seal on the folded missive: the wax was shimmering midnight blue, imprinted with a crescent moon and star encircled by a delicate wreath of flowers.

"I think it's from the Unseelie Court," said Ed, pointing to the seal. "There are runes here, and here, see?"

"I don't," said Gwyneth truthfully, "but I trust you know your runes. I don't need a rune to unlock it, do I?"

Ed shook her head as she took a bite of her jam-slathered bread. "That's the *purpose* of the rune, that only the person meant to receive the message will be able to open it."

"Clever," said Gwyneth.

"The Unseelie are very clever," agreed Caonach.

"And sometimes very cruel," added Togha in an undertone, giving a little flicker of her wings that looked almost like a shudder.

"How encouraging," murmured Gwyneth. She slid her finger beneath the seal and delicately opened the missive. A faint floral scent wafted from the parchment, and somehow, she knew it was a night-blooming flower. What else would the Queen of Night and Winter use for her perfume?

Words appeared on the parchment as though burning in silver flame, delicate yet slightly unnerving in the realistic ferocity of the wavering fire. Gwyneth read the message twice, blinking away the imprints of the bright-burning letters.

Ed made a small sound of impatience. "Well?"

"It is rude to ask another the content of their message," Togha told Ed seriously.

"It's an invitation," said Gwyneth. "To the Solstice celebration at the Unseelie Court."

"I knew it," said Ed smugly, licking jam from one finger and sitting back in her chair. "I bet Rhys that you'd be invited."

"When did you see Rhys?" Gwyneth asked quickly. She felt her heart jump a little in her chest and hoped that her burning cheeks weren't *too* obvious.

"Oh, he'll be up here soon enough, don't worry," Ed replied, holding her mug of tea in both hands. "He just got back from running a message to one of the southern *ulfdrengr* outposts. They keep a few of their younger warriors near the City, you know, to receive word from the Queens and the Paladins."

"But the *ulfdrengr* do not bend the knee to either Queen," said Gwyneth.

"Neither do we," said Togha primly.

"You have more sense than that," said Ed with a sticky grin.

"Ed," said Gwyneth, raising her eyebrows in surprise.

"What?" Ed shrugged. "It's no secret that there are those who'd rather live their lives without the yoke of a monarch." She leveled a look at Gwyneth. "Thought you'd understand, what with your people in Eire fighting the English for so long."

"It was a distant fight for us," replied Gwyneth after a moment. "My village was far enough north in the Pale that we'd only get occasional English travelers. Mostly monks trying to convert us." She shrugged. "Mother didn't allow them to sleep by the hearth. It was one of the only times I remember her withholding hospitality to travelers." After a pause, she added, "That, and Rhys."

"Both of them could have taken you away from her, and one did," Ed replied sagely, ruining the solemn effect by licking jam from her fingers.

"Your mother should not have tried to hide you," said Caonach, his wings fluttering.

"We were watching over you anyway," said Togha, sitting cross-legged by the jam jar.

Gwyneth didn't know what to say to that, so she said nothing. She held the Unseelie invitation between two fingers, feeling the fine, heavy weight of the parchment. "I suppose I should speak to Ava and Cara about the Solstice." She felt a little prickle of anger at her Instructors. Her *taebramh* stirred behind her breastbone.

"They probably already know," said Ed, leaning back in her chair. "The others will be jealous."

"No more jealous than they've been, knowing that I'm the heir to the Sword," muttered Gwyneth.

Ed chuckled. "That's where you're wrong. They're much more jealous than that, Gwyn. There will be so many *interesting* people at the Solstice – *ulfdrengr* and Merrow, Seelie and Unseelie, perhaps even Seafarers – though they prefer to keep to their ships," she added thoughtfully.

"I'm going to feel like such a dullard," said Gwyneth in an undertone, looking into the fire and feeling uncertainty rise miserably in her chest.

"Stop that," Ed said sharply.

Gwyneth looked at her friend in surprise. Ed stood and brushed invisible crumbs from her shirt, crossing her arms over her chest.

"You're the next Bearer," Edelinne said firmly, her brown eyes hard with resolve. "*They* should be grateful they get the chance to meet *you*." She moved her chin in a little nod. "You'll see, Gwyn. You'll see when they meet you."

"It doesn't *feel* – *I* don't feel..." Gwyneth shrugged.

"Particularly spectacular?" Ed suggested, a glint of mischief softening her eyes.

"Something like that," she allowed with a smile.

"But you *are*," protested Togha, leaping from the table in a blur of blue sparks. "You are the most singular Inionacha we have seen in centuries, and you are the next Bearer!"

"It's all very well to say that here," said Gwyneth, glancing around the familiar comfort of her chamber, "but...out there?" She pressed her lips together.

"Queen Mab would not have invited you if she did not want to meet you," pointed out Caonach reasonably.

"That in itself is terrifying," said Gwyneth. She suppressed a little shudder, thinking of the tales of the brilliant, beautiful Unseelie Queen, her glittering Court and the lovely ladies and Knights whose starlit allure sharpened into cold cruelty when they were displeased.

"You'll be with the Bearer," Ed said reasonably. "And perhaps a few Paladins." She poured herself more tea. "Though who would try to attack you in the stronghold of the Unseelie Queen, I don't know."

"The same who tried to attack me in the stronghold of the Inionacha," replied Gwyneth grimly. She set the folded square of parchment down on the edge of the table. Silvery smoke abruptly curled from its edges, little tongues of moon-hued fire licking the parchment into nothingness, leaving no trace of ash.

"Well," said Ed, her eyebrows slowly returning to their normal height. "I'm going to go to the library. We should read up on the Merrow and the *ulfdrengr*."

"We've been studying them – we *were* studying them, in the Tower with Ava," said Gwyneth, a sudden tiredness overtaking her.

"Then I'll speak to Instructor Ava. Perhaps she wishes to hold lessons with you herself."

"Then she can come and tell me as much herself," said Gwyneth rebelliously.

Ed sighed. "Really, Gwyn, you can't stay mad at everyone forever."

"Try me," muttered Gwyneth.

Ed shook her head and drained the last of her tea. "Thanks for tea. You should come down and practice in the courtyard with Aine and everyone, today after noon meal."

"Aren't there lessons after noon meal?"

"There haven't been lessons since the attack."

"Oh." Gwyneth felt foolish for not knowing that the entirety of the Hall had been holding its breath after the attack in the Tower. Perhaps everyone *did* care. She shifted, watching the log in the fire. "Maybe I'll come down," she said finally.

"Good," pronounced Ed with a note of satisfaction in her voice. She motioned with her chin toward the sword on the wall by Gwyneth's bed. "Bring that blade."

"I always thought that the Instructors would tell us when we could wield our chosen blades," Gwyneth replied.

"I'm not an Instructor, but I know it's time for you to pick up that blade," replied Ed enigmatically. Without waiting on Gwyneth's reply, she turned and left. The sound of the door closing behind Ed left Gwyneth feeling very alone.

"I feel like I should be excited about the invitation to the Solstice," she said finally into the silence. "But..." She shrugged. "I'm not."

"There is much for you to understand, and too much for you to feel all at once," said Caonach.

"One thing at a time," suggested Togha, landing on Gwyneth's shoulder.

It felt odd, not to have a set schedule after the years of regimented schooling. Gwyneth walked over to the books stacked on the corner of the table and chose one about the Merrow that she thought looked at least a little interesting. She should have told Ed that she already had books to read for the Solstice, she realized; but perhaps there were different tomes in the larger library available to all the Inionacha.

"Have you ever met a Merrow?" she asked Togha as she settled by the fire and rested the edge of the book on her knee.

"Certainly," said Togha. "I carried a message to one, once."

Gwyneth paused before opening the book. "What are they like?"

"Oh, they are very fierce and beautiful and proud," said Togha. "But they are also very adventuresome and wild, and they are not so cruel as the Sidhe toward those who are not like them."

"They live in the oceans beyond the Seelie land," said Gwyneth. "Out beyond Queensport."

"Yes," said Togha. Gwyneth heard the nod in the Glasidhe's voice. "They have a treaty with the Seelie and the Unseelie both, though the Seelie trade with them much more than the Unseelie just by virtue of Queensport."

"What do they trade?" Gwyneth asked, though she already knew some of the answer from her studies with the Seven.

"Oh, treasures from the sea, of course," replied Togha. "Many beautiful things that you cannot find except in the deepest waters."

Gwyneth thought of the glimmering Merrow shell on the shelf of the Tower. "And their shells, do they trade those?"

"Never," replied Togha solemnly. "The shells of the Merrow are sacred. They never trade their shells."

Gwyneth felt the brush of Togha's wings against her neck.

"They have used their shells to seal great promises and peaces," continued Togha. "It is said that the shell of a Merrow is the sincerest proof of their good intentions."

"Because of the powers that the shell can impart?"

"Yes," replied Togha. "It would be like…it would be like giving our wings to someone, if we could do such a thing. It is very…intimate."

"Embracing them as part of you," said Gwyneth slowly.

"Yes."

"We learned with Instructor Ava about the tribes of the Merrow," continued Gwyneth. Somehow, she wanted to talk rather than read. Her fingertips brushed the pebbled leather cover of the book on her lap in silent apology.

"They have their warriors and their scholars and their rulers, just as the Sidhe and mortals do," said Caonach.

"Yes, but they are *born* into it," said Gwyneth. "If I remember correctly, the outward markings of a Merrow tell their heritage."

"It is not so different from the Seelie and Unseelie," replied Caonach. "But very different from mortals."

Togha gave a bright little laugh. "Not *so* different! After all, do you not look at each other and know what part of the world from whence you come?"

"Sometimes," admitted Gwyneth, thinking of Edelinne's dark Norman coloring and Audhild's distinctive pale complexion and ice-blue eyes.

"It is perhaps natural to look at differences," continued Caonach, "but would it not be easier sometimes to look for the similarities?"

"Easier in what way?" Gwyneth asked, furrowing her brow in thought.

"Too much strife starts with simple misunderstandings," Caonach said. "We watch and we learn, because we are often forgotten because we are small."

Gwyneth didn't fully understand, but she heard herself say, "I'll keep that in mind when I am Bearer." She smiled. "And *I* will never forget you."

"We know," said Togha, tugging affectionately on the fleshy part of Gwyneth's ear.

Gwyneth spent the rest of the morning reading in companionable silence with the Glasidhe. Togha busied herself tidying the room in increments, despite Gwyneth telling her there was no need; and Caonach selected one of the smaller books from the stack on the table, turning each page with both hands and using an overturned mug as a platform so he could read more easily.

When the chimes for the noon meal sounded, Gwyneth stacked the books neatly on the edge of the table and changed into a shirt that would be suitable for practicing bladework. She paused by her bed. The sword on the wall gleamed. She reached up and grasped it, taking it down from where it had been hung for the years since she had come to the Hall. Its hilt fit in her hand as though she had always handled this sword, and at the foot of her bed she found a black scabbard sitting on the wooden trunk. The scabbard was not attached to a belt; rather, it was a bandolier meant to be worn across the chest, the strap made of soft leather with several pouches sewn into it for utility's sake.

Gwyneth slid the blade into the black scabbard and looped the bandolier over her head. She thought she heard one of the Glasidhe draw in their breath sharply as she settled the bandolier across her chest and the sword across her back, but they said nothing as she turned toward the door.

Gwyneth paused, her hand touching the doorknob. "Will you be here when I get back?"

"We have other messages to deliver," said Caonach, almost apologetically.

Gwyneth smiled. "I'm glad you visited. Thank you."

"Of course," said Caonach.

The two Glasidhe hovered in the middle of the room as Gwyneth looked at them fondly.

"Perhaps we will see you at the Solstice," piped Togha in a voice that sounded uncharacteristically choked with emotion. Gwyneth saw her touch her brother's arm, and she understood with a flash of clarity that the Glasidhe had urged her to wear this blade, the blade that looked very much like the Sword that the Bearer wore in just this manner. They were seeing her much like she would look as the Bearer, and her fondness for them only grew as she recognized the protective pride in their gazes.

"We will see each other there," Gwyneth said to them with a smile, and then she turned toward the door.

Chapter 24

The rest of the Inionacha reacted much like the Glasidhe upon seeing Gwyneth with the blade across her back for the first time. A collective hush fell over the dining hall when she walked in for the noon meal, persisting even as Gwyneth took her usual seat near Edelinne and Aine. Instructor Cara smiled directly at her and even Instructor Ava gave her a look that Gwyneth thought was approving before gesturing to the young women to begin their meal.

"I knew it was time for you to wear it," Ed said in an undertone that was only slightly smug.

"It's just a plain blade like all of you wear," replied Gwyneth.

"Perhaps," said Ed obliquely, "but it's the *way* you're wearing it, Gwyn."

"This was what was given to me." Gwyneth wondered when exactly the black scabbard and bandolier had appeared in her room.

"Exactly. Will you pass the stew, please?"

Gwyneth had thought that the other Inionacha had treated her differently once she had been named one of the Seven; *now*, with her wearing of the sword on her back, it was as though she'd given some invisible signal that it was permissible for them to openly wear their expressions of awe, pride and perhaps a bit of jealousy. She found herself concentrating on her food with unusual vigor, because each time she looked up, she met the star-struck eyes of one or another of the young women who'd once been her schoolmates and some, her friends.

Aine, thankfully, managed to act as though nothing were particularly unusual. "Did you hear, Gwyneth, that Cara is fitting Isabella for a new hand today?"

"A new hand?" Gwyneth repeated with genuine interest.

"Aye," replied Aine, "she won't be able to wear it for some time yet, but they'll at least have it crafted for her when she's healed enough."

"I haven't visited her," said Gwyneth with a bit of guilt.

"She hasn't been seeing many," said Aine. "But you were able to help Audhild, and that is something the rest of us couldn't manage." She ladled a second helping of stew into her bowl.

Gwyneth risked a glance down the long table. "There are many empty seats."

"Yes," said Aine, nodding. "Everything…many things, I should say, are different now."

"Since the attack," said Gwyneth quietly.

"And you being named as the heir."

"How does everyone know? There wasn't a proclamation or anything of the sort…was there?" asked Gwyneth in sudden dawning horror.

"No, no." Aine reassured her with a wave of her graceful, long-fingered hand. "But even though we are not the next Bearer, Gwyneth, we are all still of the Blood. We are all connected, and we all feel it."

"And…are you jealous?" Gwyneth asked softly, staring down at her half-eaten bowl of stew. Ed tore a piece from a loaf of crusty bread and placed it encouragingly on Gwyneth's plate.

Aine chuckled. "I thought you'd ask that eventually. You're not afraid to ask the difficult questions."

"Are you afraid to answer?" retorted Gwyneth, taking the sting from her words with a smile.

"Of course not," replied Aine, raising an eyebrow. She paused. "I would be untruthful if I said that there was not some small bit of jealousy. But I know that being the Bearer is not my path to walk, and nothing I do will change that."

"Brita's jealousy is what killed Catherine and maimed Audhild and Isabella," said Gwyneth darkly, vengefully tearing her piece of bread in two.

"No," said Aine. "The *syivhalla* is what killed Catherine and hurt Audhild and Isabella," said Aine in a quiet voice.

"The *syivhalla* seduced Brita with the idea that she could change her path." Gwyneth slathered some butter on her bread.

"And it would have found another way if Brita had not given it permission to use her as its host," said Aine with eminent practicality. "Now. We can keep working ourselves up over Brita's stupidity, or we can finish our meal and go do something useful."

"Like practicing bladework," contributed Ed helpfully from the other side of Gwyneth.

Gwyneth took a breath and then surprised herself by chuckling. "Are you sure you two didn't rehearse this conversation?"

"We've discussed many different ways to help you out of your...mood," Aine replied in her no-nonsense way.

"Well, it worked," said Gwyneth, finishing the last bit of her bread and brushing the crumbs from her fingers. "Let's go practice."

Aine grinned and stood. "With pleasure."

In the courtyard where they had practiced their swordsmanship so many times before, Gwyneth drew the blade from the sheath on her back. Here, at least, the other Inionacha had the good sense not to stare at her – or if they did, they waited until she could not see. It was the closest she'd felt to being one of them again since before the attack on the Tower, perhaps even before she was chosen as one of the Seven.

But you are not one of them, whispered a small voice in her head that she wasn't sure was entirely her own.

Yet Gwyneth felt a surge of affection – something very close to love, she thought – for the other young women in the courtyard as they ran through warm-up drills, blades flashing in the noon sun, shedding cloaks as they began to sweat with their exertions. Though the courtyard was protected from most snow, frost crunched under their boots, and Ed drew a warming rune to melt the ice on the stones beneath their feet in the practice rings.

Some of the more high-spirited young women exchanged good-natured insults as they began to choose their partners for the first round of sparring. Aine turned to Gwyneth with invitation in her eyes; but before Gwyneth could accept, Aine looked at someone over Gwyneth's shoulder, smiled and bowed her head briefly.

Gwyneth turned and found herself face-to-face with a woman nearly exactly her height, white-gold hair bound back in an intricate braid, catlike green eyes regarding her with a cool and distant curiosity. The woman looked very familiar, but Gwyneth couldn't place her.

"Paladin Orla," murmured Aine respectfully from behind Gwyneth.

The Paladin inclined her head slightly, her luminescent green eyes never quite leaving Gwyneth's face as she acknowledged Aine's greeting.

"I heard there was a practice of sorts going on here in the courtyard," said Orla, a slight accent rendering her words musical. "I hope I am not intruding."

"Of course not, Lady Paladin," said Aine gracefully, though Orla still looked at Gwyneth.

"Do not let me cause any undue delays," said the Paladin. "Continue on with your practice. I will take the Bearer's daughter as my sparring partner."

"As you wish, Lady Paladin," replied Aine with a smile in her voice.

Gwyneth heard and felt rather than saw the other Inionacha moving away into their own practice rings, speaking in low voices about the intent of their sessions. She felt as though she and Orla were enclosed within a sphere of their own.

"We've sparred before," she said, just barely managing not to blurt the words.

"Yes," replied Orla with a small smile. "At our Samhain celebration, though we were not wearing our own faces at the time."

"You were wearing a cat masque," said Gwyneth.

Orla did not reply, studying her silently. Gwyneth fought the urge to fidget. She shifted her grip slightly on her sword; this blade felt more balanced than her old plain blade. She tried to remember how the blade had felt in her hand at the Samhain festival, but the memory refused to surface. It felt as though years had passed since she'd used the mirror-stone to reach the wild, beautiful celebration in the depths of the forest. Gwyneth couldn't remember a time when she didn't know the feel of Rhys' lips against her own. She wrenched her mind away from *that* memory, hoping it hadn't shown too plainly on her face.

"I thought you were the heir when I crossed blades with you," said Orla with another small nod. Then she raised one brow. "Though it was not your skill with a blade that made me think so."

The droll comment surprised a half-laugh from Gwyneth. "If it was not my skill with a blade, then what was it?"

Orla remained silent for a moment. Finally, she said, "It was the way you moved among everyone, Sidhe and Paladin and Glasidhe. You did not scorn to speak to anyone, and you were not afraid."

"I was not afraid, but I was nervous a few times," admitted Gwyneth. She didn't know why she was so readily admitting such intimate details to the Paladin during their first conversation.

"It is one of my gifts," Orla said, almost gently. "Aedan has some particular skill as well, putting people at ease."

"And you both make it seem like you can read minds," added

Gwyneth, shifting her blade idly in the air, the cold winter sunlight gleaming down its length.

Orla only smiled. She didn't offer any other explanation.

A cool breeze pressed Gwyneth's shirt against her body, and though she wore a quilted vest against the chill, she shivered.

"We stand here too long speaking idle words," said Orla. The Paladin drew her own blade, longer and thinner than the sword Gwyneth held in her own hand. It was closer to a rapier than a proper sword, Gwyneth thought. "Let me see if you have improved since Samhain."

Gwyneth nearly retorted that she'd been attacked by a *syivhalla*, drained her *taebramh* Walking for the first time, and then helped to heal Audhild, so there was very little chance she'd perform better than at Samhain; but she said nothing, stepping into the sparring ring and raising her blade in the traditional salute of courtesy to her opponent.

Orla raised her whip-thin blade and then everything became a blur of movement. Gwyneth stumbled at the ferocity of the Paladin's attack, but she managed to block the savage strokes and keep her feet. Her *taebramh* awoke with a cry from its sharp hawk-beak, its wings thrusting through her chest, giving her arms steadiness and strength. White fire surged into the edges of Gwyneth's vision. Her new blade felt like an extension of her arm, as though it had once been a part of her and now had returned after a long absence.

She felt the crisp winter air streaming down her throat and into her chest, heard her own heartbeat in her ears, slowing as her *taebramh* calibrated her senses to the speed of Orla's attack. The Paladin's sword cut a glittering arc through the air, and rather than block it Gwyneth stepped neatly aside, the white fire pulsing at the edge of her sight. For the first time in a long time, she felt herself settle into that quiet place, that silent place between heartbeat and breath where she pulled a bowstring taut and aimed at the heart of a deer through a gap in the trees. Her body thrilled to the familiar feeling, and her arm moved the blade in her hand without conscious thought.

It felt like a kind of dance, like they were whirling and stepping to wild music only they could hear; through the silence of her resolve, Gwyneth felt as though the fire of the stars and the gale of a winter storm had flowed into her bones, illuminating her body with transcendent speed and fury.

They might have sparred for a minute or an hour or a day; Gwyneth lost all sense of time as she drank in the heady sensation of locking her blade with the Paladin. There was only the bright clash of their swords and the silver flash of a stroke in the sunlight and the scuff of their leather boots against the stones. As if from a distance, she realized that many of the other women had stopped their own sparring and stood gathered at the edge of their practice ring, standing silently at a respectful distance. But she did not spare them any thought; she lost herself in the thrust and parry of the match. She did not feel any pain in her body, the white fire burning through her with ferocious strength. Her breath frosted the air in calm, regular intervals.

Gwyneth spun to block a particularly fast attack by Orla. The Paladin faltered, misplacing one foot in what seemed like a strange imbalance for the cat-quick woman. Gwyneth felt her *taebramh* beat its wings and urge her to strike at the Paladin, to end the match with victory; but her blade *hummed* a warning into her palm, and she took a quick step away as a dagger flashed toward her in Orla's left hand. She heard a few cries of protest from the other Inionacha.

Expect the unexpected, accept that no fight is ever fair, and find a way to win, said an alien voice in her mind.

Orla had not even paused her attack to speak directly into Gwyneth's mind. Somehow that galvanized Gwyneth even more than the hidden dagger; she released all conscious thought and allowed her body and her blade to move as one. Orla swept down with her sword, and Gwyneth blocked the sweep, twisting her blade deftly to lock the hilts, driving Orla backward with her more powerful positioning. With a shove that gave her a bare moment to act, Gwyneth deftly changed her sword to her left hand without giving up her advantage; and she caught Orla's wrist as the Paladin arced the dagger toward her ribs. Without thinking, Gwyneth heaved Orla away using her sword as leverage, and delivered a strong front kick, her boot landing solidly in Orla's midsection.

Orla did not fall, skidding backward on her feet with uncanny balance; but before the Paladin regained her stance, Gwyneth delicately pressed the tip of her sword underneath her chin.

"Expect the unexpected, accept that no fight is ever fair, and find a way to win," Gwyneth said quietly, her *taembramh* receding from the edges of her vision.

Orla smiled and lowered her blades, straightening and stepping back where her chin no longer rested on the edge of Gwyneth's sword. "You *have* improved since Samhain, daughter of Rionach."

"Thank you," Gwyneth replied stiffly. She suddenly felt very tired and wished that the others weren't standing around the circle watching them.

"I think we will travel together to the Solstice," continued Orla, sheathing her dagger and her slim sword and speaking as though the other Inionacha were invisible. "Though we will be using a Gate, of course, we will still have a few days of travel in Unseelie lands. We will spar many more times."

Gwyneth felt her hands begin to shake. Perhaps the use of her *taebramh* hadn't completely inured her to the physical cost of the match. But she inclined her head and said, "I look forward to it, Lady Paladin."

"Just Orla, please," replied Aedan's partner. "I will not stand on formality with the heir to the Sword."

Gwyneth wondered suddenly if Orla knew anything about the passing of the Sword, or when it would take place – but she remembered that Aine and Ed and the others were still clustered around them, and she held her tongue. If they were truly going to travel together, there might be a better opportunity to ask such a question.

Then Orla straightened her shoulders and swept her piercing gaze around the gathered Inionacha. Ed and Aine were the only ones to meet her eyes, and the others dispersed fairly quickly. Aine and Ed, for their part, remained standing a few paces away from the practice ring. Ed even crossed her arms over her chest and raised her chin stubbornly. Gwyneth felt a surge of affection for both of them.

"You have loyal friends," said Orla in a low voice. "That is good. Remember them, when the time comes."

Gwyneth nodded, though she didn't truly understand Orla's meaning.

"We will meet again soon, daughter of Rionach," Orla said with a nod. And without anything more, she turned and glided away, melting into the gathering shadows.

As though a spell had been broken, Ed rushed forward, Aine following with her long-legged stride.

"We thought the match would never end," Ed said breathlessly. "She didn't cut you with that dagger, did she? Couldn't rightly see, you were moving so fast."

"No," replied Gwyneth with a shrug. "Orla wouldn't hurt me."

"Well of course she wouldn't *hurt* you, but the Paladin have a different definition of *hurt*, don't they?" replied Ed with a bit of crossness in her voice.

"A cut or two in training is nothing to them," said Aine in agreement.

Gwyneth remembered the latticework of white scars across the broad planes of Rhys' chest. "She didn't cut me," she said to the other two women, her voice surprisingly steady.

"You were sparring for nearly an hour," said Aine, raising one eyebrow.

Gwyneth realized she still held her sword in her hand. She sheathed it in the scabbard on her back without really thinking. The motion felt effortless, as though she'd been wearing a blade on her back for years. "It didn't feel like an hour."

"Of course it didn't," muttered Ed, crossing her arms over her chest again.

"There's no use in getting irritated at *her*, Ed," Aine remarked mildly.

Ed colored. "It's just…difficult," she managed after a moment.

"Difficult?" asked Gwyneth, feeling her brows draw together in confusion. Her hand touched the hilt of her sword over her shoulder.

"Watching you and wondering when you'll almost be killed again," muttered Ed, pressing her mouth into a thin line.

Gwyneth stared at her friend. She didn't know what to say.

"Let's go get cleaned up for the evening meal, shall we?" Aine suggested.

"I'm going to take mine in my room," said Ed, not meeting Gwyneth's eyes.

"Why are you angry at *me*, Ed?" Gwyneth said – it was the first thing that came to her mind that made any sort of sense. She felt unbalanced. Ed's sudden temper felt stranger and more unexpected to her than the appearance of the dagger in Orla's hand.

Ed huffed out a quick, angry breath. Then she said in a choked voice, "I'll be fine, Gwyn, just give me a few hours. It's difficult to watch, sometimes, because I…I *care* about you, *comprenez vous*? *C'est difficile, il est difficile d'etre ton ami parfois…*" She turned very red, clenched her jaw and strode away muttering a few words to herself in her native tongue every few steps.

Gwyneth stepped forward but Aine put a hand on her shoulder. "Let her go," advised the flame-haired Inionacha almost gently. "As she said, a few hours and she'll be right as rain."

"I don't understand what she meant," Gwyneth said.

"Let it settle and you will," Aine replied with a confidence that Gwyneth wished she felt. "Come now, it's time for evening meal, and you must be hungry after all that."

As if on cue, Gwyneth's stomach rumbled. Frost rimed the courtyard stones again, and shadows stretched their cloaks from the walls, the sun no longer visible. Gwyneth looked up at the darkening sky for a moment, her eyes finding the first pale stars. One flashed a greeting to her, sparkling and shining brightly as her gaze rested upon it; she smiled, her worry and confusion assuaged by the simple beauty of the star. She followed Aine toward the dining hall, touching the hilt of the sword at her shoulder again, its feel a new yet familiar comfort.

Chapter 25

As the young women who wished to take tea after the evening meal lingered around the long table of the dining hall, Gwyneth sat back in her chair and thought over the day. So much had changed in the past weeks, but she felt as though it was all apace – except, of course, the attack by the *syivhalla*. She didn't know whether she'd ever be able to forgive the weakness that had allowed Brita to succumb to the seduction of the Dark spirit.

The conversations flowed around her; the other Inionacha seemed to have regained their balance as well, and though Gwyneth still noticed a hush that enveloped her in large groups like the dining hall, it was better than the awed silence that had surrounded her right after the attack and the revelation that she was, indeed, the heir to the Sword. Now, Gwyneth felt she could engage in a conversation when she desired, and hold her silence when that was her preference. She wondered if this was what Instructor Ava and Instructor Cara felt, this ability to choose and be respected in that choice.

The sword on her back had ignited a little flurry of whispers and some craning of necks from the youngest girls, but it was nothing that surprised Gwyneth now. Aine sat to her left, speaking to dark-haired Isabella, whose bandaged wrist-stump garnered less attention than Gwyneth's blade. The Castilian woman still moved with her usual grace, her movements slow and deliberate as she became accustomed to performing all her daily tasks with her left hand rather than her right. Aine waited patiently as Isabella poured tea, accepting the teapot from Isabella, who gave her a little wry smile at the awkwardness of the hand-off.

"Tea, Gwyneth?" Aine asked, deftly pouring a stream of amber liquid into her cup.

"Yes, thank you," Gwyneth replied, taking a bit of comfort in the very ordinary exchange.

"Put in your cream and sugar, Gwyneth, and you may take it with you."

Gwyneth turned to Instructor Cara. The Seelie woman had lost none of her golden beauty, but there were shadows in her brilliant eyes since the attack on the Seven. The other Inionacha paused, as if waiting for Gwyneth to ask an explanation of the Instructor; but Gwyneth tipped a bit of cream into her tea and stood without a word, wrapping her hands around the warmth of the sturdy earthenware mug.

A hint of a smile tugged at the corner of Instructor Cara's mouth. "Come."

Gwyneth followed the Seelie Instructor from the dining hall, into the entry hall with dozens of doors and the sweeping staircases up to the first level of the dormitories.

"May I ask what's happening, Instructor Cara?" Gwyneth asked courteously as they walked toward one of the doors.

"Just Cara now, please," said the Seelie woman, turning to glance at Gwyneth as they reached a door with a brilliant swirling mosaic set into it in silver mirrored tiles. "Of course, we appreciate that you are maintaining your courtesy when among the other girls, but you are the Heir."

The way that Cara pronounced the word was different than Gwyneth had heard it before.

"Just because I'm the Heir doesn't change any of what I've learned from you and Instructor Ava," Gwyneth replied firmly.

"Of course it does," said Ava, raising her golden eyebrows. "Being the Heir changes everything, Gwyneth."

Gwyneth opened and closed her mouth, words failing her for the second time that evening. The sword on her back thrummed reassuringly, sending little vibrations through her ribs; the closest Gwyneth could come to describing the feeling in her own mind was the feeling of a purring cat pressing against her.

"And it not only changes everything for *you,* you must realize," continued Ava, her beautiful face enigmatic, "but it changes everything for all the other Inionacha, and for everyone who has a hand in their training." She turned back toward the door, regarded it for a moment, and then looked at Gwyneth again.

"I thought as much," Gwyneth said truthfully. "I've spoken about this – with Edelinne, mostly, though Aine and Isabella and Audhild have their own thoughts as well." She took a breath, watching the light of the *taebramh* globe shimmer on the silver tiles of the door. The pattern looked to her like a great spiral, fractured and curled in upon itself countless times, still an unending wave of motion despite its brokenness.

"And what are your thoughts?"

"I do not understand the Hall now," Gwyneth said. Saying the words aloud felt disloyal, but she raised her chin. She owed at least her honesty to Instructor...to Ava. "I am not sure I understood it before, but I was so busy with training and learning all the new ways of Faeortalam, after coming here so late...but now that it's known that I'm the Heir, I feel as though the Hall is merely taking away a part of the lives of the other Inionacha." She paused, trying to gather her thoughts. "I've been thinking about what will become of the other Inionacha. Some might choose to try to become Paladins. Perhaps a few will be accepted by the Scholars, and a few might have the talent to make it in the Walker's Guild. But there are dozens and dozens of Inionacha, and I feel like keeping them here is holding them back from starting the rest of their lives."

"Perhaps you will be able to discuss some of your thoughts with the Bearer," said Ava, "for it is not within my control, the comings and goings of the Inionacha."

"You are an Instructor," Gwyneth protested.

"I *was* an Instructor," corrected Ava, almost gently. There was something like sadness in her words. "But now I am merely a guardian, until the Bearer makes known her will."

Gwyneth shifted uncomfortably. "The Bearer seems to hold many hostage to her will."

"It is an honor to serve the Bearer," said Ava with a hardness that Gwyneth had never heard from the Seelie woman.

She groped for words, feeling the pulse of the sword on her back, but before she scraped together a response, a spark ignited in the center of the silver-tiled door, flashing into a thousand points of light as it traveled outward.

"Well," said Ava. "She is ready."

Ava touched the door, which swung inward noiselessly; she motioned for Gwyneth to walk ahead of her. Gwyneth took a steadying breath and stepped across the threshold into a room that pierced her with its familiarity: the stone hearth and dirt floor and rough-hewn furnishing reminded her with rending intensity of her childhood home. Her breath caught in her throat even as her feet carried her forward and her eyes swept over the entirety of the room. A moment passed, and she convinced herself that it was not actually her mother and father's stone house in the village in the Tireoghain. "It is a world away," she murmured to herself.

"Actually," said Rionach, standing up from her seat by the hearth, "it is not quite a world away."

Gwyneth stared at the Bearer, at the great golden woman who radiated such strength and surety, and thought it strange she felt nothing.

"You are my Heir and the trueblood flesh of my flesh, but that does not mean you must love me," said Rionach, none of her fierceness diminishing.

"It would make it easier if it did," replied Gwyneth without thinking.

Rionach chuckled. "Perhaps you are right." She motioned to the other seat by the hearth.

Gwyneth glanced behind her, but Ava and the silver-tiled door were gone, sealed into nothingness, the stone walls of the cottage plain and ordinary. Rionach waited impassively while Gwyneth turned back and crossed the room. She sat down and realized that she still held her steaming mug of tea from the dining hall.

"It is surprising what one can carry between worlds," remarked Rionach.

Gwyneth felt her hands tighten reflexively around the mug. "We are no longer in Faeortalam?"

"No, child."

"We are in Doendhtalam?"

"No, child."

Gwyneth stopped herself from making a sound of frustration. That would only prove her to be the child that Rionach called her with such serene patience. "Where, then?"

"This is a Place Between. Some call it the ether. It is through this place that you will travel when you Walk, and through which we pass – for a moment, at least – when stepping from Doendhtalam to Faeortalam."

Gwyneth looked at the fire in the hearth and held out one hand to their warmth. "It seems...real."

"It *is* real," replied Rionach implacably.

"How?"

"This place," said Rionach, encompassing the cottage with a wave of her hand, "is one of my homes."

"A Place Between is one of your homes," repeated Gwyneth with a hint of disbelief.

"Why would I say such a thing if it were not true?"

"I don't know," muttered Gwyneth, feeling very young and stupid. Had Rionach brought her here simply to illustrate how much she did not know?

"Of course not, child," Rionach said, her voice softening slightly. The Bearer looked into the fire for a moment, the emerald in the pommel of the Sword blinking slowly over her shoulder. Gwyneth felt her own sword trill a greeting at the Caedbranr; there was no other word for the silvery, nearly soundless song that emanated from the blade on her back.

"Ah, Ithariel remembers," murmured Rionach. The emerald brightened, awakening, and the air within the small cottage trembled with the voices of the two swords.

"Ithariel," Gwyneth repeated.

"You chose well," said Rionach. "And Ithariel you may pass down to one of your children. You have the choice in that, at least."

"Because I don't have the choice in the next Heir," said Gwyneth quietly.

"Indeed." Rionach looked again into the fire.

Gwyneth wondered if there was a daughter or grand-daughter before her whom Rionach had favored; if there had been another woman born of Rionach's daughters that the Bearer had wished to inherit the Sword.

"You will learn," said the Bearer, "that your own desires no longer tip the scales with their weight, when you carry the Caedbranr."

"Whose desires do, then?" Gwyneth asked, feeling very brave.

"You will understand in time."

"I am tired of not understanding," Gwyneth replied, thinking of the Seven in the Tower, thinking of the terrible flame in Brita's eyes as the *syivhalla* emerged from within her, thinking of Audhild's terribly scarred face and Isabella's wrist-stump. She thought, too, of the whirling fire in her blood when she touched Rhys, and the anger in Edelinne's eyes after her sparring match with Orla. There were so many things she did not understand – how could the Bearer expect her to simply accept it?

"You are very young, though you have experienced much in these past years," said Rionach. "You will understand in time."

This time, the little huff of frustrated breath escaped Gwyneth before she realized herself enough to stop it. For a frozen moment, she dared not move. The shadows contracted around the Bearer and the Caedbranr rolled its emerald eye to stare reprovingly at Gwyneth. Then a log split and fell in a shower of sparks in the hearth, and Rionach turned to look at her.

"It is easy to forget what it is to be young," the Bearer said quietly. "It has been centuries since even my grandchildren were babes. I hope you will forgive me."

Gwyneth swallowed and said thickly, "There is nothing to forgive." She licked her lips. "Would you tell me more about Ithariel, please?" She felt her sword give a little shudder of pleasure at being named.

"Perspective is the greatest gift of age, I think," Rionach said, her voice nearly a murmur. Gwyneth thought that the Bearer had not heard her question, and was drawing breath to ask it again, when the older woman shifted her gaze from the fire to the sheath across Gwyneth's back.

"Ithariel," said Rionach.

The sword gave a small, soft chime.

"Oh, do not be shy," the Bearer said, a small smile touching her lips. "You have not been properly wielded in a few centuries, but I am sure you have not forgotten anything since I last held you in my hand."

"Ithariel was your blade?" Gwyneth asked.

"Yes."

"And why did you give her up?" Gwyneth wasn't entirely sure that the blade was female in any traditional sense of the word, but she knew that she could not call the sword *it*.

"It was the right time," replied Rionach. "You will know these things. You already have a sense of them."

"So Ithariel...waited."

"Yes."

"For me." Gwyneth said the words quietly, almost shyly. She realized she sounded much like Ithariel when the sword had chimed in reply to the Bearer. The sword sent a little vibration through her spine, a warm and reassuring feeling.

"Yes." Rionach settled back in her chair. "There are a handful of Named Swords in the Two Worlds, some more powerful than others."

"The Caedbranr is the most powerful of all of them, isn't it?"

"Yes."

Gwyneth felt herself drawn toward the Bearer. She wanted to know more. She wanted to learn. Her anger and grief faded – or were overshadowed by her desire to know all that Rionach could teach her. It felt like she had a sudden thirst that could not be slaked with any ordinary draught, though she flexed her fingers around the warmth of her mug. "How does a sword become Named?"

"That is a lesson for another time," said Rionach mildly. "Now it is important for you to learn how to be partnered with a Named Sword."

A thrill ran through Gwyneth as she realized that she needed to learn how to work with Ithariel in order to become the Bearer – in order to be bound to the Iron Sword.

"You cannot be focused on the future," said Rionach quietly. "That is disrespectful to Ithariel, for one; and that future may still not come to pass. There is never any surety in tomorrow."

Gwyneth nodded.

"One of the advantages of the Place Between," continued the Bearer, "is that time passes differently here. Some cannot endure it, but I am reasonably certain that you will be fine."

"Reasonably certain?" Gwyneth repeated, her voice trembling a little.

"Yes. We do not have enough time, Gwyneth." Rionach looked at her solemnly. "I do not know exactly how much time is left before you will become the Bearer, but I fear that if I left you to your schooling, you would not be prepared." She looked back into the fire, and suddenly her face looked unbearably weary. "There are trials ahead, Gwyneth, in both worlds. I cannot part the shadows to See them, and some may land on your shoulders rather than mine..."

A chill ran through Gwyneth to see the tall, radiant, fierce Bearer look...*old.* Perhaps it was a trick of the firelight, she thought, that Rionach's face looked creased with age.

"So I brought you here to buy us what time I could," Rionach said. "Gods forgive me," she murmured.

Gwyneth drew back her shoulders in her chair. "Whatever trials lie ahead, I will meet them, Lady Bearer."

The firelight flickered, and Rionach's face smoothed into the fierce, ageless visage once again.

"And it is my duty to prepare you for them," said Rionach with a nod. She stood.

Gwyneth set her tea aside and followed suit. Ithariel quivered in anticipation.

"We must begin," said Rionach. The green of her eyes glowed with *taebramh*, and the emerald in the pommel of the Caedbranr blazed for an instant. "There is much for you to learn."

Chapter 26

"Gwyneth."

Gwyneth roused from sleep quickly at the sound of the Bearer's voice. It had become pointless to count the days in the Place Between: for one, there was no rising and setting of the sun, and for another, time seemed both faster and slower. After she'd given up trying to understand the flow of time in the ether, her training had seemed a tiny bit easier, perhaps because she was focusing her entire attention on the lessons rather than attempting to count the passing days.

She reached for Ithariel; she slept with the Named Sword close by her side, and when she did not feel the weight of Ithariel's sheath on her back, she felt naked and exposed. Slipping the strap over her head, she settled the blade against her spine and then stood, pulling on her boots with casual efficiency. She had spent enough time in the Place Between to have a precise routine upon awakening.

Her lessons with Rionach had stretched the bounds of her capabilities and knowledge. Sometimes Gwyneth could not remember all the things they had discussed and practiced until Rionach set a task and she completed it using arcane skills that flowed from her without thought. The depths of her own knowledge began to give her pause –

not *frighten* her, exactly, but sometimes it felt as though she did not recognize herself. Rionach had molded her as one molds a clay figurine, and Gwyneth knew she still had more to learn.

Gwyneth ate the unadorned meal set out on the small table: a small wedge of cheese, two thick slices of brown bread, and a few carved pieces of venison. She had never questioned the source of their sustenance in the Place Between; it became just another of the things she accepted without curiosity. Her willingness to accept strange occurrences without explanation had also expanded during her time with Rionach.

She had never seen the Bearer eat or sleep, but that had not seemed odd to her. She had already thought of Rionach as an unchangeable force, immovable as an oak and fierce as the winds of the strongest storm. After a while, Gwyneth's apprehension at being alone with the Bearer faded. It was not that she *relaxed*, because Rionach demanded concentration and hard work during their training; but she did not feel so awkward or so unworthy as she first did after Ava brought her through the silver-tiled door.

When she finished her breakfast, reciting bits of the previous day's lesson silently, Gwyneth turned to Rionach.

"You are dressed for travel," she said without any surprise. It felt as though nothing surprised her anymore.

"Yes," replied Rionach. The Bearer wore dark breeches and a deep green vest of supple leather worked with subtle gold designs at the shoulders; her spotless cream-colored shirt flowed over her well-muscled arms without any attempt to hide their strength, and she wore gleaming boots of such a deep red that they were nearly black. "And you must dress for travel as well."

Rionach gestured to Gwyneth's pallet, which sometimes disappeared when their training dictated they needed more space in the small cottage. A set of clothes much like those that Rionach wore lay on the pallet, set out with neat precision though there had been no one but Rionach and Gwyneth in the cottage.

Ithariel hummed in excitement as Gwyneth shed her plain shirt and breeches, donning the fine garments: a silken white shirt and a leather vest the color of pale spring leaves, along with soft black breeches and supple chestnut boots that reached to her knees.

"And this," said Rionach when Gwyneth had finished dressing. She held out something in her palm, a shimmering chain trailing from it. Gwyneth carefully accepted the pendant, her breath catching. It was a replica of the pendant her father had given her, the one she had taken before traveling into Faeortalam.

"It has been changed as you have been changed," said Rionach as Gwyneth took the pendant in her hand, examining it. "Iron will protect you against most Sidhe, and it is not so unusual for an Inionacha to have a token from her home."

"Won't they...know?" Gwyneth asked as she fastened the chain about her neck, slipping the pendant beneath her shirt.

"Naturally they will know," replied Rionach, arching one eyebrow. "That is to your advantage. You are no mortal to take lightly, Gwyneth."

"And they take most mortals lightly," Gwyneth guessed, her mind working quickly. She waited for the conversation to confirm her conclusion; she had learned *some* patience during her training with Rionach in the Place Between.

"They do," replied Rionach implacably. "It is in their nature to view mortals as expendable. The long lives of the Sidhe lead them to scorn those whose time is shorter than theirs. Some use them for their own pleasure, and others brush them aside." Rionach paused, watching Gwyneth. "Sometimes both happen at once."

"It sounds similar to how some men view women in the mortal world," remarked Gwyneth. She paused. "And how the rich view the poor, and those of one country view another country." She shook her head.

"It is," said Rionach, and Gwyneth thought she heard a note of approval in the Bearer's voice. "Do you believe you are ready to witness such a thing in Faeortalam?"

"I have already witnessed many things in Faeortalam, not all of them similar to Doendhtalam," replied Gwyneth after a moment of thought. "While I would not be able to look away from abuse – of any creature, Fae or mortal – I will respect the customs of any Court at which I am a guest."

Ithariel hummed approvingly.

Rionach nodded once. "You are ready. Let us go."

Gwyneth knew better than to ask where. She touched Ithariel's hilt over her shoulder, and the blade warmed to her touch. She felt true affection for the sword now, as the blade had helped her through many of the tasks which Rionach had set before them. She wondered occasionally why Ithariel had not awoken until after the attack on the Tower – until after she was sure she was the Heir – but if there was one thing above all that her time with Rionach in the Place Between had taught her, it was that she was not meant to know the reasons behind all the happenings in her life.

So rather than question where they were going – it could be the Unseelie Court for Midwinter, she thought, or it could be back to the Hall, or it could be to the mortal world, for all she could predict Rionach's teaching methods – Gwyneth collected the small leather satchel that she filled over her lessons with various herbs and implements. Though there was no garden outside the little cottage – there was no outside at all, so far as she could tell – Rionach had taught her how to request nearly any herb or object she could picture in her mind, and it would be there on the long table at the back of the room within a few hours. The more detailed Gwyneth drew the picture in her mind, the more quickly the object appeared, and she had filled the leather satchel with the most important healing herbs and instruments of the craft that Rionach taught her.

"You will most likely feel ill when you pass through the Gate again," said Rionach.

Wordlessly, Gwyneth pulled some candied ginger from one of the pouches in her satchel; Ithariel made a silvery sound of amusement.

Well, it does not have *to be candied,* admitted Gwyneth silently, smiling at the sword's cleverness. *But might as well have some sweet to gentle the bite, if anything is for the asking.*

Ithariel chimed in agreement.

"Are you ready?" asked Rionach.

"I am," replied Gwyneth. She tucked the piece of ginger into her cheek and followed Rionach toward a lovely door that appeared in the wall of the cottage. Rather than glass at the transom and mullion, it looked as though pieces of the night sky had been cut and set into the frame. Gwyneth only had an instant to peer in wonder at the stars shining in deep velvet blue and the sliver of moon visible near the top of the transom. Then Rionach sketched a rune and the door opened, the ether swirling in dizzying colors beyond the threshold. Gwyneth waited for Rionach to take her wrist or tell her to touch her shoulder, but the Bearer made no move toward Gwyneth.

"We go to the Unseelie Court," Rionach said. She handed Gwyneth a fur-lined cloak.

Gwyneth folded the cloak over her arm. She didn't want to cover Ithariel for the journey in the ether, and Rionach said nothing.

Fix the destination firmly in your mind, she thought. She had never been to the Unseelie Court, but she had read descriptions in the books that had appeared on the long table in the corner and seen detailed sketches by master artists. She pictured Darkhill as it had been described, trying to capture the essence of the Winter Court in her mind. Holding fast to that image, Ithariel humming encouragingly, she walked toward the door. One, two, three strides, and then her feet crossed the threshold, carrying her into the ether.

She felt herself pulled through the ether at a breathless pace, propelled by the force of her will. Any falter, any doubt would spell disaster. The ether whirled around her, stars and clouds of vibrant color swirling past, dark and then light, soundless yet roaring, pressing in on all of Gwyneth's senses. She held fast to the image of Darkhill in her mind and the feel of Ithariel on her back: her destination and her reassurance that she did indeed exist, that her physical body had not burst into a thousand points of light to join the rushing stars of the ether.

Gwyneth did not know whether she could breathe in the ether, and she felt the edges of panic touch her mind as she wondered if her first journey alone had gone awry – if she would be lost in the ether forever, spinning without pause among the starbursts of color and the violent changes of darkness and blinding light.

Ithariel prodded her sharply with a silver tendril, digging into Gwyneth's tender consciousness with catlike claws. Gwyneth gasped – or would have gasped had she been able to breathe – and clenched her teeth, concentrating with all her will on the image of the Unseelie Court. Not simply the *image*, but the feel: she imagined the cold kiss of winter against her skin, the silent beauty of snow falling in the Queen's Forest, ice shining silver on the parapets and walls of the Unseelie palace, the crunch of the frost-stiff ground beneath her boots. She felt Ithariel add an ethereal song that spoke of Winter and Night, the moon and stars, the beauty of the Unseelie.

With a wrench that felt as though it meant to snap her bones, Gwyneth emerged into bitter cold. Or rather, she *fell*, tumbling onto a frost-rimed ground, twigs snapping beneath her as she instinctually fell as their sword-master had taught them, twisting to the side to avoid falling on her back and breaking her momentum by sweeping one arm down to meet the ground before her body. The impact left her breathless for a moment, and even Ithariel seemed stunned; but Gwyneth blinked the spots away from the edges of her vision and awareness returned to her body.

She still clutched the fur-lined cloak against her side with her other arm. The tips of her fingers already tingled with numbness from the intense cold. She rolled to her knees and pushed herself to her feet, brushing the leaves from her breeches and shirt. Trees loomed around her, their bare branches arching overhead in a magnificent dome. She shook out the cloak and, on second thought, pulled the strap of Ithariel's sheath over her head, fastening the cloak at her throat and adjusting the strap across her chest so that Ithariel still lay free atop the cloak.

Next, she checked her satchel. Her supplies had emerged through the vortex of the ether unscathed. Checking the herbs reminded her of the ginger in her cheek. She winced at the tenderness of her cheek as she moved it with her tongue, making a mental note that traveling through the ether with anything in one's mouth was probably not advisable. In turn, thinking of the ginger reminded her of the reason she had put the ginger in her mouth, and with that, a rolling wave of nausea overwhelmed her. She managed to pull her cloak aside, at least, as she retched her breakfast onto the frozen forest floor.

Sucking on the ginger blunted the edge of the sickness after she'd emptied her stomach. Gwyneth stood shakily and wrapped her cloak tightly around her shoulders. This was decidedly *not* Darkhill, but she was reasonably sure that she had emerged in Unseelie territory. It was nighttime, though the brightness of the stars and the half-moon shed enough light to make the darkness more gray than black. She stood and listened, breathing the frigid air and trying to think through the exhaustion that settled like another cloak on her shoulders. Rionach had surely thought her capable to travel through the ether by herself, or she would not have sent her. The Bearer would not have risked the Heir...would she?

Ithariel gave a soft, reproving chime at the doubt curdling Gwyneth's stomach.

"I'm sorry," Gwyneth whispered. She turned slowly in a circle, peering into the trees and wishing suddenly for a bow and quiver. A sword in a forest felt inadequate, but Ithariel, she reminded herself firmly, was much more than an ordinary sword, just as *she* was much more than an ordinary young woman.

Where was Rionach? She had thought the Bearer to be right behind her. The first frost-like threads of fear took hold at the edges of her mind. She took a deep breath, her chest aching at the cold, and stepped closer to the nearest tree, slipping into its shadow as she had once done in the forests of the Tireoghain. Pressing a hand against the rough bark of the tree – an oak, she noted peripherally – she tried to swallow the sudden feeling of forsaken loneliness that threatened to overwhelm her just as handily as the sickness that had driven her to her knees.

Gwyneth stared into the darkness of the unfamiliar forest and took another deep breath. This was another task, another test. She pressed her lips into a thin line, pushing aside the little spark of resentment at the Bearer and calling up her stubbornness. If she was expected to navigate through a frozen forest with no supplies, then so be it. She'd show Rionach her worthiness.

Just as Gwyneth firmed her resolve, her skin prickled with her old hunter's awareness. One hand went to the dagger at her waist and the other to Ithariel's hilt over her shoulder as she crouched warily next to the tree. A quick glance upward showed that the branches of the oak were too far for her to reach with a jump. She scanned the shadows, controlling her breath even as her heart began to beat faster. Straining her senses, she caught faint movement out of the corner of her eye and whirled to face it, calling up her *taebramh* more out of instinct than conscious choice. White fire roared to life in her hands, throwing the forest into sharp relief and blinding her momentarily.

Ithariel prodded at her, trying to tell her to open her eyes and put away her *taebramh*; Gwyneth managed to dim the fire and blinked away the white blaze at the edge of her vision. She trusted Ithariel, but her heart still beat a fast tattoo as she saw the wolf standing a stone's throw away, regarding her with intelligent amber eyes. It was a magnificent beast, brindled silver and black, its winter ruff thick about its neck. Silver markings about its eyes on its mostly black face gave the wolf a distinct look – if it had been a dog, Gwyneth would have said that it looked like it was wearing spectacles, but the idea of finding amusement in such a beautiful, deadly predator fell flat. She felt herself trembling, ingrained fear shivering through her muscles even as she knew that the creature meant her no harm.

The brindled wolf twitched an ear, slitted its eyes and yawned massively. Gwyneth wondered if it had yawned on purpose to show her its long white teeth. Then it turned, looked over its shoulder at her as though to ask her whether she was coming, and glided into the shadows. Gwyneth felt herself stumble forward gracelessly, her legs cold and shaking.

The brindled wolf patiently circled back when Gwyneth did not follow fast enough and lost sight of it among the dappled shadows of the night forest. She put aside her feeling of foolishness and pressed herself to follow faster, garnering a scraped knee from a stumble and a few bloody knuckles from pushing branches away from her face as she ran through the darkness. The wolf seemed to approve, stopping every now and again to let her close the distance between them.

"Where are you taking me?" panted Gwyneth, trying to glance up through the trees at the moon to gain some sort of bearing. But the wolf, of course, did not answer her, turning and leaping over a fallen log with no more effort than she'd step over a branch. Ithariel gave a little chime of encouragement. Gwyneth climbed over the log and ran after it, the cold air burning her throat.

Finally, after what Gwyneth felt had been an hour of running through the forest, the brindled wolf slowed. Gwyneth carefully kept some space between her and the imposing hunter, her instincts still jangling in alarm at the proximity of such a deadly creature.

Then, in the distance, she heard the unmistakable murmur of voices. Straining her eyes, she glimpsed the flicker of firelight through the trees. Her feet began to carry her forward even as she realized that her lupine guide had melted into the shadows. She paused, wondering if it was some kind of trap.

"Welcome," said a voice from the shadows.

Gwyneth drew Ithariel without thinking, the silver hiss of the blade cutting through the trees. Moonlight blazed on the sword as she dropped into a fighting stance.

"Peace," commanded the voice. A man stepped out of the darkness, taller and more muscled than any of the Paladins or Sidhe that Gwyneth had seen. He regarded Gwyneth with familiar amber eyes, and there was a streak of silver in his shoulder-length black hair. The man held up massive hands and said again in a gentler voice, "Peace."

Gwyneth let out the breath she hadn't known she was holding. She nodded and sheathed Ithariel, the sword quivering in excitement. She looked at the man and a thrill of excitement coursed through her as well. A little bubble of nervousness burst as she carefully arranged the words in her head. "And peace also to you," she said in the tongue of the *ulfdrengr*. She spread her hands before her, palms upward to show she was unarmed. Her heart tripped double-time in her chest at having drawn her blade on the wolf-warrior. She spoke her next words precisely, in a low voice that only trembled slightly. "I keep my blade sheathed and my heart open to friendship."

The man grinned widely as she spoke in his language, his teeth gleaming white in the shadows. "The Lady Bearer has taught you well. Come, share our fire."

"My name is Gwyneth," she said, pronouncing the foreign words slowly and clearly.

The *ulfdrengr* touched his chest with a closed fist. "I am Kalian, and my partner Malyk was your guide." He grinned again. "I will make a few coins from that."

Gwyneth felt her lips stretch in a smile. "You bet on who would find me?"

"Of course," said Kalian jovially. "It was just a different kind of hunt with a different kind of prize." His amber eyes gleamed in the moonlight. Then he gestured. "Come. Share our fire and our food."

Gwyneth felt the beginning of a headache from concentrating so hard on translating the Northtongue, but she kept her focus. "Thank you."

Kalian walked half a step ahead of her, taking care to point out low branches and roots protruding from the ground. Gwyneth had the distinct feeling that he was treating her like a child among their people, but she couldn't blame him. She felt clumsy and graceless next to his sinuous movements.

As they neared the fire, she felt a spark of realization in the back of her head: the *ulfdrengr* had *known* somehow to expect her. Had the Bearer told them that they would find the Heir in the frozen forests outside the gates of the Unseelie Court? Gwyneth pushed aside her budding irritation at Rionach. The Bearer was the Bearer, and Gwyneth's cold-numb toes and aching hands didn't help at all with her generosity of spirit toward her teacher.

"You must be hungry," said Kalian, his broad shoulders blocking the firelight as they approached the *ulfdrengr* camp. A rune flared on a tree as they passed, silver against the dark bark, and sound washed over Gwyneth: voices of both men and women, flowing in conversation and raising in laughter; the crack and snap of wood in a great fire; the sizzle of meat being turned on a spit over red-hot coals raked into a circle of stones.

"That was a very good rune," she murmured to herself, forgetting to speak in Northtongue.

"You did not expect us to be skilled in runecraft?" Kalian asked good-naturedly in her own language.

"That is not at all what I meant," replied Gwyneth, thankful for the shadows to hide her furious blush as she followed Kalian into the camp. The *ulfdrengr* dressed wildly, but she had expected as much: both women and men wore tunics and leggings in colors that called up the forest and the hunt, red and green and fawn and black. It seemed as though they did not feel the cold, their shoulders covered in pelts of red fox and silver spotted cat and black bear, their arms and hands bare in the firelight. The women wore their hair in fantastic braids that made Gwyneth catch her breath with their complexity and beauty; some men wore their hair long as well, either loose or in a single braid down their back. Their tents were simple but well-crafted of supple tanned hides stitched together painstakingly and erected with casual mastery.

A few of the *ulfdrengr* paused in their conversations and their work to observe Gwyneth for a moment, but the swell of noise about the camp did not cease and no one stared. It was as though the *ulfdrengr* often welcomed strangers from the forest into their camp. Gwyneth could not help but feel grateful. Ithariel chimed softly, almost reprovingly.

It isn't that I don't want them to know who I am, Gwyneth thought to the sword. *I think they already know who I am, since they were expecting me. I just feel grateful that they aren't singling me out.*

Ignoring the fact that one had a guest, she thought as she followed Killian toward the center of the camp, almost made a guest feel *more* welcome. At the corner of her vision, Gwyneth saw Malyk, the great silver and black wolf, padding along beside Kalian.

"Come," Kalian said in the Northtongue, motioning to a smooth rock serving as a seat at a distance from the roaring fire. "You are still cold."

"Thank you," Gwyneth said with a formal nod of her head.

Kalian smiled. "You do not need such manners with me. I am no *herravaldyr*."

It surprised Gwyneth that the regal Malyk was not one of the royalty of the *ulfdrengr*, but she tried to hide it.

"Malyk and I, we like to fight much more than we like to rule," said Kalian, grinning. The firelight gleamed on his white teeth like the moonlight had shone on Malyk's jaws.

"Then you *could* have been *herravaldyr*?" Gwyneth asked before she stopped to consider if the question would be considered rude.

Kalian lifted one shoulder. "Malyk is of the right bloodline, but not all those that are born of the bloodline are born to rule." His amber eyes sobered. "You know this. You are one so fated."

"I do not consider it *ruling*," Gwyneth replied.

"And why is that, *ungrsverda*?" Kalian asked.

Gwyneth repeated the unfamiliar word to herself.

"In your words, it would perhaps mean *young sword*," said Kalian, not unkindly.

Gwyneth felt the color rush to her cheeks again. She held her hands out to the fire, trying not to wince as blood flowed back into her frozen fingertips.

"By the White Wolf, Kalian, you do not think to offer a fur?" said a woman nearly as tall as Kalian, and more well-muscled than even Rionach.

"The fire is hot and bright," replied Kalian without any rancor.

The *ulfdrengr* woman slid a silver fur from about her own shoulders and wrapped it about Gwyneth despite Gwyneth's half-formed protests.

"Ah, your cloak does nothing against this winter," said the woman, her dark hair gleaming like a raven's wing in the firelight. Her eyes were startlingly green.

Ithariel made a sound something like a purr at the rich fur draped over them.

"Thank you," said Gwyneth.

"Your courtesy is better-placed with Linara," said Kalian in a low voice.

A huge black wolf slid into the firelight, gazing at Gwyneth with the same bright green gaze as Linara. A thrill ran down Gwyneth's spine.

"You know that Bjarnyk and I do not stand on such courtesy," Linara said to Kalian in the Northtongue, raising one dark eyebrow.

"It does not mean that they are not deserved," Gwyneth said, speaking also in the Northtongue. She stood and bowed from the waist, careful not to let Linara's fur slip from her shoulders.

Linara grinned, her brilliant eyes sparkling. "I should have expected no less from a daughter of the Sword."

"From the Heir to the Sword," Gwyneth said quietly.

"Then you do not bow to me," Linara replied with a quick, unexpected ferocity in her words. She took a step closer, looking intently at Gwyneth. "You do not bow to me, you do not bow to my grandfather, you do not bow even to Mab herself."

"*We* do not bend the knee to Mab," pointed out Kalian.

Linara made a slicing motion through the air with her hand. "Once we did, Kalian, and never again."

Gwyneth felt her shivering ease, from both the radiant heat of the fire and the silken warmth of Linara's fur about her shoulders. Somewhere in the camp, a drum sounded, a wild rhythm taking shape in the frigid air.

"How did you journey here, sword-daughter?" asked Linara, her eyes narrowing in curiosity. Bjarnyk padded closer. His paws were nearly the size of Gwyneth's head. She suppressed her instinctual panic.

"I traveled through the ether," she answered instead, trying to focus on the conversation rather than the proximity of the massive black wolf.

"That is not easy," said Linara, a thread of appreciation in her smooth voice.

"It isn't," agreed Gwyneth. During the pause in conversation, her stomach growled loudly. She remembered that she'd heaved up her breakfast on the frozen forest floor, and the run through the cold to the camp had burned away what little remained in her belly.

"You do not give her a fur and you do not give her food," said Linara to Kalian. She shook her head at him. "What use are you, eh?"

"Say the word and I will show you," replied Kalian with a grin.

Linara raised her eyebrows, unimpressed. Kalian chuckled and strode away, presumably to fetch food.

"Men," muttered Linara beneath her breath.

Gwyneth suddenly thought of Rhys. Her chest ached with the want to see him, stealing her breath for a moment as the feeling caught her unaware.

"Ah, you have a young man of your own?" Linara said, sitting down on a stone set next to Gwyneth's seat.

"Something of the sort," muttered Gwyneth.

Linara smiled. "We do not hold with the ways of your world, sword-daughter. Among my people, women are free to love whomever they choose, whenever they choose."

"So far, I very much like your people," Gwyneth replied truthfully.

The raven-haired woman chuckled. The huge black wolf appeared behind her, pressing into her back. She ran a large, calloused hand through the fur at his chest. "I think we will get along quite well, Heir to the Sword."

Despite the long run through the cold forest, the uncertainty and confusion at her emergence from the ether into an unknown place, Gwyneth felt the tension melting from her body as the warmth from the fire soaked through her skin. She looked at Linara and something within her found kinship in the wildness of the *ulfdrengr*'s honest, open face. Gwyneth grinned, Linara grinned in answer, and the flames of the fire danced toward the cold, star-pricked sky.

Chapter 27

"How long until the Solstice celebration?" Gwyneth asked in the Northtongue, her hands wrapped around a warm mug. The *ulfdrengr* did not drink tea; Kalian had handed her a mug of a drink called *khal*. The scent rising from the mug was not unpleasant, but unlike anything that Gwyneth had ever smelled before: pungent, with a bit of woodiness and notes of cocoa. She wondered if Rhys had ever drunk *khal* with the *ulfdrengr* around one of their campfires.

"Nearly a fortnight," replied Linara without sparing any attention from the fur she had unrolled across her knees. She selected one of the slender daggers and inspected it carefully. The wild drumbeat rolled through the camp, but Kalian and Linara seemed to pay it no mind. Gwyneth found it difficult to ignore: the drumbeat and the song in the Northtongue sparked excitement in her blood. Once again the *ulfdrengr* camp reminded her of Rhys, and the thrill of traveling to the forest for the fierce, beautiful celebration of Samhain with the Paladins.

Then she fully realized what Linnara had said. "A *fortnight*?" she repeated, feeling her eyes widen.

Linara grinned. "I have not often traveled through the ether, but it is said that time can be a very tricky thing as well."

Dizziness swirled around Gwyneth; she blinked and took deep breaths, feeling her heartbeat roar in her ears. She tried to think of the practical implications: did she exist in two places at once, back at the Hall of the Inionacha and then in the Place Between while she was here in the *ulfdrengr* camp? What would happen if her two selves – if there *were* two selves – came face to face? What if Rhys or any other saw her here in the forest and then went to the Hall? She swayed. Ithariel voiced concern with a clarion chime.

"Steady," murmured Kalian, settling a firm hand on her shoulder.

"I did not intend to...arrive here," Gwyneth heard herself say as though from far away.

"We often arrive in places that we did not intend," Linara replied, her eyes glinting like emeralds in the firelight.

"It is her first such journey," said Kalian to Linara, his tone implying that perhaps Linara should be gentler.

"That does not mean that she should faint like a delicate Court lady," replied the *ulfdrengr* woman, her eyes glittering in the shadows.

At that comment, Gwyneth took a deep breath and gripped the rock beneath her with both hands, steadying herself and clutching at her consciousness with the same determination. Her wavering vision cleared enough for her to see Linara smile slightly and settle back on her seat. She hooked one foot over the other knee, glancing up at Kalian.

"See? She does not want to be some simpering maiden."

"I am *not* a simpering maiden," replied Gwyneth firmly. She sat up straighter and Kalian removed his hand from her shoulder. "Do you always arrive so early for the Solstice?"

"Sometimes," said Linara.

"There is good hunting in these forests," said Kalian.

"And not so much snow," added Linara.

Gwyneth braced herself and took a sip of *khal*. The warmth of it alone slid reassuringly down her throat and into her belly. The taste of the *khal* took her a long moment to process: slightly bitter, but not unpleasantly so, with bright notes that somehow reminded her of the oranges that her father had brought from his trading.

"What do you think of *khal*?" asked Linara.

Gwyneth knew it was a test. "It is…different," she said. "I have not tasted anything like it."

Linara chuckled. "Diplomatic," she said, with a note that may have been approval in her voice. Bjarnyk appeared again out of the shadows and yawned hugely, his pink tongue lolling over his white teeth. Linara said something to him in a low voice, her face softening affectionately as she roughed his ears with both hands.

"So, what shall you do?" Kalian asked as Gwyneth took another sip of *khal*.

Gwyneth frowned. "Well, finish drinking it, of course." The flavor grew on her, even between the first and second tasting.

Kalian chuckled. "No, *ungrsverda*, what shall you do tomorrow?"

She peered up at him. "I don't understand your meaning."

"Will you stay with us, or will you go back to your teacher?"

"Or you could perhaps travel on to the Court," said Linara, her dismissive tone making it clear that she thought that a very poor option. "I am sure that Mab would love to get her claws into Rionach's Heir."

"She does not have true claws," said Kalian in a low voice to Gwyneth.

"You do not entirely know that," muttered Linara, still combing her fingers through Bjarnyk's thick fur.

"Why go to the Solstice celebration at all, if you do not approve of Mab?" Gwyneth asked, taking another sip of *khal*.

"She is bold," said Kalian to Linara, as though Gwyneth were not sitting an arm's length away from him. "I like her."

"Bold pups often have a few scars from their missteps," said Linara, but her mouth curved in something almost like a smile. "*We* know that, Bjarnyk my love, eh?"

The huge black wolf *grinned*. There was no other word for it. Gooseflesh raced down Gwyneth's arm at the expressiveness of the wolf's face and the intelligence of his gleaming green eyes. There was no doubt in her mind that Bjarnyk understood every word of their conversation.

Still entranced by the wolf, Gwyneth said, "I would very much like to stay, if you will have me."

Kalian looked to Linara, who did not say anything right away. Bjarnyk fixed his intelligent gaze on Gwyneth. A shock rippled through her. She found that she ached with wanting to stay with the *ulfdrengr* and learn as much as she could about their ways, despite the fact that would keep her away from Rhys for longer. She would *not* be a simpering maiden, swooning after a man. Straightening her shoulders, she held Bjarnyk's gaze, threads of something that felt like starlight reaching through her veins.

"You are beautiful," she murmured in the Northtongue to the wolf. Then her cheeks colored, and she looked down in embarrassment at the unguarded comment.

Linara chuckled. "He *is* quite the handsome devil, isn't he?"

"If he were anything less, he would not have Chosen you," Kalian said, stretching his arms over his head. Gwyneth tried not to let her eyes widen at the ripple of his muscles underneath his shirt. Linara, for her part, smoothed her fingers through Bjarnyk's fur and ignored both Kalian's words and stretching.

The Paladins were mortal, so of course their forms varied, and she had only ever seen a few Sidhe men, but she was quite sure that the *ulfdrengr* dwarfed them both. Linara, too, would be a match in size for Aedan and even Rhys.

"Do you ever train with the Paladins?" she asked, taking a sip of the *khal*. It warmed her belly. She looked up, tracing the delicate latticework of the branches overhead with her eyes, picking out slices of the velvety night sky in the spaces between the trees.

"Any who come to us with open minds and honest hearts are welcome," Linara replied. "But there are few who endure the cold to do so."

"Will you train me?" Gwyneth asked, the words spilling over her lips in a rush of bright-eyed exhaustion and hope. The *khal* had helped warm her, but her body still ached from the journey through the ether and the run through the forest.

Linara chuckled, not unkindly. "You wish to match blades with us, *ungrsverda?*"

"Yes," Gwyneth replied, drawing back her shoulders. She had already made the request, and so now there was nothing to do but be bold in her response.

Linara leaned forward, resting her elbows on her knees. The movement made the muscles in her arms bulge. Gwyneth thought that she had never seen a woman with such magnificent arms. Linara met Gwyneth's eyes, the same shock rippling through her as when the wolf had met her gaze.

"There is Malit and Evedra," Kalian said to Linara.

A long moment of silence stretched over them, Kalian leaning back and making it clear he was content to let Linara continue on with her inspection, Gwyneth feeling her heart beat hard against the cage of her ribs, Bjarnyk yawning widely and standing, his black tail merging with the shadows as he looked over his massive shoulder at Gwyneth.

"I wish to learn from you," Gwyneth said, her lips numb as though from cold. Ithariel hummed encouragingly from the sheath across Gwyneth's back.

"We do not train as though it is child's play," Linara said finally, that unblinking gaze still fixed on Gwyneth's face. "We train to kill trolls. We train to fight giants. We train to defend ourselves against the frozen North."

Gwyneth nodded once, breathless.

"You are not a guest, then," Linara said. "You are one who has come to learn our ways, and we will treat you no differently than one of our own."

A thrill ran through Gwyneth, followed closely by a strange, piercing sadness. Just as the Paladins had enveloped her with their magnificent Samhain celebration, so too would the *ulfdrengr* surround her with their culture and their ways, but she could never truly be one of them. She was the Heir to the Iron Sword, and there were no other like her, not even the other Inionacha. But she pushed aside the sadness that she did not quite understand, and said, "I do not ask to be treated any differently. Thank you."

Linara raised one eyebrow. "We shall see if you are still thanking me tomorrow morn, *ungrsverda*."

Kalian grinned at that, and Gwyneth glimpsed another wolf roving through the shadows just outside the firelight. She thought it might be Malyk, but she was not entirely sure.

Without a word of farewell or explanation, Linara stood and strode away into the camp, her large form disappearing among the trees and low tents. Gwyneth looked at Kalian, expecting him to follow, but he grinned ruefully at her, rubbing his chin.

"Is it that obvious or am I that hopeless?" he said, using Commontongue. Gwyneth smiled, both in pleased surprise at his facility with her native language and his self-deprecating question.

"You speak very well," she said.

"You avoid the question," he retorted.

She laughed. "Well..." Wrapping her hands around her mug, she leaned closer to him, leaning her elbows on her knees as Linara had done. There was more to blending in than simply learning the language of her hosts. "I don't think you are *obvious*. But..." She shrugged. "I know what it feels like, so perhaps I recognize it more easily."

"What is the word for that, in your language?"

Gwyneth was grateful for the darkness as her cheeks heated. "Love?"

Kalian made a sound something between a snort and a chuckle. "I know the word for *love*." He waved a massive hand as Gwyneth began to protest that she hadn't meant any insult. "I mean when the feeling is not returned."

"Oh." Gwyneth pressed her lips together. Ithariel chimed empathetically. "Unrequited, I think, is the word you are wanting."

"Unrequited." Kalian said it slowly, testing it against his tongue.

"How do you know it is unrequited?" Gwyneth asked. She realized in a corner of her mind that her tiredness and the excitement of the unfamiliar surroundings made her bolder than courteous, but Kalian didn't seem offended. "I can't imagine that Linara doesn't find you handsome."

This time, Gwyneth lost the battle to her mortification. Her eyes widened, and she pressed a hand to her mouth. Kalian's chuckle somehow seemed worse than if he'd roared with laughter. She pressed her hands to the warmth of her mug. All the training in the Between with Rionach still had not cured her of her awkwardness. She swallowed hard as treasonous tears pricked at the corners of her eyes – how ridiculous, to shed tears over such a thing! She'd fought a *baobhan sith* before she'd even known of the existence of Faeortalam. She'd faced a *syivhalla* and seen her companions die. She'd traveled the ether and trained with the Bearer, and now she was going to shed tears over something as silly as the scorn of an *ulfdrengr* she had known all of a few hours? How ridiculous.

"I am not laughing at you, *ungrsverda*," came Kalian's voice, still rich with amusement. "If anything, I am laughing at myself."

Gwyneth blinked away the film of tears and dared a glance at him.

"You have not seen any of the *herravaldyr*," said Kalian.

"They are your leaders," said Gwyneth, glad to be able to focus on remembering her lessons rather than the damnable embarrassment writhing in her belly.

"Yes," agreed Kalian. "They are what I think in your homeland you would call royalty."

Gwyneth shrugged. "I never saw a king or queen while I lived in Doendhtalam, and it doesn't make much difference to me that I didn't."

"The *herravaldyr* are a very different kind of royalty, then," allowed Kalian. Gwyneth sipped at her *khal* and waited for him to continue. "They earn their place. Being born *herravaldyr* is not enough in itself." He looked at her with consideration. "Is it not the same with you, Sword-daughter?"

Gwyneth frowned. Another sip of *khal* bought her a moment to mull over her answer. "In a way, yes."

"You must prove yourself to be the Heir."

"Yes."

Kalian nodded. "That is good. Different than the Courts."

"How is that?" Gwyneth asked. She already had an idea – the Sidhe Queens, as far as she knew, had not had to fight for their position, and they remained as fixed and unchanging as the sun and moon.

"We do not have monarchs who demand loyalty," said Kalian. "We are led by warriors who earn it."

"You could have been *herravaldyr*," Gwyneth said, remembering their earlier words, though her mind was beginning to fog with tiredness. She pulled Linara's silken fur about her shoulders and wondered if she could just sleep by the fire.

"Not all are destined to rule," Kalian said enigmatically.

"But you think Linara is."

"I do not know many things in this world, but that is one of them." Kalian's voice dropped to a murmur so low that Gwyneth nearly lost the thread of his words.

"Sometimes," Gwyneth said carefully, choosing her words slowly, "I think it is more difficult for a woman with a great charge laid upon her."

Kalian smiled, raising one eyebrow. "You cannot give me only one line of such an explanation."

Gwyneth smiled, a bit abashedly. "Perhaps I am overstepping."

"No," said Kalian, shaking his head. His hair swung about his face like the mane of a wild creature, the streak of silver bright in the firelight. "You are young, but that does not mean you have not lived life."

"I do not know what Linara thinks or feels," Gwyneth continued, encouraged, "but for me…sometimes I wonder if the man I love will want to be with me once I am the Bearer." Somehow the dancing flames of the fire and the night sky stretching overhead and the cold air pressing against her cheek left no room to feel shocked at her admission. "When I am the Bearer, I will be more powerful than any other mortal," she continued quietly. "He is a Paladin, and perhaps the knowledge that I will be more than he will ever be will drive us apart."

"If that drives you apart," Kalian said after a moment, "then he does not deserve you."

Gwyneth wasn't quite sure if that was a compliment, but her cheeks warmed anyway. She drank the last of her *khal* and watched the fire dancing within its ring of stones. A log shifted, sending sparks flurrying into the darkness. She leaned closer as she noticed the runes inscribed on the stones. "You use many runes."

"The Paladins first learned runes from us," replied Kalian.

"My friend Edelinne would love to study runes with your people," said Gwyneth. She wondered how Edelinne had occupied her time, since Gwyneth had left for the Between. Then again, in this moment, she hadn't left for the Between yet. She blinked and drew her mind away from contemplating the problematic idea.

Kalian shrugged. "As Linara said, there is nothing that keeps one who is not born *ulfdrengr* from coming to us other than their own heart and will to endure."

Perhaps she'd speak to Ed about it when she returned after the Solstice, Gwyneth thought. She yawned.

"There is a place in a tent for you, if you wish to sleep," Kalian said.

"If I am going to train tomorrow, I should get some rest," Gwyneth said as though to convince herself, inhaling the cold night air and watching the cloud from her breath dissipate. A part of her wanted to wander off into the wildness of the *ulfdrengr* camp, letting the beat of the drum carry her where it may. The stars shone overhead. She wondered if she would ever have the privilege of seeing the stars sing.

Kalian chuckled. "Or if you do not wish to sleep, there are many who would be quite interested in showing Rionach's heir our ways."

He said the words quite casually, tipping back his head to join her in looking up at the stars. She was not sure if he meant for her to take any other meaning from the suggestion – certainly not for himself, she thought, because he clearly sought Linara's favor. Gwyneth shifted on her seat, pressing her lips together.

"What troubles you?" Kalian spoke more softly now, as though he didn't want to spook her.

She half-smiled and looked at him ruefully. "Is it that obvious?"

He grinned, his canines gleaming in the firelight. "You wear your thoughts upon your face, *ungrsverda.*" He lifted one massive shoulder in a noncommittal shrug. "It is not always a bad thing, for others to be able to see your emotions."

Gwyneth made a noncommittal sound. "For those close to me, maybe. But…as the Bearer, I don't think I'll always want others to be able to know what I'm thinking or what I'm feeling."

"Then practice. Concealing your emotions is a skill just like wielding a sword."

She nodded.

"You did not answer my question," said Kalian, raising his dark eyebrows.

"Must I?"

"Not at all. Your choices are your own. But I venture to say that I have seen a few more decades of life than you."

Gwyneth eyed him skeptically. "Decades?" she repeated.

His eyes glinted in amusement. "I am nearly a century old."

"Well," said Gwyneth, blinking. She sat back. "To read about the long lives of *ulfdrengr* is one thing, but to hear you tell it is another thing entirely," she confessed.

Kalian spread his hands. "We may bear more scars from our lives than the Court Sidhe, but I think we live more exciting lives."

"More exciting lives up in the frozen North?" Gwyneth tried to put skepticism back into her voice. She liked Kalian more for letting her guide the conversation away from his question, because she wasn't sure she had an answer for him.

"Oh yes," replied Kalian solemnly, though the firelight danced in his eyes. "Have you ever been on a troll hunt, *ungrsverda*?"

"No," said Gwyneth with a little laugh. She leaned forward and put her elbows on her knees, looking conspiratorially at the *ulfdrengr*. "But I have helped to kill a *baobhan sith* and fought a *syivhalla*."

The planes of Kalian's face hardened at her mention of the *syivhalla*. He murmured something under his breath in the Northtongue, too low for her to understand. "If you survived to tell the tale, then you are worthy of the title of Heir."

She shook her head. "I didn't kill it. I fought it. Two Paladins killed it."

"All the same," Kalian said gravely, "few live to tell of the horrors of a *syivhalla*." His eyes darkened, and he stared into the fire, looking more serious than Gwyneth had yet seen him. "You are no stranger to blood and betrayal."

"No," replied Gwyneth, thinking of Brita's purring voice and the gleaming white of her skull as the *syivhalla* peeled away her flesh. "I am not."

They were silent for a moment, the distant sounds of camp wavering about them.

"I apologize," said Gwyneth finally in the Northtongue, "for mentioning the *syivhalla*."

"You did nothing wrong." Kalian spread his empty hands in absolution. Gwyneth gazed down at the scars on his hands: feathered silver lines webbed across the knuckles, and several puckered red lines ran over the back of his left hand. She glimpsed another tangle of scars at his left wrist, though his shirtsleeve hid the full extent. It looked as though he'd caught the jaws of an animal with his left arm, she realized.

"We should speak of something more light-hearted before you go to sleep," Kalian continued.

Gwyneth smiled. "The *ulfdrengr* do not quite have a reputation for being light-hearted."

Kalian chuckled. "There are few who bother to truly understand us."

"It would feel arrogant to say that I will," said Gwyneth in a burst of bravery, "but I'm going to try my best."

"And that is the first step in any journey," replied Kalian. He tilted his head to one side. "Although we shall see if you feel so charitably after tomorrow."

A thrill of excitement mixed with apprehension bubbled in Gwyneth's belly. She only smiled, though, and they lapsed into comfortable silence peppered by the crackling of the fire.

After Gwyneth's third jaw-cracking yawn, Kalian stood and stretched.

"Come then," he said, taking her empty mug from her and offering her his hand. His giant grip swallowed her fingers as he pulled her upright. She staggered a little as her legs remembered their duty, sluggish from the cold and exhaustion.

The shadows draped around them thickly as Kalian led her away from the fire toward a tent erected alone near the perimeter of the camp. Gwyneth glimpsed a flowing form that struck a primal chord of terror before she gulped a breath and remembered that there were wolves about this camp that would not attack her. Ithariel hummed comfortingly. Kalian glanced over his shoulder, his eyes alighting for a moment on Ithariel's hilt, but he said nothing and gestured to the tent.

Gwyneth gratefully pushed aside the deer hide covering the entrance. Her exhaustion overwhelmed her as she sank down onto the nest of furs on the floor of the tent, and her last amused thought was that she had forgotten to take off her boots before sleep claimed her.

Chapter 28

An insistent voice burrowed into the warm cocoon of Gwyneth's sleep. Well – she was not exactly *warm*, she realized, despite the furs wrapping her body. She was still cold, but she had not been able to feel it while asleep. She groaned in protest, her stiff body adding its own sharp complaints as she shifted and pulled a fur over her face.

"*Ungrsverda,*" came the voice again, rumbling through the tent. "You only get one chance."

Then, like lightning flashing through the dark night sky, memory rushed back: the journey through the ether, the rush through the wintry forest, the *ulfdrengr* camp and the promise she had made to Linara. Gwyneth threw off the furs and bolted upright, clenching her teeth on a cry of pain at the sudden movement. Her back throbbed – she put a hand over her shoulder and discovered that she'd slept with Ithariel still sheathed along her spine. All the better for a hasty exit, she thought as she stumbled out of the tent.

Kalian raised an eyebrow at her and before she could say anything, he turned and strode away. She hastened to follow, feeling like one of the young Inionacha again, struggling to keep pace with one of the Instructors. About her, the camp stirred to life, *ulfdrengr* emerging from tents or rising from where they'd slept on the forest floor, wrapped only in a fur. Gwyneth winced as her legs prickled and protested such a rude awakening. She'd risen earlier and been colder in the Pale, she reminded herself fiercely, though her memory did not quite hold up to the current experience.

The trees thinned, and they emerged into a small clearing. Gwyneth could have crossed it in ten strides in every direction, and the grasses grew high about their feet. Two lithe forms detached themselves from the trees and met them in the center of the glade.

"Kalian," said the young woman. She looked to be about Gwyneth's age, though Gwyneth knew that her judgment didn't serve her well when it came to *ulfdrengr* ages. She wasn't as awe-inspiring in size as Linara, but there was the promise of strength in her long, coltish limbs and the glint of steely stubbornness in her eyes as she looked at Gwyneth. She wore her dark hair in a tight braid drawn up into a ridge down the center of her head. Gwyneth resisted the urge to put a hand to her own sleep-mussed braid.

"A new training partner?" said the young man standing beside her in Commontongue. His blue eyes flashed with mischief. He looked younger than the girl, and his body hadn't yet truly started to change. Even so, Gwyneth glanced back to Kalian. She doubted the boy would ever be a match for him.

"Yes," replied Kalian. He gestured to the two young *ulfdrengr*. "Evedra, Malit, meet Gwyneth."

Gwyneth felt both strangely grateful and a bit indignant that Kalian hadn't introduced her as the Heir to the Iron Sword.

Malit leaned close to Evedra, speaking in Northtongue. "You will beat her. She cannot even manage to braid her own hair."

"And you cannot even manage to grow a beard," replied Evedra coolly. "Is that your reason for losing to me so often?"

Gwyneth didn't catch her laugh before it escaped, and the two young *ulfdrengr* turned to her sharply, Malit with chagrin that quickly changed to defiance and Evedra with an evaluating expression.

"I do not think a beard or a braid makes the warrior," replied Gwyneth in the *ulfdrengr* language. She smiled slightly. "But I would like to learn how to braid my hair like yours, Evedra."

Evedra tilted her head to one side. "Only if you beat me."

"Fair," said Gwyneth, grinning. Her aches and pains were forgotten as she stepped forward to meet Evedra in the center of the glade, reaching over her shoulder for Ithariel. Evedra drew her own blade, shorter and thicker than the swords with which Gwyneth had sparred. At the edge of her vision, Gwyneth saw two young wolves pace around the edge of the clearing, one with sure, graceful movements and the other with spry, exuberant energy.

She turned her attention back to Evedra. She had never fought an *ulfdrengr*, not even a young one, and excitement coursed through her. Her *taebramh* sparked into awareness behind her breastbone as she paused, unsure of the courtesy to begin a sparring match. Evedra answered the question by leaping at Gwyneth with raised blade and bared teeth.

Ithariel sang as Gwyneth blocked Evedra's blow. The power behind the blow shocked Gwyneth, coursing through her arm even with Ithariel's help; her eyes must have widened, because Evedra's bared teeth curved into a grin. There was barely the pause of a heartbeat before Evedra whirled and attacked from another angle, her movement so swift that Gwyneth would not have been able to follow it but for Ithariel and her *taebramh.* Her vision whitened at the edges as Ithariel reached out, sending tendrils of awareness up Gwyneth's arm, the sword's consciousness sitting comfortably at the edge of Gwyneth's awareness.

Gwyneth leaned into the connection to Ithariel and pulled more *taebramh* from her chest, sending it coursing down her arms and into her legs. There had been a time when she had thought using *taebramh* in a sparring match constituted bad form, but one never knew the strength of one's opponent – especially when that opponent was a rangy young *ulfdrengr* who possessed far more speed and strength than any mortal except Rionach and perhaps the Paladin Gwyneth had sparred at Samhain.

For a few moments, Gwyneth allowed Evedra to direct the sparring match, parrying only when Evedra attacked and keeping out of reach as much as she could. Out of the corner of her eye, partially obscured by the bright flare of her *taebramh* burning at the edges of her vision, Gwyneth noted Malit circling the edge of the clearing, a hungry look on his face; and Kalian, standing with his arms crossed over his chest, watching the sparring match with an unreadable face.

Her training with Rionach in the Between, though confined to the strange little dwelling made of stone, had included many hours of sparring with the Bearer. Rionach had not been gentle, either, leaving Gwyneth with blackened bruises from the blunt edge of their sparring blades, and breaking Gwyneth's arm during a particularly intense match during which Gwyneth had gained an edge for just a moment on the older woman. Rionach had repaired the bone nearly immediately, but Gwyneth still remembered the sickening crack and the jolt of agony.

Evedra caught Gwyneth's sleeve with her blade, and Gwyneth felt the sharp tip of the short sword score down her forearm. She was sure it broke the skin, and with the Paladins first blood usually won the sparring match; Evedra, however, did not falter for even a heartbeat.

Fighting Evedra was not quite like fighting Rionach, but it had its similarities.

Well then, said Gwyneth silently to Ithariel, the sword tugging at her awareness eagerly, *let's get to work.*

The *ulfdrengr*, though quick, was not so quick that she could not be caught with a clever move. The beginning moments of the sparring match had given her an idea of Evedra's style, and Ithariel too had been feeling for the weaknesses in the *ulfdrengr*'s defense. Now Gwyneth opened the channel in her awareness and let Ithariel's consciousness flow into her own; she danced away from a swing of Evedra's blade and then began the counterattack.

She had longer limbs and a longer sword than the young *ulfdrengr* (which somewhat surprised her, but she supposed she'd grown during the past year, and during her time in the Between). Sweat began prickling on her brow despite the morning cold, and their warmed breath fogged the air between them in bursts. She darted close, Ithariel slipping past the short sword, her point piercing the skin of Evedra's midsection, just enough to draw blood. Gwyneth danced away. Evedra made a little sound that was no more than a huff of air, more surprised than anything, Gwyneth thought.

The *ulfdrengr* launched another quick attack, nearly landing a blow that would have sliced Gwyneth open from neck to navel; but Ithariel jerked in Gwyneth's hand and blocked the arcing of the short sword at the last moment. The clash echoed through the glade. Gwyneth's ears rang. She heard Malit yell something in the Northtongue, but her mind didn't capture the words. Her lungs began to burn as she leapt out away from Evedra, watching for another opening.

Evedra gave a low growl and stalked toward Gwyneth, looking very much like the predator to which she was bonded. Gwyneth sidestepped the swing of the short sword, reading the movement by watching Evedra's chest, and slipped Ithariel close to give another pinprick, this time in Evedra's ribs. The young *ulfdrengr*'s huff of frustration inched closer to a snarl.

Gwyneth stumbled, her footing fouled by the long grass, and Evedra gave her another shallow cut, this time on her left shoulder. Gwyneth hardly felt the sting – she berated herself for misplacing her feet, but Ithariel pushed back the frustration, directing her focus back to Evedra. The young *ulfdrengr*, though certainly a fine fighter, began to let her emotions get the better of her. Her swings became a little wilder, a little less carefully placed. Gwyneth slipped close to give two more shallow cuts and realized she did not know when an *ulfdrengr* match ended.

Blood spotted Evedra's shirt, and Gwyneth felt her own blood slide down into her left palm from the cut on her forearm. Blood certainly did not end the sparring match – perhaps disarming Evedra was the key. Gwyneth ignored the burn of the cold in her chest and the tightness in her legs. If winning this match meant she could train with the *ulfdrengr*, then she would win the match.

Ithariel observed Gwyneth's thoughts and fought accordingly, the sword an extension of Gwyneth's intent rather than her direction. They had trained together in the Between against Rionach, after all; to even survive a sparring match with the Bearer was to improve in some way. She parried several sloppy attacks from Evedra, though the blows were still powerful enough to vibrate through Ithariel's hilt. And then, rather than dodge the next stroke of Evedra's sword, she stepped to the side and toward Evedra, Ithariel flashing as the sword snaked around the *ulfdrengr*'s blade and locked at the hilt. With a sharp twist, Gwyneth sent Evedra's blade sailing through the air. Malit shouted something, his voice layered over their heavy breathing. Evedra jumped back, her hand going toward what had to be a hidden knife sheath.

Gwyneth's *taebramh* flared suddenly, sharpening her hearing. She turned just in time to see Malit hurl himself at her; she leapt to avoid the tackle, but he still caught her legs. Ithariel jerked her sword arm painfully in the rush to ensure that neither Malit nor Gwyneth ended up impaled on the blade. Gwyneth fell hard and the long grasses closed over them, reminding Gwyneth of falling into the village pond when she was barely old enough to walk. Instinctually, she kicked, and Malit grunted as her foot connected with something soft, but then he elbowed her in the stomach, knocking her breath from her lungs.

Gwyneth pushed away the edges of panic. She had definitely *not* trained in wrestling with Rionach. But that didn't mean she couldn't still fight, Ithariel reminded her with fierce pride, chiming from among the concealing grasses. Gwyneth caught Malit's next blow with her forearm and surged upward. They were about the same height, but Malit had yet to put substantial muscle onto his lean frame. He was surprisingly light as she arched her back and rolled, trying to throw him off of her while still keeping ahold of Ithariel. Malit hooked his heels around her midsection and pulled her with him – he ended up beneath her, but quick as a striking snake he threw a punch that clipped Gwyneth's left cheek. Even that glancing contact snapped her head back, her eyes instantly watering.

Ithariel sang in outrage and the sword flew toward Malit's throat. Evedra cried out. Ithariel, of course, stopped, quivering, a hair's breadth from the jumping pulse in the hollow of Malit's throat. Malit relaxed the viselike grip of his legs but did not release her, staring up at her with stubborn defiance.

Ithariel chimed a curt warning and Gwyneth thrust out her left arm without looking, catching Evedra's wrist and twisting until she growled and dropped the dagger.

"Enough," came Kalian's voice.

Malit instantly released his hold on Gwyneth and Evedra straightened, stepping away from them and leaving her dagger where it had fallen in the long grass. Gwyneth took a deep breath, throbbing pain pulsing through her cheek as she pulled back her *taebramh*. Ithariel trembled but did not protest as Gwyneth stood, sheathing the blade with calm, deliberate movements.

Evedra gazed coolly at Gwyneth, but Malit glared at her with outright hostility in his blue eyes. Gwyneth gave a little sigh. She'd meant to compliment them on their skill, but she swallowed the words that would only stoke their resentment. Evedra bent to retrieve her blade and turned away from them, crouching in the long grass to secret the knife into its hiding place.

Kalian strode toward them through the long grass, all the humor that Gwyneth remembered from the conversation by the fire gone. He looked gravely at Malit and Evedra. "You failed."

Malit clenched his jaw but Evedra nodded. "Yes."

"If that had been a real battle, you would be dead." Kalian fixed his gaze on Malit. Evedra remained silent; Gwyneth had to give the girl credit for reading Kalian. The silence stretched tensely between them. Malit nodded, his jaw set stubbornly. Kalian still waited, his massive form still.

"Yes," Malit said finally.

"Do you honor Namoryk and Vala by dying in a fight you could have won?"

"No," Malit and Evedra answered together. The intensity of their voices and their gazes sent chills down Gwyneth's spine.

The two young *ulfdrengr* seemed to be waiting for some other pronouncement from Kalian. Malit – the easier of the two for Gwyneth to read, and the younger of them, she thought – looked as though he were steeling himself.

"Go find a deer for the evening meal," Kalian said.

Malit's eyes widened in surprise and he glanced at Evedra. Evedra elbowed him, leaving a smudge of blood on his shirt, her gaze never leaving Kalian. The dark-haired *ulfdrengr* gave a curt nod, and the two younger ones turned and melted away into the trees without another word or glance at Gwyneth.

As Gwyneth's *taebramh* receded, it left in its wake the small, bright pain of the cuts inflicted by Evedra and Malit. She pulled aside her torn sleeve to look at the shallow cut on her forearm, pressing her lips together as she realized that the fine raiment intended for the Solstice celebration now bore scars from the sparring match as well. Her face throbbed sharply, muting the cuts to mere discomfort at the edges of a wave of nausea. Ithariel reached back into Gwyneth's consciousness, helping her stay on her feet and prodding a tendril of Gwyneth's *taebramh* toward her face.

"We train differently." She heard Kalian's voice as though from a distance.

Gwyneth forced herself to turn her head and look at Kalian. She smiled even though the movement sent sharp lances through her jaw and cheekbone. "You must heal quickly."

Kalian nodded. "But that does not mean we do not have scars."

She wondered suddenly what other scars Kalian bore on his massive, muscled frame, a thought that sent an unexpected flash of heat through her. She straightened her shoulders and took a deep breath against both her unruly thoughts and the throbbing of her cheek. Her treacherous thoughts segued from wondering about Kalian's scars to thinking about Rhys and his scars and comparing the two. She tried to distract herself by stretching experimentally.

"You fought well," said Kalian.

"I have the feeling you don't often give compliments," said Gwyneth. Her voice vibrated painfully through her jaw and teeth, and the motion of speaking stoked the fiery throbbing that her *taebramh* had managed to soothe down to embers.

"And I have the feeling you don't often take blows to the face," said Kalian, his tone only half-joking as he stepped close and took her chin in one large hand. She felt his callouses against her jaw as he carefully turned her face. She tried not to flinch when he ran the tips of his fingers over her cheekbone, expertly checking the planes of bone for a break. Gwyneth fought the urge to lower her gaze; instead, she watched him examine her face, his wolfish amber eyes intent.

When he released her, she said, "We do not – *did* not – often strike each other so in training at the Hall of the Inionacha, but that does not mean that I cannot adapt to your way of training."

Kalian chuckled. "I did not question that, *ungrsverda.*" One of his large hands dropped to her shoulder and he squeezed in a brief, companionable gesture. "Come. The morning meal should be nearly ready."

Gwyneth frowned. "Only one match?"

He chuckled again. "Only one blow to the head for you this morning."

She tried to think of a witty response to that and failed, so she turned instead to her curiosity about Malit and Evedra. "Are the two of them in training?"

"They have completed their first five winters with our training master," replied Kalian. She followed half a stride behind him as he led her away from the glade. "The young ones do not have formal lessons while we travel for the Solstice, but it is the responsibility of all to help to train them."

"And what was today's lesson?"

Kalian's teeth flashed white in the predawn shadows. "Humility."

Gwyneth laughed even as she felt a small spark of satisfaction that Kalian had placed such faith in her fighting skills. Then she paused, realizing it would have been a lesson in humility either way: remaining humble after besting the Heir to the Sword, or retaining grace and humility after being bested by the Heir to the Sword. *That* put a damper on her satisfaction; Ithariel chimed quietly in loving support as she followed Kalian through the *ulfdrengr* camp. Her cheek ached and the cuts on her arm and shoulder stung, but she felt happier than she'd been since before the *syivhalla* attack as she contemplated all she would learn in the fortnight before the Solstice.

Chapter 29

As Gwyneth followed Kalian through the camp toward the main fire and the communal meal, she felt again that strange sense of welcome as *ulfdrengr* passed them without so much as a second glance. Kalian occasionally nodded or exchanged a word of greeting, but there seemed to be no expectation that he introduce Gwyneth, nor was there any surprise at this stranger in their camp. Leaves crunched with frost underfoot when she stepped off the path where others had trodden; a chill wind curled through the trees of the forest as the silvery light of a winter dawn shone through their leaves overhead.

In a typical morning in the breakfast hall of the Inionacha, the conversation rose incrementally from whispers into a low hum as the young women awakened to the day. The *ulfdrengr* camp sounded nothing like that slow, building rise to wakefulness. To Gwyneth's eyes and ears, the *ulfdrengr* did not spend any time in that hazy half-awake state. They walked purposefully and gracefully, even if they looked tired, their voices sounding firm and sure. There were no yawns or grumbles. Gwyneth tucked that observation away in the back of her mind, vowing that she'd emulate the sensible approach to the beginning of the day.

At least half of the *ulfdrengr* looked as though they'd already been sparring that morning, and all of them wore at least one weapon. Gwyneth had never seen such a variety of weapons in one place: axes with short handles and long handles, daggers of every size and shape, curved scimitars that she recognized only from the pages of the books she'd studied in the Tower, short swords and broadswords, throwing knives worn on a bandolier across the chest and hardwood staffs capped with hammered metal. Gwyneth only glimpsed a handful of bows, but her fingers itched to touch the beautifully crafted weapons.

The *ulfdrengr* who bore the weapons were sights to behold as well. The men and the women dressed much the same, in well-worn shirts and breeches with furs thrown over their shoulders; some of the men kept their hair as long as the women, and any *ulfdrengr* with long hair wore it in braids that varied from simple, similar to Evedra's single braid down the center of her head, to complex woven designs that stood up in ridges and coiled like serpents. Gwyneth felt as though she didn't have enough time to see it all, to observe it all properly.

"This is what you would call the warrior camp," Kalian explained as they wove their way through a group toward a large cauldron set over the embers of the fire. A dark-haired man jostled shoulders with a chestnut-haired woman and another slim man as they ladled out something that smelled delicious from the cauldron into wooden bowls.

"There are other camps, then?" Gwyneth asked, switching to Northtongue as they neared the cauldron.

"Kalian!" said the dark-haired man, turning to them. Gwyneth saw the resemblance between them at once: though the other man was of a slimmer build than Kalian, they both had the same strong chin and a hint of almond shaping in the eyes. "This is the Heir, then? I was not surprised that you were the one to find her."

Gwyneth wondered again if her journey through the ether had truly been a mistake or if Rionach had somehow planned it – it seemed as though a good number of the *ulfdrengr* had known of her impending arrival. If it had truly been a mistake, wouldn't the Bearer have come looking for Gwyneth herself, rather than send a message to the *ulfdrengr*? She didn't think it her place to ask, so she held her tongue.

"Malyk is one of the best trackers in the North – I would have been surprised if Kalian *hadn't* found her," said the woman with the chestnut hair. Her eyes were a startling shade of pale gold, unmistakably lupine staring out from her features.

"Now, Mariel," said Kalian's brother – he *had* to be his brother, Gwyneth thought – said, switching to Commontongue. "We are being rude, complimenting Kalian in our own language so that the Heir cannot understand. She should know the prowess of her finder."

"I'm sure that I would have been found eventually, although I'm less sure I would have been found by a wolf so beautiful and unwilling to eat me as Malyk," Gwyneth said in Northtongue.

Kalian chuckled, and his brother stared at her for a heartbeat before roaring with laughter. Gwyneth thought his laughter more out of surprise at her facility with their native tongue than the cleverness of her words. The wolf-eyed woman grinned, and the slim man next to her turned. Gwyneth saw that the man was, in fact, a woman – she'd assumed her to be a man because of her short-cropped hair.

"Gwyneth, this is Mariel and Tula," said Kalian, gesturing to the two women. "And the short one is my brother Tarian."

Gwyneth almost told them that she wasn't sure that she would remember all their names – they were all starting to sound tongue-twistingly similar – but she stopped herself. If she could learn to speak Northtongue and Merrow and everything else that Rionach demanded of her in the Between, then she could remember the names of the *ulfdrengr*, especially those close to Kalian. She owed him that much at least for his kindness to her.

Tula had a sharp face that reminded Gwyneth of a fox, and her dark hair glinted with a hint of red as the breeze rustled the leaves overhead, shifting the shadows. "Did you give her that bruise, Kalian?"

"You could ask me yourself," said Gwyneth.

Rather than bristling, Tula grinned. "I could, little sword-daughter, but who knows if you have taken a fancy to our large and handsome Kalian here, eh?"

Gwyneth's mouth watered as the breeze shifted and brought the scent of the cauldron toward them.

"She has a Paladin," said Kalian.

Mariel snorted. "And what is to say she cannot have you too?"

Her face reddening, Gwyneth found herself tongue-tied.

"She is not used to our way of sparring or our way or talking," said Tula, arching an eyebrow.

"Both will be informative," Gwyneth managed.

"Well, there you are, at least she's trying," said Mariel with a grin, nudging Tula with an elbow.

"And no, I did not give her that bruise," Kalian replied, moving past them to pick up two wooden bowls from a stack by the cauldron. He ladled a portion of what looked to be porridge into one of the bowls and handed it to Gwyneth. She couldn't pick out ingredients from the foreign scent of the porridge, but nonetheless it smelled good to her. She waited for Kalian to hand her a spoon, but he walked away from the cauldron without so much as a backward glance. The other three followed him, moving easily about his larger form. Gwyneth forced her feet to move. They found a spot under the spreading branches of an oak and sat in a loose circle on the ground. She watched the others surreptitiously: Tula pulled out a flat piece of wood that she'd whittled to something resembling a spoon, but the others merely raised the bowl to their lips, using two fingers to help scoop the porridge into their mouths.

Gwyneth waited for a moment for her porridge to cool and then followed their example. Rionach had taught her that there was no room for embarrassment when following the customs of another people; that was one of the surest ways to bring insult, intentional or no. The porridge tasted surprisingly familiar, despite its foreign scent: the *ulfdrengr* made the base porridge much the same as what Gwyneth had eaten in the Hall, merely adding a good portion of roasted meat and spices to add more flavor and substance. Her jaw hurt, but her hunger spoke louder than her discomfort; she compromised by chewing the meat on the other side of her mouth.

Tarian passed around a water skin near the end of the meal. Gwyneth thought that perhaps she'd be able to rinse her fingers – it *did* feel strange to eat with her hands, despite her willingness to show the *ulfdrengr* her knowledge of their customs – but the others took a few swallows of the water and passed it on. Again, Gwyneth watched them, thinking that Mariel might be the most fastidious after Tula, who hadn't dirtied her fingers at all. Mariel wiped her fingers on a patch of moss and then on the hem of her shirt, quite unselfconsciously. Gwyneth hastened to do the same.

"So if Kalian didn't give you that bruise, who did?" asked Tula. Mariel put aside her bowl and stood, walking back toward the food; none of the others gave her a second glance. Gwyneth had the feeling breaking their fast together in the morning was a common ritual among the four of them, perfectly familiar and choreographed.

"I sparred with Evedra and Malit this morning," she replied.

Tula tilted her head to one side, looking at Kalian. "Both of them at once?"

"She is the Heir," said Kalian, as though that explained it.

"A Paladin her age would not spar two of our young ones." Tarian glanced at Gwyneth.

"I didn't think I was going to be sparring both of them," said Gwyneth. "Malit surprised me." Her face throbbed as she remembered the blow. "It won't happen that way again."

"A good lesson to learn," said Tarian. His gaze turned contemplative. "Evedra, at least, is one of the best among her litter."

"Her litter?"

"Those chosen to bond with a litter may be of slightly different ages, though they are often within a few years of one another," said Tarian patiently. "Once they are bonded and begin training, we refer to them all as a litter. All of them started training at the same time, after all."

"How many litters are there in a season?"

"Two or three in a slow season, up to six after a season when the game has been plentiful and the snows not as harsh."

Gwyneth did the calculations in her head. If she assumed there were six pups in a litter – there could be more, she supposed, but she stuck with the number – then every year there were at least a dozen new warrior-wolves bonded to their *ulfdrengr* counterpart. She remembered Malyk's sleek grace and the hairs on the back of her neck stood on end as she imagined the damage the huge wolf would inflict on an enemy on his own, much less paired with formidable Kalian.

"*Herravaldyr* litters, perhaps once or twice in a half-dozen years," added Tarian.

"It would be more if the Council would allow mixing the bloodlines," said Tula in an undertone. Tarian shifted and Kalian's face darkened just enough for Gwyneth to catch the change in his expression. She wondered what exactly Tula meant, but she held her tongue, sensing it was a topic of dissent among the *ulfdrengr*. Perhaps she could ask Kalian later.

"And then both the young wolves and their partners go into training?" she asked, trying to steer the discussion back into safer waters.

"Yes," said Tarian, but he didn't elaborate. It seemed the mention of the bloodlines had dampened the conversation.

Mariel returned to the circle carrying a fat-bellied teapot by its long handle. In her other hand, she expertly balanced a stack of earthenware mugs, of the same type that Gwyneth had seen the night prior. Gwyneth stood and took the stack of mugs from Mariel, taking one and passing the rest around the circle. Mariel poured Kalian's mug first – Gwyneth wondered whether this was because Kalian and Malyk were actually *herravaldyr*, despite his denial. To Gwyneth's surprise, Mariel turned to her next, filling her mug with steaming *khal*. Gwyneth pressed her hands against the mug as warmth seeped through the earthenware.

"Are we going to travel today?" she asked after gingerly sipping at the drink. The warmth felt surprisingly good against the throbbing of her face; she resisted the urge to press her cheek against the mug. The warmth might feel good, but it was cold that would help with the swelling and bruising.

"No," replied Kalian. Tula stretched and Tarian drank his *khal* silently. Mariel reclaimed her seat between Kalian and Gwyneth. "We are only about three days' travel from Darkhill. We will not travel for another sennight."

"It sounds as though this journey is a sort of celebration for your people as well," said Gwyneth. She took a long drink of *khal*, and when no one replied, she added, "I want to understand and experience as much as I can while I'm here."

"Training with us for a fortnight will not necessarily gain you entry into our trust," Mariel said. Tula gazed unblinkingly at Gwyneth, her light-gold eyes unreadable.

"I do not expect to be taken into the full confidence of all," replied Gwyneth, sitting up straighter as she drew upon the courtly language that she had honed during her time Between with Rionach. "I mean to say that as Bearer, I wish to have full and trusting relations with your people, and I think that learning and understanding as much as I can now will help with that in the future."

"You speak just as prettily as the envoys from the Summer Queen," murmured Tula. She hadn't yet blinked.

"Perhaps we are being too harsh with the young Heir," said Tarian, raising one eyebrow.

"She did not ask for any concession this morn," said Kalian.

Gwyneth thought that he meant it as a good thing.

"We should at least give her a chance," Mariel said.

"A chance at what?" Tula asked.

Gwyneth felt as though she were on trial. Her skin prickled – how quickly the *ulfdrengr* had shifted from amiable breakfast companions to sharp-eyed examiners.

"A chance at friendship," Mariel said.

"Friendship," muttered Tula, narrowing her unsettling eyes.

"You treated me much differently when you thought I was merely here for a day or two," Gwyneth said in the Northtongue, her stomach plunging as though she'd just leapt off a cliff. The sounds of the awakening forest filled the silence.

"Guests are much different than friends," Tula said finally. "There have been many who have tried to be friends to the North, and just as many who have broken their word."

"I make no promise other than I will be honest and forthright in my dealings with the *ulfdrengr*," said Gwyneth. A headache beat at the back of her skull and her cheek throbbed hotly. She wished she hadn't gotten hit in the face before such an important conversation.

"That is no more than we would expect from any honorable person," said Tarian, though his tone was not quite as cold as Tula.

"Then what is your expectation of a friend?" Gwyneth countered. She sipped at her *khal*, hoping that would lend her fortitude against the abominable ache in her head. Ithariel reached out with soft, silken tendrils, twining through her awareness.

"Friend is not a word we use lightly as most do," Tarian said. "A friend – a trueheart friend – would die for those they claim in friendship."

Gwyneth thought of Rhys and the Paladins. She thought of the other women at the Hall of the Inionacha, choosing their paths now that she had been revealed as Heir. She thought of Edelinne and the others of the Seven that had survived. "I do not use the word 'friend' lightly." She straightened her shoulders, Ithariel thrumming through her head, wrapping the pain enough for her to focus. Tula's eyes shifted to the hilt of the Named Sword for an instant. "I took in a wounded Paladin in Doendhtalam before I even truly knew of Faeortalam and my own heritage. I fought a *syivhalla* to save those with whom I had trained at the Hall of the Inionacha. I do not use the word lightly, and I do not intend to ever regard any friendship between us lightly."

She didn't miss the look that passed between Kalian and Tula: Tula's expression softened slightly, and Kalian raised one dark eyebrow in silent comment. Mariel hid a smile in her mug of *khal*, and Tarian regarded Gwyneth thoughtfully. She followed Mariel's example and hid her faltering expression behind her mug, blinking away the tears that suddenly prickled at the edges of her eyes.

Her face hurt with an intensity that was difficult to ignore. She could feel the swelling in her cheek, though she was sure it looked far less obvious than it felt. Ithariel and her *taebramh* could only blunt the edges of the injury for so long; besides, Rionach had cautioned her several times about using her own powers to hide the reality of an injury. Unless she knit her own flesh with her *taebramh* – a costly endeavor only to be used as a last resort – it was best to merely endure injuries like everyone else. She shuddered involuntarily as she remembered the crack and pop of her bone mending beneath the force of Rionach's *taebramh*. Gwyneth shut her eyes, took a swallow of *khal* and forced herself to breathe deeply. The cold morning air swirled in her chest.

"Are you claiming her then, Kalian?" Tarian said, his voice filtering into her awareness.

Gwyneth opened her eyes and lowered her mug, looking at Tarian sharply and then at Kalian.

"To train you," Tarian clarified, a spark of mischief in his eyes. Half a grin lifted his lips. "You certainly jumped at that, *ungrsverda*."

"Typicall a young one will have one or two…what is the word in your tongue…mentors, I think," said Mariel in Commontongue.

Gwyneth knew switching to her first language was a peace offering, so she switched as well. "I'll be happy to train with one or all."

"But that isn't our way," replied Mariel.

"Is it your way for the one being trained to choose?"

"No," Mariel replied with a smile.

The other three *ulfdrengr* looked at Kalian. For a moment, Gwyneth wondered if the huge wolf-warrior would say no; he probably had much more important things to do than look after her. He and Malyk were clearly one of the most well-respected pairs in the camp, and there had to be other necessary tasks that could use their skills.

Ithariel reproved her gently. The sword's almost-thought – Ithariel spoke in swaths of feeling and currents of emotion rather than actual words – reminded Gwyneth of her place as the Heir to the Sword. Gwyneth thought that was all well and good, but it was clear that the *ulfdrengr* did not simply take in strangers to teach their ways, despite their easy hospitality.

"I will speak to Linara," said Kalian finally.

"You would find an excuse to speak to Linara no matter what," Tula said in Northtongue with a mischievious grin, her seriousness swept away.

"One heir to train another," murmured Tarian, looking at his brother and then at Gwyneth contemplatively.

"How can you have an heir when you are opposed to bending the knee? Wouldn't an heir require a king?" Gwyneth asked, feeling bold again. She finished her *khal* and Mariel poured her more without asking if she wanted it. A feeling of belonging stole over Gwyneth once more at the easy familiarity of Mariel's movement.

"We are not bound to our king by fear of retribution," replied Tarian.

"We have a voice in who rules us," Mariel said firmly.

"If we wish to leave, nothing will stop us save our own hearts," finished Tula.

"You choose your king and your queen?" The books that the Scholars had written on the *ulfdrengr* left out most details of the power structure in the North; Gwyneth had noted as much to Rionach, and the Bearer had told her that the *ulfdrengr* did not often speak of such things to outsiders.

"Yes," replied Kalian, and none of them said anything further.

Gwyneth took a swallow of her newly refilled cup and thought that perhaps they'd speak to her of it eventually. She lapsed into companionable silence, listening to the conversations of the other four. Kalian didn't say much, but the others clearly looked to him for his opinion. He was respected, that much was clear. Tula seemed to be the youngest of the group, but she wasn't afraid to put the others in their place with deft jabs of her wry humor. Mariel seemed to be a sort of counterpoint to Tula's brazenness: she dressed with a bit more feminine flair despite the plainness of her clothes, and she laughed easily and often.

"Well then," Mariel said when the pot of *khal* was empty. "Time to get on with the day."

"It is a Solstice day, so it is a good day," said Tula with a grin.

Gwyneth looked to Kalian for explanation, but it was Tarian who answered her.

"Our entire journey to the Unseelie Court is a celebration," he explained. "The young ones do not train so hard, and we hunt only for food for the feasts. Every night there is dancing and drums." He grinned. "There will be many young ones come spring who were sired during this journey."

"That's good to know," Gwyneth replied lightly.

Tula grinned. "There you are, getting the hang of it a bit."

"Well," said Mariel, standing and brushing away a few leaves that clung to her breeches. "While you go seek out Linara, Kalian, I can take the *ungrsverda* to the *volta* so they can fix her face."

Gwyneth raised her eyebrows. "Fix my face?" she queried, deadpan.

Tula sniggered and leaned over to sling an arm about Gwyneth's shoulder. "The *volta* don't fix faces to make them more appealing to the men, little sword-sister, if that's what you're thinking."

"I don't think she needs much help in that sense," Tarian remarked mildly, earning a punch in the arm from Mariel and a cautionary look from Kalian.

Tula shook her head. "Come on then, Gwyn."

The familiar nickname struck Gwyneth like an arrow to her chest with a sudden piercing homesickness for the Hall of the Inionacha – more specifically, for Ed, who was the only one besides her father and cousin who'd used the nickname. She stood and handed her mug and bowl to Tarian, who walked about the little circle collecting all the dirtied dishes. Gwyneth found that she appreciated a man willing to share equally in a task that in her world and in the Hall would have been done by a woman. Granted, she allowed, in the Hall there had *only* been women to do the tasks.

"Kalian will find us when he's spoken to Linara, don't you trouble yourself," Tula said. "Mariel, coming?"

"Yes," Mariel replied. "Need to see Ephelia about a new rune."

Gwyneth followed the two women as they began to walk through the camp.

"You *could* just ask her to take care of it permanently," Tula said.

Mariel shrugged her shoulders. "Not completely sure if that's a good idea yet. Don't get me wrong, I want nothing to do with young ones right now, but who knows how I'll feel in two decades."

Understanding dawned on Gwyneth. "The *volta* make runes to keep you from having children?"

"Of course," replied Mariel matter-of-factly. "There's precious little time once you've bonded to train before your partner is full-grown and ready to go into battle." She shrugged one shoulder. "Last thing a wolf needs is to be slowed down that young. And then, dying in childbed never really appealed to me either."

"Are there many women bonded to wolves?" Gwyneth asked as

they passed the border of the warrior's camp. Sunlight filtered through the leaves of the trees, dappling the forest floor with shadow.

Mariel answered after a moment of thought. "Maybe one in four of the entire pack is bonded to a woman. Different clans have different thoughts on it, of course."

"Clans, like families within the pack?"

"Yes," replied Mariel.

"For getting hit in the head, you're full of many questions," Tula said.

They stopped before a tall tree with silvery bark. Birch, perhaps, Gwyneth thought. Her head hurt and made thinking clearly difficult. With her head pulsing in time to her heartbeat, it took most of her concentration to follow the conversation and conceal her growing dizziness from the two *ulfdrengr*.

Mariel sketched a complex rune in the air with both hands. As Gwyneth had seen before, a rune on the tree flared, except this rune was not to dampen sound. This rune, she saw, was to conceal the *volta* camp entirely. The air rippled silver, turning mirror-like for a moment, and then the silver dissipated like mist, curling away into the forest.

Gwyneth caught her breath. As fierce and forthright as the camp of the warriors had been, the camp of the *volta* was bright and beautiful with color. Vibrant banners in scarlet, indigo, gold and green rippled between the trees, strung from silver vines twined into the branches of the canopy overhead. At intervals, long strands of thin silk knotted with coins and pearls draped between the banners. Floating globes of *taebramh* cast light in varying shades throughout the camp, from the deep red of a sunset to the bluish white of moonlight on snow.

"Welcome to the camp of the *volta*," said Mariel, and Gwyneth followed her wordlessly into the fantastic kaleidoscope of color.

Chapter 30

Tula took the lead as they wended through the color-soaked *volta* camp. Gwyneth glimpsed the canopies of tents in fantastic, impossible shapes. She winced as a particularly bright blue banner twisted in the breeze, catching her vision. The vibrant colors did nothing to soothe her aching head.

"The *volta* enjoy the celebration more than we, I think," Mariel said in an undertone to Gwyneth. She grinned. "We hunt and dance and fuck. They drown the forest in color instead of hunt…and they may join us for the dancing."

Mariel's blunt language did not shock Gwyneth nearly so much as she expected – probably because the pounding in her head and the mounting unsteadiness that accompanied the waves of dizziness left little room for ladylike shock. She didn't know she was swaying until she felt a firm hand at her elbow.

"Come on then," Mariel said again. "Can't leave the Heir to the Sword falling about with a bruised head."

Tula led them to a tent the color of a robin's egg. "Ephelia!" she called.

A tall woman with red streaks painted on her face threw aside the entrance flap of the tent. Gwyneth couldn't properly concentrate on the woman's face. Everything looked blurry.

"Tula, it's early, you know," said Ephelia in a chiding voice, but there was the glint of a grin that Gwyneth picked out of the woman's blurry face.

"Early for *volta,*" replied Tula. "Not so early for us."

Ephelia barked a little laugh. "And what have you brought me here?"

"An *ungrsverda,* as Kalian has named her," said Tula.

The *volta* named Ephelia stepped closer to Gwyneth. She hummed. "*The* Sword-daughter, I think. Singular." She tilted her head to one side. "Well, you want me to fix her, don't you, so bring her in."

The woman whirled and disappeared into the tent. The movement sparked a particularly fierce wave of nausea and Gwyneth swallowed down bile. Mariel waited a moment before pressing Gwyneth's elbow and leading her forward.

"You should have really brought her to us before she even sparred," said Ephelia, flitting about the interior of the tent like a bird darting from branch to branch. Gwyneth took one look at the spinning constellations twinkling overhead – the stars looked bright and real – and the sculptures of deer's antler and silver wire spinning slowly in midair and shut her eyes.

"Put your finger out for me, I need a bit of blood," said Ephelia, very close to her. The *volta*'s scent reminded Gwyneth of the thick smell of rising dough and the earthen essence of moss. She obediently held out her left hand, but then the *volta* clucked her tongue.

"Don't need to prick you when there's already blood here," Ephelia said. The cut on Gwyneth's forearm stung as Ephelia touched it. "Now, you've never had a rune to heal, have you?"

"No," Gwyneth said. "Though the Bearer did knit together the bone of my arm when she broke it in sparring."

"Then you are no stranger to blood-magic, even though you have not particularly had a rune," Ephelia said.

Gwyneth opened her eyes, her curiosity overwhelming her instinct to block out the bright colors and shining baubles of the *volta* tent. Mariel lounged in a chair carved from a twisting stump, furs piled on the wood; Tula stood near one of the antler sculptures, inspecting it as she ate a piece of bread.

"Baking is my other specialty, aside from runes," explained Ephelia with a grin to Gwyneth. "Once you've had the rune, then I think you will be able to sample some of my other work."

Though her cheek still ached, and her stomach turned rebelliously at the mention of food, Gwyneth felt slightly better just standing in the *volta* tent.

"There are a few general runes, of course, that I hang about the doorway each night before I go to sleep," Ephelia said without looking up from the table where she worked intently over something small. "Visitors in the morning usually have some sort of complaint, whether they drank too much or got knocked in the head or sliced open one limb or another in training, so a few runes to bolster anyone who comes over the threshold, they save me from listening to moaning and whining while I work." Ephelia flashed a quick grin at Gwyneth.

"The men might moan, but we do not," said Mariel, standing gracefully to join Tula in plundering the fresh bread and buns set out on a cloth on a low table.

"Only when they make us," replied Tula, glancing devilishly at Mariel.

Mariel snorted. "Some of us choose to be louder than others."

Tula laughed. It took Gwyneth a moment to realize that they were talking about sex. She blinked.

"You did not blush so furiously as before, *ungrsverda*," said Mariel, not unkindly.

"If my head did not ache so badly, I would try to join the banter," admitted Gwyneth. She hoped Ephelia didn't count that as whining or moaning.

"Have you lain with a man?" Tula asked frankly, no trace of embarrassment in her voice or upon her face as she gazed at Gwyneth keenly. She broke apart another bun that had been baked in a spiral shape. It filled the tent with a delicious scent.

"Oh, those have runes baked *into* them," Ephelia said, motioning to the bun in Tula's hand. "So that when you tear into the bun, the rune makes it as though they came out of the oven five minutes ago."

"Why five minutes?" Mariel asked.

"Don't want to burn your tongue, of course," Tula said appreciatively around a mouthful of bread.

"Gwyn, you haven't answered the question," said Mariel, picking up one of the buns.

"I'm not a virgin," Gwyneth said, her throat nearly closing on the words. She'd only ever spoken with Edelinne about her trysts with Rhys, and then not in quite so blunt terms.

"Well, that's good to hear," Mariel replied. She tucked a bit of the bun into her cheek. "Ephelia, you really outdid yourself."

"Would you be able to bake these for us for the travel back?" Tula asked.

"Hmmm," Ephelia hedged. She sprinkled a glimmering powder onto the little object that she'd been working over so diligently.

"Seriously, what do you want for them?" Tula took another one, holding it close to her face as she pulled it apart and breathing in the fresh-baked scent. "I'll take you over to our camp tonight. Any night you want. Introduce you to anyone you'd like."

"I can make my own introductions," Ephelia said, tossing her long braid over one shoulder. She slid a little tool under the small object, and Gwyneth squinted at it. It looked like a miniature version of a baking peel, the paddle that the bakers used to pull loaves of bread from the oven. "Here. Open your mouth."

Gwyneth raised her eyebrows but obediently opened her mouth. Stranger things had happened in the past few years. Ithariel chuckled a little in her sheath.

"Touching it might smudge the runes, and that takes away from the power," said Ephelia. "Don't chew it, just let it sit for as long as you can stand. Tucking it beneath your tongue helps too, that will get it into your blood faster."

The *volta* deftly slid a little round flat of bread into Gwyneth's mouth. Gwyneth felt something spark against her tongue and resisted the urge to spit it out; she told herself firmly that the *volta* would not harm her, and their runes simply felt different than the *taebramh* of the Inionacha. The glittering powder that she'd seen Ephelia dust onto the bread was sugar, sweet as it dissolved. The rune popped and crackled a few more times, sending lances of pain into Gwyneth's cheek.

Ephelia must have seen her wince, because she said, "It can be a bit uncomfortable, but better than walking around with a cracked skull."

Gwyneth looked at Ephelia in alarm, raising her eyebrows in question.

"Oh yes, it was a hairline fracture, I think you would say in your language, but of course that is still a break." Ephelia gave Mariel and Tula a severe look. "Why you had her spar without..."

"Coming to you first, yes, we were idiots," Tula finished for her.

Gwyneth wondered why Tula didn't correct Ephelia – it was Kalian who'd had her spar with Evedra and Malit. The two women hadn't had anything at all to do with the decision. Perhaps it was part of the pack mentality – Tula and Mariel were clearly friends with Ephelia, but Ephelia was a *volta* and they were *ulfdrengr*. They did not pass the blame to any other *ulfdrengr*, especially not in front of a *volta* and an outsider.

Learning, Ithariel said approvingly, the word whispered at the corner of Gwyneth's mind.

Something shifted with a strange an uncomfortable sensation in Gwyneth's cheek. She swallowed against a swell of nausea, the rune-bread still soft and sweet under her tongue. Her own *taebramh* sent a curious tendril toward the rune; Gwyneth gently pushed it away, back into her chest. She didn't need her *taebramh* interacting with the Northern rune – at least not until she'd been able to study them a little bit more.

"Ephelia is the only one who gives runes like that," said Mariel.

"Takes a lot of skill," said Tula through a mouthful of bread.

"If you're going to eat an entire batch then I'd better start making more," Ephelia said mildly, looking at the low table. Two buns now sat forlornly on the cloth, crumbs scattered where there had been half a dozen more buns just moments before. Gwyneth looked at Tula and wondered how the *ulfdrengr* could eat so much.

"Running with wolves ensures that we are constantly hungry," Tula said, grinning at Gwyneth.

"I came for another rune as well, Ephelia, but we're in no rush," Mariel said, sitting again on the fur-covered chair and drawing her legs up beneath her.

"Oh, your monthly rune, of course. That won't take but a few moments," said Ephelia, walking over to a shelf and rummaging through several jars that looked to be cut from crystal.

The last of the rune-bread dissolved from beneath Gwyneth's tongue, but the sweetness of the sugar lingered, a trace of metallic tang sharpening the aftertaste. She raised tentative fingers to her cheek. When just the light touch produced no flare of pain, she pressed more firmly, feeling only a bit of an ache like from an old bruise. She opened and closed her jaw experimentally; her face felt *stiff*, somehow, like she'd just awoken from sleeping for a few days straight, but it didn't hurt anymore.

"You'll have a bit of a bruise for a day or two, but that'll fade. It was already there when you took the rune," explained Ephelia.

"Even the rune expert has her limits," Tula said teasingly.

Ephelia grinned. She was quite pretty, Gwyneth could see now; she was much physically smaller than the two *ulfdrengr* women, and she wore a brightly colored azure skirt that swirled about her legs pleasingly when she moved. Ephelia wore a belt with many small pouches slung low about her hips, and then above that she wore a scarlet shirt with a black vest that laced below her ample chest. Gwyneth had no doubt that the *volta* could find lovers without any help from her *ulfdrengr* friends.

"How do you travel with all this?" she asked, marveling at the spacious tent as she walked over to claim one of the remaining buns.

"We have our ways, of course," replied Ephelia vaguely.

With her vision clear, Gwyneth covertly watched the *volta* as she worked, gazing at the red paint that formed intricate designs on Ephelia's cheeks, chin and throat. She turned her attention to the bun in her hand, her stomach surprising her with its greedy growl. She'd just eaten breakfast barely two hours ago.

"Fighting two of our young ones should tire even the Heir to the Sword," said Tula with a knowing wink.

"I still beat them," replied Gwyneth with a shrug.

Ephelia chuckled. "She certainly has enough bravado to be one of you."

Tula grinned. "We shall see how you do when matched against the full-grown warriors, then."

Gwyneth grinned in reply. "Looking forward to it."

She wished suddenly that she could send a message to Rhys, to tell him of all the wondrous things she had already seen and done in the *ulfdrengr* camp, and all her training in the Between with Rionach. But she had not seen any Glasidhe messengers in the camp, though she knew that sometimes the Glasidhe did carry messages for the Northerners.

"You show your thoughts in your eyes, Gwyn," said Mariel. "What troubles you?"

"It isn't *troubling* me, exactly," Gwyneth said carefully. "I was just thinking of sending a message to a Paladin, but have not seen any messengers around the camp."

"Ah," said Mariel. "Eat your bread, and then I will take you to the rookery."

"The rookery?" It was not a word that Gwyneth recognized in the Northtongue. Mariel looked at Tula, who squinted in thought and then repeated the word in Common.

"Oh – you use messenger birds?" Gwyneth replied.

"We have fleet-footed messengers who carry our important missives," said Mariel, "but a love letter is not counted as such an important missive."

"That is…fair," Gwyneth admitted, even as she tamped down the urge to protest that her letter would not *just* be a love letter. She and Rhys spoke of very substantive matters in their letters to one another, even if he was a bit terser in his written word than when they spoke in person. She wondered if he'd sent letters while she'd been Between. Would he even remember her being Between, if she'd emerged from the ether nearly at the same time that she'd left?

"You think too much, *ungrsverda*," said Tula, her sharp foxlike face playful.

"Well, she will be the Bearer." Mariel paused. "That requires some thought."

Gwyneth took a bite of the bun, using a full mouth as an excuse to listen rather than contribute.

"So when will you be the Bearer?" Tula asked.

Ephelia trilled a birdlike note of disapproval at Tula, flapping one hand. Gwyneth noticed faint traces of intricate red designs on the *volta*'s palm and wrist. She thought her observation discreet, but Ephelia smiled and held out her hand for closer inspection. Tula grinned at the redirection of her friend's irritation.

"I have not forgotten your rudeness, Tula," said Ephelia without looking at the *ulfdrengr*.

"Well, it was not directed at *you*," said Tula, shrugging one shoulder. "And what was so rude about it anyway?"

Ephelia sniffed. "One does not simply *ask* about the passing of such power. It will be such a thing that we all can feel anyway."

"Maybe not all of us," countered Tula.

Gwyneth peered at the faded scrollwork on Ephilia's hand and wrist, fascinated even as she listened to the conversation about the passing of the Sword. The markings inked on Ephelia's white skin were so faded that the lines were not continuous, but they still conveyed a sense of rushing and whirling, sharpness of snow and darkness of shadow, blaze of fire and cut of ice...Gwyneth blinked and drew herself back.

"The *volta* markings speak to you," murmured Ephelia.

"It is like a whisper that I cannot quite hear," Gwyneth answered without thinking.

Ephelia gazed at her for a long moment. "Perhaps you should come to our camp to discuss this further."

Gwyneth didn't miss the small movements in the tent: Mariel sat up straighter, and Tula went very still. Would agreeing to come to the *volta* violate some sort of courtesy to the *ulfdrengr*? She racked her brain, but Rionach had never covered this situation in their lessons on Northern customs. Ithariel hummed in thought.

"Your blade has a lovely voice," said Ephelia, her gaze unfocused as she tilted her head to the side, listening.

"She does," agreed Gwyneth somewhat lamely. She cleared her throat. Perhaps the *ulfdrengr* could explain this courtesy to her further when they left the tent – if she could give a vague answer (or none at all) to Ephelia without offending the *volta*.

"Are you nearly done with my charm, Ephelia?" said Mariel.

Gwyneth glanced at her gratefully, but the chestnut-haired woman only crossed her legs coolly and yawned, displaying a very wolfish set of white teeth. Gwyneth wondered if the change in the *ulfdrengr* when they bonded to their wolves was limited to their eyes.

"First Tula with her rude question, and now you with your impatience," muttered Ephelia. "*After* you bring the Heir to me to heal, no less!"

"I said I would introduce you to whomever you'd like," Tula pointed out puckishly. "Except Kalian," she amended. "He has eyes for no one but Linara, the damn fool."

"What's so foolish about that?" Gwyneth asked. She walked over to one of the sculptures of antler and silver wire, treading softly on the sumptuous layers of fur underfoot. No one answered her. She spent the next moments tracing the curling lines of the delicate silver wire with her eyes, following it as it wrapped about tines of the antler.

"Here you are," said Ephelia, holding up a small wooden disc hung by a leather cord. The rune burned into the wood of the small circle still smoked slightly, perfuming the air in the tent.

Mariel pulled another disc on a cord from about her neck, the leather cord soft and stained with sweat. She held out the disc in her left hand, her right hand held beside it, palm down. With an air of ceremony, Ephelia held the new rune under Mariel's empty hand and covered the old one with her other hand; the *volta* closed her eyes and Gwyneth felt a little shiver of alien power in the air for an instant. Ephelia opened her eyes and turned her hands, tipping the old rune into her hand and the new rune into Mariel's. Mariel closed her fingers over the disc for a moment and then slipped the cord over her head.

"No pups for you this month," said Tula brightly.

Mariel tossed her braid over one shoulder. "Well, not for *me.*"

Tula snorted. "It's not breeding season yet and you know it as well as I."

"Nira has always been a bit rebellious," said Mariel with a shrug. "And Solstice pups would bring good fortune." She raised an eyebrow at Tula. "You know that as well as I."

Tula laughed.

"All of the buns have been eaten," Ephelia said. "Are you going to stay while I bake more? I thought warriors had more important things to do."

"Not during Solstice, we don't," countered Tula, her voice still bright with merriment. "But we'll come back tomorrow for more buns."

"Preferably not so early," Ephelia called after them as Tula swept aside the entrance hanging and Mariel led the way out of the tent.

"Not unless Gwyneth gets hit in the face again," said Tula over her shoulder.

"I don't have to have a rune every time I'm injured," protested Gwyneth, following the two *ulfdrengr* through the slowly stirring *volta* camp. A bit of lavender smoke drifted from a bright yellow tent, and embers flared to life in a fire ring without anyone tending it.

"Healing at least is something useful," said Tula enigmatically.

Mariel made a sound of agreement but waited to speak until they'd crossed the boundary between camps and the *volta* tents shimmered into invisibility behind them. "Some think that the *volta* use their power too...frivolously," she said to Gwyneth.

Gwyneth frowned, trying to reconcile this sudden change of attitude. "But we were just in Ephelia's tent...you asked her for your rune as well. You seemed friendly enough."

"Oh, we *are* friendly enough," said Tula. "But one does not always agree with one's friends."

"And that is a...broader sentiment," said Mariel. She looked at Gwyneth sharply. "Not one to be shared with the *volta*, though."

"I'm not so clumsy as that," said Gwyneth, a bit reprovingly.

"No, I do not think you are," Mariel agreed, "but sometimes it is good to say things out loud."

Gwyneth followed the two women through the cold winter forest, the bare branches whispering in the wind above them, and she thought that she had much to learn from the *ulfdrengr*, not all of it in the sparring ring.

Chapter 31

Ithariel nudged Gwyneth awake, the sword's consciousness prodding her out of sleep. She wrinkled her nose and stifled a groan of protest: why did she always have to wake in the middle of particularly delicious dreams about Rhys?

"You'll see him soon enough," she reminded herself quietly as she opened her eyes and forced her body to move. It seemed that every day with the *ulfdrengr* gave her new bruises and different sore muscles, but she had come to love being in the camp with them. This new day marked the seventh day since Gwyneth's journey through the ether, though it felt like her training with Rionach in the Between had been months ago. Time rarely felt as though it were passing in any kind of way that made sense, she thought as she pushed aside the furs and pulled on a heavy vest over her quilted shirt. Mariel and Tula had become her most constant companions in the *ulfdrengr* camp, which had surprised her at first; but Tula had explained without rancor that the *herravaldyr* had other duties to tend: Tarian and his Karala were *herravaldyr*, as Gwyneth had known Linara and Bjarnyk were as well. Kalian, for his part, seemed to have many responsibilities throughout the camp, and he tended to them all with the same attention and care that he had given to the task of bringing Gwyneth through the forest to the camp.

Gwyneth had been surprised to learn that Tarian was bonded to a female wolf; Mariel had merely raised an eyebrow and said that the wolf chooses the warrior.

"It isn't our place to question," she said.

"Unless it's a woman bonded to a male *herravaldyr*," Tula had added, her lips pressed into a line and her foxlike face serious.

"We cannot change the opinion of all the elders," Mariel had said to Tula. "Isn't it enough that Linara has Bjarnyk?"

Gwyneth had wondered at the enigmatic conversation, but she felt, as she sometimes did, that to pry would be rude. Her years at the Hall of the Inionacha made it somewhat challenging for her to fully accept the *ulfdrengr*'s idea of courtesy – many more things were said in much bolder terms in the wolf-warrior's camp than Gwyneth had ever expected to hear aloud. And as night fell over the forest, the warrior's camp descended into a wild revelry that had nearly frightened Gwyneth with its intensity the first night she observed it.

That first night, after she'd been healed by Ephelia's rune and had sparred a little with Tula and Mariel and learned from them about *ulfdrengr* tracking methods, she'd eaten the evening meal around the communal cauldron of food. Some *ulfdrengr* cooked their own meals, but a good number – the majority, Gwyneth thought, though it was difficult to be certain since they all came and went as they pleased – ate the porridge or stew that bubbled in the cauldron in the mornings and evenings. Gwyneth had sat on a log and watched the warriors come and go. On the whole, the *ulfdrengr* were larger in stature than the Inionacha, the Paladin and even the Sidhe that Gwyneth had seen. Both the men and the women were tall and well-muscled, though a few, like Tula, tended toward a more slender and wiry build.

Gwyneth had finished her stew and stacked her empty bowl with the others, cleaning her hands on a patch of moss. Strangely enough, she did not feel nervous without Mariel and Tula. She stood near the back of the gathering crowd, pleased to find that she was tall enough to hold her own with the *ulfdrengr* women.

Both the women and men braided their hair and painted their faces as the daylight faded and the forest passed into shadow. The designs on the *ulfdrengr* faces were less careful and complex than the pattern Gwyneth had seen on Ephelia's skin; the wolf-warriors favored bold stripes of color that highlighted the sharpness of their cheekbones or lines down their chin that brought the eye to the fullness of their lips; a swipe of dark paint around their eyes gave them the look of a mask, their eyes bright from the shadow of the paint, reminding Gwyneth for a fleeting moment of the Paladins' Samhain masquerade.

When full darkness fell, the camp descended into what Gwyneth thought at first was a kind of madness. Warriors who had been serious and focused during the daylight grinned and laughed with abandon; dozens of *ulfdrengr* gathered around the main fire, the flames leaping higher than the men's heads. Men and women wore their finest weapons, the blades shining and polished. From somewhere in the crowd, drumming emerged, softly at first, and then faster, louder, until one of the women added a wild, keening song that sounded to Gwyneth's ears at moments like a wolf howling. When the singer paused for breath, the wolfsong continued without her voice, the sound of the wolves raising goosebumps on Gwyneth's skin.

The drummer played faster, and the woman sang louder, and then a man joined her song. Firelight danced on the painted faces of the *ulfdrengr*, their eyes shining with a feverish excitement. Some in the crowd began to clap and stomp along with the drumbeat. Gwyneth felt the energy shivering through the air, and her initial apprehension melted into fascination. A ripple ran through the gathered warriors, and then the crowd parted to allow someone to pass through. Kalian emerged into the center of the ring, carrying a huge barrel over his shoulder with seemingly little effort. When the firelight peeled the shadows away from his face, Gwyneth saw he wore dark blue face paint in a simple but bold pattern over his face: two vertical lines down his cheeks, counterpoint to his strong jaw. A collective shout and some groans drifted up with the sparks of the fire into the darkness overhead. Gwyneth shouldered her way between two *ulfdrengr* so that she could see, her curiosity piqued. Grins flashed in the shadows and the men and women near her elbowed each other, murmuring.

"It will be a long wait tonight," said a woman with a white-painted face.

"Then perhaps the mead will last longer," replied the man next to her, his hair braided in a fierce ridge down the center of his skull. Gwyneth fleetingly wondered if Mariel or Tula would teach her to braid her hair like that, even as she wondered at their words. Ithariel hummed in thought. The sword was more awake than slumbering in the *ulfdrengr* camp, everything just as new and interesting to the Named Sword as it was to Gwyneth. Sometimes Ithariel's childlike wonder surprised Gwyneth. She thought the Named Sword would be beyond wonder after its centuries of existence.

Kalian heaved the barrel down onto the ground a few paces away from the fire, the thudding impact vibrating through the ground and causing several logs in the fire to shift, sending a spray of sparks into the air. Kalian pulled his shirt over his head in one smooth movement, tossing it aside and pulling his axe from his belt. The firelight gleamed on his muscular form, his chest painted with two more sets of vertical lines. He spread his arms and faced the gathered warriors, his dark hair held back from his face with a simple leather thong.

In the Northtongue, he shouted, "Who will fight for the mead tonight?"

"You are the ugliest goddess we've ever seen!" someone from the crowd shouted back, igniting a raucous wave of laughter.

Kalian merely grinned and hefted his axe, his teeth and the edge of his axe glinting in the shifting shadows.

"Are you sure you're the guardian of the poet's blood?" called out another voice, this time a woman. "I thought the goddess wore skirts!"

Kalian gestured to his thick thighs and muscular rear. "But then you would not have such a view as this!" he shouted back to the woman.

"I can think of another view I'd like better!" she countered, igniting a cheer from some of the crowd.

"Come and convince me with your sword!" Kalian said, tossing his axe to his other hand.

The woman laughed. "Or *you* can convince me with *your* sword later in my tent!" She emphasized her words with a little thrust of her hips. Gwyneth felt her cheeks burning, even as she found herself enjoying the bawdy banter. How shocked her prim Instructors would be at this mischievous talk!

"Ah, there you are, *ungrsverda,*" said a voice at Gwyneth's elbow.

Gwyneth turned. Tula grinned, her face painted in a wild swirl of azure.

"What is this?" Gwyneth asked.

"Ah, it is a ritual," Tula said with mock solemnity, nodding. She spoke into Gwyneth's ear as Kalian exchanged more banter with other onlookers, cheers and laughter rolling through the crowd at particularly clever or salacious bits. "You see, there was a goddess who guarded the blood of Kvasir, the wisest god who was killed by a giant. The other gods collected Kvasir's blood and realized that when they drank it, his wisdom flowed through them. They did not want to share, and so they guarded it jealously until Odan seduced the goddess and then stole the blood of Kvasir."

Tula paused while the crowd roared at a particular comment.

"So now, at our Solstice celebrations, every night there is a 'goddess' chosen to guard the mead," Tula said, her breath tickling

Gwyneth's ear. "And the challenger can either fight the goddess or seduce them. Most of the time it is fighting," she allowed. "And the one who defeats the goddess becomes the goddess for the next night, and so on."

"No one can drink mead tonight until someone wins against Kalian in a fight?" said Gwyneth skeptically.

"There may be no mead tonight," Tula said, crossing her arms over her chest and turning to watch Kalian.

An *ulfdrengr* with his hair cut short stepped out of the crowd, holding two smaller axes. Kalian grinned and strode forward to meet him.

"Ferran," said Tula into Gwyneth's ear. "Doesn't stand a chance, but he probably wants to impress someone."

The fight started a bit slowly, the two men circling one another, the crowd flowing around them to give them more room; they moved farther away from the fire, and as the crowd followed them Gwyneth felt the chill kiss of the night winter air on her skin.

Ferran made the first move, leaping into a whirling attack so fast that Gwyneth needed to focus to follow it. Kalian dodged some blows and blocked others with his axe, knocking the smaller weapons away with an ease that looked almost lazy. He stood over a head taller than Ferran, but the smaller *ulfdrengr* attacked with admirable ferocity. Gwyneth watched the two men fight, an unbridled aggression mounting in their movements as the moments passed. Ithariel crooned her appreciation, her sheath vibrating against Gwyneth's back. The *ulfdrengr* fought with tangible passion rather than prescribed techniques, a primal aggression in their actions that looked much different than the sometimes-stilted dance of sword fighting that she had been taught at the Hall. Her heart beat faster as she followed Kalian's movements. It didn't even look as though he were sweating.

Ferran managed to catch Kalian's axe at an angle with his own smaller axe, grimacing with strain as he held the massive axe back and darted his own blade toward Kalian's arm. Gwyneth winced at the cut that Ferran opened across Kalian's bicep. The huge *ulfdrengr* bared his teeth in a savage, frightening smile and with a sharp movement of his axe sent Ferran's axe spinning away to skid on the ground. In the same instant, Kalian kicked out with one powerful leg, his boot connecting solidly with Ferran's chest, sending the other man flying through the air. The crowd parted liquidly, wild cheers ringing through the air even before Ferran hit the ground with stunning impact; to his credit, Ferran rolled to his side, one axe still in hand, ready to get to his feet to continue the fight, but Kalian was already there, sliding the blunt top of his axe under Ferran's chin. Gwyneth couldn't hear, but Ferran's lips moved, presumably in acknowledgement of his defeat.

The crowd roared, and the drumbeat started again at a frantic pace. Wolf howls reverberated through the trees. Kalian extended a huge hand to Ferran and hauled him to his feet, grasping the smaller man's shoulder briefly before turning and striding back toward the barrel of mead. He ignored the blood dripping down his arm. A little knot of concern tightened Gwyneth's stomach. The cut looked deep and the rivulets of blood flowed freely. Tula muttered something to herself and tore a strip from the edge of her shirt.

"Is it against the rules to interfere?" Gwyneth asked Tula as she realized the other woman's intention.

"First thing you should learn from us, *ungrsverda,*" said Tula. "Most rules are really just *suggestions.*"

With that, she wrapped the strip of linen around her hand and darted off through the crowd. As she emerged from the edge of the crowd behind Kalian, she grinned puckishly and motioned for everyone to continue on with their conversations. None of the gathered *ulfdrengr* gave her away, though Gwyneth saw some of them grin.

Quick as a snake striking, Tula launched herself at Kalian, wrapping her legs around his waist and looping an arm around his neck.

Kalian reached back but she shifted and avoided his grasping hand, her own hands quickly wrapping the strip of linen around the cut on his arm. Just as she tied the knot, Kalian caught hold of her arm and pulled her free. She twisted away and darted back into the crowd, laughing. Gwyneth smiled.

Realization crossed Kalian's face as he looked at the bandage on his arm, but he just hefted his axe and waited for his next challenger. Two more *ulfdrengr* fought him with no more success than Ferran, though the second one managed to land a blow to Kalian's face after being disarmed; the hit didn't look like it accomplished much more than smudging the paint on Kalian's cheek.

The third fighter stepped out of the crowd and a murmur traveled through the warriors like a wave.

"That's Andorra," said Tula to Gwyneth. "Probably the best woman fighter after Linara, of course."

A question rose in Gwyneth's mind with the suddenness of a darting bird. "Can a challenger fight with any weapon?" she asked.

"It's frowned upon to actually kill your opponent, though it has happened," Tula admitted, her eyes riveted to Andorra and Kalian's match. Andorra fought with long twin blades, her skill undeniable. Gwyneth thought she had a chance – she looked slightly faster than Kalian, and she was the tallest woman Gwyneth had seen other than Linara.

Andorra launched a blindingly fast attack and knocked Kalian's axe aside, one of her blades slashing across his chest. Kalian grunted. Gwyneth's mouth went suddenly dry, but it looked as though the wound was shallow, though it stretched from his ribs in a diagonal up to his collarbone. He kicked out much like he had done to Ferran, but Andorra was ready for that, too, thrusting one blade into her belt and using that empty hand to catch Kalian's boot, throwing it upward and sending Kalian crashing onto his back with bone-jarring force.

She leapt forward but he caught her between his knees and rolled in one motion, blocking her access to the blade at her belt with one knee and catching the wrist of her other hand. Blood from the cut on his chest spattered them both. Andorra snarled and before he brought his axe to her throat, she kneed him in the groin. Gwyneth winced, and she heard some sympathetic noises from the men in the crowd, but Tula had really spoken the truth when she had said that the *ulfdrengr* did not abide by any real rules. Apparently kneeing one's opponent in the groin was perfectly acceptable, because Andorra took advantage of Kalian's split second of distraction. She freed one leg from his grip and kneed him in the chest, gaining enough space to draw the blade at her belt, which flashed toward Kalian's throat.

Kalian recovered and with a growl knocked the blade away, another cut opening on his forearm. He stood in a lightning-quick movement, hauling Andorra up by the collar of her shirt, one of his knees striking her in the midsection in mimicry of her blow the moment prior. She grunted and swiped at him with her other blade but didn't move fast enough to avoid the flat of his axe, which hit her outstretched arm with a sickening crack. The blade dropped from her nerveless hand.

Andorra dropped to one knee at the impact of the blow, gritting her teeth. Her left arm hung uselessly at her side. She clenched her fist around her remaining blade, but before she could move, Kalian snugged his axe beneath her chin.

"Well fought," he said, his voice gravelly. Blood painted his bare chest.

Andorra nodded, white-faced, and slid her blades into her belt before accepting his hand.

"Should have tried to seduce him instead!" someone called from the crowd.

To Gwyneth's surprise, Andorra smiled, though her face was tight with pain. "Why don't you come out and try that, eh?" she responded.

The crowd parted. "Perhaps I will," said Linara, stepping into the firelight. She raised one dark eyebrow. "After all, it seems as though we will not have any mead tonight if *someone* does not succeed."

Kalian went very still save for his chest as he breathed deeply after the exertion of the fight. Gwyneth watched, transfixed along with all the rest of the crowd, as Linara prowled toward him, her axe still in her belt. She pulled the laces at the chest of her shirt loose as she neared Kalian. He shuddered visibly as she reached toward him and traced her fingertips from his collarbone down to his navel. She was only half a head shorter than him, so he didn't need to lean down to kiss her. Howls and cheers of approval rose from the gathered warriors. Linara pulled herself closer to Kalian with one hand at his neck, kissing him ravenously; he dropped his axe and wrapped his hands about her waist. She moved them away from his dropped axe, pressing harder into him to direct their steps.

The crowd roared even louder when Linara drew a dagger from a hidden sheath with her free hand, the blade flashing silver as she pressed its edge to Kalian's neck. She kissed him for a heartbeat longer and then drew back, her eyes glittering. They stared at each other for a long moment. A smear of his blood trailed luridly down her chin and neck, droplets vivid against the white of her shirt. Linara pressed the dagger hard enough against his neck that his heartbeat could be seen jumping against the edge of her blade. Her other hand rested on the handle of the axe in her belt, her body coiled and ready to move if Kalian decided to fight.

Kalian didn't look away from her as he knelt, his lips curving in a faint smile. Linara relaxed slightly and returned her dagger to its sheath. She left Kalian kneeling and strode over to the barrel of mead. The drumbeat started again and the gathered *ulfdrengr* cheered in approval as two men ran forward with a long trough. They set it by the barrel and one of them handed Linara a circular stake with a sharpened end. She drew her axe from her belt, positioned the stake over a specific point in the barrel – the bung, Gwyneth remembered, reaching back to what she'd observed in the village pub. Linara struck the stake twice, driving the sharpened end into the soft wood, and then with a mighty wrench she pulled the stopper free to the thunderous approval of the crowd. Mead flowed into the trough and one of the men handed Linara two copper mugs. She filled both directly from the stream of mead, held them up to the crowd and shouted, "Begin your night, my fellow warriors!"

With a cheer, the festivities began. Gwyneth watched as Linara threaded her way through the crowd back to Kalian, who had stood and picked up his axe again. She handed him one of the cups of mead and said something to him; he grinned, downed the mead in one long pull, and followed her away from the crowd into the shadows.

"I think Kalian won more than he lost tonight," Tula murmured to Gwyneth. Then she pulled at her arm. "Come on then, let's see if you can hold your mead, *ungrsverda*."

The night passed in a blur of music and dancing and ribald humor, and in the morning, Gwyneth woke with the worst headache she'd ever had in her life. Ithariel was unsympathetic, and so too were Mariel and Tula, who arrived at her tent to awaken her shortly after dawn.

Gwyneth had sparred with Tula first for three bouts – she won the first, Tula won the second, and they called the third a draw after nearly half an hour.

"You do know what you're doing with that sword," Tula said approvingly as they drank some water. Then the shorthaired woman tossed Gwyneth an axe. "But let's see how you are with this."

Each day brought a new weapon and new lessons to learn, and each night brought a new boisterous fight against the 'goddess' to claim the mead for the evening. Gwyneth learned that one or two mugs of mead was quite enough for her to join in the raucous revelry but didn't leave her with a pounding headache the next day; and she learned the value of a full waterskin prepared that afternoon, waiting for her when she returned to her tent for the night.

She wasn't sure if Mariel or Tula – or perhaps even Kalian – had warned the *ulfdrengr* not to pursue her, but she found herself both strangely grateful and oddly put out that none of the wild, handsome wolf-warrior men approached her with that gleam in their eyes. But she reminded herself of Rhys and thought of him as she drifted off to sleep every night.

Now in the half-light of dawn, Ithariel chimed sleepily as Gwyneth settled her sheath against her back. It seemed so much longer than seven days that she'd been in the camp. She ran a hand over her braided hair; Tula had obligingly styled it for her prior to the last evening's festivities. Some of the *ulfdrengr* had looked at her differently with her hair drawn up into three braids, one at each side of her head and then one down the center. Gwyneth wondered if they didn't approve of her wearing the style, but she trusted Tula. She was starting to consider the two women her friends.

After rinsing her mouth with the last of the water in her waterskin, Gwyneth left her tent and made her way toward the cauldron to fetch her morning cup of *khal*. She'd become quite fond of that drink, too. She liked its sharp taste and the lift in energy it lent her.

Tula and Mariel met her at their usual spot where they ate before heading to find a place among the trees to spar with the weapon of the day. Often, they didn't say much, but ate in companionable silence. Gwyneth finished her porridge and *khal*; when the other two were done, they all stood. She followed half a step behind them. Mariel led them to a different part of the camp. The trees opened into a narrow but long clearing. Gwyneth saw a ring painted on a tree at the other end of the clearing.

"I have heard you have some skill with the bow," Mariel said, picking up one of the three bows leaning against a tree.

Gwyneth grinned and slung one of the quivers over her shoulder, her fingers already tingling in anticipation. The bow felt like an old friend as she strung it in one fluid motion. Mariel smiled.

"Well," said Tula, an arrow already nocked to her bow, "let's start the day off right, shall we?"

Still grinning, Gwyneth joined Tula on an imaginary line, drawing her arrow back and sighting on the target, feeling her past and her present and her future all existing at once as she stood in the clearing of the *ulfdrengr* camp, a Named Sword on her back, and practicing archery with the wolf-warriors of the North.

Chapter 32

"I said once that you knew what you were doing with a sword," said Tula as they walked down the length of the meadow toward the tree with the target painted on its trunk. "But now I think I must say that you're better with a bow."

Gwyneth chuckled. "I've been hunting with a bow since I was old enough to hold one."

"I do not know much about Doendhtalam," said Tula as they reached the tree. "But what I have heard sounds like a world full of contradictions." She clucked her tongue against the roof of her mouth. "You won this match as well."

Gwyneth didn't need to count her blue-fletched arrows against Tula's red-fletched ones; she'd known before the match even started that she would win. She'd won the last five against Tula. Mariel had left them to more matches after Gwyneth had beaten her three times; the wolf Nira had slid out of the shadows at the edge of the meadow and Mariel had promptly abandoned archery to run with the wolf.

"Why do you say Doendhtalam is full of contradictions?" Gwyneth asked Tula as they began to pull their arrows from the painted rings of the target.

"Well," said Tula, examining an arrow for damage before she slid it back into the quiver at her hip, "I've heard tales that women cannot rule nor own land, nor choose their own partners." She shrugged. "And yet here you are saying you were given a bow soon as you were old enough to hold it."

"Different places within Doendhtalam are different," Gwyneth replied, running her fingers down the shaft of an arrow to check for any small cracks. "My village in Eire was not so restrictive about what women could and could not do."

"So women could rule?"

"I don't know," admitted Gwyneth. She thought of the village council. "I suppose I didn't really pay much attention to it. I was young."

"Young ones observe more than we think," said Tula.

"In the place where I was born," Gwyneth continued as they pulled the last of their arrows form the tree, "I am told that women held power for much of the past centuries. Druids."

"Druids," repeated Tula.

"That is what most of the Blood was called, I think," Gwyneth said. She slid the last arrow into her quiver. "We still honor the old ways, though I could see that fading in the years when I was old enough to notice such things."

"The Sidhe observe the happenings of the mortal world much more closely than we," said Tula, "but I have heard that there is a tide of change sweeping your world."

"Isn't that the way of history?" replied Gwyneth. "There is always something new approaching that which is old. The old fades, the new becomes old, and the cycle begins again."

Tula paused and peered at Gwyneth. "You sound older than your years."

"I feel older than my years," confessed Gwyneth. It was difficult for her to believe that only a handful of years had passed since she'd found Rhys wounded in the forest, since Rionach had stepped over the threshold of her old home in Eire.

"That is the way of it, when you know there is great power awaiting you," Tula said. "Linara, if you can believe it, was only a season ahead of me in training. She and Bjarnyk were tremendous even when they were young, of course, but everyone expected so much of her."

"She is the daughter of the one you call your king?"

"She is the daughter of the one who wears the mantle of king," said Tula with a nod. "And her mother is the closest thing to a queen that we have. She is the king's consort. They have had no one but each other for nigh on a century now."

Gwyneth knew that *ulfdrengr* lived as long as the Sidhe – centuries and centuries, provided no sickness or wound killed them; but she still felt a little burst of surprise, even now, when centuries were mentioned so casually. She held her tongue and hoped that Tula kept talking.

"Some thought that Linara would be *volta*, because of her mother," continued Tula. "*Volta* begin training a few years younger than us, because it would be dangerous for them not to understand how to control their powers."

"Is it only the *volta* who have *taebramh*?" Gwyneth asked.

"No," said Tula. "Most of us have something. Some of the *ulfdrengr* train with the *volta* in basic runes and such – the stronger ones, I mean." Tula sat down on a log and motioned for Gwyneth to join her, pulling her flask from her belt.

"And are there those who are neither bound to a wolf nor blessed with the power of the *volta*?" Gwyneth asked. It had been a question in her mind for a few days now as she observed the camp.

"Of course," replied Tula. She offered the flask to Gwyneth. "They are our craftsmen and our farmers, our bakers and tanners."

"Is their camp here as well?" Gwyneth took a swallow from the flask and found it to be liquor. It burned down her throat and warmed her belly. After a morning spent in the cold, she rather enjoyed the sensation.

Tula chuckled. "They do not travel to the Solstice."

"Oh." Gwyneth took another sip from the flask and handed it back to Tula, feeling a bit foolish.

"No need to be embarrassed. There are those who think that all of us are bound to wolves. But what use would that be? Not all can be warriors. We need bakers and tanners and smiths just as we need warriors."

"Do some *ulfdrengr* train in other things, like forging weapons?"

"Full of questions this morning," said Tula with a smile. "Perhaps you are feeling bold after beating me so soundly in archery."

"Perhaps," allowed Gwyneth with a smile.

"Yes," answered Tula. "The forge seems to be a favorite of many *ulfdrengr*. It helps us to be able to know what is wrong with our weapons and perhaps sometimes we can repair them ourselves, if there is no smith nearby."

Gwyneth nodded. "That sounds very practical."

Tula grinned. "Now you are just trying to soothe my wounded pride."

"By saying that something sounds *practical*?" Gwyneth chuckled.

"Compliments come in many forms, *ungrsverda*," said Tula. She stretched her legs and then stood. "So. Tell me what I am doing wrong."

Gwyneth felt her eyes widen but then tried to school her face into a neutral expression. "Doing wrong?"

Tula picked up her bow. "You are a much better archer than me. Watch, and tell me what I am doing wrong."

Gwyneth slung her bow over her shoulder. "All right. Shoot three arrows and then we'll make some adjustments."

Tula grinned. Sunlight filtering through the branches overhead glinted on her short reddish hair. She nocked an arrow to her bow and sighted in on the target.

Time passed with astonishing speed as Gwyneth watched Tula's technique and made small adjustments to her grip, to her stance, to her draw, even to the way she nocked the arrow. Tula took each change in stride, and Gwyneth rarely had to correct the same thing twice. The *ulfdrengr* did not complain, even though Gwyneth knew that so many draws of a bowstring in a row was painful even for one used to the bow. The shadows lengthened.

"Let's have another match," said Tula after they finished a break.

"All right," said Gwyneth, flexing the string of her bow a bit. "Give me ten shots to warm up."

Tula shot well and strode quickly toward the target to score the match. Gwyneth followed at a more sedate pace. Ithariel stirred on her back; the blade tended to drift into something like sleep when Gwyneth practiced archery.

"You still won," pronounced Tula as Gwyneth reached the tree. She grinned. "But only by three."

"That's a tremendous improvement," Gwyneth said, feeling an answering grin on her own lips. Tula's enthusiasm for developing her skills felt contagious. Gwyneth found that she respected the *ulfdrengr* more because they were not afraid to admit when someone else possessed greater skill than them, and they were not shy in asking that person to critique their form.

"Yes," said Tula in satisfaction, surveying the target with hands on her hips. "That first match you beat me by eight."

Gwyneth smiled. "It feels good to have a bow in my hand again."

"Well, perhaps you should carry one more often," suggested Tula. She gave the target a last long look, as though memorizing the tangible evidence of her improvement, and then began pulling her arrows from the wood.

"May I carry this one, for now?" Gwyneth asked, her fingers trailing down the longbow's length. It was a well-made weapon, though the strings used by the Northerners were a bit thicker than what she had used at the Hall of the Inionacha.

"Of course," said Tula.

"I was surprised to see that you wear your quiver at your hip," said Gwyneth as she began to pull her arrows from the tree and slide them into her own quiver. "Some think that archers wear it on their backs."

Tula shrugged. "I saw you put yours there and I wanted to see if I liked it, too." She thought for a moment. "I like being able to see my arrows, but I think it would be difficult to run with it. Archery is not one of our primary skills as *ulfdrengr*, but we are taught the basics."

"If you're carrying a lot of arrows for a long time, then they can be transported on the back," said Gwyneth, brushing a splinter from the hem of her shirt. "But really hip quivers are the most practical. And if you run with a blade at your hip, then I don't see how running with a quiver is much different."

Tula tilted her head. "You make a good argument."

"I do my best," replied Gwyneth.

"Come on then," Tula said. "Time for the evening meal."

"Already?" Gwyneth peered up through the trees, trying to gauge the time.

"The day passes quickly when you are doing something you love," said Tula.

Gwyneth slid the bow over her shoulder and followed Tula back toward the camp. A shadow detached itself from one of the trees and glided toward them.

"There you are, Veta," said Tula affectionately.

The wolf Veta shared some of Tula's sharpness of face, and of course their eyes mirrored one another.

"Would you like to come into camp with us, or are you going to go hunt?" Tula continued. Gwyneth wondered if the *ulfdrengr* was speaking aloud for her benefit. She'd seen the *ulfdrengr* communicate silently with their wolves, though she was not sure if actual words passed silently between them.

Veta yawned and licked her chops, flicking an ear.

"She already hunted today," Tula said to Gwyneth, grinning and running one hand down sleek Veta's back. "We may not be the biggest, but we are the fastest, eh?"

Veta turned and prowled toward Gwyneth. After a week at the camp of the *ulfdrengr*, Gwyneth had not been any closer to the wolves than her time with Malyk as he led her through the frozen forest. Now, as then, she reminded herself firmly that the predator pacing toward her was not going to attack her. Veta stopped in front of Gwyneth, gazing at her with dark, intelligent eyes. Gwyneth felt her legs trembling, but she did not move as Veta nosed at the air around her, taking in her scent. Even as a small *ulfdrengr* wolf, Veta's head nearly reached Gwyneth's chest.

"It is an honor to meet you," Gwyneth said softly in the Northtongue. Veta went very still. Gwyneth felt certain that the wolf understood her, so she swallowed and continued, "It has been an honor to train with Tula. She is quite skilled. I am glad I am able to meet her partner in battle."

Veta flicked one ear again and looked at Tula briefly, as though to say, *Well, I suppose I agree with you.* Tula grinned.

"Tomorrow I think all of us will be training with our partners," she said, "so perhaps you will be able to watch, Gwyn, or perhaps not. I think Linara will tell us."

Gwyneth didn't look away from Veta. She nodded, fighting back the feeling of disappointment. Despite her earlier promise, Linara had not appeared during their training sessions to spar, and though Gwyneth thought it would be strange for a *herravaldyr* not to follow through on a promise, she also thought it possible that she had misunderstood Linara to begin with.

Veta paced around Gwyneth in a circle, and in walking back toward Tula, the wolf bumped Gwyneth's hip with her shoulder. The contact sent a thrill through Gwyneth – at first she thought perhaps it had been accidental, but then she reminded herself that these were the legendary wolf-warriors, and they did very few things accidentally.

Tula smiled as Veta leaned against her. She buried her fingers in the wolf's thick ruff. "The Solstice travel is a break for the wolves as well," she said. "We train every day in the North. Here, we all may do as we wish for a few weeks."

Veta half-closed her eyes in pleasure at Tula's touch. Gwyneth watched the two with a hint of envy. Would she ever have such a connection with another being? Ithariel chimed reprovingly. Gwyneth touched the hilt of the Named Sword in apology and reassurance. It was quite a different thing, though, to be bound to a wolf than to be bound to a sword, she thought.

They walked back to the camp, Gwyneth finding that she knew the way without having to follow Tula. Veta wove between the trees, visible one moment and concealed by shadow the next. As she sometimes did when her mind settled into a moment of silence, Gwyneth wondered what occupied Rhys. What was he doing at that moment? Perhaps sparring with the other Paladins, his blade flashing; or maybe practicing runes with one of the older Paladin. Would Aedan and Orla be at the Solstice as well? She couldn't imagine them *not* attending such an event, since it seemed that all the luminaries of every part of the Fae world attended the Winter and Summer Solstices.

Veta disappeared as they reached camp proper. Tula stopped by her tent to stow her bow; Gwyneth kept hers over her shoulder, the weight of her quiver at her hip comforting.

"Andorra is the goddess tonight," Tula said conversationally as they walked toward the common area.

"She's a very good fighter," Gwyneth replied.

Tula glanced at Gwyneth's bow and said, "Aye, she is."

A prickle of awareness ran down Gwyneth's spine at Tula's unspoken suggestion. A knot formed low in her belly. She remembered Andorra fighting Kalian – the woman was ferocious and nearly twice her size. Deep in thought, she burned her mouth on the stew; grimacing, she set her bowl aside and waited for it to cool.

The *ulfdrengr* valued courage, but they also valued cleverness. Not all their warriors were huge like Andorra and Linara and Kalian; Tula was slender but had a reputation as a fast and ferocious fighter. Even Andorra had resorted to kneeing Kalian in the groin, after all, which the *ulfdrengr* looked upon with practicality. Taking advantage of an opponent's weaknesses was not scorned, no matter what form that took. She thought about the usual setup of the fighting ring, losing herself in contemplation of different possibilities for so long that when she did remember her stew, it was nearly cold. She hastily ate and deposited her used bowl in the pile as usual.

"Where are you going?" Tula asked her, brow wrinkled as she watched Gwyneth pick up her bow.

"I'll be back," Gwyneth said in what she hoped was a reassuring tone. Part of her hoped that someone defeated Andorra before she returned, but part of her also thrilled at the possibility of a bit of glory in the *ulfdrengr* camp. She loped back toward her tent, hoping that the item she needed was still in the pack that she'd taken from the Between. As was the way of things, she *thought* she'd packed it, but she couldn't visualize the instant of putting the object into her pack.

She reached her tent as she heard the drumbeats start. Hastily conjuring a small *taebramh* light, she grabbed her pack and rifled through it. With a sound of frustration, she dumped its contents onto one of the furs, cringing at the childish move but urged on by the thought that another fighter would defeat Andorra before she returned. Beneath the silvery light of her *taebramh*-glow, she sorted through her once carefully organized pack, her hands starting to shake from a spike of anticipation. Finally, her fingers closed around a neat skein of cool, silken thread. She made a sound of triumph as she held up the spidersilk; this batch she had made particularly fine, nearly invisible except for in the right light; and her heart began to thump in her chest. She had her materials, now she had to see if she had the courage to go through with her plan. Tossing one of the furs over the jumble of her belongings, she quickly drew two arrows from the quiver at her hip and worked over them for a moment. Her trembling fingers made tying knots difficult, but finally she felt satisfied. She extinguished the light overhead with a twist of her hand.

"Here we go, for good or ill" she muttered to herself. Ithariel hummed in excitement as she ran back toward the main fire.

Someone had, indeed, stepped into the ring with Andorra, but the big *ulfdrengr* seemed unconcerned by the challenge, fending off his attacks easily, her eyes glittering as she advanced on him. Gwyneth slid through the crowd, looking for the huge barrel of mead; Andorra stalked around the other fighter, her twin blades flashing in her hand. The *ulfdrengr* woman attacked savagely, her braids flying as she gave her opponent no quarter. It ended with one of her daggers buried to the hilt in his shoulder. Gwyneth's mouth went dry.

You've endured more than that, she reminded herself.

Yes, but this is different, said the small, practical corner of her mind. *You are doing this voluntarily. By choice.*

Andorra's opponent yielded, and she hauled him to his feet. He staggered but then regained his footing and without a grimace, pulled her blade from his shoulder, offering it to her hilt first. She grinned at him and took it. The crowd roared.

"Who else?" Andorra shouted, spreading her arms just as Kalian had the first night that Gwyneth had watched the contest.

Wait for another opponent to tire her, whispered the practical part of Gwyneth's mind.

"The plan does not depend on her being tired," Gwyneth said in a low voice to herself. No one paid her any attention as she grasped one of the two arrows in her quiver. "It depends on my cleverness."

Her whole body alight with a trembling awareness, Gwyneth watched until Andorra moved toward just the right position. She slid her bow off her shoulder and pushed her way to the front of the crowd, her heart leaping into her mouth as she nocked the arrow and sighted down its length at her target. She drew the arrow back smoothly, the fletching brushing her cheek as she loosed the missile. It sang through the air, missing Andorra by a hand's breadth and burying itself in the wood of the mead barrel.

Andorra turned sharply. Gwyneth was already moving, and she heard the *ulfdrengr*'s words as though from a distance.

"If you wish to use arrows, *ungrsverda,* you should aim truer!"

Gwyneth wasn't sure if the crowd had quieted or was roaring. All she could hear was her own heartbeat thundering in her ears as she ran toward Andorra, the other arrow already in her hand. She couldn't afford to let the *ulfdrengr* see her plan, so she thrust the arrow into her belt, careful to keep the spidersilk untangled and unspooling as she ran. Her *taebramh* roared to life in her chest as Andorra swung her blades at Gwyneth; Gwyneth saw the long daggers as though in slow motion, and she threw herself to the ground, sliding feet-first beneath Andorra's lunging strike.

Nearly there, she told herself, even though there were a thousand other things that could go wrong with her plan. *Keep moving, keep moving*. And she rolled to her stomach, pushing herself off the ground and leaping to the side as Andorra swiped at her again.

"Stand and fight," growled the *ulfdrengr* as Gwyneth danced out of reach again.

As Gwyneth gauged their distance to the barrel, she realized in dismay that they'd gained more distance than she anticipated. She'd have to close with Andorra if the plan were to work. Back near her original position facing Andorra and the barrel, her blood roaring in her ears louder than the crowd around them, Gwyneth nocked her second arrow. She ducked another swing and went to one knee with the bow drawn, loosing the second arrow as she felt a line of fire down her back. The wound didn't feel deep, and the odds hadn't been in her favor to avoid every one of Andorra's strikes. Without watching to see the second arrow hit its mark – she knew it would in her bones – she dropped her bow and her hand found Ithariel's hilt, drawing the sword none too soon as she deflected one of the long blades in the instant her arrow was in flight.

Then as she danced away she heard the solid *thunk* of her arrow hitting the barrel. Andorra lunged, and a look of surprise flashed across her face as the loop of spidersilk arrested her movement, snapping her legs together and throwing her off balance. As Andorra fell, Gwyneth pounced, helping the *ulfdrengr* find the ground with a knee to her back, laying Ithariel's edge neatly against the side of Andorra's neck.

"Yield," she said quietly into the shocked silence.

Andorra grimaced, and Gwyneth felt her test the strength of the spidersilk binding her legs together; Gwyneth leaned more of her weight onto the *ulfdrengr*'s back, keeping Ithariel carefully still against Andorra's neck.

Then the *ulfdrengr* released both her daggers, holding up her empty hands. Gwyneth carefully stood, keeping Ithariel pointed at Andorra, breathing heavily. The whole gathered crowd could probably hear her pounding heart, she thought. Andorra rolled to her side and delicately pushed the point of Ithariel away from her face with one finger. She grinned up at Gwyneth, blood beginning to drip from her nose.

"I yield, clever little *ungrsverda*," she said, loud enough for the crowd to hear.

Gwyneth almost dropped Ithariel as her limbs went weak with relief. She sent a spark of *taebramh* down Ithariel and cut the spidersilk – only her *taebramh* on a blade would separate the spidersilk she'd made. She'd thought it clever, though Rionach hadn't been impressed. Andorra pulled the silk loose from her legs and accepted Gwyneth's hand. The weight of the *ulfdrengr* nearly pulled Gwyneth off her feet, but she gritted her teeth and hauled Andorra upright. As her hearing returned, she realized the crowd was delirious with delight, howling and cheering around her. Someone handed her the tap and a mallet; she stumbled toward the barrel of mead, tapping it between her arrows and accepting the first cup.

A large hand found her shoulder and she turned to find Kilian smiling down at her. "Well done," he said, and she finally felt a rush of triumph.

"Well done indeed," said Linara, appearing beside Kilian. She filled her own cup at the spout of mead and then saluted Gwyneth. "Tomorrow at dawn, we shall spar."

Gwyneth raised her cup to Linara, tongue-tied, her face flushing with victory as the *ulfdrengr* howled around her.

Chapter 33

Gwyneth sparred with Linara and Kalian every morning for the rest of the days they were camped in the winter-frosted forest. She lost every time she fought them, but she felt no shame in the losing; and with every loss she felt herself improve. She had not beaten Rionach in sparring, either, but the style of the *ulfdrengr* fighters still surprised her sometimes with its ferocity and disregard for conventional techniques. She learned quickly to expect a well-aimed kick or a quickly thrown punch with just as much certainty as she expected the clash of blade on blade.

Mariel and Tula had found her the night she'd defeated Andorra to open the mead cask for the festivities, grins alight on both their faces. They saluted her with their cups.

"That was a fine little bit of trickery," Tula said in approval.

"Didn't know if it would work," Gwyneth confessed into her cup. She didn't even have to travel back to the barrel for refills: as soon as her cup was nearly empty, an *ulfdrengr* pressed another full one into her hand. She grinned lopsidedly at Tula, swallowing her mouthful of mead.

"How many cups have you had?" Mariel asked.

"Thought that was the point of the Solstice," Gwyneth said, trying to pronounce her words very carefully. She'd had, what, three cups? In less than an hour, after the heady rush of the fight. She shrugged. "'Swhat you said, after all." She toasted Mariel. "Fighting and drinking and…what's the last?" Even inebriated, she couldn't bring herself to say the crass word, and congratulated herself for making a joke of it instead.

Mariel muttered something to herself and pushed her way back through the crowd. Tula chuckled and clinked her wooden cup against Gwyneth's copper one. "Didn't think you wanted to partake in that last one, *ungrsverda*. Your Paladin, remember?"

Gwyneth shrugged. "No law against it."

Tula raised her eyebrows. "Well, this is certainly a new side of you."

Gwyneth *did* feel daring and bold, fortified by the mead and her victory over Andorra. Granted, it had been a trick, but everyone had raucously approved all the same. She tried not to think of the next night, when she'd have to fight all challengers herself. "Can't help I'm so stiff sometimes. I try not to be. But…" She shrugged.

"You're not *stiff*," said Tula. She tilted her head. "Well, maybe a little. But you aren't a Northerner, Gwyneth, you're the Heir to the Sword. We don't expect you to act the same as us. Matter of fact, we don't expect anyone at all to act like us." Her teeth gleamed in the shifting light. "The world can only handle so many *ulfdrengr*."

"How do the Sidhe Courts handle the *ulfdrengr*?" mused Gwyneth aloud, punctuating her thought by another draught from her cup.

"Very courteously," replied Tula, that lupine grin still stretching her lips. "We will have our main camp outside the walls of Darkhill, and only a few of the *herravaldyr* will take their quarters inside."

"Linara will be inside then," Gwyneth said seriously.

"Most likely," agreed Tula.

The drumbeat began again behind them to cheers. Gwyneth turned, smiling as she watched the *ulfdrengr* leap into a wild dance just as unpredictable and ferocious as their fighting. They did not discriminate in their partners: men danced with men and women with women, though Gwyneth found herself watching the men and women dance together more than any of the others. With their faces painted and hair braided, their muscled bodies half-clothed in breeches and vests, the *ulfdrengr* were one of the most beautiful, visceral, primal sights that Gwyneth had ever seen. Where the Paladins' celebration of Samhain had been glinting with mischief and subtlety, the *ulfdrengr*'s celebration sent a fire through Gwyneth's bones. She felt their desire for one another, not concealed beneath any veneer of propriety or restraint; as the dance continued, she saw a couple veer away from the fire, the man sweeping his partner into his arms as she grinned and wrapped her legs around his waist.

Gwyneth took another drink from her cup and thought, for the first time, about joining the dance.

"Watching is fun, but participating is even more fun," said Tula by her shoulder.

With a grin, Gwyneth said, "Nothing wrong with watching." She laughed a little, thinking herself quite clever. Ithariel tried to say something, but she couldn't hear the sword's delicate chime over the wild drumbeats and ululating song. She drained the last of the mead from her cup.

A tall man with hair that had a reddish glint like Tula held out a cup to Gwyneth, but before she took it, Mariel appeared and pressed another cup into Gwyneth's hand instead, neatly taking the cup from the man herself.

"Thank you," Mariel said to the tall *ulfdrengr*, who looked over her shoulder at Gwyneth, visibly disappointed. She felt a little flare of interest, leaning slightly forward so she could meet his gaze.

"You're welcome," the man said to Mariel, but he was still looking at Gwyneth.

"Fell," said Mariel, "don't cause trouble."

"Why would I be causing trouble?" Fell said. His eyes were an icy blue. "I merely wanted to give our champion a drink."

"You want to give her more than a drink," Tula said bluntly.

"Perhaps I do," said Fell, smiling at Gwyneth. He was handsome, in a long-faced way; Gwyneth thought that it was the unconcealed interest in his eyes and the warmth in his voice that sparked the heat in her belly. She took a swallow from her cup and found it to be water. The taste of it awakened her thirst, and she drank the rest of the cup in one long draught. The fire seemed less bright and the flames did not sway so much.

"Would you honor me in the dance, *ungrsverda*?" asked Fell.

Part of her wanted Mariel to rebuke Fell, but the two women remained silent. Hadn't they told her more than once that the *ulfdrengr* believed in choice? She gripped her empty cup, her eyes traveling to the wild dance and then back to Fell. "Perhaps another drink first," she said, stepping toward him. Tula grinned and caught Mariel's arm, pulling her away.

"Whatever the champion wishes, she shall have," Fell said, his eyes glinting in pleasure as they walked around the edge of the dance toward the barrel of mead. He dipped a cup from the trough, and when he handed it to her, their hands touched. Gwyneth felt a shock as though an errant spark from the fire had burned her. He stood very close to her while they watched the dance, close enough that she could feel the heat of his body but not so close that he was touching her. She felt his glance every few heartbeats, and she felt a heady rush much like when she'd disarmed Andorra.

"Have you fought in the North?" she asked suddenly. She swallowed thickly, wanting more water but not wanting to interrupt…whatever this was. Her entire body felt alight with anticipation and a pleasurable kind of uncertainty.

"Yes," replied Fell, the firelight sparking in his pale eyes. "Trolls, mostly, though sometimes a giant or a dragon will come down out of the mountains."

"You fight the trolls with your partner, yes?"

"Yes. Udlyk is one of the best trackers," Fell said with a hint of pride.

"Not as good as Malyk," she said without thinking.

Fell looked at her sharply. She felt her face burn.

"It is your choice," Fell said, "but if Kalian has laid claim to you…"

"He has not," Gwyneth said before he finished the sentence, more forcefully than she intended. Why, oh why was she mucking up the first chance she'd had to talk to an *ulfdrengr* interested in her as a woman? In the back of her head, a small voice reminded her that Rhys had laid claim to her, but she pushed it away. Rhys was not here. Rhys had spirited her away to the Samhain celebration, yes, but Rhys was gone on Paladin business more often than he was able to be there for her. She drew back her shoulders and met Fell's eyes as she took a fortifying drink of mead. "No one has," she said when the cup left her lips.

Fell smiled and leaned down – he was taller than her by a head, nearly as tall as Kalian – and kissed her. He kissed differently than Rhys, more forcefully, and he tasted of mead, but Gwyneth felt liquid fire racing through her. Fell dropped his cup and wrapped his large hands around her waist, picking her up as though she weighed nothing at all and moving both of them farther into the shadows.

Fell pressed her against a tree, his hands roaming over her body; she slid her own hands under the hem of his shirt and he shed it with barely a pause, his torso rippling with muscle and sinew. White and red scars laced his chest and shoulders; she pressed her palm against them as he trailed kisses hungrily down her neck.

Ithariel's sheath dug uncomfortably into Gwyneth's back, an annoying undertone to the heat racing through her body. She ignored it, instead focusing on the gentle spinning of the forest around them and the feel of Fell's callouses against her skin and the sound of his breath as he made sounds of want…one of his hands slid lower, pulling at the laces of her breeches, and cold washed suddenly over her.

Gwyneth wanted to ignore the voice that told her this was not Rhys, that she did not truly want this *ulfdrengr*; but she couldn't deny the pit that opened in her stomach. Too much mead and too little sense, she told herself. Fell kissed her neck and she put a hand on his chest, finding her voice.

"No," she said, a tremble running through her. There were dozens of *ulfdrengr* a stone's throw away, but she felt her throat close around any further sound. She could call up her *taebramh*, she could draw Ithariel, she could do any number of things if he did not listen to the one word she uttered. But she felt frozen, the glow of the mead fading and leaving her feeling stupid and cold and vulnerable.

The moment stretched into a crystalline line of suspended time. Fell, with one hand against the tree behind her and the other still at the laces of her breeches, did not immediately move. The pit in her stomach opened wider and the cold in her chest choked her. She wasn't sure if she could call up her *taebramh* if she tried. She kept her hand firmly against his chest, even though he was stronger than her and likely nearly twice her weight.

Then Fell stepped back. Gwyneth took a shuddering breath and dropped her hand. He stood bare chested in the shadows and said, "I did not mean to push too far." He bowed his head in mute apology.

Gwyneth felt a sense of wonder fill her – what was so different about the *ulfdrengr* that their men listened so readily to women's voices? A wave of shame washed over her. She tightened the laces on her breeches with shaking fingers.

"Are you all right, *ungrsverda?*" Fell asked, genuine concern in his voice.

"I…" she started, but the words seemed ridiculous even in her head. She felt slightly sick from the mead and from the tangle of emotions in her chest.

He spread his hands in invitation. "It is all right." He smiled. "Not every invitation must end in a tryst." The smile widened to a grin. "Though that would be very nice, eh?"

Gwyneth managed to return his smile shakily. She cleared her throat as she straightened her shirt. "I just…I'm sorry, I…"

"No," he interrupted her firmly, his pale eyes blazing with sudden ferocity. She swallowed and waited for him to elaborate. "Do not ever apologize for knowing your own mind, Gwyneth." He tilted his head slightly to one side. Gwyneth wondered if he was related somehow to Tula; they shared the same reddish hair and a few mannerisms.

She nodded. After a moment, she said, "I thought for a moment that...I have many unpleasant memories from my time in the mortal world."

Fell looked at her with a question in his eyes.

"No," she said quickly. "No, I was never forced. But I just knew...I knew that a woman's voice did not count for much in most of the world. Our village used to be different, back when the druids ruled, but..." She shrugged. "The world changes."

"*That* should never change," Fell said. "A woman's word is not less than a man's. Her body is her own. Just as you would not force me, why would I force you?"

Gwyneth felt very foolish. "I don't have an answer for that. It sounds...it sounds ridiculous."

The forest floor tilted under her feet. She thought that the effects of the mead had receded, but apparently not. She stumbled and Fell caught her arm, keeping her from falling.

"I think perhaps you have had enough mead for the night," he said. "Though the choice is yours, as always."

Gwyneth felt tears burn at the corners of her eyes – from the mead, from Fell's unexpected kindness, from embarrassment at her own assumption and anger at the memories that had created that assumption so deeply seated within her.

"If you are crying when we return to the feast," Fell said solemnly, "I am sure Mariel and my cousin will beat me soundly." He held her elbow with gentle firmness.

Gwyneth hiccupped and swiped at her eyes. "Being foolish," she muttered.

Fell released her elbow long enough to find his shirt and pull it over his head; he rested a hand on her shoulder and said earnestly, "You are not being foolish, Gwyneth. We all feel many things. It is not foolish."

His words helped. She swallowed and smiled a little. "You should go find someone else, someone willing to..."

"Why?" he asked simply. "I am here with you. I am enjoying our conversation."

She gave him a disbelieving look. He gazed at her unflinchingly.

"It is not every day one gets to speak to the Heir to the Sword," he continued.

Gwyneth chuckled. "Well, if you have any burning questions..."

Fell smiled. "Not in particular." He tucked an errant strand of hair carefully behind her ear. "Though I would like to know the name of the lucky man."

She narrowed her eyes. He linked his arm through hers and began to lead them back toward the fire.

"I have been told my skills as a lover are not wanting," he said conspiratorially, "and so it cannot be that."

"Oh, of course it cannot be *that*," said Gwyneth, laughing. He laughed along with her and they rejoined the shifting group of *ulfdrengr* around the main fire. Fell gallantly fetched Gwyneth a cup of water (and more mead for himself), and they watched the leaping dancers. Gwyneth still felt the heat of his kiss on her lips, and part of her wished that she hadn't stopped him, but it was only a very small part. Another part of her wondered if she would tell Rhys that she had kissed Fell, but she tucked that worry away for the morning. Mariel reappeared, gave Gwyneth an appraising look and took up station on her other side; Fell asked over Gwyneth's head where his cousin had gone.

"Do you even need to ask?" Mariel replied, arching one eyebrow with a smile. "You're blood kin, after all."

Fell grinned. "Tula and I have a bit of a competition sometimes during the feasts," he said to Gwyneth.

"I don't want to know," she said immediately, making both Fell and Mariel laugh. She drank her water and thought that overall, the night was not a complete disaster.

The next morning, she awoke with a splitting headache and her shirt stuck to her back – she hadn't tended to the long shallow cut inflicted by Andorra. Tula, in bright spirits, had tutted at Mariel for being so remiss. They visited Ephelia briefly, and on the walk back to the *ulfdrengr* camp, Linara found them.

"Follow me," she said to Gwyneth.

Gwyneth was grateful that she'd at least received Ephelia's rune before the sparring session with Linara, though she knew she would probably have more cuts soon. She followed Linara, realizing that Tula slipped away through the trees without another word. Linara stopped at a small copse and turned back to Gwyneth.

"You favor the sword?" she asked.

"Yes," Gwyneth answered, her hand already reaching for Ithariel.

"Very well," replied Linara with a grin.

Gwyneth did not have time to wonder that they were alone, that Linara asked no one else to join this sparring session, before the *ulfdrengr*'s blade flashed and she leapt from its path, Ithariel emerging from her sheath with a bright silver hiss.

Fighting Linara was nothing like fighting the two younger *ulfdrengr*. It felt like going from sparring with Edelinne to sparring with Rionach – Gwyneth winced at the comparison as she waited for feeling to return to her sword-arm after Linara caught her in a cross-body lock and neatly disarmed her. Ithariel vibrated with anger.

"We can wait a moment," Linara said, watching Gwyneth flex her hand.

Gwyneth cleared her throat. "I will be a better partner after a few rounds, I think."

Linara chuckled. "You think I need practice, *ungrsverda?*"

"Everyone can always improve," Gwyneth replied with her best guileless expression.

Linara's chuckle bloomed into a laugh that rang through the trees.

"Do you mind…may I ask a few questions?" Gwyneth said.

"Of course," Linara said, "though I prefer more fighting than talking in my sparring sessions."

Gwyneth smiled. "Are there those that come to study with you, perhaps to live with you and be one of you, if they are chosen?"

"And who do you ask this question for?" Linara turned her wolf-eyes to Gwyneth. "Or do you want to know in case you do not become the Bearer?"

Ithariel gave a strident peal at the rudeness, the impossibility of such a question – the Named Sword's voice cut through the forest-sounds like a knife through butter. Linara raised one eyebrow at the sword.

"I meant no insult," she said calmly. "I simply want to understand the Heir's question."

"You have heard of the creature called a *syivhalla*?" Gwyneth asked.

Linara went very still, reminding Gwyneth of a predator before its strike. "Yes."

"I studied with six other young women, all of the Blood," said Gwyneth. Her hand was nearly ready to spar again, but she knew that they needed to finish this conversation first, just from Linara's reaction. "They called us the Seven. It was before Rionach made it known that I was the Heir."

"But you knew already," said Linara in a low, certain voice.

Gwyneth looked at the *ulfdrengr* sharply. She smiled and spread her hands.

"I am one of the few who might understand how you felt," Linara said. "How you knew."

"Perhaps," Gwyneth said slowly.

The other woman motioned for her to continue.

"In any case…the *syivhalla* tempted one of the Seven. She came to the Tower for our lesson and…" Gwyneth paused. She felt her hands shaking. It surprised her – she'd thought that she was beyond being affected by the memory of the attack.

"The *syivhalla* attacked," Linara finished quietly.

Gwyneth nodded. She swallowed hard and tested her grip on Ithariel with her sword-hand. "The *syivhalla* attacked," she said firmly. "We were all wounded. Catherine died. Isabella lost a hand – the creature had laid a curse on the door. And Audhild very nearly died as well." She met Linara's eyes. "They protected me. They knew, too. I fought it at the end, and I held it off until the Paladins broke the curse on the door, but the other Inionacha…they knew, and they tried to keep the creature at bay."

"Which of these women wish to come and live among us?"

Gwyneth felt a spark of something like hope. She hadn't even allowed herself to think of the possibility that she would actually convince the *ulfdrengr* to accept Audhild. After a heartbeat of frozen silence, she found her voice. "Audhild," she said. "Her name is Audhild, and she is very good with both the sword and axe already, and she comes from the North in Doendhtalam."

"You say that as though it matters to us here," Linara said, passing her sword through the air a few times almost lazily. The air whistled around her blade.

"She knows how to live in the North," Gwyneth pointed out. "That is what I meant."

"She knows how to live in the North of the mortal world," countered Linara without any malice. "You should know, Gwyneth, that this world is more beautiful and more dangerous than the world of your birth."

"And Audhild knows it as well," Gwyneth said. She paused. "Forgive me for assuming anything about your people's homeland. I care deeply about Audhild and owe her my life. Living with your people is a dream she has held close for a long time. After I become Bearer, there will not be a Hall of the Inionacha any longer, and I hope to help find all who wish a place in this world that makes them happy."

"Pretty words," said Linara, again without rancor, "but do you mean to say that you are going to personally place all the Inionacha?"

"I will help all those who wish it," replied Gwyneth.

Linara smiled and passed her sword through the air again. It had snowed lightly the night before, and the whitened forest floor crunched beneath her boots. "I would do the same for my people," she said finally. "Your Audhild may come to us, if she wishes."

Gwyneth felt the grin spreading across her face and did nothing to stop it. She'd send a messenger back to Audhild at the Unseelie Court. She drew in a breath.

"Don't thank me," Linara said, raising her sword. "Back to practicing, *ungrsverda*."

They fought four more sword-bouts, each time ending with Gwyneth at the point of Linara's blade. But each time she lasted longer, and the last bout she opened a cut on Linara's shoulder. The *ulfdrengr* grinned as they sheathed their weapons.

"Not many make me bleed my own blood," she commented, surveying the stain on her shirtsleeve with interest.

Gwyneth snorted, glancing at her own sleeves, tattered now from her mornings sparring with Mariel and Tula, her arms laced with the fresh red lines of healing cuts. Even with Ephelia's runes, the blades still left their mark.

"Now then," Linara said. "Let us test your skills with the axe."

Thankfully Gwyneth caught the axe Linara tossed her by the handle – she grabbed for it out of reflex, not any real conscious thought. She looked at the *ulfdrengr* as she sheathed Ithariel, hefting the weight of the axe in her hand.

She wondered if Rionach had known that the *ulfdrengr* would teach her such skills....and then she realized she did not much care what Rionach did or did not know anymore. With a grin, she lowered into her fighting stance, the unfamiliar weapon heavy in her hand, awaiting the onslaught of the unknown.

Chapter 34

"It's hard to believe that I've been with you less than a fortnight," Gwyneth said, her hands wrapped around a mug of *khal* as she sat with Mariel and Tula in the common area of the *ulfdrengr* camp. "It feels as if I've been here much longer."

"Each day seems much longer when you fill it with worthwhile tasks," Mariel agreed.

"Each hour seems like an eternity when you're sparring Linara," rejoined Tula with a grin.

Gwyneth smiled. "I've learned a lot." She felt as though she'd learned nearly as much with the *ulfdrengr* as with Rionach during her time Between, though the comparison was inadequate. Living with the *ulfdrengr* had thrust her into an entirely different culture, immersing her in a language that she had learned but did not speak daily, pushing her to understand social interactions from an entirely different point of view. She didn't truly care anymore, but she thought now that Rionach had deposited her purposefully in the dark, cold winter forest; her time with the *ulfdrengr* had proved fruitful in more ways than one. She'd adopted a few of their habits, at first unwittingly – all small things, like rolling up her sleeves to her elbows in the morning despite the wintry bite of the air.

"You've bled a lot," Tula replied drily, eyeing the reddish lines crossing Gwyneth's forearms.

"Ephelia says that she always makes a rune for you now, the night before, just so she doesn't have to trouble her head about it in the morning," Mariel said.

"Well," Gwyneth said, "that sounds like a sensible solution. She sees me most afternoons anyway for lessons." She grinned. "I've become predictable in so short a time."

"When you spar with Linara..."

"And Kalian," Tula interjected.

"And Kalian," Mariel added, "then yes, it's predictable that you'll end up bleeding." She shrugged and took a sip of *khal*. "You fared no worse than any of us would, training with them." She nodded at Gwyneth, the motion no more than a thrust of her chin in Gwyneth's direction. "As I said before, you learn quickly."

Gwyneth brushed the handle of the axe at her belt with one hand. Linara had gifted it to her yesterday in honor of their last training session before the *ulfdrengr* joined the Unseelie at Darkhill for the Solstice celebration. "If I didn't learn as much as I could while here...that would be dishonoring the gift I've been given."

"The gift of being the Heir, or the gift of making our acquaintance?" asked Tula with a spark of mischief in her eyes.

"Both, I suppose," Gwyneth said, her words overlaid by a chuckle.

"If you weren't the Heir," Tula continued, leaning back on one hand and drinking her *khal* between phrases, "then would you want to stay?"

Gwyneth thought about it for a moment, watching the steam rising from her mug, curling up into the frigid morning air. She thought of the wonderful partnership between the wolves and the warriors, the brightness of the *volta* and the fierceness of the Northerners' pride, accentuated by their hospitality and generosity. They were a people shaped by the harshness of their homeland and taught by the loyalty of the wolves bonded to them. They valued independence and forthrightness, but also respected cleverness and trickery. It was a complex, beautiful world in which they lived, and Gwyneth knew she had only experienced a very small part of it.

"If I were not the Heir," she repeated quietly. She paused. "To think such a thing is to wish myself to be a different person, and I cannot do that."

Tula snorted. "I see why you and Linara get along. You're entirely too serious."

"Just because you don't have a grand destiny doesn't mean you should scorn those who do," Mariel said, raising her eyebrow at Tula in mock chastisement.

"Grand destiny," said Gwyneth with a grin. "I don't quite see it that way."

"Well, you should." Mariel drained the rest of her *khal* and stood. "Come on then, lazybones, we need to pack and be ready to travel."

Tula groaned theatrically. "I still don't understand why the *volta* can't pack for us, too."

"How do the *volta* pack?" Gwyneth asked curiously, finishing her own *khal*. The activity around the camp had begun to take on a different character than the normal morning movements: she saw *ulfdrengr* striking their tents and bundling the furs into packs, wolves slipping through the busy camp every so often with grins of anticipation and a quick spring to their step, some of them licking the remnants of a predawn hunt from their jaws.

"With their *fjalkynja,* of course," replied Mariel sensibly.

Gwyneth had learned that while the *ulfdrengr* recognized the word *taebramh,* and that was still the word she most often used in conversation with them, they had their own word for the sorcery of their *volta*: *fjalkynja.* As Gwyneth understood it, the *volta*'s power was based largely in blood-magic and tied much more to their ancestors and the tradition of their craft than *taebramh.* It was possible for any mortal to possess *taebramh,* Gwyneth knew, and the *ulfdrengr* were surprised to learn. She'd spent a few hours discussing the finer details with Linara, who possessed both the *volta* bloodline through her mother and the *ulfdrengr* bloodline through both her mother and her father. Gwyneth gathered that many of the most powerful rulers of the *ulfdrengr* resulted from a mingling of the two bloodlines. She still wondered if there was anything to be said for intermingling the bloodlines of the Inionacha and the Paladin – though they were in their entirety descended from the children of Rionach, distant cousins all.

"You are expected to have children once you are Bearer," Linara had said as they sat on a log, eating some *kajuk* during a break from training.

"Yes," said Gwyneth, feeling heat rise to her cheeks though her voice remained steady enough. "To continue the bloodline."

"And your bloodline is only through daughters. What if you do not have any daughters?"

"I've been told that…doesn't happen," Gwyneth said, feeling foolish.

Linara had gazed at her for a long moment, and then Bjarnyk had appeared silently out of the forest, looking at Linara expectantly. Without another word, Linara had unfolded her legs and followed the wolf into the trees, leaving Gwyneth to stare after them and wonder if she had said something offensive.

She hadn't, of course – Gwyneth was only just beginning to understand now, at the end of her time with them, that the *ulfdrengr* did not view courtesy as the Inionacha or the Paladin viewed courtesy. In Northern culture, there was nothing rude about cutting short a conversation out of necessity with no explanation; neither party took offense, and everyone merely went about their business. Gwyneth saw the practicality of it – no time wasted in polite excuses or explanations, but it still caught her off guard.

"Come on then," Mariel said. Gwyneth had caught herself using the chestnut-haired *ulfdrengr*'s common phrase a few times over the past few days. "The *volta* construct our camp outside Darkhill," she explained as they went to the nearest deerskin shelter and began packing it. The shelters and furs were all commonly owned among the *ulfdrengr;* any belonging with important personal value was packed separately and carried on the warrior's person. Gwyneth had fortunately been told of this, and she'd worn her small traveling pack, beltpouch and weapons to the morning meal.

"The next camp needs to be grand enough to impress the Unseelie," Tula said in a voice that was half-scathing and half-amused.

Mariel shrugged. "One less thing for us to do."

Between the three of them, they had the tent and furs packed in a neat bundle in a handful of minutes, and Tula took the bundle to the common area while Mariel and Gwyneth began packing the next shelter. They packed three more, and then there was a general movement of *ulfdrengr* toward the common area. Without any direction, the *ulfdrengr* picked up bundles, most of them carrying at least two of the heavy bundles slung across their backs. Gwyneth saw Malit and Evedra as she bent to pick up one of the packs; Evedra smiled at her in easy companionship, and Malit eagerly approached her.

"You've been training with Linara?" Malit asked her without preamble as he finished tying a length of heavy twine between his two bundles. He slung one bundle over his shoulder and settled the other at his chest.

"Yes," Gwyneth replied, eyeing her bundle. She decided to shift Ithariel's sheath from its place on her back, and with her own length of twine rigged two straps on either side of the bundle, slinging it over one arm and then settling it across her back instead. It was almost comfortable, save for the thinness of the twine – she made a mental note that it might be worth it to carry her own straps, if she traveled with the *ulfdrengr* in the future.

"And how has it been?" Malit continued, his eyes bright with curiosity.

Gwyneth held up her forearms, showing him her new scars. "Well, you can see for yourself." She smiled, a bit ruefully.

"Scars well earned," Evedra said approvingly. She nodded to Gwyneth. "Good to see you again."

"And you," said Gwyneth. To her mild surprise, Evedra held out her arm. Gwyneth gripped the young *ulfdrengr*'s forearm in the traditional Northern greeting of friendship.

"Will you be staying with us during the Solstice?" Malit continued. They moved away from the rapidly dwindling pile of bundles. Gwyneth saw Tula and Mariel a small distance away, making the last adjustments to their own packs. It seemed that the older *ulfdrengr* did not associate with the youngest ones in social settings – to separate instructor from student, Gwyneth supposed.

"By *us*," Malit clarified hurredly, "I mean…the *ulfdrengr*. As a whole." He cleared his throat.

Gwyneth caught the fond but exasperated look that Evedra gave Malit, and she realized with a sort of embarrassment that Malit…she groped for words in her head. Found her attractive? That was the best phrase she could tolerate.

"Well," she said, "I think I will rejoin the Bearer."

"Ah," Evedra said, "so you will be staying in Darkhill proper, then."

Malit's face fell, but he hid it quickly.

"I'm sure I could come and join you for a morning of sparring," Gwyneth offered, wanting the young *ulfdrengr* to understand that she held nothing against him.

"At your convenience, of course," Evedra said. She slipped her arm through Malit's elbow and towed him away.

"You are entirely too softhearted," Tula said in Gwyneth's ear, almost making her jump.

Gwyneth rubbed at her ear where Tula's breath tickled her. "What was I supposed to say?"

"Tell him you have a Paladin," Tula replied. She shrugged. "Or, if you have more than one lover, just tell him straight that you don't want to add him to the group."

Tula's blunt language still made Gwyneth blink in surprise sometimes as well. "I don't see the need. It's not as though we'll meet again often after this."

"You never know," said Tula enigmatically. Then she shifted her attention to a distant point in the forest, listening to something that Gwyneth couldn't hear. "Time to go – want to run with me?"

"Run with…?" Gwyneth didn't have time to finish her question, because the *ulfdrengr* started forward at a run all at once in response to some invisible signal. Gwyneth stretched her legs to catch up with Tula. The pace was not particularly fast but navigating the forest with the heavy pack on her back certainly made things more interesting. The *ulfdrengr* ran through the forest, braids flying about their shoulders, some of them with axes in hand, calling out to each other from time to time in the Northtongue. Wolves wove between them every so often, surefooted and fleet, giving little yips of enjoyment as they ran.

At first, Gwyneth feared she would not be able to keep pace; but to her mild surprise, once the burn in her legs faded and her lungs became used to the cold air, she felt an exhilarating sense of her own abilities. Her *taebramh* glowed behind her breastbone – not the cause of her speed, but a part of her that pushed her onward nonetheless, and Ithariel sang happily at her hip, enjoying the rush of the wind past her pommel.

Tula's wolf-partner, sleek reddish Veta, ran alongside them for the better part of an hour, allowing Gwyneth to observe one of the *ulfdrengr* wolves closely for an extended amount of time. Between checking her own footing and weaving between the trees, Gwyneth watched the wolf, awestruck by the sinewy muscles rippling beneath her pelt and the languid grace with which she navigated the complex terrain of the forest, looking as though she were flowing over the ground rather than running.

When the noon sun shortened the cold shadows beneath the canopy of the trees, another invisible signal called a halt. The *ulfdrengr* ate some *kajuk* and hard biscuit, drank some water and ale, and then continued on. Gwyneth felt a small, hard kernel of pride at her own endurance. Her shoulders ached from the weight of the pack, but she made no move to touch the straps; her thighs began to burn as they started again at a decent pace, but she pushed the discomfort aside. She had trained for a fortnight with the *ulfdrengr*, and while she understood that was nothing like going with them into battle or anything of that sort, she was loath to give up any of the respect she may have earned during her time in their camp.

The trees began to thin as the afternoon light slanted golden through the leaves of the trees. Gwyneth wasn't sure if she imagined it because she was tired, but it felt as though the *ulfdrengr* increased the pace, their strides lengthening and their eyes gleaming. The wolves surged forward and then circled back, flowing around the warriors and then leaping to the front of the great group with graceful bounds. Gwyneth began to feel their excitement, and it buoyed her tired body. She did not even lift a hand to wipe sweat from her brow. Ithariel began to hum in her sheath at Gwyneth's hip.

Through the sound of her own breath and heartbeat and the footfalls of the *ulfdrengr*, Gwyneth heard a great tolling of bells. It sounded as though dozens of bells, all different in their voices and timbre yet harmonizing perfectly, were sounding at once, shivering through the trees. This time Gwyneth heard the howl that signaled the halt, and then the wolf-song rose all around her, counterpoint to the tolling of the bells – the bells that she now realized belonged to the Unseelie palace. She glanced at Mariel, who grinned and motioned for her to follow as the great company moved forward at a more sedate pace.

They emerged from the trees to the cold brightness of the winter sun, a great plain before them that rose up into a steep hill, and atop the hill behind tall, glittering dark walls emerged the parapets of the gleaming Unseelie palace, the pride of Queen Mab's kingdom: Darkhill. Gwyneth paused for a bare moment, her eyes sweeping across the beautiful, imposing structure, taking in the lustrous stone and the windows set into the towers like burnished gems, reflecting the light with diamond brilliance. The palace glimmered beneath the pale winter sky like a jewel laid upon a fold of white silk.

"The Merrow aren't here yet," said Mariel with a note of satisfaction, "so we've the choice of camp."

The *ulfdrengr* and *volta* held at the edge of the trees as a column emerged from the main gate of Darkhill: three Knights in shining armor, and behind them a brilliant figure who radiated such a light that Gwyneth knew without asking that it had to be Queen Mab. Beside the Queen rode another, slimmer woman who looked younger; the Queen's younger sister, the Princess Andraste, Gwyneth remembered. The Unseelie all rode upon graceful *faehal*, the Knights upon gray mounts and the Queen and Princess upon black.

Five figures, too, emerged from the Northern contingent: Linara striding first, flanked by Kalian and Andorra half a step behind her, followed by a man almost as large as Kalian walking arm-in-arm with a woman as tall as Linara. The wolves ranged around the warriors, Bjarnyk largest among them, larger even than the huge wolf that bore many scars and a whitened muzzle, the one that Gwyneth supposed was bound to Linara's father.

"Vinramryk, the Greatking," said Mariel in a quiet, reverent voice, "and his lady, Saela."

"His lady has no title?" Gwyneth asked, matching Mariel's quiet tone.

"They call her the Kingbreaker," Tula answered from her other side with a grin.

"When he was young, Vinramryk was wild," said Mariel, her voice dropping into the lilt of a storyteller. "He had no interest in ruling, no interest in taking a wife or a lover to continue the line of his father, the Secondking."

"Vinramryk's father was the second king of the *ulfdrengr*?" Gwyneth did not want to interrupt, but the question escaped her anyway.

"We have long been separated, according to our lineage and customs," said Mariel. "Different clans had their rulers, and they held council together every decade or so."

"It was not a bad way to govern," Tula said, lifting one shoulder in a shrug.

"But then the Firstking rose above them during the first war with the trolls," said Mariel. "The giant Illiligr learned to speak the language of the trolls…"

"Such as it is," interjected Tula with disgust, wrinkling her nose.

" – and banded together to make war upon us. The Firstking was the Gifrbana before the other kings elevated him to rule over all."

"Gifrbana," said Gwyneth. "Trollbane."

"Yes." Mariel smiled a little. "You are very good with our language, Gwyn."

"I enjoy languages," Gwyneth murmured.

"Do you speak Merrow?" Tula asked with bright, sharp interest as they watched the *ulfdrengr* close the distance across the field to the Unseelie procession.

"Not very well," said Gwyneth, even though Rionach had deemed her spoken-word Merrow quite sufficient.

"I've heard it's very difficult," said Tula. "Not many can even remember a few words, much less speak it at all."

The Unseelie Knights dismounted. Two of them took the reins of the Queen and Princess' mounts; Gwyneth frowned. She remembered reading that the Sidhe rarely used what she would view as traditional tack on their mounts, but the reason became clear as the wolves approached. The *faehal* hesitated, their eyes widening and nostrils flaring. The firm hand of the Knights kept them from bolting. The Knights' chargers, for their part, stood watching the wolves alertly, delicate ears pricked forward.

Gwyneth realized suddenly that her vision seemed much better than she remembered. She could see the expressions on the faces of the beautiful Unseelie Knights as they walked toward the *ulfdrengr*. They looked haughty and cold to her, the fairness of their pale faces too perfect, the sculpted elegance of their bodies apparent even beneath their shining armor. She could see the ripples of Linara's shirtsleeves in the breeze and the leather thong tying the end of Kalian's braid. She made a note to ask Rionach about her heightened senses later; perhaps it was just a consequence of her training in the Between.

Or perhaps it means you are edging closer to becoming the Bearer, the voice in the corner of her mind whispered.

The Unseelie and the *ulfdrengr* met near the center of the great, flat plain. Gwyneth watched the expressions on the faces of the Knights: they all looked as though they were carved from marble. None of them so much as betrayed a hint of their thoughts on their faces. Then Linara gave them a nod and the Knights bowed to her slightly from the waist, and the Knights and *ulfdrengr* warriors parted smoothly, allowing their rulers to greet one another. Queen Mab and her sister dismounted gracefully, and one of the Knights led their *faehal* back to where the chargers stood.

Gwyneth noticed that Princess Andraste did not speak at all, but rather looked with interest at the wolves. Bjarnyk yawned, displaying his white teeth, and Andraste grinned. Gwyneth couldn't see Linara's face, but she thought that perhaps the two daughters of the rulers were sharing a moment of levity.

King Vinramryk and Queen Mab spoke for more than a few moments, but short of a long while. Saela – Queen Saela? wondered Gwyneth – spoke to the Unseelie Queen as well. Mab wore a diadem that shone like a star, its luminescence making Gwyneth's eyes ache after a few moments of watching the meeting intently. Then Queen Mab motioned elegantly toward Darkhill, and the *ulfdrengr* king and his *volta* queen walked with the Queen and the Princess toward the gates, the Knights and *ulfdrengr* warriors following behind them. The wolves flowed around them and disappeared over the hill, racing around the walls of Darkhill, Gwyneth presumed both to explore and to find their evening meal.

To Gwyneth's surprise, it was Fell who stepped out of the trees and whistled sharply. A lean gray wolf bounded ahead of him into the long grasses of the plain. More wolves followed in an unbridled romp, their sleek bodies weaving through the long grass as the small animals of Mab's kingdom dashed away in sudden terror through the underbrush.

"Time to set up camp," Tula said brightly.

"You're only excited about it because the *volta* are handling the tents," pointed out Mariel as they began walking forward.

"Of course," replied Tula. She grinned and pulled at Veta's ear as the red-hued wolf paused to nip at her hand before rocketing away to join the other wolves chasing rabbits through the grass. "Like pups again, they are," Tula said affectionately.

"You'll be wanted in the palace, I think, Gwyn," Mariel said.

"Well," said Gwyneth, feeling suddenly sad at the prospect of leaving the *ulfdrengr*, "I'll go when they summon me."

Tula grinned. "That's the spirit!"

Gwyneth grinned in reply. She wondered if Rhys and the Paladins were already within Darkhill, a thought that pulled at her heart with excitement; but she also wanted to spend one more night of revelry with the fierce wolf-warriors who had taught her so much over the past days. She followed Mariel and Tula toward the place that Fell staked out for their camp, tucking away her curiosity at what the coming days of the Solstice celebration would bring.

Chapter 35

To Gwyneth's mild surprise, no Glasidhe messenger found her that first night the *ulfdrengr* camped on the plain outside of Darkhill. Gwyneth watched the *volta* raise the magnificent tents of the camp, the jewel-colored fabrics billowing as though lifted by an unfelt wind and arranged by unseen hands. Mariel and Tula chose an emerald-hued tent. Gwyneth drew in her breath when they crossed the threshold; much like Ephelia's airy abode, the tent was much larger on the inside than it looked from the outside, rich rugs and furs strewn underfoot and piled in several intervals to make beds.

"This is why I love it when the *volta* make our camp for Solstice," sighed Tula, falling rapturously into one of the piles of furs.

Mariel stacked their packs neatly in one corner. She pulled off her boots and laid back in one of the piles as well. Gwyneth watched them both a bit bemusedly: this was rather odd behavior from the ascetic, disciplined fighters who had told her stories of digging snow caverns on long troll-hunts in the dead of a Northern winter.

"We can enjoy a bit of comfort," Tula said, her voice muffled by the voluminous woven blanket that she'd pulled over herself.

"Once or twice a year," agreed Mariel with a blissful sigh as she finished removing her socks and buried her bare feet in the pile of furs.

"Well, now I know that I just have to offer you luxurious lodgings to stay on your good side," Gwyneth said teasingly.

Tula's only answer was a light snore.

"If you want to catch some sleep before the real festivities begin, better take it now while you can, *ungrsverda*," Mariel advised. She yawned and burrowed deeper into the nest of furs until only the tip of her nose and a few locks of chestnut hair remained visible.

Gwyneth wandered around the tent, peering at the silken hangings that shimmered and twisted in the unfelt breeze that seemed common to all *volta* constructs. She remembered that she had ripped the good shirt that she'd first worn through the ether, and wondered whether Rionach would send other, proper clothes. Part of her bridled at the thought: after her time among the *ulfdrengr*, she certainly didn't think that clothes mattered much at all when it came to the skills of a warrior. But the part of her that had been trained at the Hall of the Inionacha knew that with the Sidhe, looking the part one wanted to play was almost as important as possessing the skills to fulfill the role itself.

Gwyneth glanced fondly at the lumps beneath the furs that were Tula and Mariel. She'd meant to take a rest as well, but suddenly she found that she was not tired at all. Ithariel hummed in interest as she turned and slipped outside into the *ulfdrengr* camp – and nearly collided with Linara. The *herravaldyr* woman stepped neatly aside without so much as an intake of breath while Gwyneth recovered her footing from stumbling.

"Well, that was convenient," remarked Linara, raising one eyebrow at Gwyneth.

"That's one way to put it, I suppose," Gwyneth agreed.

"My grandfather sent me to you," continued Linara, her green eyes brilliant as emeralds in the afternoon light. She switched to Commontongue, her words lightly accented. "He wanted to ensure that you are properly attired for your introduction to the Unseelie Queen."

"I thought the king was your father," Gwyneth said as she followed

Linara through the camp, *ulfdrengr* pressing their thumbs to their forehead in salute as Linara passed.

"No," she answered. "Truly he is my grandfather once more over – what is that called?"

"Great-grandfather," said Gwyneth, trying to do the calculations in her head.

"We are very long lived," said Linara, "but that does not mean we are immortal." She glanced at Gwyneth. "Much like you."

Gwyneth ran her thumb along one of the tender new scars along her forearm.

"You want to ask," Linara continued.

"Are your grandparents and parents..."

"Still alive?" Linara paused and smiled, emerald eyes glittering. "My mother died bearing me. The *volta* say it is because the power in my blood was too great for her."

Gwyneth winced. "That is cruel of them to say."

Linara shrugged. "It is not cruel if it is true." She turned and entered a shimmering gray-silver tent. "My mother's parents did not approve of her union with my father, so I never knew them. My father's parents were killed by a winter sickness a century past. And my father was killed by a giant."

"Do you remember them?" Gwyneth asked quietly. The inside of the silver tent was furnished more sparsely than Mariel and Tula's dwelling, conveying a sense of restraint.

"Only my father," answered Linara, almost brusquely. "Vinramryk and Saela are the ones who raised me, along with the pack."

Gwyneth nodded and then bit her tongue. She would not ask any more probing questions.

"Don't be ashamed of asking," Linara said with that preternatural sense of Gwyneth's thoughts. "We have become something close to friends, have we not?"

"I would be honored to call you my friend," replied Gwyneth honestly.

"Well then, be greatly honored," said Linara, smiling slightly. Then she turned to a long, low table upon which were laid selections of clothing. "Now. Let us choose what would be suitable for you."

"Oh," said Gwyneth as she realized that she would be dressed from Linara's wardrobe. "I…really, Rionach should supply something…"

"Nonsense," said Linara, surveying the table. "What does it say about our hospitality if we send you to the Solstice after ruining your clothes sparring?"

"Well, it says that I should be better at sparring, and then my clothes would not have been ripped half so often," quipped Gwyneth.

Linara chuckled. "You have certainly been spending time with Tula. Her quick wit and sharp tongue are matched by few."

"I've enjoyed my time spent with all of you." Gwyneth touched one of the shirts, cleverly woven so that it looked silver in one light and blue in the next. Linara packed up the shirt and held it against Gwyneth's chest.

"That will do," she said with a nod. "It sets off your eyes nicely."

Gwyneth couldn't help the snort that escaped her. Ithariel chimed reprovingly. "I wouldn't have guessed you considered fashion closely," she said to Linara, feeling daring.

"Don't we all?" replied the *ulfdrengr* evenly. "Even the men, though they will not admit it." She fixed Gwyneth with a serious look. "Do not let anyone ever tell you that you must choose between being a warrior and a woman."

"Nothing will change my being a woman," Gwyneth said, feeling her eyebrows draw together.

"Even in this world, sometimes it is thought that being a woman and being a warrior are two different things," Linara said. She paused. "By that I mean that some think beauty means you cannot be strong. Some think strength means you are not a woman because you are not bearing children and tending a hearth. Some think toughness means you are coldhearted."

Gwyneth watched the silver and blue flames dancing on a black disc in the center of the tent. "I have not experienced all that you have, but your people are the most...equal-minded...that I have ever encountered."

Linara pressed her lips together. "We still have our...conflicts."

"I am sure that any group of people do. Not all are going to think exactly alike."

The *ulfdrengr* smiled tightly and selected a pair of black breeches, laying them alongside the silver-blue shirt. "That is true." She looked at Gwyneth again. "You will be in a position of unquestioned authority, Gwyneth."

It took Gwyneth a moment to realize that Linara spoke of when she would become the Bearer. She lifted her chin and forced herself not to shy away from the subject. "Yes."

Linara considered and added an intricately woven black leather belt to the outfit. The air went very still as she turned to Gwyneth. "I know you will use your power well." The corner of her lips turned upward. "You have a mind of your own, and you will not bow to the will of the Sidhe."

Gwyneth wondered if Linara was implying that Rionach had bowed to the will of the Sidhe, but she didn't ask. She simply nodded and allowed herself to accept the warm glow from Linara's praise – sparely worded praise, yet praise nonetheless from the unyielding *ulfdrengr*. After a moment, Gwyneth found words. "When you take the mantle of leadership from Vinramryk, I know that you will do the same."

Linara smiled but did not reply. She considered the clothes and then crossed the tent, opening a lacquered black box. "You might as well change now," she said over her shoulder to Gwyneth. "Princess Andraste has invited a small group to join her for an afternoon meal."

A little thrill ran through Gwyneth. She shed her traveling clothes, any self-consciousness long forgotten, and slipped into the well-made *ulfdrengr* attire. To her surprise, the clothes fit well. Linara turned back toward Gwyneth as she surveyed the fit of the breeches.

"It seems the changes are progressing fast," Linara said with little inflection in her voice. "You look as though you spent half a year with us, not merely a fortnight."

It was true that Gwyneth had been sore every single day of her training with the *ulfdrengr*, but surely her body had not changed so visibly...she gave up on evaluating herself. "Well, if you say so."

"I do," replied Linara. And then she held out a magnificent necklace toward Gwyneth, displaying the collar between her hands. It was undoubtedly a piece made for an *ulfdrengr*, beads carved from a jet-black stone woven on black leather thin as a spider's web, interspersed with long ivory-colored beads that looked to be bone. Small silver beads decorated the edge of the collar. The pattern of black and white was striking, fierce and elegant, all at once.

"This belonged to Saela once, in her younger days," said Linara. "We would consider it a gesture of the friendship between the Bearer and our people if you would wear it to the Solstice."

Gwyneth opened her mouth and closed it again. Rionach had not prepared her properly to accept such gifts, she thought. Even as she thought quickly of what she could give in return, she smiled. "I would be honored."

"There is no need for a gift to us," Linara said, stepping forward to fasten the necklace around Gwyneth's throat. She touched one of the carved bone beads, her gaze turning throughtful, and then she put one hand on Gwyneth's shoulder with a nod. "It looks well on you."

"Thank you," said Gwyneth in the Northtongue.

"And you will accept Princess Andraste's invitation?" Linara continued. She crossed the tent to the black lacquered box again and selected another necklace, this one bearing unmistakable claws, the construction of the piece more of a display of a trophy than a tribute to beauty.

Gwyneth folded the clothes she had shed and set them neatly on the table. "I think it would be rude not to accept such an invitation."

"You think right," said Linara, "though the Princess is young enough that she might not take offense. She is not half so cold as her sister the Queen."

"Will Bjarnyk join us?"

Linara chuckled. "No. He likes the confinement of stone walls even less than I do."

"Will there be others in attendance?"

"I imagine so," said Linara.

Gwyneth smoothed her hair, wondering if she should redo her simple braid.

"You look entirely acceptable," Linara said. "More than acceptable, I would say, after your time with us." She tossed her dark braid over one shoulder. "And if your Paladin does not think so, well then, I think many of my brothers in the pack would contradict him." Picking up a silver fur, she handed it to Gwyneth without another word.

Linara's words brought to mind the feel of Fell's skillful kiss and the chiseled, sinewy muscles of Kalian as he fought bare-chested in the ring. Gwyneth took a deep breath and followed Linara from the tent, wrapping the fur mantle around her shoulders as she walked. One hour at a time, she told herself, grateful for the chill of the air that cooled her burning cheeks. Would she ever stop blushing so furiously? After all, she was nearly eighteen, though she felt much older than that. Every day in the Hall of the Inionacha had felt like a week, and every hour with Rionach in the Between had felt like a day. She had seen and done so many things in such a short time – how was it that her awkwardness had not abated? If she'd stayed in the mortal world, she ruminated as she followed Linara beyond the magnificent tents onto the plain before the Unseelie palace, she'd most likely be bearing her second or third child at the very least, if she'd not already died in childbirth.

Gwyneth shivered. She realized that she had not thought of her cousin Siobhan in a long time. For a moment, her mind drifted. She wondered if Siobhan had married, if Siobhan had borne children already. She wondered if her mother and father looked upon her cousin with love or with bitterness, bereft of all their children: two daughters to Faeortalam, and one son to the dark sleep of death. Gwyneth suddenly felt certain that there had been other babes aside from the three of them, babes that had died in the womb or shortly after birth. Perhaps that was why her mother had let her attend to births much sooner than Gwyneth had anticipated, why her mother had been so insistent on trying to protect Gwyneth against being taken by the Bearer. She felt a pang of something like regret or sadness, but she pushed it away.

Kalian and Andorra met them on the plain, greeting Linara and Gwyneth with easy nods, and they began to climb the hill to the great gate in the dark, glimmering walls of the Unseelie palace. For a moment, Gwyneth felt small beside the huge *ulfdrengr* and the great parapets of Darkhill; but then Ithariel chimed reassuringly, a sound only for her ears, and her *taebramh* stirred within her chest. She looked up at the beautiful, mighty Sidhe stronghold silhouetted against the deepening gray of the sky and drew back her shoulders. She was the Heir to the Sword.

Then they were walking through great gates, larger than anything Gwyneth had ever seen even in the White City. The Guards at the gate did not question Linara, but neither did they salute her. A little prickle of indignation expanded in Gwyneth's chest – did they not know that Linara was equal in rank to their Princess? She turned her head to look at one of the Unseelie Guards, and when she met the Guard's eyes, she felt as though she spun in an endless, starless night. She blinked and managed not to stumble, grateful for the solid warmth of the fur mantle around her shoulders.

They walked into a large courtyard, the *ulfdrengr*'s boots silent upon the stone, Gwyneth matching their tread as best she could.

Banners of radiant silver and midnight blue hung at intervals, and the stone walls of the keep glittered with delicate patterns of frost, complex and beautiful. They passed surprisingly few Sidhe – perhaps they were all readying for the feast, Gwyneth thought. Linara led them toward a small door. A young Unseelie stood with his hands clasped behind his back, clearly waiting; he bowed gracefully when they approached, brushing a curl of dark hair out of his eyes when he straightened.

"I am to escort you to the Princess's courtyard," he said, his voice just as beautiful as his face. Gwyneth thought that he and the Princess might be of the same age, though it was difficult to tell with the Sidhe. The Unseelie boy turned and pressed his hand against the door, which had no handle; the door swung inward noiselessly. He gestured for them to follow him. Gwyneth caught the edge of a look that Linara slid toward Kalian – Linara with her lips pressed together as though to prevent a smile, and Kalian with an evaluating look. Commentary on their young guide, Gwyneth thought, though she didn't understand what Linara thought so funny.

Too solemn, Ithariel chimed into Gwyneth's thoughts, the words shimmering and half-formed.

Gwyneth understood a little more as she walked with the *ulfdrengr* down the hall, *taebramh* lights flickering and glinting on diamond-carved ice encrusting the walls with kaleidoscopic coruscation. The beauty of the Unseelie seemed frozen, cold.

Too cold, she thought to Ithariel. The Named Sword knew she was not speaking of the chill in the air, though that, too, increased as they strode deeper into Darkhill. Every now and again, they passed a vein of *taebramh* pulsing in the dark stone of the wall. Gwyneth had read about the *taebramh* that flowed through the walls of Darkhill: it was the very heart of Queen Mab's kingdom, the seat of her power and the deepest connection to her land.

"Are you ready, *ungrsverda*?" murmured Andorra in the Northtongue, falling back slightly to walk beside Gwyneth.

"If I felt ready," Gwyneth answered quietly, barely able to hear herself over the beating of her heart, "I think that would be the first sign that I am not."

Andorra smiled. "It is a gentler introduction, this little tea-party with the Princess."

"Is she very young?"

"For the Sidhe, yes," replied Andorra.

Gwyneth wondered briefly if their young guide spoke Northtongue, but he walked gracefully a few strides ahead of Linara and Kalian. Even if he did speak the *ulfdrengr* language, he might not be able to hear them, although, Gwyneth corrected herself, Sidhe hearing was quite good, better by far than that of a mortal.

Not quite mortal, Ithariel shimmered. The Sword's voice seemed clearer within the glittering crystal halls of the Unseelie palace.

If their guide *did* hear them, then he gave no sign. He led them through the corridors, passing no one else, until they emerged into a courtyard, the light blooming around them as though they had surfaced after swimming underwater. The raven-haired Unseelie lad bowed to them and then disappeared into the shadows.

Linara surveyed the courtyard, clotted with small groups of graceful figures, *taebramh* lights shimmering as they drifted overhead in clusters, weaving through the air as though borne by an unfelt breeze. The Unseelie had some taste in common with the *volta*, Gwyneth decided as she peered up at the lights. Kalian pressed her elbow, subtly motioning her forward until she stood aligned with Linara, Kalian flanking them on the right and Andorra on the left.

Flowers blossomed improbably on the frosted walls of the courtyard, white roses the prominent flower, their heads nodding heavily and glittering with ice crystals. The young Unseelie Princess sat on a plain but elegant silver chair. It was more her posture that brought to mind a throne than the chair itself. Her gown echoed the simplicity of the furnishings, though the closely fitted bodice and silver embroidery at the cuff and hems emphasized her finely formed, slender body. The Princess wore her hair in a simple braid pinned around her head like a crown.

A hush fell over the courtyard as those gathered realized the presence of the *ulfdrengr*. Gwyneth's heart leapt into her throat as she caught a glimpse of a familiar face among the beautiful Unseelie, a flash of dark golden hair among the midnight tresses of the Sidhe. She felt a smile tilt her lips as Aedan met her eyes from across the courtyard and inclined his head in greeting.

"I am so glad you accepted my invitation," said the Princess into the rippling murmurs. She stood and glided toward them, her grace effortless and her beauty ethereal. Gwyneth felt as though the Princess were not quite real. No woman could be *that* beautiful, that...perfect. It was the word her mind supplied, though she told herself that there was no such thing as perfection, even among the otherworldly allure of the Sidhe.

"How could we not accept something so prettily worded?" replied Linara with a small smile. She allowed the Unseelie Princess to walk nearly the entire distance between them before taking a few steps forward. Gwyneth wasn't sure if she imagined the looks passed between a few of the Unseelie courtiers.

"Well," said the Princess, tilting her chin upward to look at Linara and then Kalian. She seemed delicate as a porcelain doll next to the tall, sinewy *ulfdrengr*. "I welcome you to Darkhill. The Seelie have not yet arrived – they so dislike the cold, I think, that they delay their arrival as much as can be courteous." The Princess laughed lightly, and a few of the courtiers joined her. Two Unseelie women drifted toward them, murmuring to each other and plainly eyeing Kalian. They stopped behind the Princess.

"I do not believe you have met the Bearer's Heir," said Linara.

The Princess blinked, her long lashes dark upon her snow-white cheeks. Her cupid's-bow mouth formed a little moue of surprise. "You mean to tell me the Bearer means to give up her position?"

Linara turned to Gwyneth, clearly not willing to answer for her.

"Not give up her position," Gwyneth answered, her voice ringing louder through the courtyard than she intended. "Pass on the Sword as intended."

"As intended," the Princess repeated to herself, tilting her head slightly to one side. She turned to one of her ladies. "Rose, is it not surprising?"

The taller of the two Unseelie ladies curtseyed to the Princess and said, "It is, of course, my lady, very surprising indeed." Her smile revealed fetching dimples. Upon closer inspection, Gwyneth decided the two ladies must be sisters. They possessed the same heart-shaped face and slight tilt to their eyes, though the one who had not curtseyed was almost a full head shorter than her sister.

"It is also surprising," said Linara, her voice pitched low so that it was more difficult for all to hear, "that you have not greeted the Heir as befits her station, Princess."

The Unseelie Princess blinked again – she really was very young, Gwyneth thought. Then the Princess gathered herself and clasped her hands in front of her demurely. "Forgive me," she said smoothly. "I am Princess Andraste of the Unseelie Court."

"Gwyneth O'Connor of the Inionacha, Heir to the Iron Sword," said Gwyneth, feeling a little spark of pride at the steadiness of her voice.

"I am pleased you extended my invitation to Gwyneth, Lady Linara," Andraste continued, smiling without showing her teeth as she looked at Linara.

The *ulfdrengr* woman returned the same smile, keeping her gleaming white teeth covered. "I thought you would like to meet the next Bearer before your sister."

Something flashed through Andraste's eyes, more quickly than Gwyneth could follow. Then the Princess motioned. "Please," she said. "Come. Enjoy yourselves." She turned and began walking back toward her silver chair, clearly expecting them to follow. "I extended an invitation to Melusina of the Ritheaghlach, but I do not know if she will attend. And, of course, there are a few Paladins here already." She gestured with one white long-fingered hand in Aedan's direction. Gwyneth thought it a bit dismissive, but she tried to school her face into a neutral mask. She felt the gazes of the Unseelie courtiers from all sides. There were only a few dozen in the courtyard, but the small space and shifting light and their gleaming beauty made their numbers seem greater to Gwyneth.

"Perhaps if you had invited a few of the Laochra, my lady, the *ulfdrengr* would have more companionable conversation," said the Unseelie woman whom the Princess had called Rose.

"The Laochra would likely not accept such an invitation," said the smaller Unseelie woman.

"Even warriors must have civilized conversation every once in a while," quipped Rose, sliding a glance at Kalian to see whether he had smiled at her cleverness.

"Is this your first Solstice, Lady Gwyneth?" asked the smaller woman, deftly changing the subject.

"Guinna, you are no sport at all," murmured Rose.

"It is," replied Gwyneth. She wondered why Linara had accepted the invitation from the Princess – the prim, frosted courtyard was a far cry from the wildness of the *ulfdrengr* drums throbbing through the darkness of the night.

"And you have been hosted by the *ulfdrengr* for a few days?" Guinna continued.

"A fortnight, actually," replied Gwyneth. "I've been training with them."

Princess Andraste settled back into her silver chair and her ladies rearranged themselves around her like birds fluttering through the branches of a tree to find the most agreeable perch.

"Want some *vinaess*?" Andorra asked Gwyneth. She winked. "Don't worry, it's nothing as strong as what you've been drinking with us."

"In that case, certainly," said Gwyneth. She turned back to Andraste, but the Princess had already become engrossed in a conversation with one of her ladies, and a few of the young men gathered at the edge of the group gathered their courage enough to approach. Soon, the young Princess laughed gaily, the sound echoing from the walls of the courtyard like a merry cascade of bells.

"Our Princess is young," said Guinna, suddenly very close to Gwyneth. She looked pointedly at Ithariel on Gwyneth's hip. Gwyneth glanced at the *ulfdrengr* and realized with a sinking feeling that none of the three wore any visible weapons, but then she drew back her shoulders.

"Ithariel is a Named Sword," she told Guinna, pretending to mistake the Unseelie woman's look for one of curiosity. "She has been my companion in my training with the Bearer." She paused. "You certainly do not expect the Bearer to part with the Caedbranr when she steps within Darkhill, do you?"

Guinna smiled. "That is a matter I leave for Queen Mab, as she is the nearest equal to the Bearer."

Ithariel hummed at Gwyneth's hip. Was it a thinly veiled insult or simply ignorance? Gwyneth felt herself go very still. "I will choose not to take that as an insult, Lady Guinna, because none are the Bearer's *equal*."

For an instant, Guinna met Gwyneth's eyes and the air tightened between them. Guinna looked away first, and then Gwyneth heard a familiar voice.

"What an unexpected and pleasant surprise."

"Aedan," she said warmly, turning away from Guinna to greet the Paladin. She didn't watch to see Guinna's reaction; she had no need to play the silly girls' games that the Princess and her ladies seemed to espouse. They were Sidhe, but they were young, and it seemed some things did not change between the mortal and Fae worlds after all.

Aedan clasped her hand in greeting. The feeling of his warm, calloused grip brought Gwyneth more comfort and familiarity than she anticipated.

"Is Orla here?" Gwyneth asked, glancing around the courtyard for Aedan's partner.

Aedan smiled. "I thought you would ask about another Paladin first."

Gwyneth chuckled even as she felt her cheeks warm. "Well, of course I want to know if Rhys is here, but..." She shrugged slightly, unsure of how to express her misgivings about asking such a personal question within the Princess' courtyard.

"He is," replied Aedan simply. "Not *here* in the courtyard, but he is here at the Solstice."

A burst of warmth and giddiness whirled through Gwyneth. She felt herself nod, trying to keep her expression contained. "I'm glad to hear it."

"You are more than glad," said Aedan almost fondly, "but this is not the place to speak of it."

Gwyneth smiled. "You're certainly right about that." Andorra pressed a silver cup into her hand as she passed by, and Gwyneth took a sip gingerly. The *vinaess* reminded her of wine, though the flavor was brighter and colder than anything she'd ever tasted. "How are you?" she asked Aedan, turning back to him and scrutinizing him fully. The edge of a fresh red scar emerged from beneath the collar of his shirt. Gwyneth wondered if Rhys had any new scars.

"Ready to celebrate the Solstice," replied Aedan. "It is always an experience to travel to the Courts, but it means that I am not doing anything else during these days."

"There are other tasks you to which you would rather devote your attention," murmured Gwyneth.

"Though it is perhaps not quite polite to say as much," agreed Aedan. He held her at arm's length as she took another draught of *vinaess*. "Rionach took you into the ether, didn't she? She trained you Between."

"Did she send word to you?" Gwyneth asked curiously.

Aedan shook his head. "No. You have the look about you."

She frowned.

He chuckled. "I simply mean that when one stays Between, time passes. It passes differently. You are obviously not the same young woman that I met not even half a year past."

"It feels like years have passed since the Tower," said Gwyneth with a nod.

"And for you, they have," replied Aedan. "Your time with the *ulfdrengr* has changed you as well."

"I certainly have the new scars to show for it," she agreed good-naturedly.

"Rionach has planned well," Aedan said quietly, almost to himself.

Gwyneth finished her *vinaess*, feeling the warmth of the Unseelie drink spreading through her limbs, a pleasant counterpoint to the chill in the air.

"It is high time you visited the Paladins' Tower," continued Aedan. "I think you will find it most illuminating."

"I look forward to it," replied Gwyneth. They stood in companionable silence for a few moments, watching the gentle churning of the groups of courtiers, knots forming and then dissolving as the Unseelie, most as young as the Princess, shifted and angled for a position nearer to the Princess and her ladies.

"Why did she invite us if she is simply going to gossip with her ladies and flirt with the young men?" asked Gwyneth, glancing at the silver chair and the perfect Unseelie Princess.

"She is young," Aedan said, "and she is trying to find her own way within her sister's Court."

Gwyneth pressed her lips together. Aedan's reply didn't satisfy her, but she thought it best to let the question go unanswered.

"The young men might speak to you as well, despite your scowl," Aedan said teasingly, his tone brotherly.

That surprised a little laugh out of Gwyneth. She looked down into her empty cup and then glanced at Aedan. He gave her an encouraging smile and, thus bolstered, she set out across the courtyard to find more *vinaess*, feeling as though she were striding into an unknown land.

Chapter 36

Gwyneth found Aedan again when the number of those in the courtyard seemed to be thinning; she supposed the Sidhe needed to go dress in their finery for the evening's feast.

"And how did you manage?" Aedan asked, sipping at his silver cup, his gold-flecked eyes sweeping over the courtyard every now and again.

"Quite well, I think," Gwyneth replied boldly, though she knew part of her newfound boldness had much to do with the *vinaess*. She felt it reaching its pleasurably warm tentacles out from her stomach, wrapping her spine and cradling the back of her head gently. She also felt Ithariel checking on her every so often, the Named Sword touching Gwyneth's consciousness for a moment and then retreating, circling and waiting and watchful in her sheath at Gwyneth's hip. Gwyneth didn't quite understand why Ithariel was so awake – perhaps Darkhill and the presence of the Sidhe made the sword restless. Gwyneth cleared her throat and continued. "The younger Unseelie are more difficult to read than the Paladins, of course, since they are Sidhe and not mortal, but I think I was successful in my conversation with them."

Aedan smiled. "I believe so."

"You didn't answer me earlier." She looked at Aedan and though that he ought to speak to her truthfully – she was the Heir, after all. She'd be Bearer someday, though she grimaced at the thought. It might be years still – maybe even decades – before Rionach passed the Iron Sword to her.

"When you asked me why the Princess chose to invite us," Aedan said, the hint of a smile on his lips.

"Yes," said Gwyneth. "And where's Orla?" she added, thinking that he might as well answer more than one question at once.

Aedan gently but firmly exchanged his cup for Gwyneth's, and she found that by the time she realized what was happening, he already had her cup in his hand. She also found that his mug was delightfully warm, and she raised it to her nose, smelling the delightful fragrance of the tea.

"You can hold your *vinaess*," Aedan said with a trace of approval in his voice – or did she imagine that. "But it would be best for you to have all your wits about you at the feast."

"Why?" she asked, obediently raising the warm cup to her lips. The vibrant tea shocked her tongue with its luscious, tart berry flavor – the fragrance paled in comparison to the actual taste. Gwyneth blinked and found her thoughts clearer already. She took another sip, and the warm tendrils of *vinaess* retreated from the base of her skull.

"I'm sure you know who will be there," Aedan said, watching as a trio of young Unseelie men took their leave of the Princess, with much courtliness and lowered lashes and half-smiles.

"The Unseelie, of course," Gwyneth said. "The Seelie. The Paladins. The *ulfdrengr*. The Merrow, possibly the Seafarers, though from what Rionach taught me, they are not the most reliable of guests."

"They would not be Seafarers if they were entirely predictable and courteous," said Aedan. He swirled the liquid in his cup. Gwyneth suddenly felt guilty for drinking his tea, and she offered the cup to him. "No, I'm quite fine, thank you," he said. "I thought you might need it."

"So, you were waiting for me to come to speak to you, just so you could take my *vinaess* and give me this tea?" Gwyneth said with a hint of incredulity. "This *delicious* tea," she added in an undertone, taking another swallow and relishing the bright flavor.

"I would have come to speak to *you*, if you hadn't come over here," said Aedan. He smiled and shifted, his lithe form ever coiled and ready. "And I will answer your question."

"Both my questions?" she said hopefully.

"Both," he said with an air of indulgence. She grinned. The Unseelie Princess's laughter rolled through the courtyard like chiming bells. "I believe Princess Andraste is searching for her own identity, like any young person. And she is positioning herself as the young, bright foil to her sister. To her mind, that means collecting luminaries, cultivating an image of lighthearted and beautiful merriment that also converges with thoughtful conversation."

Gwyneth pressed her lips together. "I don't much like the idea of being part of anyone's *collection*."

"You are the Heir," said Aedan. "It is something to which you must become accustomed. It will only increase after you have become Bearer."

She resisted the urge to ask Aedan how exactly he was so certain, because *he* wasn't the Bearer – the words sounded childish even in her own thoughts, so she took a sip of tea instead.

"And Orla tolerates these events even less than I," Aedan continued. "She is otherwise occupied, but even if she were not, she would prefer to avoid it."

"Orla is fearless," Gwyneth said without thinking, almost in protest.

"No one is fearless, but she would smile to hear you describe her so."

Gwyneth thought of the woman wearing the white cat masque at the Paladin's Samhain celebration. She remembered the fierceness in Orla's voice from the other side of the Tower door as she broke the *syivhalla*'s curse. "Well," she amended, "she is the closest to fearless that I have seen."

"Then you have not spent enough time with us, *ungrsverda*," said Linara in the Northtongue, saluting Aedan with her silver cup before taking a long draught.

"Did you switch *her* cup with tea?" Gwyneth asked Aedan in a stage whisper.

"He most definitely did *not*," said Linara in Commontongue. She grinned at Gwyneth and crooked her finger at Gwyneth's cup. "That's *good*," she exclaimed after tasting it. "Why did you *not* give me some of that splendid brew, Paladin?"

Aedan smiled. "The *ulfdrengr* are not particularly known for their love of *tea*, Linara."

Linara mock-scowled at Aedan. Gwyneth watched in amusement – the *ulfdrengr* certainly held their *vinaess* better than she, but Linara was certainly freer with her words and smiles after a few glasses. "Just because I do not proclaim my love for something does not mean that it does not exist," she pronounced.

At that moment, Kalian joined their small group. Gwyneth was fairly sure she didn't imagine the slight pink in Linara's cheeks at his timely appearance.

"Kalian, would you like some tea as well?" Aedan asked without missing a beat.

"It's very good tea," Gwyneth said gravely, lifting her cup.

"If the *ungrsverda* pronounces it good, then I'll try it," said Kalian, smiling at Gwyneth.

Gwyneth felt her own cheeks heat, and she gave Linara a look of solidarity. Or at least she hoped the fierce *ulfdrengr* knew it was solidarity. It wasn't that she shared Linara's feelings toward Kalian, it was simply that she recognized Kalian's raw masculine power and its effect on her. Ithariel hummed in amusement at her hip. Gwyneth touched the blade's hilt with one hand – why did Ithariel chuckle at every little prick of feeling that Gwyneth experienced? Sometimes it felt as though Ithariel laughed *at* her.

Ithariel sent her a rush of reassurance and affection. The jewel in the

Named Sword's pommel warmed beneath Gwyneth's touch. Gwyneth realized with sinking feelings that she didn't know what would become of Ithariel when she became Bearer – would the Caedbranr allow her to continue to have a relationship with another Named Sword?

Do not worry, Ithariel shimmered, her voice soothing now.

Gwyneth finished her tea just as Aedan arrived with more. Kalian and Linara had been conversing in low tones, but they rejoined Aedan and Gwyneth now, accepting their cups of tea with nods of thanks.

"Are we going from here to the feast?" murmured Gwyneth.

"Yes," replied Kalian.

"That is *our* plan," said Linara. "Perhaps the Bearer will wish to speak with you."

"I expect the Bearer will still be at the Queens' Council," said Aedan.

Understanding washed over Gwyneth. "*That* is where Orla is," she muttered, mostly to herself. She narrowed her eyes at Aedan. "Shouldn't you be there as well?"

Aedan smiled. "I think we know what is best for us, Gwyneth."

The rebuke was mild, but it still smarted. Gwyneth hid her face for a moment behind her cup of tea as she took a swallow from the refilled cup. Then she drew back her shoulders. "You're right, of course."

"Then I do not understand why the Princess would expect Melusina to be here," said Linara conversationally.

"We do not know with certainty that Melusina has been anointed," said Aedan in a tone that suggested this was not the first time they had spoken of the matter.

"If she is at Council, then I think that would be proof enough," Linara replied.

"You know they cannot discuss it," Aedan said.

"Cannot, or will not?" Linara murmured, draining the last of her tea and setting the silver cup on a small table. Gwyneth followed her example.

"Perhaps both," the Paladin replied in his mild but unshakeable manner.

"Have you attended many Solstice feasts here?" Gwyneth spoke the words to no person in particular.

"A handful," Kalian said.

"A dozen," said Linara after a quick pause.

Aedan smiled. "If I tell you how many Solstice celebrations I have attended, you will think me old."

"Well, I am sure you are not older than Rionach," Gwyneth said reassuringly. "She has attended almost three centuries' worth of Solstice celebrations."

"How exhausting," muttered Andorra from just behind Linara.

"Well then, if you will not answer that," Gwyneth continued light-heartedly, "then perhaps tell me your favorite event of the celebration."

"The tournament," Linara and Andorra said together. Kalian said nothing.

"The feast tonight," said Aedan.

"How boring," muttered Andorra.

"It is an opportune time to observe many of the luminaries of this world," said Aedan.

"That doesn't happen often," said Gwyneth thoughtfully. She nodded. "I see your point."

"I do not," retorted Andorra, raising her eyebrows. "I cannot understand how one would prefer a feast over fighting."

"Perhaps some of us have already fought much more than we prefer in our lives," said the Paladin, the gold flecks in his eyes catching the shifting light. The *ulfdrengr* looked at Aedan with varying expressions of incredulity, Kalian being the hardest to read and Andorra letting her skepticism show plainly.

"I would think that the Queen would have the feast after the conclusion of the tournament to honor the champions," said Gwyneth. "I understood that to be the tradition." It was a similarity between the mortal world and the Fae world, slight as it was.

"Oh, there is a feast to celebrate the champions," said Andorra with a nod. "This is the opening feast, and everyone is welcome."

Gwyneth tried to envision a feast hall that would accommodate all the *ulfdrengr*, warriors and *volta* alike, as well as the emissaries from the Seelie Court, the Seafarers, and the Merrow.

"Well, not *all* will come to the Great Hall," amended Andorra. "There will be food brought out to the camps as well."

"Ah, I see." Gwyneth wondered if they were going to go take their leave of the Unseelie Princess as her courtiers were doing, one by one; Linara answered her question by glancing at Aedan and reaching some unspoken agreement with him. Aedan walked over to the Princess seated in the silver chair, bowed slightly from the waist and spoke to her, his posture and expression the model of courtesy. He bowed again and then returned to their small group.

"Shall we?" he said, motioning toward one of the doors.

Gwyneth fell into step with Kalian behind Andorra and Linara. Aedan led them through the twisting passageways of Darkhill without faltering. The veins of *taebramh* in the glittering dark stone walls pulsed and shone with eerie light, painting their faces with pale luminescence.

"Your teacher, she told you that there might also be other mortals here at the feast?" Kalian said in Northtongue without looking at Gwyneth. Neither Andorra nor Linara gave any sign of interest in his words, though they were sure to have heard them.

"I know it is a possibility," Gwyneth replied in the same language.

"And there is the possibility," the big *ulfdrengr* continued, "that they will be…under the power…of the Unseelie."

"Yes." Gwyneth glanced at Kalian. "What is troubling you?"

"The Unseelie think it sport," he said in a low voice that was very nearly a growl. "We think it very close to slavery."

A little shock rippled through Gwyneth. "Slavery?"

"What other word do you use when choice and free will are stripped away?" The growl in Kalian's voice became unmistakable.

"Rionach spoke of it to me," said Gwyneth as they rounded a bend in the passageway, their small corridor opening into a larger thoroughfare. A group of passing Unseelie nodded to them politely even as their eyes raked over each member of their party, lingering on Linara, then Kalian…and then Gwyneth.

"They would not dare try any of their craft on you," said Kalian, "but it will be a temptation to them."

"And the Paladin?" Gwyneth thought of Rhys amid the cold perfection of the Unseelie women.

"They are protected."

"Protection does not mean that they cannot make the choice," murmured Gwyneth.

"Just as you could make such a choice, if you wished," said Kalian.

"Why did we not speak of this before we were here?"

"I did not wish to…prejudice you."

"I should hope I am capable of making my own judgments." Her words came out a bit more tartly than she'd intended.

Kalian fell silent for a few moments, and then he said, "You are right, *ungrsverda.* Nonetheless, you have lived with us and trained with us, and I feel it an obligation to say such things, even if it should have been said long before we stepped foot in these halls."

Gwyneth nodded. "I understand, and I thank you." She thought she saw the hint of a smile on Kalian's lips as he returned her nod.

The thoroughfare in turn opened into a wider hall through which a steady stream of Unseelie moved – and through the crowd Gwyneth glimpsed pale gold and tawny skin, the flash of colors bright as springtime. The flowing current of darkly dressed Unseelie parted before the Seelie entourage, which suddenly changed direction toward their small group. Aedan stopped, and Linarra stepped up beside him, Andorra and Kalian flanking her. Without prompting, feeling bold and uncertain both at once, Gwyneth positioned herself by Aedan's other side. Ithariel warmed reassuringly beneath her hand as the splendid Seelie made their way toward them, and others stopped to watch the encounter, until onlookers formed a ring with the *ulfdrengr* and Aedan and Gwyneth at the center.

Gwyneth found her mind struggling to comprehend the woman leading the Seelie: she looked youthful yet wise; she walked with the statuesque grace of a matron but her eyes sparkled like a maiden; her face was at once both beautiful and searing. It felt as though Gwyneth stared at the sun, though she kept her eyes fixed on the woman. Her *taebramh* sparked in her chest, rising to some unspoken challenge from the Seelie woman's power.

Behind the Seelie woman walked three men, quite nearly as blazing in their beauty. The Unseelie were moonlight and stars, darkness and ice, Gwyneth thought; and these Seelie were dawn and brilliant noon, midsummer heat and the rush of a river's crystalline waters.

The Seelie woman glided to a stop before them. Aedan bowed deeper from the waist than he had before the Unseelie Princess, and the *ulfdrengr* inclined their heads respectfully. Uncertainty struck Gwyneth with terrible force – should she bow or curtsy or nod her head like Linara? She quickly chose to follow Aedan's lead, executing a slight bow from the waist.

"Aedan," said the beautiful woman, her voice warm and familiar.

"Queen Titania," said Aedan respectfully.

"Come now," the Seelie Queen said, her eyes dancing, "we know each other better than to stand on such ceremony." She laughed, and it was a rushing, warm sound that wrapped around Gwyneth's shoulders like a length of sun-doused velvet.

"You flatter me, my lady," the Paladin replied.

Something flashed through Titania's eyes that could have been displeasure – did she expect Aedan to bow to her will, whatever the implication of such familiarity entailed? But the Seelie Queen turned her attention to Linara. The two women gazed at each other for a long moment. Finally, Titania smiled brilliantly. "I hear you have bonded to the most splendid wolf, Linara."

"That has not changed since last Solstice feast," Linara replied.

"Each Solstice brings new changes to all of us," Titania said with a little tilt of her head, seeming unaffected by Linara's reply. The Queen's eyes shifted to Andorra, and then to Kalian, lingering on the big *ulfdrengr* for almost as long as she had locked eyes with Linara.

Then Titania turned her attention to Gwyneth. It felt like the full force of the noon sun's rays were focused entirely on her; with an effort, Gwyneth reached for her *taebramh*, and when the fire roared to life in her breast, the Queen's effect faded from unbearable to almost pleasant.

"Ah," Titania said, as though she had felt Gwyneth's *taebramh* push back against her power. "And you must be Rionach's Heir."

"Yes," replied Gwyneth simply – at least her voice did not tremble. She felt the pulse of Ithariel beneath her palm like a second heartbeat, but the Named Sword remained silent.

Titania contemplated Gwyneth for what could have been a single moment or may have been an hour – Gwyneth focused on keeping the brilliance of the Seelie Queen from overwhelming her. Finally, Titania smiled without showing her teeth, her sumptuous lips curved beautifully, a courtly counterpoint to the lupine grins of the *ulfdrengr* to which Gwyneth had become so accustomed. In the Sidhe Courts, Gwyneth thought, the realization coming to her clearly and fully formed, power existed beneath the veneer of beauty; the Northerners lived in a raw, exposed manner in comparison to the impenetrable perfection of the Sidhe.

After the interminable length of time, Titania gave the barest of nods to Gwyneth. "I am sure we will speak again soon," the Seelie Queen said, and with that, she turned and swept toward the Great Hall, her three Knights – her Named Knights, Gwyneth saw now – wheeling in concert like huge, graceful birds behind her. The precision of their movements seemed eerie to Gwyneth. Murmurs followed the Seelie Queen like ripples through water.

"Well," said Linara, "Titania *never* changes."

Gwyneth smiled at Linara's clever play on the Seelie Queen's words. She turned her attention back to the flow of feast-goers around them.

"If you are thinking to catch a glimpse of the Merrow, they are not so fond of glitter and glamor as Titania," said Aedan. He motioned toward the door. Gwyneth started forward, her feet carrying her of their own volition. They passed through a great arched doorway, the double doors thrown back against the stone walls, and as they stepped over the threshold, Gwyneth felt her breath leave her in speechless wonder at the magnificence of the Great Hall. Silver lights were arranged overhead to look like stars in the sky, though upon closer inspection Gwyneth picked out figures within the stars – portraits of the luminaries gathered to celebrate the Solstice. Two great tables stretched down the length of the immense hall, benches lining both sides; and both the benches and tables looked to be carved of *ice*. Frost traced delicate patterns on the stone walls, graceful and beautiful whorls that dazzled the eye with their complexity. And then the feast itself was already laid upon the table, silver platters bearing a variety of dishes that confounded Gwyneth's sensibilities. Pitchers cut of crystal gleamed, some full of *vinaess* scarlet as blood and others full of amber liquid or a clear draught.

"This is…magnificent," said Gwyneth, almost begrudgingly.

Aedan smiled. "Welcome to the Winter Solstice at the Unseelie Court."

Chapter 37

They had just finished their first course – Aedan and Linara had both assured her that it was expected they begin to eat before the Unseelie Queen arrived, if she attended at all – when Gwyneth saw Rionach enter the hall. An unexpected rush of affection and familiarity overwhelmed her for an instant when she recognized the Bearer's imposing figure. She took a drink from her goblet – just water, flavored faintly with mint – and stood, clambering over the bench.

Rionach wore the same plain white shirt, embroidered gold vest and dark breeches that she had worn when she had entered the cottage of Gwyneth's parents. The plainness of her garb did nothing to detract from her imposing figure; in actuality, Gwyneth thought as she walked toward the Bearer, the simple raiment amplified it. Here was a woman who needed no decoration to declare her authority.

"Gwyneth," Rionach said, placing her hands on Gwyneth's shoulders. "You look well, blood of my blood."

"I *am* well, Lady Bearer," Gwyneth replied. She did not need to tilt her head so much to look up at Rionach anymore.

The Bearer wore her hair in a simple braid, and a streak of white stood out against the dark gold of her locks. There were lines at the corners of Rionach's eyes and around her mouth. Gwyneth did not remember the Bearer ever looking so tired.

"And are you well, Lady Bearer?" asked Gwyneth quietly, feeling concern crease her forehead.

Rionach smiled humorlessly. "You are observant."

"Because you have trained me to be so," Gwyneth replied.

"Come," said Rionach. "Let us speak where not all will be watching us."

"Do you not want to eat something first?" Gwyneth suggested.

Rionach did not answer. She had already turned and begun striding toward the great doorway. Gwyneth glanced over her shoulder at Aedan, Linara, Kalian and Andorra – but she would be able to find them again to resume the celebration after her talk with Rionach. She stretched her legs into a near run to catch up to Rionach, swallowing a laugh at the abrupt familiarity of the scenario. She was forever running to catch up with Rionach, whether it was in the forest or in the Unseelie stronghold. As she drew even with the Bearer, she realized that Rionach had been speaking.

"...my mistake, you see, and I must apologize to you now, Gwyneth," Rionach said. "I did not think my time would be so short."

"Your time is not short," protested Gwyneth as they passed through a grand courtyard. The Unseelie Guards saluted Rionach as she swept past them. They crossed the drawbridge, their steps echoing hollowly on the wood. "Rionach," Gwyneth said, touching the older woman's arm. "Your time is *not* short."

Rionach paused, acknowledging the greeting of a few *ulfdrengr* passing on their way to the feast. "Gwyneth," she said, her green eyes tired, "I had hoped to give you more time. But then again, I received the Sword when I was barely older than you." She smiled, the fading daylight illuminating her pallor. Then she turned and resumed her long-legged lope.

"I don't understand," Gwyneth said through numb lips as she followed Rionach toward the forest. They skirted around the *ulfdrengr* camp, the Bearer only glancing cursorily at the fantastic tents.

"What is there not to understand, my daughter?" Rionach said as they entered the treeline. She twisted through the trees, following some invisible path that Gwyneth could not see. "You are my Heir."

"I am," agreed Gwyneth. "But I do not understand why we are striding into the forest when the Solstice celebration is about to begin in Darkhill."

"Because I am treading the line as it is," replied Rionach cryptically. She paused, the lines on her face terribly drawn. It looked as though another white streak had sprung up in her braid, though that was impossible. It had to be a trick of the fading light. "My own arrogance could have been our downfall, Gwyneth. Remember that, heart of my heart. Trust yourself and take counsel from others only sparingly. Above all else, you must trust yourself." Rionach nodded, closed her eyes for a moment, and then turned, continuing on through the forest.

Gwyneth dutifully followed, letting Rionach's word settle into her mind. It was good counsel, of that she had no doubt; but she still did not *understand*. Ithariel thrummed at her hip, suddenly very awake. They journeyed through the trees until full dark, and Rionach did not weave a *taebramh* light to illuminate their path. Gwyneth found it much less challenging than she'd thought to navigate the dark forest.

"Nearly there," murmured Rionach.

Was the Bearer breathless? Gwyneth gripped Rionach's arm as the older woman stopped. "Are you ill, Rionach?" she asked, terror nearly closing her throat.

Rionach turned to her. "No," she rasped. "But my time is short."

"You've said that already," Gwyneth said. "What do you *mean,* if you are not ill?"

"There is only so long that each Bearer is given, and I thought in my arrogance that I could stave off my appointed time for a while longer." Rionach swallowed with difficulty. "You must understand, Gwyneth, that I did it out of...out of love for you."

"Of course," Gwyneth said as Rionach drew herself up and strode forward again with renewed vigor that belied the exhaustion in her eyes.

Gwyneth felt something shift in the air, and then the trees parted. They stood at the edge of a glade. The stars shone overhead in the velvet-dark night sky. A white rock rose from the earth in the center of the glade like one of the bones of the earth revealed.

"Come," said Rionach, drawing back her shoulders.

Ithariel shuddered in her sheath as Gwyneth walked through the long grass of the glade. A movement in the shadows caught her eye – a massive stag lifted his head at the far edge of the glade, regarding them solemnly with one liquid eye.

"Blessed be," murmured Rionach. "I have not done so much wrong that the gods have turned from me."

Some unnamed fear knotted Gwyneth's breath in her throat. Her steps faltered. Rionach turned and took her hand, the Bearer's hand feeling cold and corpse-like. Gwyneth tried not to recoil. The feel of it only added to her fear, but she swallowed down the dread and allowed Rionach to lead her to the white rock.

"First you must commit Ithariel," Rionach said in the firm voice of an Instructor.

Gwyneth felt as though she were standing on the edge of a cliff. She felt her knees go weak, but she clenched her teeth.

Do not worry, shimmered Ithariel, the words tinged with sadness and fear and acceptance, breaking Gwyneth's heart cleanly in two as she drew the blade from her sheath.

"Must I?" she said, her voice trembling now. Tears prickled at the corners of her eyes.

"You must," Rionach said gently but firmly.

Gwyneth did not know how she knew what to do. Rionach had never taught her any ritual such as this. But she knew, marrow-deep, and she raised Ithariel over her head, pain searing her chest as she drove the sword down and buried it into the broken bone of the earth, the blade slicing into the slab with absurd ease. She felt her hand pulled from Ithariel's hilt as the Named Sword was drawn into the rock by an inexorable force. A sob escaped her as the jewel in Ithariel's pommel flashed one last time and then was swallowed. Gwyneth did not care that tears wet her cheeks. She had *loved* Ithariel.

"Gwyneth," said Rionach.

Gwyneth turned to the Bearer, her teacher and her forebear, her chest still aching, tears spilling down onto her cheeks. Rionach drew the Iron Sword from its sheath upon her back.

"Take what you will, when I am gone," Rionach said, gesturing to the bandolier across her chest.

"I…must it be now?" Gwyneth cried out, feeling as though her heartbreak would overwhelm her.

"It must be," Rionach said solemnly. She held the Sword aside and gathered Gwyneth to her with her other arm. They had never embraced, and Gwyneth felt a keen sorrow that it would never happen again after this night. After a few moments, Rionach stepped back. She held up her closed fist to Gwyneth, opening it to reveal a pendant of the great Ancient Tree, a near-identical replica of the pendant that Gwyneth had taken from her home in Doendhtalam.

"Wear your iron emblem with pride," Rionach said, pressing the pendant into Gwyneth's hand.

"I will," Gwyneth said, her voice choked. Everything was happening so fast.

"You will claim the Sword when I release it," said Rionach. She stepped back and looked up at the night skies for a long, silent moment. A breeze rippled through the glade, and she inhaled deeply. "It is time," she said, and she slid the Iron Sword into the white rock.

The rock did not swallow the Caedbranr. The Iron Sword gleamed with its own silvery light, and a sudden wind whipped through the glade. The emerald in the Sword's pommel brightened and gleamed and fixed its gaze on Gwyneth.

"Now, Gwyneth," commanded Rionach through the wind.

Gwyneth reached for the hilt of the Sword. Her *taebramh* roared in her chest. When her hand closed around the hilt of the Sword, white fire rushed into her, filling her, sweeping away everything else. She was simply a vessel for the indescribable power of the Sword, the next in a long line that stretched behind her in the mists of the past. She heard their voices and saw their faces as the fire of the Sword consumed her.

Gwyneth.

She felt the coolness of the night earth beneath her knees. She opened her eyes and drew in a shuddering breath.

Gwyneth.

The Sword spoke again, insistently, clearly. Gwyneth looked at her hand: she still gripped the Sword, and she had drawn it free from the rock. With a hiss, she peeled away her hand from the hilt, her palm bloody with an angry burn. But the physical pain seemed small – she shuddered as the power of the Sword rolled again through her.

And then she saw the bones. With a cry, half of horror and half of protest, she staggered to her feet, closing her bloody hand around the Sword again, and stood looking down at the crumbling bones that were the only remnant of Rionach. As she watched, the bones crumbled into dust, leaving a plain white shirt, dark breeches, a vest embroidered with gold, and the sheath of the Iron Sword.

Gwyneth stood in the glade for a while holding the Sword and breathing. Eventually, long after her tears had dried, she bent and hooked a finger beneath the bandolier that bore the sheath of the Sword, pulling it free of Rionach's raiments. As she stood, she saw the stag, still watching at the edge of the glade. She raised her chin. The stag bowed its regal head to her and then turned, walking into the darkness of the forest.

Clumsily – she did not want to set the Sword down for an instant – Gwyneth pulled the bandolier over her head and arranged the sheath on her back. She held the Iron Sword before her, gazing at her own reflection and the stars above shining on its blade.

"If you had felt ready, you would not have been ready," she whispered to herself. She glanced at Rionach's garments and thought it fitting to leave them by the white rock. She pressed a palm to the rock, willing Ithariel to know her love and understand; and then she slid the Sword into its sheath on her back.

Gwyneth, said the Sword again, as though it were cementing her name in its awareness.

Gwyneth straightened her shoulders and looked to the stars, performing a quick calculation on the quickest way back to Darkhill from the glade. Once she had fixed her position, she turned in the direction of her path. She took a deep breath and began striding through the darkness of the forest, her footsteps quick and sure.

She was the Bearer of the Iron Sword, and her journey had just begun.

Epilogue

Gwyneth emerged from the edge of the forest, the night sky glittering above her. She felt the weight of the Caedbranr upon her back as she stepped alone through the long grass, skirting the edge of the *ulfdrengr* camp just as she had done with Rionach as dusk had fallen.

She drank in a breath of the cool night air and stopped as the ground began to slope upward to Darkhill. While she still had the cover of the velvety darkness, she pulled the edge of her sleeve over the heel of her left palm and daubed at her cheeks. If her eyes were red from the tears, there was little she could do about that, but at the least she could dry her face. Then she drew back her shoulders, took another breath and began climbing the hill toward the drawbridge.

The power of the Sword thrummed through her bones as she approached the Guards at the gate of the Unseelie palace. They showed no hint of surprise to see her returning alone, and they saluted her as they had saluted Rionach. She nodded to them once, as she had seen the Bearer do, and walked through the grand courtyard through which she had followed Rionach. Her burned palm smarted and stung, but she paid it no mind. She felt like she was Walking, her body and her emotions peeled away from one another.

The hum of voices in the Great Hall echoed through the hallways, intertwined with music and other sounds of festivities. Gwyneth heard her own breath louder than it all as her footsteps carried her closer and closer to the feast. She did not let herself stop. If she paused, she might think better of presenting herself to the hundreds of luminaries of Faeortalam gathered for the Solstice celebration.

"You are the Bearer," she reminded herself in a whisper, her lips numb. The words almost felt like a lie. She swallowed hard. Rionach had trained her. Rionach had placed faith in her.

You are the Bearer, said the Sword into her mind, speaking to her more clearly than Ithariel ever had. A lance of pain pierced Gwyneth's chest, a flash of grief at the loss of her training companion *and* the loss of Rionach in one night. But just as she pushed away the sting of her burned hand, she set her jaw and forced herself to bury her sadness. She would do Rionach proud, just as she had vowed on her very first day in Faeortalam. She strode toward the great doors of the feast hall, the sounds of revelry flowing around her as she stepped over the threshold, walking down the center of the hall between the two long, shimmering tables. The beauty of the Unseelie feast did not pierce her numbness; it was as though she observed it from afar. She set her gaze on the dais at the end of the hall, lit by the brightness of the Seelie Queen's beauty and the cool starlight of the Unseelie Queen's magnificence.

A hushed ripple followed her from the back of the hall. She did not slow, not even when she heard words in the Northtongue. The ripple became a wave of silence that flowed down the great tables as the hundreds of feasting Sidhe, *ulfdrengr* and Paladins fell quiet at her solitary procession. Even the delicate music faded as the raven-haired, terrifyingly beautiful Unseelie Queen motioned with one marble-white hand at the rosy-cheeked mortal girl plucking the strings of the harp behind the dais.

Aedan was seated by the Seelie Queen and Orla by the Unseelie Queen – fitting, Gwyneth supposed, for the Paladin leaders not to show favor to one Court. Beside Orla sat Princess Andraste. The *ulfdrengr* King and his *volta* Queen sat on the other side of the Unseelie Princess, their wild, weathered beauty a counterpoint to the Princess's youth.

And at either end of the dais sat a man and a woman whom Gwyneth had never seen. The man sat beside the *ulfdrengr*, his keen eyes fixed upon Gwyneth with unnerving intensity. He wore his dark beard long and plaited with beads carved of ivory and some shining black stone, and his face, like the *ulfdrengr*, showed signs of long, hard journeying in the sun and wind.

Seafarer, said the Sword.

A little thrill ran through Gwyneth, breaking through the numbness as she neared the dais. At the other end of the dais sat a woman who Gwyneth thought looked young, but she could not be sure; the woman's skin shimmered in the silvery light of the Hall, and even seated she was taller than Aedan. Colors shifted through her hair like shadows through water, and scales gleamed at the woman's neck and forearms, visible through her diaphanous tunic. The woman's almond-shaped eyes met Gwyneth's for a moment, the Merrow woman's gaze evaluating but somehow almost compassionate. Gwyneth felt a thread of kinship with the Merrow that she could not have explained in words.

You are both new-blessed, said the Sword.

Gwyneth stopped before the dais, the quiet in the Hall gathering with the tension of a growing thunderhead. She drew back her shoulders and met the impenetrable gaze of the Unseelie Queen.

"Rionach has returned to the stars," Gwyneth said into the thick silence, her words surprisingly loud. The power of the Sword, still half-foreign, rolled through her as a murmur rose behind her proclamation.

"Long live the Bearer," replied the Unseelie Queen, her clarion voice carrying over the Hall. Silence fell again in the wake of Mab's resplendent voice. She raised her silver goblet in one long-fingered white hand, and Gwyneth saw and heard the rest of the Hall follow suit. Aedan and Orla stood as they lifted their goblets, the rest of the Paladins following suit. With a small smile, Queen Titania rose to her feet, and the *ulfdrengr* were raising their glasses to her from their feet as well. The Seafarer stayed seated, leaning back in his chair and lifting his cup almost jauntily; the Merrow woman flowed to her feet and grasped her goblet in a hand with delicate webbing between its fingers.

"Long live the Bearer," declared Queen Titania.

"Long live the Bearer," echoed hundreds of voices throughout the Hall, raising gooseflesh on Gwyneth's arms.

There was an empty seat on the dais between the two Queens where there had not been an empty seat the moment before. Gwyneth hid any sort of surprise as she turned and acknowledged the toast from the gathered revelers with a simple nod and smile. The Caedbranr approved of her reserved response.

"Come and join us in the feast, Lady Bearer," said Queen Mab, her voice glittering like the stars overhead that had watched as Rionach's bones crumbled into dust.

Gwyneth walked around the dais, nodding in turn to the Unseelie Princess, the *ulfdrengr* and Orla as she passed. The Seafarer raised one eyebrow and looked at her in a way that made her wish he wasn't a leader of his people and she could tell him exactly what she thought of his leer. But she raised her chin and walked past him without a word.

With a twist of her fingers, Queen Mab ordered the mortal girl to begin playing the harp again. Gwyneth took her seat between the two Queens. Music filled the Hall and after a moment the conversation began to rise again until the sounds of revelry eclipsed their prior volume.

"It is not like Rionach to leave so suddenly," said Titania, as though Rionach had simply decided the feast wasn't to her liking.

"I do not think she owed any of us an explanation," replied Gwyneth.

"Of course she did not," said Mab, taking a sip from her silver goblet. "It would be a strange world in which a woman of power owed anyone an explanation."

Gwyneth did not know what to say to that, so she said nothing. She'd expected the Sidhe Queens to be more inscrutable, though she couldn't quite say that she *liked* them.

"Ah, look, here is the next course," Mab said with a note of anticipation in her voice.

Young Sidhe emerged from cleverly concealed doors at the sides of the feasting hall, each of them holding a pair of snow-white rabbits in their arms. The large, plump rabbits did not struggle as the young Sidhe, all dark-haired boys, walked to their assigned stations. A second line of young Sidhe, all dark-haired girls, followed, each taking up station next to a boy holding two rabbits. Gwyneth felt her mouth going dry as she watched the girls set up three silver sticks on small black dishes. She barely watched as the young Unseelie wrung the necks of the rabbits and with another flick of their wrists skinned them by some trick of rune or sleight of hand. The smell of roasting rabbit soon filled the Hall, and more servers brought out platters of herbs, spices and sauces.

"Quite clever," said Titania to Mab as she watched the rabbit roasting on its little spit before them. "But I prefer not to see blood before I eat."

"It is a small but significant pleasure," said Mab silkily, "to see the death of the creatures whose flesh will sustain us."

"Crown-sister, it is a bit macabre, even for you, to call witnessing death a pleasure," replied Titania in a tone of gentle remonstrance, as though Mab were simply joking.

"Oh, but I am quite macabre," purred Mab, "so it is fitting."

Gwyneth ate small portions of each dish and listened to the conversation at the high dais; she spoke only when the Queens spoke to her, or when she had something to say.

"You do not waste your breath on idle chatter," Mab commented as the servers began to bring out decadent desserts.

"No," Gwyneth said.

"In that, you are much like Rionach," Mab said, turning her attention to a drink set before her upon which blue and silver flames danced.

As the feast drew to a close, Gwyneth noted that her hand no longer hurt. She looked down and saw that it had healed. As she moved her hand in the light, white-gold markings gleamed on the tender new skin of her palm, complex whorls that reminded her of the sacred marks that the druids painted upon their skin. The design wrapped around her wrist and disappeared beneath her sleeve.

"Melusina will find your war-markings quite beautiful," said Titania, glancing over at Gwyneth's palm.

"As I find her markings quite beautiful as well," Gwyneth replied smoothly, laying her hand in her lap again. She suddenly wished that the feast would end soon – she felt terribly tired.

The Queens lingered over the desserts, each new confection more fantastic than the last. A young mortal man playing a lute replaced the rosy-cheeked harpist; Gwyneth glimpsed one of the Unseelie Queen's Three leading the pretty mortal girl away through one of those clever doors at the side of the Hall.

"I believe it is time to release these beautiful creatures to their own amusements," announced the Unseelie Queen with a languorous smile. She turned to Gwyneth. "I will have one of the pages show you to the Bearer's chambers."

Gwyneth suddenly could not stand the thought of sleeping in the bed that Rionach had occupied just the previous night. "Thank you, Queen Mab, but I believe I will lay my head elsewhere tonight."

"As you wish," said the Unseelie Queen, pressing her luscious crimson lips together in a small smile.

The *ulfdrengr* King and Queen took their leave first, followed by the Seafarer captain, his gaze still raking over every womanly form within his sight; Gwyneth stood and meant to excuse herself, but found herself drawn to the Merrow woman at the end of the table. Aedan graciously gave her his seat and went to sit with Orla at the other end of the dais.

"Bright sun and fresh sky to you," she said in the Merrow tongue, using a traditional greeting that Rionach had taught her.

The Merrow woman's eyes brightened and she almost smiled. "Deep waters and good hunting to you," she replied. "It is not often that we hear our own tongue from an outsider."

Gwyneth smiled. "As the Bearer, it is part of my duty not to be an outsider."

The Merrow tilted her head. "I am Melusina."

Gwyneth nodded. "I am Gwyneth."

They studied one another for a long moment.

"You are young," said Melusina finally. Gwyneth said nothing, and the Merrow added, "As I am."

As Melusina shifted in her chair, Gwyneth noticed that the Merrow's sheer tunic left little to the imagination; though scales covered Melusina's chest like a rippling plate of armor, the curves of her breasts were still visible in detail. Gwyneth reminded herself that the Merrow did not view their bodies as things to be covered and hidden. In the ocean, they wore almost nothing, and even at such a celebration as this, they still wore very little.

"Will you be here for the rest of the celebration?" said Gwyneth.

"Yes. One of my warriors will be fighting in the tournament of champions, of course," said Melusina, her eyes sparkling.

Gwyneth wondered briefly if a Paladin fought in the tournament. "Then I wish you and your champion luck," she said, "and I hope to speak to you more tomorrow."

Melusina nodded gracefully. "It has been a long and trying day for you," she said. "We will speak more on the morrow."

As Gwyneth departed the dais, Rhys appeared from the crowd of revelers beginning to stream from the Hall into the great courtyard.

She stopped short, her breath stolen as their eyes met. He smiled and walked toward her, bowing from the waist as he approached. "Lady Bearer."

"Paladin," she said, all her tiredness washed away by the fire in her blood sparked by his nearness.

"May I walk with you?" he asked.

She nodded, and they made their way with the crowd into the courtyard, but then they continued to the gate of Darkhill.

"I don't want to sleep in the bed where Rionach last rested," confessed Gwyneth in a low voice as they crossed the drawbridge. "And there are…so many eyes watching me."

"They are simply curious about the new Bearer," said Rhys. He twined his fingers through hers as they walked down the hill toward the *ulfdrengr* camp. She brushed her thumb over his knuckles, feeling the ridges of scars.

"It is…exhausting," she said, her voice catching.

"You are still allowed to feel," Rhys said.

"Perhaps I will feel something tomorrow," she said. "I'm just so tired."

"Then let's find you somewhere to sleep," he said as they walked into the *ulfdrengr* camp.

"Gwyneth!" Tula yelled joyously. "Thought you'd been captured by the ice queen."

Gwyneth smiled tiredly as Tula loped up to them. The *ulfdrengr*'s eyes glittered as she surveyed Rhys.

"Ah, you just went to capture your Paladin, eh?" Tula grinned. She ran her fingers through her short copper hair. "Well, I'm off to our fire – take the tent, Gwyneth, I'll tell Mariel." She winked at Rhys. "Though you can put a rune of your own on the entrance, if you'd like."

Gwyneth chuckled, the knots of tension loosening as she let Tula's easy humor wash over her. "Happy hunting at the fire, Tula."

"Always." Tula's teeth gleamed white in the starlight.

Rhys followed Gwyneth to the tent she'd shared with Mariel and Tula, and just as Tula suggested, he sketched his own rune over the entrance as Gwyneth carefully slid the bandolier of the Iron Sword over her head. She again felt the loss of Ithariel keenly.

A fire sparked to life in the brazier in the middle of the tent. She set the Sword down on a pile of furs and turned to Rhys.

"You are magnificent," he told her in a quiet, earnest voice, stepping close and cupping her cheek with one calloused hand. She smiled tiredly. "We are all very proud to have you as the Bearer," he said, the firelight silvering his gray eyes.

His touch soothed her, but she still needed to ask. "Are you afraid to be with me now that I am the Bearer?"

He gripped her chin gently but firmly, tilting her face up toward him. She was only half a head shorter than him now.

"I would love you if you were not the Bearer," he said, his voice wrapping around her, "and I would love you if you were the Queen of England." He smiled and brushed his thumb over her lower lip. "I love you because you are Gwyneth."

She smiled. "And I love you because you are Rhys." She kissed him softly. "It does not change that I am the Bearer and you are a Paladin."

"There is nothing wrong with the Bearer taking a Paladin lover," Rhys said earnestly, smiling his half-smile. "It has happened in the past."

"And what if I do not want you merely as a lover?" she asked. "What if I want…more?"

Rhys looked at her with such intensity in his eyes that it sparked a flame in her core. "Lady Bearer," he said, "are you asking me to marry you?"

She grinned. "Must *I* ask *you?"*

He pretended to consider. "Well…you *are* the Lady Bearer." He took her face in both hands and kissed her fiercely. "I want no other," he said, "and if you will have me I will gladly tie my fate to yours."

For the first time in a day of wrenching change, Gwyneth felt truly happy. Her tiredness did not weigh as heavily on her and her sorrow receded as Rhys kissed her again, this time slowly, languidly. He chuckled as she tugged at the laces on his vest, her fingers finding the hem of his shirt after she'd made short work of the vest.

"No need to rush," he said, his gray eyes dark with desire. "We have centuries, after all."

She looked at him and smiled. "Centuries still seem too short a time with you."

"We will make every day count," he promised, pulling his shirt obligingly over his head. "I *am* a Paladin, after all."

Gwyneth followed suit and bit her lip as she drank in the sight of his bare torso. She reached out and traced the scar on his side with one finger, the intake of his breath at her touch kindling answering excitement within her. "I think I'm starting to like the Paladin philosophy."

He chuckled. "Come here, you magnificent woman."

She obeyed, and the Caedbranr hummed in its sheath.

Whatever the future held, they would face it together, the Bearer and her Paladin, two not-quite-mortals from a small village in the Pale of Eire.

OTHER NOVELS BY JOCELYN A. FOX,
AVAILABLE ON KINDLE AND IN PAPERBACK:

The Iron Sword
The Crown of Bones
The Dark Throne
The Lethe Stone
The Mad Queen
The Dragon Ship
Midnight's Knight: A Fae War Chronicles Novel

THE FIRST THREE NOVELS ARE ALSO COLLECTED IN A
SPECIAL EDITION, AVAILABLE ON KINDLE:

The Fae War Chronicles Omnibus Edition

Acknowledgements

This has been a year of such change.

With every ending comes a beginning, and so it is with writing as well. There has been a beginning in the Old World Trilogy, which tells the story of the end of the Golden Age of the Fae world. Gwyneth's journey through training has echoed, in some ways, my own, and I first have to thank everyone who has helped me over the past year as I transitioned to my new life: my family and friends, my classmates and most especially my best friend and adventure buddy (who still insists that he will play the role of Quinn when the Fae War Chronicles is adapted into a television series.)

And as always, many, many thanks to my patient and dedicated editor, Ronn Dula. Thank you to Peter at Bespoke Book Covers for his lovely and professional designs, and Maureen Cutajar at GoPublished Formatting Services for putting the final polish on these novels in preparation for releasing them into the world.

I hope you've enjoyed your journey into Gwyneth's world—get ready for more tales of the Old World with the rest of the trilogy! Thank you for reading, and if you liked the book, please consider hopping on over to Amazon or Goodreads and leaving a review.

Indie authors depend on readers like you to help get the word out about great books.

Believe in magic and unlikely heroes; live your adventure and make the world a better place.

Until the next book,
Jocelyn A. Fox, November 2018

About the Author

Jocelyn A. Fox is the bestselling author of the epic fantasy series *The Fae War Chronicles,* which include *The Iron Sword, The Crown of Bones, The Dark Throne, The Lethe Stone, The Mad Queen,* and *The Dragon Ship.* The series also includes a full-length prequel novel, *Midnight's Knight. Druid's Daughter* is her eighth novel. She believes that storytelling can change the world, superheroes do exist in real life, dogs are the best kind of people, and there is no such thing as "too much coffee."

You can find her on the following platforms:

Facebook:
www.facebook.com/author.jocelyn.a.fox

Twitter:
www.twitter.com/jafox2010

Instagram:
@jocelynafox

Amazon Page:
www.amazon.com/Jocelyn-A.-Fox/e/B0051DX7G0

Made in the USA
Coppell, TX
30 November 2021